He had her tight and controlled, like he'd done this hundreds of times. She couldn't move except to blink.

"Don't fight me, beautiful," said the voice of the thing from Central Park—the thing that was probably Strada. The sound was nothing but a masculine rasp against her ear, and the hand against her mouth felt hot enough to thaw glaciers. "You won't win."

Camille drew hard on her elemental fire, using the already overheated dinar to expand her pyrogenesis. Flames broke out along her neck and hissed down her arms, sizzling holes in her battle leathers and sending a shock of alarm through her Sibyl tattoo. Smoke poured around her, blurring her vision—but the asshole holding her managed not to let go.

"Keep it up," the man murmured, so quiet no one else in New York could have heard him. "I like it hot."

How the hell was he still holding her?

Camille couldn't see him, couldn't sense any elemental essence that would help him absorb her fire, but—

She shifted her energy into pyrosentience, stabbing at his flesh with focused beams of blue flame. He didn't react to her probing, but he didn't stop it, either. This time she got off a good blast, enough energy to finally tell her what she needed to know.

He wasn't demon. Wasn't Rakshasa. Not Strada, but he didn't feel completely human, did he? Well, the muscled arms, the way-ripped pecs pressing into her shoulders—those were definitely all man.

ALSO BY ANNA WINDSOR

Captive Spirit

Bound by Shadow
Bound by Flame
Bound by Light

CAPTIVE SOUL

A NOVEL OF THE
DARK CRESCENT SISTERHOOD

ANNA
WINDSOR

BALLANTINE BOOKS • NEW YORK

A Ballantine Books Mass Market Original

Copyright © 2010 by Anna Windsor
Excerpt from *Captive Heart* copyright © 2010 by Anna Windsor

Published in the United States by Ballantine Books, an imprint of The Random House Publishing Group, a division of Random House, Inc., New York.

BALLANTINE and colophon are trademarks of Random House, Inc.

ISBN 978-0-345-51390-8
eBook ISBN 978-0-345-51679-4

Printed in the United States of America

www.ballantinebooks.com

9 8 7 6 5 4 3 2 1

For my family, again, who did without me
for weeks on end, again. You guys are the best!

The soul is dyed the color of its thoughts.
—HERACLITUS

❨ prologue ❩

On the day everything changed, Camille Fitzgerald was in trouble—as usual.

"Stop running, you little freak!"

She tore away from the taunting voice, her bare feet pounding over cold, smooth stone. She sensed the older girls gaining on her from behind. They could hear the *slap-slap-slap* of her steps or maybe the wheezing jerk of her breath. Her clenched fists moved up and down, up and down as she tore through the twisting corridors, one rock hallway looking just like the next, but Camille knew the castle better than her own reflection. The castle was her only friend, her only haven. Here the hallway smelled like potatoes and roast from the kitchens. And around the next corner she'd catch a whiff of bitter oils and leather from the weapons room and see golden wall sconces instead of silver, with only every other torch lit. After that, it got colder and blacker and the air started smelling like mushrooms and water and rot.

Down she went, deeper into the stone fortress, heading for the endless maze of tunnels and storage rooms and pits far beneath Motherhouse Ireland. Where all the unwanted things ended up. Where all the mad things lived. Some of those tunnels probably ran all the way to Connemara, or maybe to other secret places. Camille hadn't yet opened all the doors or followed every carved hollow to its final destination. She figured she hadn't even found them all yet—but she'd found enough. If she could make it into the darkness, the older girls would have more trouble hunting her. Fire made light, but it also made *scáth*—shadow. Shadow had always been much kinder to Camille.

Almost there.

Another minute. Another few steps.

One of the girls shouted, "You're just making it worse on yourself, you pathetic coward."

Póg me hón—kiss my ass. It was the first thing that came to Camille's mind. She almost said it, but she decided to run faster instead. She didn't want a beating today. Older girls meant practice swords. Fists and feet she could handle, but wooden sticks hurt like hell, especially when it was Maggie and Carlyn and Lee. They were the best fighters in their training class.

She knew she had to cover more ground. Push harder. Stretch. She threw all her energy into her next stride—too long! She pitched off balance and stumbled forward through patches of light cast by the few sconces overhead. The corridor's nearest wall stopped her when she hit it full-on, slamming into the cold rock. With a loud curse, she ricocheted back into the corridor and fell hard on her knees.

Camille yelped as pain knifed up both legs. Before she could scramble to her feet and take off again, the older girls whipped forward and surrounded her in the big, empty stone space. Maggie Cregan, the oldest and tallest, blocked Camille's path to the lower reaches of the castle, and she stood in ready fighting position, teeth bared. Her short, thick red hair was damp from the class they had just finished, and from chasing Camille halfway through Motherhouse Ireland. Flame reflected in her pale green eyes, changing them from creepy to flat-out psychotic.

Camille kept her fists up and her eyes on Maggie, though she was just as aware of Carlyn and Lee closing in behind her. They weren't as tall as Maggie and they had longer brownish red hair and brown eyes. Still, with their jeans and matching long-sleeved T-shirts all smeared with soot, the three of them looked like sisters. They sort of were. All three girls were boarders, and close friends the way boarders tended to be when there were more than one of them in a training class.

Camille's pulse raced as she tried to control her breathing and keep her wits. Her skin ached as if her body knew the punches were coming, because the punches always came, didn't they? She still had bruises that hadn't healed from the last time somebody chased her.

"You were supposed to have my back when we were sparring." Maggie's dead-quiet voice made the stones feel colder. Nothing but Maggie's mouth moved when she spoke, and a steady cloud of smoke rose from her shoulders, framing her like a *deamhan* who'd just walked out of hell.

Maybe the older girl had actual demon blood running through her veins. After all, Maggie's ancestors were executioners—the meanest in history.

Camille's muscles tightened. "I did have your back."

Maggie laughed, and the sound wasn't nice. She pointed at the side of her head. "You let Cynda Flynn smash my skull with a rock."

Camille lowered her fists a fraction so she could see Maggie better. "There were too many girls from the other class jumping you. I couldn't fight them all at once."

"You could have if you'd used fire." Carlyn gave off her own smoke as she worked to catch her breath. "That's the point."

Camille did her best to bluff, giving all three girls a defiant scowl. "Leave me alone. It's over. What's done can't be undone."

"You're supposed to be a Sibyl." Lee wasn't smoking, but her sarcastic tone bit like fire. "A *fire* Sibyl."

"I'm a fire Sibyl in training, just like you," Camille shot back, not worrying about Lee or Carlyn as much as Maggie.

"You're nine years old," Maggie said. "I made flames before I ever took my first step as a baby. If you haven't done it by now, you won't. You don't belong here."

Camille met Maggie's gaze and immediately wished she hadn't done it. Those eyes—they were just freaky. "That's up to the Mothers, not you."

Maggie kept her scary eyes as flat and unchanging as the big practice sword belted at her waist. "Most of the Mothers say the same thing. You're too little and too quiet. You'll never make it."

Camille's jaw clenched against those stabs. Was Maggie telling her the truth? Most of the Mothers didn't like Camille, that much was right—especially Mother Keara, who was always pissed because Camille's fire making didn't work right.

But did the Mothers want her out?

The thought made her insides curl into a tight, painful ball.

She was no boarder like these girls, here for the weekdays and home on nights and weekends. She'd been born at Motherhouse Ireland. If the Sibyls put her out, where would she go? It was enough to make her breath squeeze deep in her throat, and she started to sweat.

"Leave me alone," she said again. Crap. Her voice was shaking. Anger and humiliation burned through her like the world's hottest flames, and she wished she could make fire, fire, and more fire whenever she wanted and not just by accident every now and then. She wanted to burst into roaring heat and light more than anything. "You better go away. I'm warning you."

Lee laughed at her this time, and her laugh didn't sound any nicer than Maggie's. "The Mothers told us to toughen you up or you'll never turn into a real fire Sibyl."

"I *am* a real fire Sibyl." Camille spoke through her teeth, seeing the red heat she felt inside, seeing fire in the air all around her. "I was *born* here, remember?"

She grabbed at the ambient fire with all the energy in her body, touched it, willed it to do what she wanted, to cook Maggie and Carlyn and Lee right where they stood.

They hesitated like they were waiting for the attack, getting ready for it—but nothing happened. No smoke. No outside heat coming together in a furious orange arc.

Nothing.

Stupid, awful nothing.

Just like always.

"Stand in the fire and speak when no one wants to hear your words," Camille yelled, hating herself and wishing she could turn into a dragon and breathe a gout of flames all over Maggie's stuck-up, better-than-you smirk. "Let the flames burn as you speak when cowards would choose silence. Speak until no smoke obscures the truth. *That's* our job in a fighting group, and I'll be able to do it just fine."

"Mortar, pestle, broom." Maggie jabbed her index finger at the tattoo on her right forearm, the same tattoo they had all been given when they came to Motherhouse Ireland—or in Camille's case, when she came into the world. It was a picture of a mortar, a pestle, and a broom in a triangle around a dark crescent moon. The sacred mark of the Dark Crescent Sisterhood. When Maggie touched the pestle, she ran her short fingernail across the outline of the stone grinder. "This is us. The strongest Sibyls in any fighting group. The toughest. The best fighters."

"Some warrior of the Dark Goddess," Lee said. "Look at her hands shaking."

"Can you even make a spark?" Carlyn reached into the air, pulling at ambient bits of fire until flames jumped from each of her fingers.

"It's a Sibyl's job to protect the weak from the supernaturally strong," Maggie said as she raised her own hand and lit her fingertips. "If some demon blasts fire right in your face, the best you'll be able to do is spit on the flames and hope for the best."

Camille focused her energy on drawing the fire off Maggie's fingertips into her own body. A second later, the flames snuffed out, leaving trails of smoke reaching toward the stone ceiling. She had no problem with pyroterminus, which was absorbing or ending fire energy. She was fair at pyrokinesis, which was moving fire that had already been created, and good at pyrosentience, or sensing and tracking fire or impressions left in fire energy by stuff that touched the fire.

It was pyrogenesis—drawing building blocks of fire into her body and making new, whole flames—where she fell short. And that was the only thing most fire Sibyls cared about. Camille glared at the smoke rising off Maggie, Carlyn, and Lee, and part of her hated them. Pyrogenesis came so easily to them that they made fire when they didn't mean to and burned up clothes and sheets and furniture. Camille hardly ever did that. She only made fire now and then—and not that much of it—because she was . . .

Weak.

Her gut ached as Maggie drew her wooden practice sword and took a single step forward. Two more, and she'd be close enough to smack Camille with the flat of the dull blade.

"Stop me," Maggie demanded.

Camille raised her fists higher. "I'll kick your ass. I mean it."

Maggie's next words came out in a growl. "Stop me with fire or you'll regret it."

Camille screamed. Fury. Frustration. Helplessness. She didn't know why she yelled and she didn't care. This wouldn't help. Threats and fear just made everything worse. She had as much chance of making flames as an earth Sibyl, an air Sibyl, or the ancient water Sibyls that had been washed away in a tidal wave at Motherhouse Antilla and didn't exist anymore—which was exactly zero.

Carlyn and Lee stood back as Maggie lunged at Camille and swung the practice sword.

Camille smashed her fist into the wood. Pain blasted across her knuckles and down her wrist, all the way to her elbow. Tears blurred her vision and she wanted to scream her guts out and fall down and hold her hand, but she didn't. Maggie staggered, eyes huge from the shock of how hard Camille had hit the wood.

Before Maggie could recover, Camille kicked her in the ass just like she'd promised, and let out a crazy-sounding laugh as Maggie slammed into the corridor's stone wall. She didn't wait to watch her fall. Holding her throbbing hand, Camille whirled on Carlyn and Lee, who had their swords drawn.

"You're nuts," one of them muttered.

No way to beat two at once, so Camille went low, throwing herself at Carlyn's legs and bashing into her knees. The two of them went down hard in a tangle of legs and arms as Lee swore, threw down her practice sword, and tried to snatch Camille off Carlyn.

Camille jerked out of Lee's grip, rolled to the side, and grabbed the discarded sword. Seconds later she was on her feet, dull blade at the ready, and the fight felt more equal.

Maybe I am crazy.

The thought didn't bother Camille.

All she wanted was out—out of this situation, out of the main part of the castle, and down into one of the dark tunnels, where she could be alone and safe. She wanted to go where nobody thought she was stupid or worthless or broken. Where maybe she wouldn't think that, either. If she ran far enough, maybe she'd get away from herself, too.

All three girls were in front of her now, standing between her and the route back up to the main castle. Carlyn and Maggie rubbed at cuts and bruises while Lee fumed and smoked and glared at the practice sword she'd lost to Camille.

"I'm so gonna make you pay for this." Maggie mopped blood off her nose with her sleeve and raised her own practice sword, which was easily twice as long and twice as broad as the one Camille held. Her hair flickered, then the ends caught fire, along with the wooden blade. Smoke billowed into the long hallway as flames licked toward Camille, heating her fingers and arms.

Tears streamed down Camille's cheeks even though she didn't want to be crying. She could barely breathe and hold her sword, her fingers hurt so badly, but they were healing. Sibyls healed fast, which was a good thing, because she was about to get the shit kicked out of her.

Maggie's eyes got big as she stared at Camille, and Camille figured she was picking the first place to bash Camille with that enormous wooden sword.

Before Maggie could move, Carlyn threw down her sword. The sudden clatter of wood on stone made Camille jump, but she held her position and kept her stance.

Carlyn and Lee backed away from her.

What the—?

Camille tried to look as pissed and mean as possible. Her tears slowed as Carlyn and Lee kept giving ground. Both girls spun away from her and fled back up the corridor, toward the castle. Maggie shook her head once, then twice, like she was trying to rattle her own brain back to reality. A moment later she uttered a squeak of uncertainty, then turned and shot away as fast as the other two, sword swiping up and down as she ran.

Camille stood there gasping for air, feeling weird and stupid, then looked at her hands and the practice sword to see if she was growing scales or hair or something that would have scared the older girls that badly.

It was right about then that she felt it.

A strange pulse of energy behind her, something she'd never even sensed before—and it was strong. And dark. And moving up from the earthen tunnels beneath Motherhouse Ireland.

Something was coming, and Maggie and Carlyn and Lee had seen it and had run away. Camille didn't want to turn around, and she didn't want to keep standing there, either. Her heart squeezed and froze, slowing its pounding until she got dizzy. She couldn't keep standing there. But she did, because she couldn't figure out what else to do. Her vision swam until she was sure she'd faint. She had nothing but a wooden sword and a busted hand. Fear flooded into her mouth like bitter copper, choking her, making her breathe even harder, like she really was dying of a heart attack.

You're a Sibyl, she told herself, but Maggie's taunts lingered in her mind. *Too little. Too quiet.*

"I'm a fire Sibyl," she said out loud. Her hands shook harder. Remnant smoke drifted all around her, settling in the corridor like a thin white fog.

A noise sounded behind her, like a strangled scream, hoarse and crackly and utterly terrifying.

Camille had been in battle training since she could walk. It was stupid to let an enemy take her from behind. She had no defenses—unless she turned around.

Goddess, she didn't want to do that.

The scent of sulfur and hot metal drifted through the waning haze surrounding Camille.

The scary noise went right on, making her skin tighten and crawl, but it didn't seem to be coming any closer.

Turn around, she told herself, but her cursed weak knees wouldn't obey. *Turn around, coward.*

Legs leaden and wobbly, Camille felt a fresh wash of the strange energy, but as it touched her, it didn't feel so strange. It felt metallic and warm and powerful, yet familiar. Fire Sibyl energy, but very unusual. An image of her mother danced through her mind, but her mother had been killed in battle in some faraway city, and that was a whole year ago.

The energy wrapped her and fueled her, chasing back her fear and steadying her knees and hands. She used the momentum to make her head move, then her shoulders and torso and hips and legs, until she was finally, finally widening her stance, pivoting, still holding her wooden sword tight as she turned to find—

The smallest person she had ever seen, standing directly in the middle of the corridor behind her.

Camille stopped breathing for a moment.

The woman was dressed in a black tunic and breeches, which was odd in a place where most grown women wore green robes, but her clothing wasn't what riveted Camille's attention. No. It was the woman's face that absorbed every ounce of her awareness. Her bald head, smooth and spotted as a pheasant egg on a forest floor, gleamed in the light of the single sconce above her. The skin below that was white, with a thick, knotty scar over her puckered, empty left eye. Her damaged mouth was partially open, like she was about to snarl or breathe fire all over Camille, and Camille had to battle with her own insides not to slam her eyes closed.

This woman was almost too scary to look at directly, like some *taibhse*, a ghost, come back from the dead still bearing the wounds that killed it. Very few fire Sibyls ever got burned, much less scarred, given how well and fast Sibyls healed, so what had happened to her?

"Who are—what—" Camille couldn't find the right question, and she ended up with, "Are you a Mother?"

The scarred woman's dangerous expression faltered

and shifted. She made a terrible crackly wheezing sound, her one eye fixed so hard and harshly on Camille that it watered from lack of blinking. That wheezing came again, louder, longer, and Camille began backing away from her. If she could make it a few steps, she could turn, maybe run far enough and fast enough before the old ghost could catch her or knock her silly and burn her with a fire blast.

But—

Wait.

The woman wasn't wheezing at all.

She was . . . laughing.

Camille's heart raced and raced, but she kept herself steady, staring at the scarred lips, which were turning upward as much as the scars allowed. A few seconds later, words cranked out of the woman's injured mouth, raspy and slow, like she hadn't spoken in years. "Mother." She wheeze-laughed some more. "I am . . . many things . . . never that. Never." When she finished seeming to hurt herself with the laughter, she spoke more plainly, adding, "I'm ancient and decrepit and ugly, so I can see where you'd make such a mistake."

Ancient and decrepit—was she joking about the Mothers? Had she just called the Mothers ugly? Camille's eyes narrowed with surprise. Nobody joked about the Mothers, even out of earshot. They had ways of hearing everything.

"My name is Ona," said the scarred woman, and Camille flinched.

"Ona," she repeated, not quite believing that could be true. She'd heard stories, just like every adept in training. A few whispers and snatches before the Mothers glared or sent singeing blasts at their butts, hissing about the dangers of rumor and folly.

Oldest living Sibyl . . .

Something dark . . .

Something unspeakable . . .

Monster . . .

Camille had heard that Ona had turned into something less than human. Some girls said she was a vampire or an old-style witch, or maybe a werewolf. For her part, Camille had always imagined Ona as one of those shadow creatures who slinked up to kids' beds at night and snatched them over the side, carrying them away forever, maybe to feed them to scary demons.

She had no idea what to say to this tiny woman, not at all a monster even with those horrible scars, so she settled on, "I—I didn't think you were real."

Camille realized her voice sounded almost reverent, but she didn't care. It wasn't every day she got to look one of Motherhouse Ireland's legends and mysteries right in the face. Then she noticed that Ona wasn't smoking from the arms and shoulders like most fire Sibyls did even in civil conversation. Until that second, Camille had never met another fire Sibyl who didn't smoke.

"I'm real enough," Ona said. "And so are you."

Camille blinked at the little apparition as her features seemed to shift and change in the torchlight. Tiny chills broke out along her neck and shoulders, and she had to go stiff to keep from shaking all over.

I'm real.

What did Ona mean by that? It had to be important, but Camille felt too jumbled to work it out.

"You'll understand one day." Ona's words conveyed a certainty Camille didn't feel. "Now go. Study. Learn what you can. The universe will teach you the rest when the time comes."

Was she about to leave?

No!

Camille didn't want her to leave. She wanted to run toward Ona and grab her so she couldn't get away, but a small, sane part of her brain told her that would be a really bad idea. "I try to do my best, really, I mean it, but the other girls—"

"Won't bother you in the future." Ona's smile terrified Camille way more than her strange energy or her scars, and put to rest any thought of chasing after the old woman, or even trying to find her later in the dark tunnels under Motherhouse Ireland. "I'll pay them a visit. We'll have . . . tea and a chat."

Camille tried to figure out how to answer, but before she could, the sconce overhead flickered, and Ona was gone.

Camille gaped at the spot where the old woman had been standing.

Ona hadn't walked away or run or jumped or anything. She was just . . . gone.

That wasn't possible.

Real flesh-and-blood women didn't disappear like spirits. They couldn't just evaporate into thin air. And Ona—she'd been real enough for Maggie, Carlyn, and Lee to see her and be terrified and run away from her.

Camille had a sudden image of the three older girls sitting with cups and saucers in shaking hands, trying to have a "chat" with the monster who lived underneath Motherhouse Ireland. She could almost see their huge, white-ringed eyes as they tried not to spill their tea, as they tried not to scream or run or make complete fools of themselves.

Laughter burst up Camille's throat before she could stop it, echoing in the empty stone corridor. She felt older than she had an hour ago, though she didn't know why. She had a sense that Ona would be true to her word, that life would be different from now on, but she couldn't say how, or if everything would be better or much, much worse.

"Everything just changed," she said out loud, wondering if she was still in trouble—maybe worse trouble than ever.

Camille figured it might take a very long time to answer that question.

(1)

July

Something was following her through Central Park.

Camille wasn't sure about many things other than the fact that she shouldn't be out at night without her quad, her fighting group, searching the streets and parks of New York City alone—but she sensed a presence lurking through the darkness behind her, somehow just out of her sight and awareness.

She knew it was there.

She knew *he* was there, as surely as she saw lights twinkling in skyscrapers rising over the imposing dark edge of Umpire Rock.

Whatever it was, it just felt—male.

But it didn't feel completely human.

"What am I doing?" she muttered to herself. It wasn't like she could whip out her cell and make a quick call, because cell phones never survived Sibyl energy longer than a few hours. Neither did handhelds, computers—laptop or desktop—or any other fancy electronics.

"I mean seriously, what the *hell* am I doing out here alone?"

But the answer came immediately to her in the form of three faces—Bela Argos Sharp, Dio Allard, and Andy Myles—the earth Sibyl, air Sibyl, and water Sibyl in her quad. Those three women had been willing to take a chance on her, to welcome her into a fighting group even though all the Sibyls in her first group had been killed. Even though she'd been hiding away from the world for years. Even though her own Sibyl Mothers had tried to convince them that Camille was unstable and unworthy.

Bela, Dio, and Andy.

That's why she was out here with whatever was sneaking across the park behind her, probably figuring she didn't know it was there. Camille intended to protect Bela, Dio, and Andy from the consequences of a big mistake she'd made, so she had to keep working on the one thing she was good at—pyrosentience. And she had a demon to find.

Not just any demon. An ancient tiger-monster known as a Rakshasa.

Rakshasa were shape-shifters who could travel as blue flames, adopt one natural human form for long periods, and imitate just about anybody for a few minutes at a time. They had no conscience, no mercy. They were totally evil, and they were a bitch to bring down. Last year Camille had let one of them escape a firefight with her quad, Strada, a Rakshasa leader who was likely to hunt them all down to get his revenge for the ass kicking his little army had taken from the Sibyls. The demons had fled New York City, but Camille knew that was temporary. They wouldn't stay gone forever, especially not Strada. She had made a terrible error in judgment that left her quad at risk, and if she had to come out every single night her quad wasn't on patrol and flex her pyrosentience trying to track the furry bastard, she'd do it to set that mistake right.

The coin on the chain around her neck, a strange and unusual talisman given to her by—well, something that never should have had a generous impulse—lay still and cool against her skin, held close by her tight cotton undershirt. The coin was an ancient Afghan dinar, used in the time of the Kushan emperor Huvishka, thousands of years ago. It reacted to and repelled Rakshasa, but it also had properties that allowed elemental energy to move through it, so she could use it to enhance her own abilities. Well, her one very solid elemental ability—pyrosentience.

Rather than pulling fire to her or creating it from the core ingredients in the atmosphere, she could pull the energy *into* her and release it again, mingled with her own essence and super-focused on the purpose she intended. Focusing projected fire energy allowed her to read the environment around her even if she couldn't blow shit up and burn down buildings with a snap of her fingers. She could gain a better understanding of objects, people, and other types of energy by sending her awareness out through her fire energy, then drawing it back and trying to understand what she had sensed. With pyrosentience, she could track almost anything, so long as it came into contact with the world's ambient or actual fire.

The dinar could also help her magnify the fire energy she took in with her pyrosentience, but that drained her down to nothing, and usually it wasn't worth the price. She shouldn't count on the coin to help her shore up her weaker talents. Using the dinar that way could be unpredictable and dangerous, and the Mothers didn't approve of it, though they had stopped short of forbidding it, just like they had screeched to a halt just shy of forbidding her to use the coin altogether.

Well, screw the Mothers. Let them think about how small and quiet and weak she was, how she wasn't worth assigning to a fighting group, and how they had no idea why Bela chose her and went to war with the meanest Mother in Ireland to get her. Camille was using the dinar whether they liked it or not. In fact, she had learned to make metal that was similar in its properties, and she had given her whole quad projective charms with the same capacity—and they were using those charms whenever they wanted, too. Her quad had unusually good sentient abilities, which was one reason they were more compatible than anyone had thought they would be.

Usually paranormal energy made the dinar vibrate, heat up, or both, but tonight Camille was getting nothing. She might as well have been wearing costume jewelry from a secondhand store.

Instead of comforting her, the dinar's inactivity made her more nervous. Whatever was following her might be powerful enough to know how to regulate its elemental signature and keep itself concealed. That meant it wasn't the demon she was looking for, but it might be something just as bad, or worse.

Camille kept to the edges of Heckscher Playground, out of the open expanses. Leaves rustled above her head, and a faint breeze raised chills along her neck and shoulders even though the air was still seasonably warm. The night smelled like freshly mowed grass and dirt from the nearby ball fields, and the playground itself radiated the salty, happy smell of all the children who had occupied the big space earlier in the day.

Whatever was following Camille, she didn't think it was happy. Sibyls could sense states and traits, and fire Sibyls were particularly adept at judging emotional energy. The strange part was, she didn't pick up much negative feeling from the thing. It seemed . . . intent. Almost overly focused on its mission—which appeared to be following her.

Well, that's nothing new in my life, is it?

Camille had spent more hours than she cared to count sneaking through Motherhouse Ireland to dodge other adepts hunting for her, or hiding out in one of the castle's hidden rooms to avoid angry Mothers who wanted to teach her a lesson. She could hold her own in any battle, but when everybody wanted to pick a fight at the same time, she had learned it was best to minimize opportunities.

Not exactly what she was doing now, out alone in Central Park, almost daring something to give her grief.

Camille walked faster, purposeful, not panicked. She wasn't prey, so she didn't intend to look like prey. She tugged the zipper on her battle leathers as high as it would go. The bodysuit was designed and treated to deflect elemental energy, but it didn't shield her from a fresh round of shivers. She thought about pulling on the leather face mask she had stuffed in her pocket. Thought about it, but didn't do it. The stupid thing made her feel like she was suffocating.

Camille's fingers flexed. The worn ivory hilt of her Indian *shamshir* felt cool as she brushed her palm against it, though these days she usually called the weapon by its Americanized name—scimitar—because she heard that so often from her quad. Her mother had given her the weapon before she died, and she had taught Camille how to take a head with a single strike. Scimitars had a curved edge made for hacking, and Camille liked the fact that nobody expected a small woman to draw such a long, deadly blade, much less swing it like the Grim Reaper.

Everyone except her quad underestimated her strength—physical, emotional, and otherwise. Since she sucked at making fire, enemy misperceptions about her abilities were her greatest advantage in any type of fight.

Her heart rate picked up to a steady *beat-beat-beat*.

Would she be taking a head tonight?

Camille moved quietly around a copse of trees and bushes, letting the thing behind her gain a few steps. If this needed to come to blows, it was better that she pick the moment and the location. Yes. This little clearing would do. Shielded from view, plenty of moonlight, enough room to swing, but not enough room for too many surprises.

Her mouth felt dry when she tried to swallow. Her quad would be so pissed if she got herself beaten to death or eaten tonight. They'd have no idea why she was out without them, or what she was doing—or that she was doing it for them, to make up for that big mistake.

Let's get this over with.

As soon as Camille heard the rustle of brush near the clearing she had picked, she ripped her scimitar from its sheath, spun toward the noise, and pulled the blade back for a strike.

The thing in the bushes went totally still.

Camille blinked at the spot where all sound had stopped. She had expected the creature to run or fight, not just stand there and wait for her to hack it to death. What the hell was that about?

It occurred to her to kill the thing first and figure it out later, but what if this creature was friend, not foe? Just because something had powers didn't make it evil. Sibyls worked with all manner of supernatural practitioners, and even some kinds of man-made demons. Most natural demons—and the man-made kind, too—were nothing but soulless murderers. The Asmodai the crazy Legion cult used to create, for example.

Camille's insides clenched.

No.

Don't think about Asmodai.

Brainless elemental golems. Strong as hell, targeted on one victim, bent on killing no matter what got in their way.

She'd lost one of her first fighting group to an Asmodai. She would never forget its towering bulk, its blank, hateful face, or the fire pouring out of its mouth and nose and eyes.

Let it go. Now.

No time to dwell on Asmodai, because some demons were a lot more complex, and a lot more human. Cursons, half-breeds, with human mothers and human souls, were Sibyl allies now, and so were full-blooded Astaroth demons. Most of those had been human children when they got converted into demons, so they still had human intelligence and emotions. Hell, Cursons and Astaroths had even married Sibyls. And then there was Duncan Sharp, Bela's husband, a half-human, half-Rakshasa creature called a Bengal. Even their next-door neighbor Mrs. Knight was half demon, a Bengal like Duncan.

So maybe this thing in the bushes was more like Cursons and Astaroths and Bengals—something new to Sibyls and paranormal police officers of NYPD's Occult Crimes Unit, but friendly and a little shy. She still didn't sense any malice from it. It was hard to behead something that gave off the energy of a distracted kitten.

She could almost see it, a man-like outline in the deep shadows under the trees, but even her sensitive Sibyl vision couldn't make out details. Weird. Was it doing something to throw off her perceptions?

"Show yourself," she demanded. She didn't make any threats, because Camille never made a threat she didn't plan to back up in full.

The thing refused to move, but its energy . . . it was— what? Amused?

That pissed her off enough to begin drawing fire power into her essence, intending to use her pyrosentient talents to send the energy back out, to channel it so she could use it to explore Tall, Dark, and Shady Silence over there.

"You're out past your bedtime, beautiful," the thing said to her in a startlingly human voice. "And that's one hell of a pocketknife."

Camille's grip on her scimitar loosened, and she almost dropped it.

My big mistake.

She needed to get hold of herself, but she barely managed a complete breath. It took all she had to keep hold of her blade. She knew she was overreacting, because if this was the Rakshasa she had been looking for, it would have attacked already.

This was something else. It had to be—but that voice. So raw and low.

So familiar and enticing.

She was losing it.

Even though she'd been searching night after night, she had to admit she'd never expected to actually find what she was looking for, much less have it find her and not try to tear her to pieces.

If it is him, he's a deadly demon, and I can't forget that no matter how many new tricks he's learned. Not this time.

But why would he play with her? Rakshasa weren't prone to dicking around. They killed. Then they ate what they killed. Pretty simple formula.

"Step out of the shadows and let me see you." Her voice still had some authority even though she felt like the tree leaves over her head were rustling through her chest and belly instead. Thank the Goddess for small favors, and for scimitars. One look and she'd know if this thing was her demon or something else entirely. "Come out now."

"No," it said, and its tone suggested it didn't think Camille could force the issue.

Moonlight spilled into the clearing. Camille knew she was lit up like a silvery neon sign, but the thing in the bushes stayed dark and inscrutable. The sense she had of it now wasn't demon at all. It was human. Completely.

Yet not.

The confusion that had gripped her a year ago, the same confusion that had led her to make that big mistake, seized her again.

Kill it, she told herself. *Don't take a chance. Chop it into pieces, and if it turns out to be a good guy, apologize to its kin and make peace with them later.*

If it even had any kin.

"Who are you?" she whispered, and now her voice was shaking like the rest of her. She tightened her arms to make sure her weapon stayed in ready position. "What are you?"

The thing in the bushes didn't answer immediately, and the rush of emotion it put off went by too quickly to read.

Then the dinar resting against Camille's chest grew faintly warm.

"You know who I am," it said, and that intense voice curled across her body like she wasn't even wearing her battle leathers. She felt the sound *everywhere*.

"I don't." Too fast. Like a lie, except it wasn't.

I do.

No, she didn't.

I've sensed this man before.

But she hadn't.

She wished she could stop shaking. She wished her nerves weren't shivering from the sound of that voice.

"The Rakshasa demon pride isn't back in New York City yet," the thing in the bushes told her, and Camille gave up on her plan to cut it to ribbons.

She surrendered to the confusion and uncertainty and lowered her scimitar. "How the hell do you know what I'm looking for?"

The thing let out a breath, actually sounding as tired as she felt. "Because I'm hunting them, too. When those assholes get back to New York, I'll make sure you know, but don't come looking for them alone again."

"Fuck you." Camille squinted at the big shadow. "You're not my mother—but *who are you*?"

"You know who I am," it said again, hot and devil-sexy,

and before she could argue, it was gone. Park bushes rustled in its wake, and a soft fall breeze brought his scent back to Camille. Light, spicy, and masculine. The perfect aftershave.

"Not possible," she said aloud to nobody as she jammed her scimitar into its sheath. Then, much louder, "Not possible!"

Her mind pulled away from her and she tried to snatch back her focus, her awareness, but it was too late. The memory from last year struck her with the force of a fist, making her stagger back and sit right down on the wet, dark grass.

Dio's voice rang out through the cold, dark alley, strong as the wind. "Camille! Get the demon!"

Camille charged forward. Strada, a big white-furred monster with claws and fangs like a prehistoric saber-toothed tiger, was choking Duncan Sharp with a gold chain.

Choking him.

Choking him to death.

Not happening.

Camille launched herself at Strada, swinging her scimitar as she jumped, right at the demon's head.

The blade came down in a perfect arc—

And hit something like electric concrete.

"Shit!"

Her voice echoed in her own brain as her bones seemed to compact from the blow and white-hot agony seared every muscle she owned.

The hilt tore out of her hands. She stumbled to the side, fighting for balance as she saw Duncan's face go blood red and dark, his eyes closed.

Dying.

Seconds left.

Since Camille had no real fire making to draw on, she knew what she had to do.

Damnit, no choice.

She had to!

Dio and Bela shouted at her, and Andy, too, but Camille got her balance, charged toward Duncan and the demon, and dropped to her knees beside Duncan and the Rakshasa. She pulled deep inside her own power, to her own well of elemental energy, and willed her awareness of fire to bring itself forward.

Pyrosentience was all about channeling the fire energy, drawing it through her instead of into her. Simple. Different from fire making. Infinitely more powerful—and infinitely more dangerous. Her whole quad had a touch of sentient gifts with their elements, and the Mothers had all but forbidden them to use these powers, because nobody really knew what could happen.

"I'm saving Duncan's life," she muttered to herself as she opened her senses and tiny lasers of firelight broke across her fingers. Fire energy, pulled through her, escaping to the world again in controlled bursts through her skin.

She pushed at the demon, but his energy turned hers away.

Strada tightened his grip on Duncan, who lost consciousness.

Not strong enough!

More screaming from her quad—but Camille couldn't listen to them or Duncan was a dead man and this demon bastard would have them all for dinner. Focusing every bit of her fire awareness into her hands, she grabbed the coin on the end of the chain Strada was using to choke Duncan.

The dinar, she knew, had projective properties—it could take in energy and feed it out again in big, concentrated blasts. The coin would magnify her pyrosentience hundreds of times over.

The second she made contact with the metal, it seemed

*like every stray ounce of fire energy in the universe chan-
neled itself through her.*

Hit by lightning.

Blown apart.

*Camille screamed as the force of it seemed to tear her
apart.*

*A roar like a thousand volcanoes erupting crushed
against her ears. Her skin—was it coming off?*

*All she could do was scream and try to shove back
against the onslaught. Barely there. Barely able to focus
on anything. She couldn't possibly be in one piece, but
somehow she knew she was, still screaming but making no sound now, eyes open but seeing nothing but a
huge swirl of golden, pulsing fire energy going to war
with the dark power pouring off the bellowing tiger-
demon.*

*This time when she hit Strada, she made contact.
Enough to get her free hand on the chain. To take control of it and ease the pressure on Duncan's neck.*

A stench—hot desert winds and fresh blood—

The connection, Duncan Sharp to her to Strada.

The golden storm around them—

Duncan coughing himself back to awareness—

*And then the ghost in Duncan's head, the ghost of his
dead best friend, starting to move, to set itself free and
finally fling itself off this mortal coil—*

Camille sat in Central Park, breathing slowly and
steadily so that she wouldn't cry, not wanting to think
about what had happened next on that terrible night,
but she couldn't help herself.

The ghost that was inhabiting Duncan Sharp's head, a
man named John Cole, a man she'd never met before in
her life, had suddenly been in that alley beside her. He
was there, and then he was gone.

Only he wasn't gone.

Many, many times in Camille's life, she'd been convinced she was losing her mind, but all of those times paled in comparison to that night, and now this one.

In that alley, John Cole *had* been there, with his green eyes and dark hair. She'd touched him inside and out for that one moment. She had seen him, heard him, and smelled that enticing, spicy aftershave she wouldn't ever forget, and then he was gone.

He. Wasn't. Gone.

"Yes, he was." Camille scrubbed her palms against her cheeks to keep herself in the now, in today, in the reality of middle-of-the-night and dangerous-as-hell Central Park.

John Cole was gone.

She'd told herself this every time she allowed herself to remember what she'd done that night, how she'd saved Duncan and set free the spirit of John Cole. Then how she'd gotten confused and let the demon Strada convince her that somehow the wandering spirit of John Cole had ended up in his body. That's why she had let Strada escape.

Damn me.

Strada had gotten away. Duncan had gotten better. John Cole was gone forever to wherever spirits went after their bodies died.

I looked in that demon's eyes, and they were John Cole's. The demon spoke to me in John Cole's voice.

And it had to have been a trick. A brilliant move on Strada's part to save his demon ass.

But the way he looked, the way he smelled, that voice . . .

Camille wanted to pound her head on the ground.

The man who'd been following her tonight, she did know him. But she couldn't, because he couldn't possibly have been there. Camille was as sure of that as she was of the skyscraper lights, her earlier sense of being followed, and the fact that she shouldn't be patrolling alone.

Camille didn't have a clue what else to do, so she curled up on the grass and hugged her knees to her chest.

The man who'd been following her tonight couldn't have been there, because that man—the one man she had ever really, truly, deeply touched, even if only for one literally shining moment inside a shimmering golden cloud of madness—had died a year ago.

And Camille had just let Strada, leader of the Rakshasa demons, play her all over again.

Jesus, but seeing that woman up close and personal again felt like torture.

He kept moving, through Central Park, around Central Park, because he didn't know what else to do. John Cole—on the inside, even if the outside was not what anybody might expect—got far enough away from her that he thought he could keep himself from following her as she headed home. Then he dropped onto a bench on Balcony Bridge because one place was as good as another.

He leaned forward and let his head hang toward his knees, but that didn't block his view of the darkened walkway at his feet. In the strange night lighting, it seemed like a cracked stone slab, and his mind flashed on the entrance to that godforsaken temple in the mountains of Afghanistan near Kabul, which he and others had explored during the war. The scorch marks. The heat fissures.

Looks like it got cooked. That's what he'd said to one of the ten men from Recon who went with him and the contingent of Vatican priests. Then, to his commander, Jack Blackmore, in lower tones, *What the hell are we doing here, Blackjack? What are all these high-level priests doing here? They won't tell me anything, and I'm supposed to be one of them.*

Standing orders. Blackjack had eyed the big stone door with its burn marks, top to bottom. Twilight made the rock look like it was still on fire. In the distance in the big valley around the temple, John saw shadows and more stones. The ruins of an ancient village? More like a city.

We've had a description of this place since we hit the ground, Blackjack had added. *Straight from military intelligence. They left details on what to do if we found it.* After another few seconds, Blackjack said, *I think the orders are old. Like, passed down for decades. Maybe centuries.*

Great. John remembered thinking that. *Old orders about some ancient temple. That can't be good.*

Blackjack had pulled out then, taking half of Recon with him to seal the valley and deploying the rest to form a perimeter around the temple. John's instructions were simple enough: get the priests into the temple, let them do whatever it was they had to do, then get them back out again. Recon would escort them back to the valley's mouth, then they'd all beat it back to camp before they got their asses shot off.

Only it hadn't quite worked out that way.

Stop.

Leave it alone.

John refused to let the tension in his neck and shoulders get worse. He wouldn't let the memories roll over him again, not here, not now. Too many years and too many miles ago, not that he'd ever get the war or the Valley of the Gods out of his mind and heart, no matter how far and how fast he ran, and no matter how much he tried to atone.

Camille—she was like that, too. Lodged inside him, maybe forever.

She was as beautiful as he remembered.

"You don't know anything about her," he reminded himself, his voice seeming to echo across the deserted bridge. "She's nothing but a fantasy to you."

Only that wasn't really true, was it? He'd spent some

time with Camille Fitzgerald and all the Sibyls in the South Bronx fighting quad after his best buddy, Duncan Sharp, got himself attacked by Rakshasa demons. John had died trying to save Duncan from John's worst enemies, the creatures he had been hunting every single day of his life since he accidentally helped set them free from their prison in the Valley of the Gods.

John's body had died, but a strange paranormal accident involving the ancient dinar John had given to Duncan to shield him from the Rakshasa had left John's spirit alive and well and hanging out in Duncan's head—until Camille had done whatever it was she did in that alley.

Golden light.

John remembered that, and he remembered giving her the dinar she now wore around her neck, but more than anything, John remembered her. The light in her eyes. The rich tones of her auburn hair. The feel of her, not just physically but spiritually. It was like he had moved through everything that made her. Like he had connected with her on every level.

Yeah.

On his way to this new body, which she could never see. She or any of her Sibyl buddies.

That thought brought him more grief than he expected, the kind of grief he remembered from the war, when somebody had died right beside him—or when he'd seen the Rakshasa start to take down Duncan Sharp, the only person in the world he'd truly cared about saving until he touched Camille.

The possibility of never really seeing her again, except from a distance, of never getting to truly talk to her or know her or hold her—it kicked him in the gut so hard he wanted to roar.

And something *was* roaring.

That was the real bitch of this whole situation, wasn't it?

John almost laughed out loud, but he was afraid it would be a madman's lunatic braying, because something in his mind was definitely making a lot of noise. The thing in his mind, it wasn't quite dead or alive, but he knew it was dangerous. And definitely, definitely evil.

Dark energy surged forward, wrong energy, perverted and twisted and nauseating. John slammed his head against his fists, letting the shock of pain help him focus. Bile surged in his throat, and the darkness around him swam in sickening, expanding, contracting ways.

In his days as a priest, before he lost his faith and his collar and his freedom, John had known true evil like the thing in his head, but he had never known insanity up close. Crazy had to feel like this, taste like this, smell like this. He was crazy now, and that's all that was left of him.

He had to put this fantasy with Camille away and focus on his only purpose. John Cole knew his spirit and knowledge had survived for one reason, and that was to kill Rakshasa, to make sure every last one of the demon bastards got wiped off the face of the earth. Then and only then could he leave crazy behind, set himself free, and take the lingering soul and essence of the last demon with him.

The demon living in his own head.

"You're fucked, Strada," he whispered to the monstrosity trying to chew its way through his brain.

And the Rakshasa in his head howled, and howled, and howled.

The man stood on a path in Central Park near West Sixty-third, across from one of the park entrances and in front of the brownstone where his gods-cursed enemies chose to reside. A warm, comfortable breeze stirred leaves and branches in nearby trees, making the night crinkle and rattle around him like it had some secret duty and purpose, much as he did. Moonlight lit the few steps leading into the three-story dwelling he sought, but he sensed no powerful energy and saw no sign of activity from within. The plain white curtains in the windows remained still, and all the lights were off.

Too bad.

He had come here hoping to observe, to begin the long and arduous process of learning the Sibyls' new patterns, and perhaps their new weaknesses.

Caution. Calculation. They won't expect those things from me.

The man—though he wasn't a man at all—knew his enemies anticipated his loud and forceful return to the city. They believed he would make a show of strength and draw attention to himself, that he would behave impulsively, leaving himself and his pride vulnerable to attack.

The fools.

He would not put his true brothers, his Created brothers and sisters, or his allies at risk. He was the pride's *culla* now, and he had much to learn and accomplish.

Such as remaining comfortable in human form.

Not an easy task for him. He felt confined in this flesh, but holding this strange shape was already becoming easier. Still, his senses seemed duller than they should, and he needed to learn more focus. If he directed his energies properly, he should suffer no loss of his acute hearing, vision, and sense of smell simply because he wore the skin and shape of a human male.

With tremendous force of will, the man concentrated all of his efforts on the brownstone, and slowly, slowly his eyes let him see the brilliant colors of the elemental barriers the Sibyls had constructed and reinforced to protect their lair. Earth, air, fire, and water energy had been layered together and locked so tightly that any paranormal creature attempting to enter the brownstone or any other house on their block without their consent would be repelled—and violently, perhaps stumbling into the traffic of the busy road in front. The barriers could be broken, of course, but at high cost to the invader's energy and strength.

He closed his eyes and let the colors fade, then opened them again and gazed at the brownstone with only human skill and perception.

Just a quiet home in New York City, with all occupants apparently asleep.

After a time, the man determined that he would gain no useful information this night, and he walked silently and quickly into the nearby bushes. With a sigh of release, he stepped out of his human form, shifting to his natural state as easily as another creature might change positions during a fitful night's sleep. Dark fur flowed over him as his teeth expanded to their fierce and proper length, and his claws curled out of his powerful paws as his muscles flexed and pulled into their true and superior form.

In his former life, Tarek would have roared, challenging the world to come to him, to try to defeat him and fail—but he had learned much in the last year. Challenge was best reserved for times when he was certain he could win the contests.

With his numbers few in comparison to his enemies, he had to plan carefully and strike with overwhelming advantage. To do that, he must increase his allies and the force he could bring to bear. More soldiers. More weapons. Which would of course entail more money to be spent, and garnering more power to be wielded.

"Soon," he told the sleeping occupants of the brownstone, confident that they would find nothing, that they would have no hint of his plans before his trap was sprung. He'd throw them crumbs. He'd lead them this way and that, but in the end he would destroy them with a single, glorious move.

Bordering on excited and cheerful, Tarek turned to make his exit from the park.

He had taken only a few steps when a scent came to him—familiar, yet strange at the same time.

Demon? One of his own?

But no. How could that be?

Tarek was *culla* of the Rakshasa. He knew every member of his own demon ranks, and if this were some renegade Created—hybrids formed when humans were attacked but not killed by Rakshasa—he would be able to tell by the weak spoor.

This scent was too strong. Human, yet tiger. Ripe, but distant from his current location.

He crept toward the smell, making certain to keep to the overgrowth as he moved toward his quarry. He covered ground, crossed a path, and skirted some water— yes, there, just ahead. Perhaps atop the bridge looming in the lamplit city night.

Just as Tarek prepared to leave the relative safety of the plant cover to explore this situation more thoroughly, a woman ran past his location.

A woman dressed in leather.

The shock was so great he barely held back a roar.

One of the Sibyls here—now! He could leap out and take her down with a single swipe. He could tear out her throat before she had a chance to draw her weapon. His own blood thrummed in his ears as he imagined the taste of hers. The night painted itself red as battle lust seized him, and it took every ounce of his new knowledge and self-control to hold himself in check.

Killing her would weaken his enemy but also enrage them. It would announce his return to New York City before he and his allies were prepared, and before he gathered more soldiers to fight in their battles. Perhaps worst of all, he would reveal the fact that one of his allies had developed new but meager protections to make it more difficult for the Sibyls and other paranormals to sense his presence.

Tarek lifted his paw to a thin chain hanging around his thick, powerful neck. On the chain hung a bit of iron around a tooth forged and treated so that it dispersed elemental energy. Not much. Just enough to create confusion for anyone attempting to read his energy or understand what kind of creature he might be. They would perceive him as a flicker across their awareness, not human but not malevolent or threatening, perhaps nothing but a trick from an overactive and worried mind.

No.

He couldn't do this thing.

He couldn't go after the Sibyl no matter how desperately his baser instincts wanted to do just that.

He forced himself to breathe slowly, imagining calming vistas and comforting textures. He let himself take in the smells of dirt and grass and water and earth until the battle lust waned and at last set him free. For good measure, he slipped back into human form to place yet another obstacle between himself and impulsive self-destruction.

When he returned his attention to the bridge and found his strange quarry gone, he almost lost control all over again, but once more kept hold of himself.

"Not this night," he said aloud, his voice more a snarl than human words. "But soon. I'll find you both."

(3)

August

Asmodai in her dreams.

Asmodai in her daydreams.

Since Camille had been hunted by, then hunted, that thing in Central Park, her old nightmares about the Asmodai demons who'd slaughtered her sister Sibyl right before her eyes had come roaring back. There hadn't been a single Asmodai reported anywhere in the world since the Legion fell, but the big, ugly, smelly bastards were alive and well in her twisted mind.

An omen?

A portent?

Stop it.

The fact that Camille hadn't found—or been found by—the thing in Central Park again was the only thing sparing her sanity, and now this ceremony-for-the-past shit was threatening to burn up her inner peace more brutally than any Asmodai could ever manage.

She stood on a stone battlement at Motherhouse Ireland with about twenty other women, hating the wind that stung her eyes and whipped her auburn hair into knots she'd never comb loose without yanking herself bald. Heavy clouds turned the landscape gray and damp and miserable, and any second the heavens would open and rain would wash them all away.

Sometimes the hidden valley near Connemara, Ireland, seemed to spread for miles, fresh and green and beautiful beyond words. Sometimes the castle grounds bustled with frenetic energy that couldn't be equaled, that demanded enjoyment and excitement and smiles and wild, optimistic outlooks. Sometimes Motherhouse Ireland was a haven and a sanctuary, and the only place Camille wanted to be.

But sometimes the place just sucked.

Today the entire world sucked, as far as Camille was concerned.

At least she and her companions had on their battle leathers, though, being fire Sibyls, few of them were wearing the masks. Too confining. Though she figured she'd regret that choice when the rains came and froze her cheeks solid before she could get inside.

She frowned at the fields below the Motherhouse, which were covered with Sibyls about to experience an old-fashioned Irish gully washer. On her left stood the earth Sibyls and brown-robed Mothers from Motherhouse Russia, no doubt trying to be earthy and steady and helpful. In the center, green-robed Mothers and fire Sibyl adepts and warriors huddled together, giving off steady clouds of smoke. Air Sibyls from Motherhouse Greece occupied the field on her right, with their blue robes and windy, breezy gestures and expressions. Just about in the middle of the mix, in her glowing yellow robe, was Andy, the world's only fully trained water Sibyl, who had arrived an hour ago from Motherhouse Kérkira, in the Ionian Sea. Andy was anything but breezy, and even at a distance, Camille's keen Sibyl vision showed her Andy's scowl and tightly folded arms.

Looking at so many Sibyls, Camille felt the absence of her first fighting group like a constant ache in her chest. The two women who had first made her their sister Sibyl were lost to her, gone forever. That was why she had to stand on this stupid wall once every three years, when it was Motherhouse Ireland's turn to host the remembrance ceremony, and try to keep herself together. Her new fighting group, the only quad in existence, stared up at her from the crowd—Andy in her idiotic yellow robes, Bela in her brown robes, and Dio in her blue robes. They had been together just over a year, but so far they had managed not to kill one another.

What happens if I let them down again?

Camille's left eye twitched even as she tried to hold her face perfectly still.

What happens when *I let them down again?*

Tears made Camille blink, worsening the twitch until she surrendered and closed her eyes. Couldn't the worries leave her alone for just one day?

Heat prickled against her cheeks, and the pungent scent of wildfire and smoke forced her eyes open again. Mother Keara, one of the oldest Irish Mothers, reached the top of a set of steps leading up from the castle. Her unbelievable warmth came and went like an orange wave as she passed Camille on her way to the center of the battlement, without sparing Camille so much as a glance.

Typical.

Camille had never known deep relationships at Motherhouse Ireland after the Sibyl who gave birth to her had been killed in battle. There was one time, before she was even ten years old, when she'd met an old woman down in the tunnels, an old woman she thought might have been a Mother, no matter what she said. Camille had thought that woman might turn out to be a friend, especially after she somehow put a stop to the bullying that had plagued Camille in her early years. Yet Camille had never seen her again. She figured Ona had died or finished going insane, or simply lost interest when she saw Camille really wasn't going to develop any definitive talent for pyrogenesis. Whatever happened, it didn't matter, because what was done couldn't be undone. Camille had finished her training with high accolades in everything but battle skills, and she had never bothered currying favor with her fellow fire Sibyls or the Mothers. She doubted she would ever experience their love or support, but that was old news, and not worth the time it took to cry about it. She needed to stay in the present, and the present was the ceremony, no matter how much she despised every moment of it.

Tiny and wrinkled but still spry, Mother Keara stepped onto a small raised area of stone so she could see the grounds and the Sibyls below. The ropes of gray hair spilling down her shoulders were too heavy to move in the wind, but her green robes snapped in the sharp gusts. Without preamble, she raised both gnarled hands and loosed two massive gouts of fire from her palms. Her orange flames shot toward the thunderous sky, rebellious, seeming powerful enough to part the clouds, but the sky didn't stir.

"Aban, Angela," Mother Keara shouted without looking at notes. "Abel, Victoria. Abhen, Westra."

Her voice blasted against the clouds, as forceful as the flames she had released.

The names.

Goddess, the names.

All those lives. All those women.

Camille listened to the list with growing numbness as Mother Keara recited them all, any killed in battle all the way back to the time before Sibyls even called themselves Sibyls, and the numbness gave way to a slow burn in her gut when her mother's name rang out in Mother Keara's lyrical Irish brogue.

By the time the older woman's recitation moved on to air Sibyls, Camille didn't bother trying not to cry.

"Carmella, Bette," Mother Keara said soon, too soon. Camille coughed from the blow, mostly to keep from sobbing out loud. Bette had died in battle, right beside Camille. They had been ambushed by Asmodai demons in Van Cortlandt Park, near the Old Croton Aqueduct. Nothing anyone could do.

Sure. Just keep telling yourself that, and you'll get Dio killed, or maybe Bela or Andy. Sibyls always worked in groups, with earth Sibyls serving as the mortars, responsible for picking the group and holding it together. As a fire Sibyl, the pestle of the group, it was Camille's job to handle communications and close-quarters fighting. Simply put, she was supposed to keep her mortar alive at all costs. Air Sibyls served as the brooms, battling from a distance, charged with keeping perspective—and sweeping up messes. Water Sibyls were supposed to be in charge of flow, but Andy was the only water Sibyl in a fighting group in the world right now, and she wasn't so good with regulating her own emotions, much less helping her fighting group regulate theirs. As for healing, the special talent of water Sibyls, Andy hadn't quite figured out that skill, either.

Their quad was far from perfect.

Oh, hell.

Their quad was a train wreck waiting to happen, but Camille loved her new sister Sibyls desperately. She'd die before she'd let any harm come to them.

"James, Alisa," Mother Keara announced.

Camille's heart lurched.

She hadn't realized Mother Keara had moved on to the earth Sibyls lost in battle.

Hold it together. Hold on, hold on . . .

But she couldn't. Not really. Alisa James had claimed Camille for a fighting partner and taken her away from Motherhouse Ireland. Then Alisa had been locked up at Rikers Island for a crime she didn't commit and murdered in jail. Camille had never had the chance to protect her.

Her thoughts tore free and floated toward the rain-swollen sky, and for a few seconds nothing seemed true or concrete or tangible, not even her own body or the hard stone beneath her leather boots. She felt like crap. She felt like before, when she was a little girl who couldn't find any safe place, or later, when she ran away from the deaths of her fighting group and hid for years inside the thick stone walls of Motherhouse Ireland.

Bela. Dio. Andy. Camille recited the names to herself, imagining them like anchors pulling her down from the clouds.

They were still alive, and she had a responsibility to them. She absolutely couldn't allow herself to go to pieces again, especially not on some frigging stone wall in front of just about every living Sibyl on Earth.

Bela. Dio. Andy.

Camille's emotional fog started to clear. She couldn't let anything happen to this fighting group. She had to keep finding ways to be better at what she *could* do, to be stronger so she could do her part to keep her quad whole and safe.

The woman next to her elbowed her, and Camille raised her chin.

The reading of the names had ended, thank the universe. Mother Keara was talking about Sibyls and strength and determination, and about ridding the world of perverted energies and evil creatures who used the elements to do harm.

Camille realized she was shaking and weeping, and the sigh she released seemed to come all the way from her toes. Losing both of her first sister Sibyls within weeks of each other had shattered her, but some of the pieces had been glued back together. Bela had come for her, claimed her for a new fighting group, and challenged her to return to the land of the living. Bela had challenged her to fight.

"We fight," Mother Keara announced, echoing Camille's thoughts as she finished the remembrance. "We fight for fairness. We fight for honor. We fight for the world. Let our strength burn in your souls now and always, until we meet again."

Once more she lifted her arms and fire blasted from her palms.

The Sibyls around Camille gave off dense smoke and let fly with their own flames. Camille raised her hands for Bette and Alisa, and for the bits of her own soul that had died with them. The fire energy around her glowed like the sun in her eyes. She could taste it, smell it, touch it, even glory in it, but no flames burst out of her body. She barely smoked and she didn't drop so much as a trickle of sparks.

Her teeth clamped together, and she wanted to swear and cry and kick something. Her chilled fingers curled into fists. How was it possible that she was a fire Sibyl, born and trained in a Motherhouse, and she couldn't create her own element with any reliability? Not even now, when she would give a body part to honor her dead fighting group with a show of her own strength.

The disgusted, pitying expressions of the other fire Sibyls around her made silent comments about that strength—or lack of it. Mother Keara was looking at her, too, and the old woman's blazing green eyes held the same judgment.

Too little, too quiet, too weak.

Camille *really* wished she had her scimitar, just to draw the blade and stare down each of the women on the battlement, Mother Keara included, until they moved away from her and went back down to the castle. Without her weapon, she had nothing but matted hair, wet eyes, and freezing fingers. Paltry heat rose in her cheeks— embarrassment, not power—and she felt nine years old again, failing in most of her lessons, shunted to the side as a reject who probably wouldn't make the cut to fight, and running for her life down endless, dark stone corridors.

On the fields below, the crowd began to disperse and head into the keep before the storm struck. Camille spun away from Mother Keara and her glare, and elbowed past the Sibyls separating her from the steps.

Retreat.

Why did that always seem to be her best option?

Ah, screw it.

She more or less ran down the steps before any of them could see her cry again and slammed open the door at the foot of the stairs. When she stormed into the dark, quiet hallway leading toward the main entrance, she almost crushed a tiny figure standing directly in the middle of the corridor.

The woman's scarred, white face and puckered, empty left eye were as unmistakable as her pheasant-egg bald head. Camille almost cried out from the shock of seeing Ona standing there like a spirit straight from Camille's past, from the childhood she didn't really want to commemorate.

"Figured you would be the first one down, like all the times before." Ona spoke as though no time had passed since their long-ago meeting near the tunnels under Motherhouse Ireland. She had no accent, and obviously, she still spoke so rarely that it left her voice sounding rough and hoarse.

"I hate that ceremony," Camille muttered, processing what Ona meant—that the old woman had seen Camille fleeing from these ceremonies before.

"I hate those ceremonies, too, and most others, which is why I don't attend." Ona studied Camille with her good eye, which was a strange, shadowy shade of black. Her unlined face had no discernible expression. "Why do you put yourself through that torture?"

"It's—I—" Camille fished for an explanation, but she was too rattled by Ona's appearance and the question to find an answer. "It's expected," she said after a few seconds, then realized how lame that sounded.

"Expectations. Rules." Ona raised a slender hand and gestured toward the stone walls and ceiling. Gold bracelets glittered along her arm. They seemed too still, fixed in place, not like bangles or normal jewelry. "The likes of us, we don't do so well with edicts and pointless traditions. From this day forward, do what feels right instead of what you're told is right."

"Yeah, okay, like that's so easy." Camille's shame and anger faded as she tried to absorb the sight of the barefoot enigma, who still wasn't wearing the green robes of the Motherhouse. Today Ona had on a white tunic and black cotton breeches that made her look like a throwback to medieval times.

Who knows? She might have been acquainted with King Arthur and Merlin, too, as old as she is.

Had Ona's mind finally collapsed? Was that why she had come out of hiding again to give Camille this do-what-feels-right lesson after leaving her hanging for all these years?

Movement disrupted the silence behind them, and Camille felt Mother Keara's distinctive heat and energy roll into the corridor. A second or so later, Mother Keara walked past Camille and hesitated at the sight of Ona. The Sibyls behind Mother Keara stopped, too, all of them staring at the little woman with almost matching looks of shock.

"We've a lot goin' on today," Mother Keara said, irritation mingling with a hint of surprise and maybe even kindness in her tone. "What can we do for you, Ona?"

Ona never shifted her gaze away from Camille, and she didn't bother with being pleasant. "You can move along. I have no business with any of you."

Camille's mouth came open, and her gaze darted to

Mother Keara, who had been one of the worst terrors of her young life.

Mother Keara's face turned a deep, hectic red. A cloud of smoke wreathed her gray braids. Camille readied herself for the blast of fire and temper, but Mother Keara didn't ignite anything at all. It was almost like she couldn't, like the fire refused to obey her will, form itself, and explode outward to express her anger.

"Fine." Mother Keara stared at Ona another few heartbeats. "I was just bein' polite, for all that gets a person with you."

Ona gave her no response. She just kept staring at Camille.

Camille barely kept her mouth from falling open.

She had never seen anybody show Mother Keara such open disrespect except for Bela, who had an unusually close relationship with the old witch—and Bela was usually kidding or being affectionate.

Mother Keara sniffed, but she didn't say anything else. Instead, she stumped off down the hall in the direction of the entryway, trailing curtains of smoke as she went. The other Sibyls from the battlement followed her, single file, none of them looking over their shoulders.

"Rules and expectations," Ona said loudly enough to be heard by Mother Keara. "Pointless. By the time councils and kings get around to making rules, the trouble they're set to fix has already happened. Why bother? I never saw rules teach anybody anything. Do what feels right, Camille."

Mother Keara walked faster and smashed the corridor's wooden door against the stone wall when she opened it. When the last Sibyl went through, she closed the door firmly behind her, as if to lock trouble away for good.

"You live in New York City now," Ona told Camille, stating fact instead of asking a question. "You live with a . . . a water Sibyl."

Camille felt her eyes go wide. "You—I—yes." Her mind was still reeling from watching Ona take Mother Keara down a few pegs, and she couldn't quite believe she'd heard Ona correctly. "Sorry. I'm surprised you keep up with details like that."

Ona shook her head once. "I don't care about details, girl. It's you I'm keeping up with."

If Camille had been surprised before, she was stunned now. She didn't know how to respond, and Ona didn't seem to have anything else to say, either.

Chills broke out along Camille's neck and shoulders as Ona kept staring at her, and she remembered having the same reaction to her when she'd seen her as a child. Ona's gaze was more like probing than simple staring, like Ona was reaching inside her to pry out—what?

And why?

"Okay, well." Camille tried to keep her composure as she ran her fingers through her hair to tug out some of the wind knots. "I guess I should go find my quad. We have to get back to the city for patrol tonight."

Ona's expression shifted to something like sadness, but by the time she nodded, her scarred face had become unreadable again.

Camille moved past Ona carefully and slowly, wondering what the hell had just happened. It wasn't like Camille needed any more stress, complications, or weirdness in her life. She was trying to work with a fighting group with a lot of issues, she'd just had her nose rubbed in her losses and failures and weaknesses *again*, she was dealing with the world's only water Sibyl—and oh, yeah, Bela, the mortar of her triad, had gotten married and kicked Camille out of the bigger bedroom she'd had on the ground floor of the brownstone where they all lived, consigning her to the basement. That was quite enough for now, thank you.

As she reached the doorway separating the corridor

from the main entryway, she heard the dull, distant thunder of conversations, lots of people moving, and rain beginning to fall on Connemara's boggy land. She got hold of the door's metal handle and gave it a pull, and from somewhere behind her Ona said, "I may see you soon."

Camille let go of the wooden edge of the door and whipped around to ask Ona what that meant, but Ona was gone, as if she'd never been in the hallway at all. A tiny patch of stone in the center of the corridor seemed to flicker and shimmer like a small pool of water in the moonlight, but when Camille blinked, the area was normal again, gray and solid.

Okay, maybe all that time she'd spent hiding out in the lower reaches of Motherhouse Ireland to regain her sanity after Alisa and Bette died hadn't worked after all. This was definitely crazy. Sibyls worked with the elements, like all supernatural practitioners. There was no such thing as "magic" in the mythical storybook sense—only enhanced abilities to control, channel, and shape the natural energies of the earth. Way back before Sibyls started writing everything down, people used to call their elemental abilities "magicks" or "old magicks"—but those were just words, not reality.

Ona couldn't have gotten out of sight that fast, and she couldn't have disappeared.

Right?

" 'I may see you soon,' " Camille repeated, her heart beating faster as her words echoed into the empty hallway. "Was that an offer or a threat?"

She waited. That sense of things changing came back to her, just like it had when she was little, the first time she met Ona.

"Ona?" she called into the empty hallway.

Then she waited a little longer, but she got no answer at all.

(4)

September

John Cole's knees hit stone so hard his teeth slammed together.

The growling in the back of his mind morphed into roaring, and he wished he could rip the sound out of his head. He'd had this body for a few months now, and he'd figured out a few things about how to put it to good use—but he hadn't figured out how to unplug that god-awful noise, especially when something was pissing him off.

Four massive hands shoved down on his shoulders and neck.

Yeah. That was pissing him off.

John jerked against the weird iron cuffs locking his hands behind his back, surprised they could hold him. His new body was super-strong, more powerful than five men put together, but something in the cuffs drained away some of that strength. He bit into his gag and strained to catch a glimpse of something through the thick black fabric tied around his eyes.

Nothing but darkness.

Wherever he was, the place smelled like shit. Well, shit and mold and water. And dirt and rock and sweat. He had a sense of people, lots of them, moving into position all around him.

Metal rattled on metal.

Swords being drawn?

Swords.

You gotta be kidding me.

He knew only one group of warriors who fought with swords, and the six huge assholes who'd jumped him tonight in the alley were definitely not good-looking women in leather bodysuits.

Sharp, cold steel pressed against the back of his neck.

Great.

He'd survived childhood in the rural South, seminary, the Army, a nightmare in Afghanistan, leaving the priesthood, then years as a black ops agent hunting demons—and now he was about to die in some New York City sewer, thanks to a bunch of sword freaks he didn't even know.

Cloth rustled.

The space around him went grave-still and tomb-silent, and a new smell made him try to lift his head even though the blade bit into his skin.

Rosewood.

A trickle of blood flowed down his back, drenching his best T-shirt, but John ignored that. Rosewood reminded him of his grandmother, of everything regal and formal and really, really old.

Cloth whispered in front of him again, stirring against the stone where he had been forced to kneel. The sword at his neck moved once, slicing through the gag. It fell away from his face. Another slice of the sword, and his blindfold fell away, too. The blade didn't return to his neck, and the hands restraining him turned him loose.

John Cole found himself staring at feet. Very small feet, withered and ancient, clad in sandals beneath a flowing silver robe.

He raised his head.

The first thing he registered was the fact he was in a candlelit stone chamber roughly the size of a football field, and it was full of silent men standing in straight lines, arms behind their backs like soldiers at parade rest.

After his time in the Afghan mountains, John didn't much like stone chambers. Too temple-like. But at least he didn't see any fire marks on these walls. As for the soldiers or whatever they were, most of them looked vaguely foreign, with dark hair and dusky skin, like they might have come from a desert nation. Each wore modern-day jeans and T-shirts, but their overshirts barely concealed scabbards holding broadswords. Arched tunnels led away from the chamber, and more men lined those tunnels. They were probably in some forgotten offshoot of the Old Croton Aqueduct. The masonry looked to be from the mid-1800s, around the time the aqueduct was built.

The second thing John registered was the small elderly woman staring down at him with completely white eyes. *Blind,* his mind told him, and he knew she had to be, yet he sensed she was seeing him more keenly than a sighted person might. She had dark brown skin and a cloud of short hair as silver as the strange robe she wore. The robe and her hair seemed to glitter even in the dim light of the stone chamber. Strange pinkish scars covered all of her that he could see, forming no particular pattern, almost like somebody had dipped her in hot wax or oil, then left her to burn. Supernatural power frothed in the air around her wrinkled skin, and his entire being prickled as he sensed her probing into his essence, his energy—and his thoughts.

"Fight me if you wish," she told him in a clear, strong voice. "You won't stop me from taking what I want to know, demon."

"My name is John Cole." John kept his gaze on her reflective eyes, forcing himself to allow her invasion into certain areas of his mind—but definitely not all of them. His new body had reflexive knowledge of mind talents, and John put that to use, protecting what he didn't want anyone to see, yet careful not to push the woman's energy away from him. He was outnumbered, but also he sensed the woman might be useful to him if he could win her trust. Something about her reminded him of every military officer he had ever known, and power like she seemed to command usually proved to be useful in a war.

In the depths of his essence, the snarling of his body's previous owner never stopped. "I'm not a demon," John said, ignoring that racket as best he could. "I haven't gotten rid of the fuck—ah, sorry, the monster—who used to own this bag of bones, but I kicked its ass, and I'm the one in control now. Dig through my thoughts if you have to. See for yourself."

The scarred old woman in the silvery robes moved closer to him, slow but supple as a year-old cat. The soldiers nearest to them shifted positions, just enough to defend her if John made some sudden move.

Don't worry, boys. I'm pigheaded, but I'm not stupid.

John's skull tingled as the old woman leaned in even tighter. Hot prickles lit up his brain like it was nothing more than a bunch of wires slammed into a wall jack.

Okay, maybe the not-stupid part wasn't spot-on.

He breathed through the fiery jabs, flexing his fingers. Somehow he managed not to move any more than that, and to let the old woman do what he'd invited her to do—dig around his head until she found all she needed to know.

When she finished, she was frowning. "You say your name is John Cole, but you're wearing the skin of our worst enemy. Why should I let you live?"

John reminded himself to watch his mouth in the presence of a lady, and he gave her what he hoped was a polite smile. "Because I slaughter Rakshasa, and I'm good at it."

John sensed a fierce surge of approval from the woman. Whatever she was, she had no love for those creatures.

Good.

Killing the bastards had been his one purpose since he walked away from the first Gulf War.

The snarling in his brain got worse.

John ground his teeth to tamp down the noise in his brain. It distracted him. That's why six of this woman's henchmen had been able to sneak up on him, club him stupid, cuff him, blindfold him, gag him, and drag him down to this godforsaken set of tunnels. Why the men hadn't killed him in the alley, why they'd taken a chance on bringing him to what was obviously a hideout or staging area to meet this woman who was obviously their leader—those were questions he needed to answer.

The old woman backed off a step, then closed her blank white eyes for a few seconds. She seemed to be adding up everything about him and trying to come up with some description that made sense.

Yeah. Good luck with that.

The men protecting her didn't so much as twitch as they waited, but their mistrust buzzed like wasps against the back of John's neck.

Tiger, his overly sensitive nose told him, picking out the acrid musk from the old woman's rosewood and the musty odors of the aqueduct. *Yet not tiger.*

"You're a priest who gave up your collar," the old woman said, her eyes still closed. "You're a soldier who gave up your stripes. You're a man so determined to complete your mission that you escaped death and stole a demon's body to complete it."

John kept his expression as friendly as he could manage, given the circumstances. "That about covers it."

"You have the look of Strada, leader of the Rakshasa Eldest." The woman's puckered face eased into a semblance of peacefulness, and she finally opened her eerie eyes. "You have his human form, but not his energy. Mind and flesh are yours, John Cole, but the struggle for this body's soul is far from over."

How old was she? A hundred? Two hundred? John had a suspicion she was much older, and maybe some of her soldiers were, too. The Rakshasa Eldest had spent a millennium trapped in a temple in the Afghan mountains, in the Valley of the Gods, until a special-forces expedition—an expedition he had been part of—accidentally set them free from that bombed-out temple. Was it possible that the woman and some of her friends had encountered the tiger-demons before the Rakshasa had gotten ensnared in the temple's containment?

"I am *taza* Elana." The woman gestured to herself, then to the silent, staring men in the chamber and the tunnels. "Since you've retained your host's supernatural strength and senses, what do those senses tell you about us?"

John frowned and sampled the air again. "That you're demons—but also not demons. I smell as much human as I do tiger."

"Yes." Elana lowered her withered hand. "We were once human, all of us, before we were scratched or bitten by Rakshasa."

"You're trying to tell me that you're Created?" John gazed at Elana, then glanced at some of the fighters again. No patches of fur, no tails, no crazy fangs or wild eyes like most people turned into demons by Rakshasa wounds.

No way.

These were normal-looking guys, not insane killing machines with shoddy control over their demon essences. They looked like an out-of-uniform army regiment standing around a four-foot-tall blind colonel.

"All Created go mad," John muttered, repeating the rule he had followed since he started hunting Rakshasa. No Created could be trusted. All of them lost their minds and started slaughtering anything in their paths.

"Not all." Elana reached out to touch the arms of her

nearest fighters, two big bubbas who could have been WWF wrestlers before they ended up in an aqueduct under New York City. "We call ourselves Bengals, and we keep ourselves apart from the creatures who stole our lives—when we're not hunting them. The Rakshasa Eldest and their minions would force us into slavery or murder, or claw us to shreds on sight."

John's gaze traveled from Elana and the bubbas to the six guys who had taken turns whacking at him with dumpster lids in that alley. "They were tracking Strada to kill him."

Elana's nod confirmed his suspicion. "When they found you, they sensed something amiss in your essence. You weren't what they expected, so they brought you to me instead of taking your life."

John brought his focus back to Elana. "Now that you've made your inspection, you know I'm telling you the truth. I'm John Cole, and I've got Strada's body. So, what now? Do we make an alliance and help each other wipe these demons off the face of the earth?"

"Perhaps." Elana folded her thin arms. "But first I want to know how you came to possess that flesh."

John sighed.

There it was.

The question he didn't want to answer, and the information he'd kept Elana from reading in his mind when he let her go sifting around in his consciousness. "That's off-limits. Sorry."

Elana's expression sharpened, like she was sorting him out all over again. Then her strange eyes narrowed. "I think I understand. You want to protect the woman."

Her casual statement jolted John so deeply he almost jumped to his feet and let out one of the snarls echoing from the back of his mind. His fists clenched as crazy came charging at him, and there was nothing he could do to stop it, or the memories he didn't really want to ignore.

Auburn hair, so long he could wrap his hands double in the soft strands.

Wide, sad eyes, aquamarine like the ocean after a storm.

An exotic scent, floral, like the yellow fawn lilies he used to gather for his mother in the spring when he was a kid back in Georgia.

He'd used remnants of Strada's knowledge to shut those images away from Elana, he was sure of it.

So how did she know?

And she *did* know. He could tell from her posture, from the look on her face. She had some of the information, and she was expecting him to supply the rest.

"You can't hide thoughts from me, John," Elana said, gesturing for him to stand. "I've been on this earth far too long. When it comes to understanding the ways of the mind and how such powers work, I have almost as much experience as the one who once lived in that body."

John barely heard her as he got to his feet. He struggled with himself, with a weird, tingling burn starting in his feet and trying to more upward to cook his legs.

What the hell was happening?

It didn't feel right, and he wanted it to stop.

The snarling in his head got louder. Way too loud.

John sucked in a breath, then let it out slowly, imagining he was back in the desert on a throat-parching hike.

Ignore the heat. Keep the pulse low. Muscles easy. Mind clear. That's it. Focus. Drive it back down.

He shook his arms like he was loosening up for a run. *Drive it back down. . . .*

John eyed the multitude of Bengal fighters standing at an approximation of parade rest. He had spent so many years keeping secrets, it sucked having anyone see him nearly lose control, much less a bunch of demons. Half demons. Whatever.

Yeah. That's it.

The burn in his feet slowed, then slowly faded. The snarls got quieter, too.

Down . . . down . . .

Elana raised her small hands and made some gestures, and the chamber and feeder tunnels began to empty. The two big bubbas beside her took off with everybody else, but the six fighters who had brought John to the tunnel stayed near their leader, standing three on either side of John, positioned to cut him off if he made a sudden move for Elana. These had to be her personal guards, and John was betting only the best of the best got that honor. That was why she'd chosen them to go after Strada, even if it put her at some personal risk, unprotected while they were away.

When she turned her attention to John again, she studied him, this time with sympathy and maybe some compassion. "The transition is disorienting, I know. Growing accustomed to holding the supernatural in your own essence and learning to control it, it's very difficult."

John stared at her, caught between rattled and pissed. "What just happened? Did you do something to me?"

Elana shook her head. "You experienced a deep emotional shock, and you almost shifted to tiger form. That's how most Rakshasa learn to shift in their early days."

"Tiger form." John's own voice fell into the stone chamber and seemed to land flat, echoing in his mind. He knew he had Strada's strength and senses, but he hadn't given a thought to having the demon's shape-shifting abilities.

Not possible.

Not good.

No. Uh-uh. This was just a body with some extras. He wouldn't be letting his bones and sinews stretch, his skin grow ugly white Strada fur—not happening.

"I can—I almost—" John rubbed the back of his neck. "Am I a Bengal now, like you?"

Elana shook her head again, this time more slowly. "You're a man in a demon's body. There is no word for you."

John's pulse surged in his ears, the volume of the snarls in his mind cranked up, and his muscles went tight all over again. His feet tingled for a second, but he stuffed down the sensation.

No word for me.

Well, he knew a word.

He had learned it what felt like a million years ago, in tiny Southern churches dotting the Georgia countryside.

Abomination.

Elana's personal guards looked like they were thinking the same thing. Their very human but large hands twitched against sword hilts, like they truly wanted to use the blades to rid the world of John and the compressed, barely restrained essence of Strada that John was still hauling around in his head.

Abomination.

Shape-shifter.

Tiger-demon.

No fucking way.

Elana's unblinking gaze held no judgment. "I think you're more Bengal than anything else, John Cole. You have control of Strada's spirit, but I think it's wise that you don't allow yourself to delve too deeply into his more powerful skills. I also suggest you do not shift to tiger form, even if you gain understanding of how to make the transition on purpose. Strada could overtake you."

"Won't be happening." John made himself breathe carefully, slowly and evenly, holding on to every inch of his awareness. The snarls in his mind died back to a tolerable level. When he was sure he could speak normally again, he asked, "So how do I get rid of what's left of Strada's consciousness?"

"You don't." Elana gave him another sympathetic look.

"Battling with the demon king you carry in your mind, that's the price you pay for this second chance at life."

Another surge of emotion threatened John's control, but this time he beat down the sensation before the snarling got louder. His thoughts shifted to the moment when his spirit had entered this body—and, before that, the moment his awareness had passed through the woman who had helped him claim Strada's flesh.

Camille.

He had shared space with her, only a second or two. A moment of the most perfect peace he had ever known, being part of her, mingling his essence with hers.

"You're thinking about the woman again," Elana said, from what might have been a thousand miles away. "She's a Sibyl, isn't she."

Not really a question.

Good, because John didn't want to answer.

Elana's smile was gentle. Encouraging. "You would have learned about Sibyls last year, after the Rakshasa attacked your best friend, Duncan Sharp."

She really did know everything. Whether she'd gotten it from his mind or somewhere else, John didn't know, and he figured it didn't matter. If this woman really was as old as she claimed, if she knew as much as she seemed to about powers of the mind, he needed her help—and maybe, just maybe, she needed his.

"Duncan was a detective with the NYPD." John made himself loosen up again, until he was standing in front of Elana more like a normal guy than a tense soldier ready to grab for a weapon he hadn't even brought to this fight. "He started investigating Rakshasa killings and thought I was the murderer. The night he finally found me to arrest me, I was tailing the Rakshasa and he got caught in the cross fire. A group of Sibyls saved him."

Elana's unseeing eyes fixed on his with eerie accuracy. "Sibyls are an ancient order of female fighters, trained from birth in Motherhouses around the globe. They have elemental power—earth, air, fire, and now, I believe, the water Sibyls are making a comeback from the long-ago tragedy that destroyed them, thank the Goddess." This time her smile turned very sad, then a little wry. "Like me, some Sibyls can live a very long time."

"They saved Duncan," John repeated, still not wanting to mention the woman he was determined to protect, even though Elana probably already knew her name. "Their fighting skills, and the medallion I gave Duncan to keep him alive. It's a dinar from the Afghan temple where the demons were trapped, and it repels Rakshasa."

Camille's still wearing it now, I hope.

"You chose death at the hands of the demons," Elana said, "but Duncan Sharp used the dinar to hold your essence in this plane of existence. For a time, you resided with him, inside his body. We learned this from Duncan himself, when he was making his own transition into a Bengal from his Rakshasa wounds."

John hated the thought that Duncan had become part demon because of him. Just another sin and failure to stack on top of his ever-growing mountain of mistakes. Since the moment he saw the Rakshasa break out of their temple prison, he'd been adding crap to that teetering pile, starting with failing to reach the young soldier who had so stupidly wandered into the containment design etched into the temple floor and picked up the dinar.

Elana's expression had shifted back to interested—and almost needy, in a weird sort of way. "Duncan couldn't tell us what occurred in the alley the night your spirit left his body. What happened with the Sibyl who helped you, John? That's what I wish to know, and this time, please, leave nothing unsaid. Your secrets are safe here with me and my guards."

John didn't respond. He was fairly certain Elana and

her Bengals were good guys, that they'd be no danger to Camille Fitzgerald, but that risk was hard to take.

"I know she's a fire Sibyl," Elana added, as if to get him talking. Her white eyes flashed. "And I know her name is Camille."

John's muscles tensed, and the nearest Bengal guard reacted immediately, drawing his sword and jabbing the tip against John's chest. John figured he had Rakshasa resilience now, so if the guard didn't spear him in the heart with specially treated metal, cut off his head, burn his body and head, and spread the ashes in different locations, he'd reconstitute. Just come back to life, like a cartoon character springing up after getting whacked with a grand piano.

He wasn't completely certain about that, though.

"I'd die before I let anyone hurt her." John kept his gaze level on Elana's face, ignoring the sword drawing blood directly over his heart. "I'll kill anyone who tries, no matter who, and no matter how long it takes me to find him. Are we clear on that?"

Elana opened her arms and turned up both palms, as if she were sealing a solemn vow with a prayer. "Completely." She carefully pushed her guard's sword away from John, and after a stern look from her, the guard sheathed his blade.

"Talk to me, John," Elana said. "Tell your story so we can both understand what happened. If I have that information, I might know better how to assist you with controlling Strada's essence—and how to help you keep Camille safe from all those who would harm her for what she did . . . or what she might do."

John thought things over for another minute or so. He did trust the old woman, though he couldn't put into words why. A soldier's instincts, or maybe a priest's, or maybe just the hope of a desperate, tired man who needed allies. Whatever it was that drove him, it was John's turn to close his eyes, shut out the world, and let his thoughts turn fully back to that moment in time when he stopped being a ghost in Duncan Sharp's head. When he left Duncan and took the body he had now.

When John spoke, the words carried him back, until he could feel and smell and taste the entire scene, and that's how he related what happened, as best he could.

Camille had never been afraid of dying—but as she had learned all too well, everything in life was subject to change.

Tonight she was scared half out of her mind. The tattoo of the Dark Crescent Sisterhood felt dull and lifeless on her skin as the dark alley near East Harlem pressed against her senses, and her heart pounded harder with each step she took.

Closer.

She was moving closer to death.

Camille could taste death's coldness in the early fall air and feel its icy stillness biting into her chilled fingertips. Her Sibyl instincts screamed for her to break off, to get the hell out of the alley, but Camille made herself keep walking.

The streets of New York City seemed quiet after a late-season rain. Her black leather boots splashed at the edges of puddles, and blood rushed in her ears. So loud. Too loud. Her breath came out in whispers, stirring against the freckles on her cheeks and her long auburn ponytail.

Her scimitar swung in its leather scabbard and tapped against her calf as she walked. On a chain around her neck, tucked beneath the zippered leather of her bodysuit, the dinar burned against her bare chest like it usually did when she used it to magnify her weak skill at pyrogenesis, but that was the only heat Camille knew in the increasingly cool night air. Damnit, if she were better at making fire, she could at least warm herself up and keep hunting longer.

She really hated giving up early. It felt like letting down Bela, Dio, and Andy all over again. If she didn't find that cursed demon soon . . . well, she would. End of it. Her instincts gave a little shiver, and not for the first time in the last month, Camille had an eerie sense that she was running out of time.

She swallowed a fresh rush of dread and fear and knelt in the pitch-dark alley. Her leather-clad knee hit wet gravel as she eased her scimitar's tip up and back, to give herself enough room to move. Some creature or energy had blown out all the safety lights before she got here. Her Sibyl vision allowed her to see well enough in the dark, but that kind of seeing wasn't what Camille was after.

She stretched out her right hand over the pavement in front of her. With her left hand, she tugged down the zipper of her battle leathers and slipped her fingers inside, to the chain and then the coin underneath.

Drawing a breath of air so chilly that it stung her nose and burned deep in her chest, Camille summoned her fire energy. Tonight it came easily enough, flowing into her from the sparks she could see dancing at the edges of her vision. She pulled it into her essence, then released it again, sending it out through the dinar and her fingers until the ground beneath her outstretched hand seemed to change.

Rippling rain eddies and water-soaked asphalt took on a translucent glow, silver, then pearl, then clear as a sheet of glass. Thin streams of blue flame crackled from Camille's fingertips, touching the pavement below. As her fire made contact with the ground, dozens of colors blazed into her awareness. She picked up the dull brown energy of human footprints, and the gray nothingness of tires and oil and gasoline. Then pulsing reds and yellows and golds and silvers—different signatures from the city's myriad of paranormal creatures and humans with elemental talent. And underneath those colors, or more like to the side of them—

There.

The trace she'd been following.

The tracks formed a wide line, radiating a poisonous green and giving off perverted energy that made her stomach lurch.

"Demon," Camille said out loud, startling herself with the sound of her own voice.

No question about it, and no question about which type of demon had made them. This time she had the bastard, and this time she was sure.

The Rakshasa had definitely returned to New York City.

Camille took in a breath, then blew it out, wishing she could spit fire like some of the fire Sibyls she knew. Instead, she studied the disgusting traces of energy, using her fingers and her fire much more than her eyes.

Rakshasa came in two flavors, Eldest and Created. The Eldest were the original demons, larger and more intelligent, and definitely more powerful than the Created, demons they made by infecting human beings. The trace on the left, Camille couldn't quite read. It seemed to alternate between natural and unnatural, strong and weak. Probably a Created, or something she hadn't seen before.

The other one, the trace on the right—judging by the sheer pulsing power of it—had to have been made by one of the Eldest.

Camille used her fire to sample the energy again. Bile surged up her throat, and she had to let go of the dinar and jerk back her hand before she threw up the half pot of amaretto coffee she'd drunk before sneaking out of the brownstone.

This trace was strong. Too strong. It had to have been made by Strada.

The Sibyls and their law enforcement partners, New

York's semi-secret Occult Crimes Unit, had been searching everywhere for that bastard just like she had, and he'd been right here in this alley, maybe only minutes ago.

Strada was probably still close by.

Camille's hands started to shake.

He wouldn't fool her again. No way. Nothing he said, nothing he did—she wouldn't even listen to him.

"Like it's that simple," she said, as if anyone could hear her. As if anyone outside of her own quad even cared. Half the Sibyls in the city still gave her weird looks because they knew part of what had happened that night a year ago—that Camille had prevented her quad from chasing after Strada and finishing him off.

"Not that simple," she mumbled again, but she wondered if she was lying to herself. Camille reached up and brushed the outline of the coin hanging around her neck, feeling its gold ridges beneath her leathers.

Golden light . . .

Blinding, blinding light. So much fire. Fire energy like I've never seen, never known.

The power that had moved through her that night, the energy that her essence had moved through in return, it defied any description.

Golden light.

That's all she could call it.

As for the apparition with John Cole's dark green eyes, black hair, and light, spicy aftershave—whatever.

Even as Camille rested her hand against the proof of Strada's proximity, that horrible confusion tugged at her.

In the middle of all that pain and wildness and golden light, how was it possible that John Cole had seemed so real and present that she could have reached out and caressed the stubble on his cheeks?

He had been there, the entirety of him, only without his flesh.

Then came the light and the fire. Like lightning, burning through her and into her even as she almost fried herself throwing her essence into that energy, and she'd felt John Cole as he disappeared. Almost like his soul had moved through her own. She had wanted to grab hold of him, to call him back, but the light had exploded into nothing.

Then Strada had reverted to his human form, healed himself, and opened his eyes.

His dark green eyes.

And that's what made no sense, no matter how many million times she'd gone over this with herself, because Strada's eyes had been black before—

Before the golden light.

It was the next part that *really* made no earthly sense, and the next part that had kept Camille from using her scimitar to take the demon's head.

Strada gave me the dinar. He put this coin over my head, and he helped me to my feet.

Nothing about him had seemed evil or murderous or . . . demon. At that moment, Strada hadn't felt like Rakshasa at all. He'd felt as human as that thing in Central Park a couple of months ago—that thing that was probably Strada, too.

That's why Camille had let him go. That's why she'd kept her quad from pursuing him. That's why she was so confused now.

She dug her fingernails against the hard pavement, scraping at the demon trace as it slapped at her senses.

No more confusion.

This disgusting bit of left-behind energy told its story without any lies or tricks or distortions. It was truth, and it was demon.

Rakshasa.

She had to have been out of her mind to let a killer like that just run off into the night two separate times.

And now Strada was back again, maybe this time with allies.

Camille wanted him dead before her own weakness and choices came back to haunt her, before the demon or some of his Created hunted her sister Sibyls or any of her friends.

Tonight was the night.

Tonight she wouldn't lose her nerve.

(6)

"We—Duncan, with me in his head—we were down on the pavement in a dead-end alley," John said, raking across every second of the night he took a demon's body for his own as he tried to relate the experience to Elana. "No air. We couldn't breathe, because the bastard was choking us. "

He told the story in as much detail as he could. He told it openly and honestly, and soon enough, no matter what he wanted, he fell into the past as he spoke, and he lived it again.

Duncan beat at Strada with both arms as the Rakshasa, still in human form, used the dinar's chain to strangle the life out of him. Now that Duncan was changing into a Created Rakshasa from his wounds, the dinar no longer repelled the demons—not with its bearer sharing their essence.

John poured all the energy left in his soul into Duncan's fight.

No use.

Black spots danced at the edge of their vision.

Everything faded—

Until fire exploded all around them.

She came flying through the air like a leather-clad ninja, her red hair streaming behind her and her scimitar raised and flaming with the force of the elemental energy she commanded. Camille landed and swung her sword toward the demon's neck in one smooth motion.

Made contact.

Elemental energy exploded in a crackling blast, knocking the sword from her grip. She stumbled. Almost fell.

Duncan's senses failed him and his eyes closed even as John bellowed for him to stay in the game, to find a way, but he knew it was hopeless. Duncan was history. Both of them were history.

Then John saw her again, even though he was teetering with Duncan on the edge of unconsciousness.

He smelled her. Lilies. Wild lilies.

She knelt beside Duncan and John in the alley. Her touch—fiery heat, warming Duncan and John's body, surging through John's essence most of all.

From somewhere else in the alley, people started yelling at Camille to stop—the other Sibyls from her fighting group, trying to save her life. John tried to move Duncan's lips to tell her the same thing, but nothing worked.

Camille grabbed the dinar with both hands.

John felt the contact like lightning. Felt Duncan's body jerk like it had been hit with a set of shock paddles. The demon jerked, too, and yanked the chain around Duncan's neck harder.

"Do something!" somebody screeched, but fire energy fed through the dinar and swept around them like a glimmering golden wall, cutting them off from the rest of the world.

Hot wind beat against Duncan's face and body. John tried, but they still couldn't move. Strada seemed frozen, too, as was Camille. Fixed in position. The energy flowing out of Camille's hands into the dinar wrapped around Duncan's head and shoulders. It wrenched at John like a hot crowbar, ripping him loose, pulling him forward, hauling him out of Duncan so fast he thought he'd fly straight into the pavement, all the way to hell.

Instead, he passed through something soft and warm, vibrating with a power he couldn't begin to comprehend. Everything left him, past, present, and future. He was nothing and everything, and he could smell the desert and New York City at the same time, and he never wanted to leave that perfect place, that perfect moment, and—

I'm out.

I'm out of Duncan's body.

And I'm out of . . . her.

With a jolt, John realized he'd shared Camille's body for a second, maybe two.

He gazed at her without the filter of Duncan's perceptions, seeing her, really seeing her for the first time. Gleaming waves of auburn hair tumbled down her shoulders. Freckles stood out against her cream-and-roses cheeks. Her big aquamarine eyes got even wider as she stared back at him.

She's perfect.

He had left the priesthood long ago, when his only mission in life became killing demons. Good thing. He had no doubt he'd have broken his vows over this woman.

Reality slammed back to him then.

The alley.

With one hand Camille held the dinar against Duncan's nearly lifeless chest. Her other hand gripped Strada's wrist, pressing it down to take away the force of his pull on the dinar's chain.

Strada. Right here, in easy reach!

John lifted his hands—and saw nothing but a shimmering, silver image of himself.

Camille stared at him, wide-eyed.

He wasn't supposed to be here.

He couldn't possibly be here.

But he was, and she could see him, and John knew what had to happen. She was about to send his spirit to wherever spirits went. It was over.

Yeah.

If he had to finally die all the way and head to hell, this was the sight he'd take with him, and he'd thank the heavens for the gift.

I understand, *he mouthed, hoping she knew he meant it.*

Her pretty eyes closed.

Energy blasted into John. Another lightning strike, louder, stronger, hotter, this time pushing instead of pulling—

Shoving him straight into Strada's body.

For a split second, John's senses swam, but the demon's essence was weak and distant, damaged by repeated attacks and by contact with the dinar.

Yes!

John flung his own energy into all available space and took Strada's body for himself. The demon's consciousness tried to rise against him, but no way was John turning it loose. He crushed Strada into a tiny speck of darkness in the back of his mind, and—

And he was looking at her again. At Camille, only from a different perspective.

Duncan rolled away from them, coming to rest against the back alley wall—breathing. He was okay.

Camille knelt beside John, the dinar still gripped tightly in her fingers.

John looked at his own hands and realized he had hold of the chain.

"Don't let him fool her," *someone said.* "He'll kill her!"

But he could never do that. He would never allow anyone to do that.

All John could do was look at Camille, and she looked back at him, searching his face, locking her eyes on his.

"Who are you?" *she whispered, so softly that only he could hear.*

John didn't trust himself to speak. He pulled the dinar

out of Camille's hands, shook out the chain, then slipped the necklace over her head. The coin crackled and sparked, then settled against her leathers.

The coin had keyed itself to her. It would protect her from Rakshasa now, and John was glad.

"You have to get out of here," she murmured.

John didn't need to be told twice.

He grasped that he was in Strada's body, that he looked exactly like the Rakshasa that Camille and her sister Sibyls had come here to kill. Even Camille wasn't certain what or who he was. He gently separated himself from her and got to his feet so that he could help her stand. Then both of them looked toward the back of the alley at Duncan, who had his eyes open now.

Duncan's breathing came shallow and fast, and John winced at the tiger fur beginning to spread across his best friend's face and arms.

"Can't hide, sinner," John said, quoting a line from their favorite gospel song, hoping Duncan would understand and know that John was still around, that he'd help Duncan any way he could.

Then John turned and hauled ass out of that alley, without a single clue what he was supposed to do next.

"I got sick after that," John whispered. He'd have paid real money for a chair, or even a glass of water.

"I hid out in Central Park and came in and out of consciousness, but gradually I got my thoughts together. I accessed some emergency funds I had stashed in cash in a bus locker, and I got myself a flat in Harlem. I've been watching for the Rakshasa who survived these last few months. Tarek is *culla* now. I know he'll bring his pride back to New York City any minute now, and they'll be worse than ever."

When John finished, he rubbed his eyes with his thumb

and forefinger, wishing he could make better sense of what he had said, of what he knew, the bits and pieces. He'd told the old woman everything, even the parts he'd wanted to leave out. That should have surprised him or at least made him angry, but all he felt was relief. Saying it all out loud made it feel real.

He was still here. He was still alive and on earth—and he was still John Cole, even if he was wearing a demon's skin.

Elana seemed lost in her own thoughts for a time, and John waited, talking himself through a series of mental exercises he'd learned in the service to keep himself calm and steady.

"Camille used the medallion—the dinar—to enhance her own powers. You believe she channeled her fire energy into the metal and through it. You're certain of that?" Elana gave him one of her spookily accurate glances. "*Through* the metal?"

"Yes." John had no idea why that was important, but Elana seemed entranced by that detail.

She remained silent another long few seconds, her face captured by a wistfulness that seemed strange and sad to John. In his other life as a priest, he would have been offering her comfort or, if she was Catholic, the opportunity to take part in the sacrament of confession. As it was, he gave her time, and watched as she slowly collected herself.

When she finally spoke, it was to say, "You're right about Tarek. Strada was a monster, but Tarek—that one knows nothing at all but blood and death. He'll come back to this city and he'll seek your Camille as soon as he can, since he believes she bested Strada. You should go to her right now. I fear time is short."

"I'm watching her as often as I can, but I can't approach her." John's chest tightened, feeling even more

certain of that now, after learning that he could accidentally go all tiger and lose ground to Strada. "Not with a
demon sharing my soul, if there's any chance he could
take over my awareness."

Elana waved this off with an impatient gesture. "Your
Camille can take care of herself, but she'll be strongest
with you at her side. I suspect the same is true for you—
that you'll be more firmly your better self in her company."

"Have you worked with the Sibyls before?" John
couldn't help staring at her, already guessing at the answer. Still, Elana's look of pain sent a ripple of shock up
his spine.

"That was a long, long time ago, and it's something
best left at rest," she said. "For the present, my people
need your help, and you need our help exploring Strada's
essence and the abilities you can safely use. You'll also
find yourself wanting a people to call your own. All we
ask is that you reveal our existence to no one who doesn't
already know about us."

John knew he should consider her offer and weigh the
pros and cons, but the relief he felt at telling his story
still had hold of him. Relief . . . and reality . . . and a
positive instinct about the old woman and her Bengal
fighters, even the ones who had jacked him in the alley
and forced him to come to the tunnel.

He extended his hand to Elana. "I'll keep your secrets."

She shook his offered hand, and she gave his fingers a
squeeze. "I would like one other favor from you, one
you've already taken as a personal mission, I think."
The look of pain he had seen before made another quick
appearance. "Kill Tarek. Kill as many Eldest as you can—
but keep Camille Fitzgerald safe."

"That's definitely a mission I plan to complete," he told

Elana as a fresh, new instinct seized him. He turned his gaze to the ceiling of the aqueduct, as if he could see through the stone straight to Camille, wherever she was—and whatever dangerous-as-hell thing he sensed she was doing. "But I've got a feeling Camille won't make it easy."

Camille heard whispering, tried to listen to it.

Roars?

What was roaring?

It sounded interesting somehow, like if she could just make out what the roars were saying, she'd finally understand something important. She strained to listen, then shook her head and realized the noises were in her mind.

She'd been lost in thought, examining the energy traces with her pyrosentience and trying to convince herself that this time she really would kill Strada.

Time tended to get away from her when she sank too far into fire energy or pulled too much into herself in order to use her pyrosentience. She shook her head again, this time to clear it, but it felt too heavy, like it might snap right off her neck just from the weight of its movement.

"Get a grip," she mumbled, the sound muffled by the pavement all around her. She had to get herself together before she started imagining giant Asmodai lurching out of the shadows to cut her down.

There are no Asmodai. No Asmodai left in the world, and nobody left to create them. Let it go, Fitzgerald.

If she crept to the end of the alley, if she looked into the next alley, or maybe the side streets that led east and west back toward main avenues, she might find stronger remnants of Strada's trail. Camille checked the trace one more time, then eased her energy back into her body and stood, swaying from the fatigue of using the dinar to enhance her pyrosentience. The coin drained her, probably because it pumped so much power into her elemental skills. She gave herself a count of three to get her thoughts together, then gripped the hilt of her scimitar and headed toward the alley's mouth.

A cold wind stabbed at her through her battle leathers, and her fear drove the chill into her arms, her legs, her chest.

Enough. I'm not some adept fresh out of training.

She squeezed the scimitar's hilt tighter.

She had to do this. She owed it to everyone she cared about.

She was almost to the alley mouth, and so far there was nothing out of the ordinary. Just brown fall leaves and fire escapes and dumpsters and the wooden gate at the end to close the alley off from traffic. The gate hung open with one hinge busted.

Maybe Strada had passed by this place and kept going.

Camille inched forward.

If Strada had friends with him, she didn't plan to fight them all alone. She'd follow and stay close enough to track him to his lair. Then she'd alert her quad and the rest of the Sibyls in the city, they'd make a battle plan with the OCU, and they'd take down the Strada and the rest of his Rakshasa once and for all.

If he was alone, though—

At the end of the alley, Camille stopped and stared.

Fresh paw prints glistened on the far side of a puddle.

Big paw prints.

Then human prints, like the paws had slowly morphed into human feet, shoes and all.

Strada in his human form.

He had dark green eyes.

Camille gripped the scimitar's hilt so tightly the ivory

patterns dug into her hand. No way. She wasn't going there. Not now, damnit!

Those eyes should have been black. She was positive about that, based on what her own eyes had seen and the drawings one of her quad had made.

It didn't matter.

Soon enough those eyes would be nothing but dust and ashes on the street, and it wouldn't matter what color they were.

Camille eased out of the alley.

The dinar suddenly scalded the skin on her chest.

She yelped, grabbed for the coin—and powerful arms seized her and snatched her back into the alley's cover.

Camille's pulse rocketed. She rammed her elbows back and hit a hard wall of muscle as someone—something—hauled her behind one of the alley's dumpsters. A massive hand clamped over her mouth, cutting off all sound, but leaving her able to breathe.

Human, her instincts told her. *Sort of. Definitely male.* Totally, completely male.

The coin around her neck felt like it might explode from the heat it was generating.

Camille tried to bite the hand over her mouth. Tried to stomp the man's instep.

Nothing.

He had her tight and controlled, like he'd done this hundreds of times. She couldn't move except to blink.

"Don't fight me, beautiful," said the voice of the thing from Central Park—the thing that was probably Strada. The sound was nothing but a masculine rasp against her ear, and the hand against her mouth felt hot enough to thaw glaciers. "You won't win."

Camille drew hard on her elemental fire, using the already overheated dinar to expand her pyrogenesis. Flames broke out along her neck and hissed down her arms, sizzling holes in her battle leathers and sending a shock of alarm through her Sibyl tattoo. Smoke poured around her, blurring her vision—but the asshole holding her managed not to let go.

"Keep it up," the man murmured, so quiet no one else in New York could have heard him. "I like it hot."

How the hell was he still holding her?

Camille couldn't see him, couldn't sense any elemental essence that would help him absorb her fire, but—

She shifted her energy into pyrosentience, stabbing at his flesh with focused beams of blue flame. He didn't react to her probing, but he didn't stop it, either. This time she got off a good blast, enough energy to finally tell her what she needed to know.

He wasn't demon. Wasn't Rakshasa. Not Strada, but he didn't feel completely human, did he? Well, the muscled arms, the way-ripped pecs pressing into her shoulders—those were definitely all man.

His energy, though . . .

Before Camille could struggle again, the man's grip tightened. "Watch—and knock off the fire, or we're both dead."

Something in the man's tone made Camille react immediately, pulling her energy back so fast the effort nearly made her dizzy. The smoke around them drifted away, blending with the wet walls and fire escapes until Camille had a clear view of the end of the alley even though she was fairly certain no one on the other side of the dumpster could see her.

The dinar around her neck stayed red-hot, then seemed to get even hotter.

Just outside the alley's walls, a dark-haired man in a camel-colored silk suit strode into view. Average height, decent build, light tan—he could have been of almost any heritage, and nothing about him stood out as unusual or memorable. He stopped near the alley's mouth and glanced at his watch.

When he looked up, the pain from the hot coin on her skin made Camille yelp against the hand covering her mouth.

The man's black eyes burned with an inhuman fire at the center, and the foul, perverted energy that rolled off him and hit her full in the face would have driven her to her knees if her captor hadn't held her upright.

Rakshasa.

Eldest.

But Camille didn't recognize him.

All she knew was, this one wasn't Strada.

He's so powerful. How could that be?

Another figure approached, human in appearance, likely male, wearing jeans and a black hooded sweatshirt. He came toward the demon waiting for him without a hint of fear, and didn't hesitate or shrink back when the demon growled at him.

"Nice threads," the human said.

The demon growled again, this time louder.

Again, the human didn't seem to have any reaction to the threat. "Come with me," he said. "They're waiting for you."

The demon kept growling, but it gave a quick, sharp nod. Then it followed the man in the sweatshirt away from the alley and down the long, darkened side street.

The heat in the dinar started to drain away, and Camille realized the coin had been reacting to the presence of Rakshasa—or maybe just to danger, or more likely to the presence of such concentrated perverted energy.

When the demon and its companion had been out of sight for a few seconds, Camille's captor eased his grip—a little. "That was Tarek," he whispered in her ear. "Eldest, and the pride's *culla* now that Strada's gone."

Strada—gone?

If Camille could have turned around and challenged the asshole holding on to her, she would have. How could Strada be gone? She'd just been tracking him—but if Tarek was Rakshasa and Eldest, it might have been his trace she had been following.

"Tarek never valued taking human form before he took charge of the pride," the man said. "Now he's gotten good at it. Calls himself Corst Brevin, and stays away from fur and claws most of the time. Bad for business."

Camille didn't try to figure out how the man knew any of this, but her Sibyl instincts told her he was telling the truth. For reasons she couldn't begin to explain, she not only believed everything he was saying but had no sense that he intended to hurt her. In fact, the whole time they'd been watching the Rakshasa, she'd felt safe with him. She had even felt protected.

Not that she needed protecting.

"I need to understand—are you hell-bent on feeding yourself to the Rakshasa?" The man's voice sounded teasing yet serious, and Camille recognized the long vowels and rhythms of a Southern drawl. "Is that why you keep coming out here without your fighting group, playing with fire, and trying to sneak up on a *culla*? I'm beginning to think you've got a death wish, beautiful."

The man took his hand off Camille's mouth, and her words flew out in a rush. "Let me go, you son of a bitch—and who the hell are you, anyway?"

She tried to jerk herself free again, but he held her just as tightly. She caught his scent. Light, and spicy, and familiar. Her head started to swim.

"You know who I am," he told her for the third time, and his bass rumble sent ripples of gooseflesh across her neck. "Tell me my name before I let you turn around."

Camille shoved against his stone-strong arms.

"Tell me my name," he said, his lips so close to her ears that his warm breath gave her crazy shivers as rain started falling again in tiny, tapping drops.

Golden light . . .

"John Cole." The name spilled out of her even though she felt played all over again. Elemental energy blasted up from her depths, blazing through the dinar and covering her entire body with red-orange fire. "Now let me go before I burn you to the ground."

The strong arms pinning her behind the dumpster turned her loose, and Camille sprang away from its metal wall. She drew her scimitar as she wheeled to finally, finally get a close-up look at the man who had captured her so easily and completely—and her blade burst into roaring flames, channeling her gut-level shock and disbelief.

The dark green eyes she remembered so well, too well. But the black hair, the tanned skin, the tall, muscled frame and that handsome, arrogant face—no more confusion.

Not now.

Not ever again.

"Strada." The snarl tore out of her as she lunged forward through the rain, but the bastard used the dumpster for cover to keep her from getting off a good swing.

"I've got Strada's body." Strada made no effort to fight back, but he looked loose and ready to get out of her way. "You gave it to me. You know I'm telling you the truth."

Camille screamed with rage, wishing she could scrub off the feel of the demon's arms around her and wash out the lingering tingle of his deep voice in her ear. She used her shoulder and her Sibyl's strength to shove the dumpster sideways.

Strada kept pace with the dumpster's movements, staying just out of her range. "Strada was dying. You'd have finished him off if you'd taken his head and cooked his remains, but you helped me out of Duncan's head and gave me what was left of Strada—with the dinar."

Golden light . . .

Camille shoved the dumpster again and got an angle on the smooth-talking jerk, but the thought of that golden light, of that explosive energy moving through her as she held the dinar . . . She hesitated.

Three other Sibyls came roaring into the alley from its other end.

Bela led the way. The earth Sibyl had her serrated blade drawn, and her wavy black hair streamed out from beneath her zipped leather face mask as she ran.

Andy wasn't wearing her face mask, but she had her underwater dart pistol drawn. Puddle water and rivulets from the buildings around her swept into waves, soaking her red curls and washing grime off the alley walls.

Dio had her face mask off, too, and she was walking. Her wispy blond hair stirred and swirled around her shoulders as her wind did the running for her, building into towering funnels as she drew her deadly three-sided African throwing knives.

Camille's heart surged at the sight of her quad, and she knew they were answering the distress call she'd sent them through her tattoo when Strada first grabbed her.

Strada kept the dumpster between him and her onrushing saviors, and his expression never changed. "Next time you take on Tarek, beautiful, make sure you bring your friends. They're almost as dangerous as you."

He moved so fast she barely saw him go, pivoting and leaping into the darkness of the side street.

"No!" Camille charged after him. "You are not getting away from me a third time."

But he *was* getting away. The side street was still and quiet and absolutely empty.

Camille ran a couple of steps, then let out a fire-laced roar, magnified a hundredfold by the dinar around her neck. She spun back toward the alley, stormed into it, kicked the dumpster so hard it smashed into the wall, then hauled off and hacked a corner off the bin. The severed corner clattered against the wet pavement, still glowing red from the heat channeled through her blade, and the acrid smell of melting metal filled the air.

Bela got to her first and grabbed one of her arms before she could lay into the dumpster again. Bela had pulled her face mask off and sheathed her own sword, and her dark eyes were wide with concern. "Was that who I think it was? Were you just fighting with Strada?"

"Something like that." Camille lowered her smoking scimitar and gently pulled herself free from Bela's grip.

"The Rakshasa are back in New York City." Andy stopped beside Bela and let the waves she'd brought with her crest against the wounded dumpster. "Fuck me. That's all we need."

Dio's wind smashed directly into Camille's face, pasting her lips to her teeth and pelting her with pebbles as it passed. By the time Camille's eyes stopped tearing enough for her to see, Dio had stopped in front of her and had her finger right in Camille's face.

"What the *hell* were you doing out here without us?" Dio's gray eyes crackled with energy, and somewhere in the distance thunder rumbled. "I'm the broom of this quad, but you better not leave me sweeping up your body parts because you did something jackass stupid!"

Dio jerked her finger away, then let her arm fall to her side. Camille glanced from Dio to Bela to Andy, seeing their concern and their frustration with the chance she had taken. All of them, Camille included, had suffered terrible losses in their pasts, and what she'd done tonight—what she'd been doing for months—no doubt brought back fear, mistrust, and worry for everybody.

"I was tracking him," Camille admitted. "Tracking Rakshasa."

That sounded lame. She wanted to ram her head into the dumpster. Her quad had finally achieved something that passed as a fighting rhythm, and now she'd thrown them all off again. "I'm the one who let Strada go. It's my responsibility to find him and kill him—and besides, I thought I needed the practice with my pyrosentience to be more useful to all of you. I'm sorry."

Andy frowned, her pretty face so atypically serious that Camille couldn't keep looking at her. "It's a great thing, working on your pyrosentience," Andy said, "but using projective elemental energy is dangerous all by itself, and you've been doing it all alone, then adding Rakshasa to the equation. I'm getting better at this whole water Sibyl healing thing I'm supposed to be able to do, but I can't sew you back together if you melt yourself or let a cat-demon eat you for dinner."

"I know—" Camille started, but Bela cut her off.

"When I chose you as the pestle for my quad, I knew you weren't strong with pyrogenesis, and I didn't care." Bela's tone stayed even, but Camille heard the fear-driven anger in each syllable and understood it. "Making fire on command, that's not what's important to me or any of us. If you take a risk like this again, we're going to have problems."

"I'm sorry," Camille repeated, wishing she could find something better, or some promise that might make a difference. If that threat had come from Dio or even Andy, it would have stung Camille, but from Bela, the mortar of her quad, the woman who held them all together, it cut like a blade against her throat.

For a few moments nobody said anything.

Then Dio hissed out a breath and tapped the throwing knives sheathed on her belt. "Yeah, well, next time we come face-to-face with that ass-wipe demon, he's going down."

Andy grumbled something Camille didn't quite get, but she caught the part about chopping Strada's dick off before they moved on to hacking off his head.

Bela put out her hand. "Come on. We need to call the OCU about the Rakshasa, and get the word out to other Sibyls that the demons are active in the city again. Then we need to get home without waking Mrs. Knight next door and get some sleep. We're back on patrol—*together*—in about fourteen hours."

Camille took Bela's hand, but as they started for home, she couldn't help glancing down the dark side street where Strada had made his escape.

Or . . . it might have been John Cole.

Don't be stupid. Of course it was Strada, screwing with you to get more intel on the Sisterhood.

Or something like that.

Maybe he wanted the Sibyls to kill Tarek so he could have his pride back without a fight. Really, Camille didn't know what game the Rakshasa was playing, and she didn't give a shit. She was through falling for his lies.

Flames broke out in her mind, even though no fire found its way to her skin and no smoke puffed from her shoulders in the dark, rainy night.

Like Dio said, the next time Camille crossed paths with that tiger bastard, the demon was going down.

(8)

October

Tarek sat beside Griffen in the opulent high-rise conference room, taking in the shades of mauve and taupe in the wallpaper and expensive accents and paintings. The oak chairs and long, rectangular conference table had been polished to a perfect shine along with the hardwood floor, leaving a faint scent of lemon in the air. Even the drapes, blinds, and windows had been rendered spotless.

Pity.

Much of it would have to be replaced when this meeting concluded.

Tarek realized that since the death of his beloved oldest brother, Strada, he had begun to abhor waste of any sort, even blinds and curtains that would be ruined, or hours spent cleaning a room that was about to be soiled so badly it would have to be stripped to studs and rebuilt to scrub away the filth.

He glanced down at the dark silk suit he had chosen to highlight his tanned skin and dark hair. Strada had always preferred silk. Tarek had thought his brother foolish for his choice of clothing—for wearing clothing at all and staying in human form so frequently.

Now that he was *culla*, he understood Strada's reasoning.

With Strada gone, and with the damage done by the cursed John Cole and the Sibyls, the Eldest Rakshasa left in the world numbered only twenty-one. Tarek felt incredibly responsible for each of those lives. If he and his true brothers were to thrive in this modern landscape after a millennium of captivity in the Valley of the Gods, they had to find allies, strategies, and safety. They had to both blend in with and stand out among the humans teeming across the planet, and they had to learn how to better use humans to achieve Rakshasa goals of wealth and power . . . and survival. Remaining in human form helped Tarek understand his potential friends and enemies much better, and presenting himself in a handsome flesh-and-blood shell made negotiations much easier than showing up with fur, fangs, and claws.

Most of the time.

"Three minutes." Griffen smoothed his short blond hair and adjusted his own brown suit—also silk, but low-grade, and not among his favorites. The sorcerer knew they would be sacrificing much of what they wore today, but the means would be worth the end. "Are you ready?"

"I am." Tarek glanced at the clock over the conference room door, then noted that Griffen must have closed the room's hall-side blinds before he arrived.

The conference room door opened, and their host, Ari Seneca, strode in reeking of confidence and spices. Modern aftershave. Tarek managed not to wrinkle his nose to close out the cloying scent. The big man, dark-haired despite the years obvious in the wrinkles at the corners of his oil-black eyes, had another underlying odor, one Tarek couldn't identify, but he thought it might be the acidic tang of serious illness. He filed this fact for later consideration, then noted that the man's black suit hung at the shoulders and chest, as if Seneca had recently shed weight and hadn't yet had his clothing tailored to account for the difference.

Seneca left the door open and surveyed them, his eyes lingering on Tarek, as if surprised Griffen had only one associate in attendance. Tarek stood with Griffen and shook Seneca's large hand, giving nothing away with his even, practiced expression and his new human name, Corst Brevin. It impressed Tarek that Seneca was willing to place himself at risk and come to this meeting alone, save for a newly hired set of allies. Ioannis Foucci, Seneca's rival, likely would arrive armed and flanked by personal guards.

"I'm confident we can resolve this situation today," Griffen was saying as Seneca seated himself at the head of the conference table.

"I am more concerned about the aftermath." Seneca's European accent was thick, and his dark eyebrows pulled together as he spoke.

Griffen's smile seemed relaxed. "My associates are very talented, and you've given all the staff on this floor the afternoon off."

Seneca leaned forward and propped one elbow on the polished table. "Foucci is no fool. He will have plenty of support. Contact times. Contingencies."

"He's out of his league." Griffen's smile stayed full even as his blue eyes took on a colder edge. Seneca made a rumbling noise deep in his throat. Not a challenge. More of a surrender. *You have no idea of the power you've purchased,* Tarek thought, studying the man who had hired them. *But you're about to understand.*

From down the long hallway outside the conference room, Tarek heard the soft ring of an elevator bell.

Seneca got up from his chair, moved to the open door, then exited the conference room to allow three very large men with obvious firearm bulges under their gray suit jackets to enter. The men glanced around the room, then adopted smug expressions Tarek assumed to be related to their superior numbers. As they positioned themselves, Seneca greeted his opponent with widespread arms, a jovial smile, and much false camaraderie. Tarek glanced toward the hallway and saw his target, Foucci, familiar to him from photographs supplied by Griffen, pull back from Seneca's embrace. A fifth bodyguard stood directly behind Foucci, this one smaller than the rest, but with more intelligent eyes. His gray jacket concealed two bulges, and Tarek saw a third at his right ankle.

Foucci had silver hair and a face lined and tanned from years of outdoor labor before he'd moved up the ranks of his crime clan. The older man was thin but fit, which made Tarek frown.

Stringy and tough. Not his favorite sort of meat.

He didn't let this thought occupy much of his attention as Foucci, Seneca, and the fifth guard came into the room. Foucci sat while the fifth guard took a spot directly behind his chair. Seneca closed the conference room door, and by the time the heavy wood settled into place, Seneca's expression had changed to something darker and less inviting. He came to sit on Griffen's left, leaving Tarek with a direct line to Foucci if he stood and walked around the right side of the conference table.

Tarek gave Foucci a polite smile.

Seneca's voice was rough and low when he spoke, gesturing to the room full of armed men arrayed around Foucci. "I'm disappointed in this show of force, my friend."

"We are not friends." Foucci's thin lips pursed between statements, like he was smelling something unpleasant. "And I have no intention of surrendering any territory east of the Hudson."

Tarek assessed Foucci, from the pace of his heart to the scent of the sweat breaking out beneath his high white collar. Nervous but determined. Definitely dangerous, as humans went. Seneca was wise not to tangle long with this one. He might have proved a menace.

Seneca waved a hand toward the covered windows, to

indicate the city spreading out beneath them. "All the territory in Manhattan was mine before your arrival. I still consider it so."

Foucci's pulse grew louder and faster, and strips of color crept into his thin, pocked cheeks. "And you back your claim with what, fancy buildings?" His dramatic sweep of the arm indicated Tarek and Griffen. "Crooked lawyers or foolish underlings?"

"Do you believe in magic?" Seneca smiled at his fractious guest. "I speak of witches and ghosts—and let's not forget vampires, as those legends are so uniquely our own."

The question seemed to give Foucci momentary pause, and Tarek felt the shifting of elemental energy in the room as Griffen began to tamper with the weapons carried by Foucci's guards. Griffen drew off the power rising from the Coven's rituals in the basement and channeled it through himself, his fingers occasionally jittering against the table's surface as he targeted key parts of the firearms. Ammunition. The trigger mechanisms. Chambers.

Seneca continued with his assigned task, keeping Foucci engaged until Griffen had had time to complete his work. "It's not such a hard question, really. I've come to believe in a great many things since my arrival in New York City. Witches have particularly captured my interests. Perhaps I should call them sorcerers, since that's the term some prefer when they dabble in the darker arts."

Foucci's guards exchanged glances. One made a strange gesture involving his finger and his temple, and Tarek assumed they were casting aspersions on Seneca's sanity. Foucci himself could only sputter for a few moments, but at last his voice caught like a gruff engine and roared loud in the otherwise still room. "I haven't come here to talk madness and fantasy, you bastard! Either acknowledge my rights to the territory we dispute, or fight me for it. My clan is prepared for whatever you bring to us."

Seneca let his guest double his fists and pound them against the oak table once, then again, before answering with a clipped "I doubt that."

Foucci shoved away from the table and stood, shaking, though Tarek couldn't tell if it was from rage or frustrated confusion. "This was a waste of time."

"Sit down," Seneca said, his voice growing more deadly with each word.

Foucci remained on his feet, glaring at Seneca, ignoring Griffen and Tarek completely. "Witches. Sorcerers. If I had known you were mad, I wouldn't have bothered with this formality."

His guards tensed, and Tarek saw their hands slip toward the weapons Griffen was adjusting.

"I'll ask you once more: sit down," Seneca said, his tone positively icy now, his black eyes blazing a warning any fool would have recognized as lethal.

Griffen pressed his palms flat on the table, a pre-arranged message to Seneca that they had nothing left to fear from the conventional weaponry possessed by their opponents. "We are leaving." Foucci gestured to his guards, but before he could step away from the table, Seneca got to his feet and transformed his face into a false mask of sorrow.

"Poor choice, my friend."

"I told you, I am not—" Foucci began, but broke off, staring at Tarek.

Tarek smiled at him and let his fangs show, along with the paws and claws he had revealed only moments before. The fabric of his suit began to rip at the seams since it was actual clothing instead of aspects of his own body he had transformed into clothing-like layers.

Seneca was too focused on his opponents to look at Tarek, which was a good thing. Tarek had no doubt the man would have reacted, given that Griffen hadn't shared this aspect of their plan.

"Holy shit," the guard behind Foucci muttered, ripping a Colt out of one of his chest holsters as his four companions drew a variety of automatic pistols. He pointed the weapon at Tarek and squeezed the trigger.

The weapon didn't so much as give a click, its firing mechanism welded into place by Griffen's targeted heat.

The guard glanced down at the weapon and cursed as his associates opened fire—or tried to.

Two of the guns backfired due to strategically plugged chambers, killing their shooters instantly. The stench of gunpowder and burned flesh rushed through the room, but the fire alarms had been disabled, and Seneca had already cautioned other workers in the building that there might be some minor bangs and loud noises as they addressed plumbing and electrical problems on the upper floor.

The other two weapons didn't fire, but Seneca had removed two small knives from his pockets. Before the other two shooters could understand what had happened, they struck the conference room floor with blades buried in their skulls, directly between their eyes.

Foucci's last standing guard, the smart one, had tried all of his useless pistols by then. He pitched the last one at Tarek, grabbed his charge, and thrust the old man behind him.

Tarek, fully in tiger form now, approached the two men in an unhurried fashion.

"Holy God," somebody muttered, and Tarek realized it was Seneca, moving farther back, toward Griffen, as the man finally grasped the totality of the force he had brought to bear. Griffen was using his pocket telephone— cell phone, yes, that was the term—to summon his half sister Rebecca, the Coven, and the Created from the basement. They would come by way of the stairs, to avoid distressing workers on the floors below.

Foucci lapsed into the language of his birth, using old words that Tarek recognized.

Albanian. Yes. He knew this speech.

"Djall," the man growled in his native tongue, his dark eyes wild as he pressed himself against the conference room wall, using his guard as a shield. A painting crashed to the floor beside them.

"Djall," Foucci said again, then in accented English, "Devil!"

"Dreqi," Tarek corrected, preferring the Latin-influenced alternative, which formed the root for the Romanian name Dracul and conjured up all sorts of terrifying, bloody legends. "And thank you for the compliment," he added in flawless English before he threw the guard across the conference table, seized hold of Foucci, and tore the man's silver-haired head off his shoulders.

Blood frenzy seized Tarek as the delicious liquid filled the air, the room, his senses, his mind, his consciousness. He ate with abandon, not caring what he tore or ripped or destroyed. When he finished, the Created would feed from the carcass, and the Coven would clean away all trace of the kill, burning the room down to basics, then painting it anew. Seneca would have to deal with obtaining new carpeting, drapes, and furniture at his leisure, but Tarek assumed a Balkan crime lord could handle such minor details with ease.

He was only partly aware of Seneca's continued expressions of shock and Griffen's calm, soothing voice.

"You asked for a thorough job," Griffen was telling Seneca as Tarek swallowed the last bit of stringy meat he chose to endure. "And I told you—my associates are more than capable of any task."

"What is he?" Seneca asked, gripping Griffen's shoulder as Griffen dragged the last living guard off the floor by his collar.

Griffen didn't answer that question, keeping his attention on the guard. The semi-conscious man groaned as Griffen slammed him down on the conference table.

Tarek shifted back to human form, brushing off the rags of his soiled, torn clothing and altering some of his outer essence to resemble the dark suit he had just destroyed. Following Griffen's lead, he didn't speak to relieve Seneca's anxiety and doubt, but instead allowed Griffen to finish the last bit of their plan.

After just seconds of persuasion, the guard started babbling to Griffen, giving him telephone numbers, names, and locations, and explaining all the contingencies Foucci had established to see to his safety or, in the event of a poor outcome, his vengeance. The key player in setting these plans in motion was Foucci's eldest son and heir, still residing in Albania.

Griffen worked the man over with some elemental fire, then jerked him sideways on the table to get a look at his beheaded boss. Tarek leaned across the table and growled in the guard's ear.

"You have more meat on you," Tarek whispered. "You'll be much more tender."

This time when the guard started babbling, his words had little direction or purpose beyond begging, pleading, and raving.

Griffen used an untraceable, disposable cell to place a call to Foucci's eldest son while Seneca stood beside him, still trembling and eyeing Tarek.

To the man's credit, he said nothing as Griffen verified that he was indeed speaking to Foucci's heir.

"We have a situation here," Griffen told the man. "One of your employees has turned up at our place of business. He has no explanation for why Mr. Foucci has failed to keep his appointment, and Mr. Seneca is not pleased."

Griffen glanced at Seneca, who tore his eyes away from Tarek, seemed to reach inside himself and grasp hold of his manly parts, and give himself a quick, mind-rattling jerk. He cleared his throat and took the phone from Griffen before the man on the other end of the connection even finished firing off questions.

"What is the meaning of this outrage?" Seneca demanded. "I agreed to a meeting, and I get nothing but a bloodied underling, babbling about monsters and demons?"

He held out the telephone for Foucci's son to gain a taste of the guard's newborn madness.

Then, for the listener's benefit, Seneca said loudly to Griffen, "Relieve me of his suffering, please."

Griffen extracted a Glock with a silencer and shot the guard once in the head, ending the man's desperate chatter.

Seneca put the telephone back to his ear. "You find that carrion carcass you call a father, and you tell him I want payment for my wasted time—and my soiled carpet. Your clan will regret this stupidity."

He slammed the device closed, and by the time Seneca looked at Tarek again, he seemed as collected and in control as the moment he had entered the conference room.

Tarek sensed the beginning of a long and fruitful alliance.

Elemental energy surged down the hallway as Griffen's Coven arrived, twelve men of similar stature and ability, dressed in jeans, faces obscured by black hooded sweatshirts. The Created brushed past them, scenting a meal, fangs bared, and Tarek moved aside to allow them to enjoy the leftovers. Griffen's sister, a strange and thin girl with very blond hair, eased into the room behind the Created, her bright blue eyes wide at the sight of Foucci's blood sprayed on the walls and ceiling and pooling all around the dead guards. She licked her lips, and Tarek thought he caught a flash of silvery energy around the edges of her pointed face.

Just as fast, it was gone, likely some trick of the light on his meat-satiated senses.

Rebecca draped herself across a chair and watched the Created eat, a disturbing smile playing at her pale lips as the Coven used their joined energy to keep the Created calm. With quiet gestures, they directed the Created in their devouring of much of the legal evidence, simultaneously rewarding them for a week of hard training and reasserting the Coven's dominance over their trainees.

Seneca took in the scene without shrinking from it, though he had gone pale, and Tarek heard the irregular hammer of the man's heart as he fought to control his reactions. Tarek imagined he could also hear the man's mind adding and subtracting possibilities, and smell the friction of his greed rubbing against his instinctive terror.

"Your organization and mine could do much together," Seneca told Griffen.

Seneca's gaze shifted to Tarek, and Tarek knew the man was coming to understand who held the title of *culla* in this room—and in New York City.

"Mr. Brevin," Seneca said with an appropriate note of respect, "I would like an exclusive contract with Premium."

Tarek gave the man a single nod of acknowledgment. Then he offered his response in his best human voice, with only the softest of growls. "I'll consider your request, but I must warn you, Mr. Seneca—I demand a very, very high price."

9

Four Bengal fighters circled John. They were half tiger, half human in form, and all fucking muscle. John kept his fists up, ready to defend like they'd been teaching him. Similar techniques to military hand-to-hand fighting, but a lot more effective. The room reeked of ammonia and sweat. The lighting sucked, but John didn't need good light, not with his cat's vision. When he was feeling good and sarcastic, he thought of himself like Spider-Man, bitten by something radioactive and learning to manage bizarre new powers, some of which seemed pretty stupid, at least on the surface.

"Use the demon's strength," the biggest one told him. The guy called himself Ben Seti, and he looked Egyptian, but not quite modern. More regal and king-like—and the asshole was big. As the commander of Elana's private guard, he was without question the best fighter in their army. "Access Strada's power, but do not allow it to control you."

John gave a grunt of understanding, staying focused on Ben, because Ben was the biggest threat.

Ben charged at John. So did the other three.

John shouted and swung with both fists, with all the speed and force he could muster. Two Bengals went down. A third fighter dropped. John barely felt the impact on his knuckles. He kept his gaze locked on Ben's smooth face, on the way his mouth had opened to show tiger fangs.

John blasted a punch at Ben's nose.

Ben swung faster.

Pain exploded through John's jaw and he dropped to one knee.

Strada howled in his mind. John suddenly hated Ben. He wanted to pull Ben apart, from his too-handsome smirk to his big bare feet. He wanted to rip out his organs. He wanted to bite hard through his flesh, until Ben kicked and screamed and couldn't escape. More than ammonia and battle stink filled John's nose. The Bengal's blood smelled of copper and water and enemy. John heard the fluid pounding, pounding through Ben's chest, into his vulnerable neck.

Everything felt . . . dark.

Kill.

Now.

John's muscles bunched. His lips pulled back from his teeth. Damn, but his head hurt. Were his teeth getting longer?

Ben didn't come at him. The three Bengals who had fallen scrambled away into the shadows.

Kill . . .

"No," John growled, grabbing his head with both hands, like he could keep his brain from ripping in half.

Second by second, he reclaimed his thoughts, his self-control. He refused to lose focus, like when he used to be in battle, bullets flying. No panic. No distractions. Eyes on the goal and nothing more.

After a time, he lifted his head to see Ben staring at him, fully human and frowning. He was back to jeans and a sleeveless T-shirt, and he looked modern enough now, except for the giant sword belted to his waist. The angular, exotic lines of his face made him seem stern and even more regal, like a pharaoh displeased with a subject at his feet. "You fought better, John, but you must keep Strada managed. In a true battle, he would have had you."

John couldn't do anything but nod, swear to himself, and hate the Rakshasa bastard in his head for turning him into a liability and holding him back. How could he return to any kind of real fighting or real life, even just long enough to wipe out the Rakshasa, if he couldn't keep Strada stuffed where he belonged?

"It did take longer this time," Ben allowed, as if he might be trying to make John feel better. "And a harder blow."

The energy in the room shifted, and John stayed down on his knee because he knew Elana had just entered the sparring chamber.

Ben and the rest of the guards bowed, then moved to a respectful distance as the little woman approached John. Elana glowed in her silver robes. Today her silvery hair had been braided down the center, making the ribbon-like scars on her face tighter and more visible. After weeks of working together, Elana had stopped bothering with introductions and pleasantries where John was concerned, and she usually came straight to the point.

"Are you watching Camille?" she asked. "Carefully?"
Couldn't stop if I wanted to.

"Every day." John stood and lowered his head once, quickly, to acknowledge Elana. "I come here when she's sleeping, but otherwise, wherever she is, I'm close."

Elana's frown eased, but not by much. "Does she have much contact with other Sibyls?"

"Outside her own group? No. She attends meetings with the Occult Crimes Unit before and after patrols, but I don't see her socialize." John rubbed his sore jaw, impressed at how fast it was feeling better from Ben's punch. Strada's body healed about as fast as Sibyl bodies healed, which was pretty fast.

Elana paced back and forth in front of John for a few seconds. "Have you ever noticed some of her own kind watching her outside of her awareness?"

This question disturbed John, and he scrutinized Elana more carefully. She looked a little distracted, but otherwise pretty much normal. "You mean—fire Sibyls?"

"Yes. The older ones."

"The Mothers? No." John glanced at the chamber ceiling reflexively, half expecting to see through it to the streets of New York City so he could discreetly hunt for ancient Irish women giving off smoke. Elana stopped pacing and faced him, gazing at him with her strange white eyes. "If the Mothers come close to you, Strada's essence will react to them, I think. Not in a positive fashion."

She looked like she might be ready to walk off and end their contact for now, but John managed to get out a question before she turned away. "Do you think Camille's own people might move against her? Why would they do that?"

Once more Elana hesitated, and she seemed to choose her words very, very carefully. "I honestly don't know what the fire Sibyls might do, but yes, that's one possibility I'm guarding against. The why of it—let's revisit that later." She gestured to one of her guards, who brought forward a polished wooden staff John had gotten to know a little too well for his own liking.

He stood straighter, then loosened his stance and got ready, regulating his breathing and throwing all of his focus on Elana.

Elana's smile revealed tiger-like teeth, extending. Sharp claws dug into the staff as white fur lined her tiny arms.

John sank to his knees, eyes straight ahead, chin up, watching and waiting for his cue. His fists were clenched, for all the good it would do. Would she strike first this time, or give him a warning? He never knew.

Ben and his boys formed a line in the distance, watching just as closely.

"Get up, John Cole," came the growled command. "Get up so I can knock you down again."

10

Camille crouched at the warehouse's basement window and squinted to see through the low, smeared glass. The reflections from nearby building lights and streetlamps obscured most of the room, which seemed darker than the moonless night they'd endured so far, even to her very sensitive eyes. Cold air burned her nose, yet it barely numbed the dead-skunk stench of blood and dung and perverted elemental energy. The dinar around her neck felt warm and tingly, but it wasn't giving off the frenetic heat she had noticed the night she came close to the Rakshasa Eldest. With no sign of those bastards anywhere despite repeated searches, they were back to regular patrol schedules, some strategizing, and a lot of grumbling and worrying.

Bela knelt beside her on her left, completely zipped into her bodysuit and mask, gripping the copper half-moon charm Camille had fashioned for her after their first round of battles with the Rakshasa. The metal, crafted to remove any impurities and treated with elemental energy, helped Bela magnify her terrasentience—her ability to sample the earth and see what had touched it. Since they were dealing with a basement, Bela was the logical choice to check it out.

"Perfect," Andy grumbled from Camille's other side, droplets of water freezing on her leathers and face mask as she leaned to the side to see if she could get a view of the warehouse basement. The iron half-moon charm Camille had made for her bounced against her ample chest. "Nothing like the Garment District at midnight when it's already frigging cold. I think the OCU hates us. Couldn't we be the group hunting for potential Rakshasa hideouts on the Upper East Side?"

"I might have pissed off Calvin Brent," Dio muttered from Andy's right. She was on her hands and knees trying to see through a spiderwebbed crack in the glass, and she wasn't wearing her face mask, either. Her long blond hair looked stiff in the frigid semi-darkness. "He asked me out and I turned him down."

Camille and Andy glanced at Dio at exactly the same time.

"You turned down—" Camille started, but Andy finished.

"The acting director of the OCU. Fucking wonderful. He'll be sending us to explore all the landfills next, or maybe the sewer treatment plants."

"Why'd you say no, Dio?" Camille watched fog rise with each word she spoke. She did her best not to think about John Cole's green eyes and the way his deep voice made her breath come short, or the fact that he'd probably never be able to ask her out. "All that thick brown hair and that big smile—Cal Brent is gorgeous. Plus he's refined and classy, kinda like you."

Dio's cheeks flushed as she fiddled with her own half-moon charm, pure silver, and maybe the prettiest and most delicate pendant Camille had made, with its carefully etched wind rune added after Dio chose it. "I don't date. And neither do you, so don't give me any shit."

"I'm not saying date." Camille rubbed her hands together, wishing she could feel her fingers, and wishing that every mention of men and dating didn't take her right back to the same mental place. Strada was a demon. A *demon*. Not the new home for John Cole's soul. She'd never even known John Cole, and he was dead. Gone forever. "Why don't you just go out with Cal, Dio? Give it a try and see what happens."

"Unlike other people at OCU headquarters, Cal's not an asshole," Andy added, leaving it unsaid that the unit's current acting director, Jack Blackmore, on sabbatical visiting all the Motherhouses, *was* an asshole—or at least a great big stubborn jerk.

"Not an asshole." Dio shifted her weight to get a closer look at the window. "Yeah, see, that's where Cal Brent and I would be a lousy match."

Andy tugged at the edges of her face mask. "Hey. You've mellowed. You haven't blown down any buildings for, what, a few months now?"

"I think the perverted energy is from a voodoo ritual, not Rakshasa activity." Bela broke into the conversation before Camille could offer her opinion on whether Dio had mellowed—which was . . . sort of. Maybe.

Bela sat back and let go of her copper charm. "That's the good news. The bad news is, the priest—the *houngon*— is nobody we've dealt with before, he's definitely practicing voodoo, not Vodoun, and the energy feels too wild and strong for humans to manage."

Camille bit back a groan. Interrupting a voodoo ritual could be more dangerous than letting it run its course. Half-conjured gods could get really pissed, and they were a bitch to send back to their own plane of existence. Even worse, with Vodoun and its dark perversion, voodoo, it wasn't just about having a good grip on the paranormal and all the aspects of a proper ritual. If the gods—the *loas*—didn't know you personally or really appreciate your offering, there was a good chance they'd eat you.

Camille's back went stiff as the taste and smell of flames in the air doubled, then tripled. "There's fire down there. A lot of it. Gunpowder, too. I'm going to use the coin to get a better sense of what's happening."

Bela agreed with a fast nod.

Camille's heartbeat increased with each fraction of a second, and the dinar around her neck gave off a low vibrating hum. She rested her fingers against the agitated metal and let her energy flow into the coin. Her mind reached out, out, and—

An image of red-robed dancers slammed into her awareness.

"Spinning," she said aloud, trying to keep her breath and balance as she watched the crazed women whirl past her mind's eye. A fast, hard rhythm thudded in her ears, in her blood. "And drums. Two guys on goatskin drums."

The warehouse basement unfolded before her, illuminated by her pyrosentience, bathed in the essence of fire. The big space seemed to pulse. Then it rippled. Then it started to change.

Crimson smoke.

Gunpowder burning.

The sweet, sweet smells of rum and blood and pork made Camille's stomach flip.

Pigs. Pig blood. Lots and lots of pig blood.

Not good.

No straight-up Vodoun ritual involved the sacrifice of pigs.

Camille's fingers burned against the dinar and her teeth started to chatter from the force of the energy rushing through her enhanced connection with fire. "Petro," she managed to get out of her mouth. "Fire magic. There's a *bókó*—a sorcerer, and he's perverting energy, calling on evil. He and his boys are summoning one of the Petro *loas*. My money's on Kalfou."

The crimson air in Camille's vision shifted, and she had the vague impression of a leering skull with horns, then a huge, wicked-looking man who could double for portraits of Lucifer.

Fire. Rage. Vengeance. Murder.

That's what she tasted now.

Smoke blasted all through the warehouse basement.

The drums went quiet.

"They lost control." Camille's words choked in her throat, but she forced them out in a hot, fast rush as her sense of the dancers splintered. No more dancers. "Kalfou's here. He ate them."

Bela grabbed Camille's arm and yanked her away from the warehouse windows. Andy and Dio dived in the other direction just as all the glass in the warehouse basement windows exploded.

A blast of Dio's wind energy blew a thousand shards away from them, but it didn't do much for the heavier wave of pig blood. Dio shoved herself up, swearing and wiping pig blood off her face and dispersing clouds of glass dust as Camille staggered to her feet and managed to yank her scimitar out of its scabbard. The blade was burning, but not because she set it on fire. Flames scorched half the alley, crackling against bricks and walls and stones. Andy was smoking and washing herself with water energy at the same time, but she was coated in elementally charged pig blood, and it wasn't coming off. Bela tamped the fire on her hair with a burst of earth power, and Dio's wind pushed the heat back into the warehouse, but it just kept coming.

"Draw him out to us," Bela shouted from behind Camille. "Better to fight in the open than close quarters."

Breath catching hard in her throat, Camille charged toward the ruined windows, opened herself to the flames billowing into the alley, and pulled the fire into her essence. It filled her. Crammed into her. Her skin ached and swelled outward, and her jaw locked as she held back a scream from the pain and pressure. Not enough. Not yet.

Keep going. More. More!

She soaked up as much of the blaze as she could stand, and still more. She had to stop. She was going to explode, but the coin drew the fire even faster, even harder.

There. Enough. Might just be enough.

Sword in one hand and dinar in the other, she let out the scream she'd stifled, firing all the pent-up fire energy with it, straight out of her mouth. She focused her strike at the center of the warehouse basement, at the wide expanse of perverted energy running like lava in every direction.

Contact, then—

Heat blasted back across Camille's face, into her, *through* her. The dinar seared her palm. She hit her knees so hard that pain cracked through her legs and back. Her scimitar stayed in her grip, but she let go of the scalding coin and felt the sizzling metal bounce against her bodysuit. Her senses went dull from the shock and weight of Kalfou's backwash, and she saw the onrushing *loa* through a red-orange haze of disaster.

Camille got up. No strength. She couldn't lift her blade. She could feel her quad behind her, needing her to make a good first strike, and she couldn't do anything at all.

The angry god stormed through the warehouse basement wall like it was made of spit and paper. Bricks tumbled. Plaster pelted Camille's cheeks like dozens of stinging fists. Pig blood seemed to rain down from the sky. Kalfou towered over her, towered over all of them, huge and red and horned and lighting up the night. The god was growing, roaring so loudly the sound seemed to drill to the center of Camille's mind.

Wound him.

She had to do something, had to help her quad do damage to Kalfou. Enough pain and injury, and the god would retreat back to where he belonged. They needed to cut him with elemental metal. They needed to batter him with elemental energy. They needed to hurt whatever they could see, whatever they could touch.

"Hit him!" Bela yelled. "Hit him now. Hard! Hard!"

Andy's darts and Dio's knives whistled past Camille as

she shook her head back and forth trying to dislodge the numb, dead feeling in her head and arms. Bela ran by her, taking the lead, swinging her serrated blade at the big god's ankles.

Kalfou swiped a clawed, flaming hand at Bela.

Camille hurled herself forward, scimitar dragging, and knocked Bela out of the way.

What felt like a thousand pounds of stone and fire slammed into Camille's side. Sulfurous clouds choked into her lungs as she wheezed against the agony. Fireballs blasted around her as she flew and fell out of control, flailing, trying to keep hold of her scimitar. Gone. No weapon. Heat cracked brick and asphalt in every direction, or maybe it was her head and shoulder when she slammed into the pavement. She didn't feel the impact.

That couldn't be good.

Water washed over her, and wind, and earth energy. Her chest—ribs—Goddess. Squeezing. She couldn't breathe. She couldn't see anything but a mountain of fire with claws and horns and red, hungry eyes.

Get up.

Mindless now. Experience. Instinct. She drew in the flames the thing was throwing off, then let them go again.

Bela was back at the god, hacking at his legs. Darts riddled his belly. African throwing knives lodged in his face, glowing silver-red, dripping down across his curled, snarling lips.

Get up.

Kalfou was coming straight toward Camille. He seemed to know she was the one who had poked him with fire energy when he was still in the warehouse, and he was way beyond pissed. Whatever. She coughed, and some of her own blood splattered the pavement in front of her face, sizzling to black stains in the crushing storm of heat. She'd been knocked down in combat training at Motherhouse Ireland dozens of times. Hundreds.

Get up and fight.

"Screw you," she mumbled at the god through her cracked, bleeding lips. When she rolled over to get to her knees, she cried out from the stabbing pains in her chest and ribs.

"Stay down. I'll take care of this." John Cole's voice rumbled through Camille's awareness, cutting under the god's bellowing.

She saw the barest flash of movement as he ran past her and leaped at the god, just a blur of jeans and T-shirt and glowing silver.

My blade. He's got my scimitar!

Cole—Strada? Whoever he was, he was swinging the sword in wide arcs, sending sprays of burning pig blood in every direction. His T-shirt burned in ten places at once, leaving bare muscle to flex and scorch as he fought. Some kind of power rolled off him in waves, dueling with the god's elemental energy as he cut the creature. His skin had to be on fire, blistering, but he never slowed down, never stopped hacking with her scimitar again, again, again.

Her quad's battle cries ripped into her consciousness, yanking her to her feet, but she couldn't quite stand. Half her body felt broken. Somehow she got her right arm up, got hold of the dinar as Bela, Andy, and Dio drew closer to Kalfou, exploiting the damage Strada—or Cole, or whoever he was—was creating.

The big god kept roaring, kept swinging his sledge-hammer fists.

Camille squeezed the hot coin in her hand.

If I use this thing, I'll melt where I stand.

But if she didn't, her quad and the demon-man might get crushed before she managed to suck in a full breath of air.

Camille pulled in all the fire energy she could manage and shoved it back out again, through the dinar, straight toward the god's big horned head.

Kalfou lurched when her blast hit him, and that was all the demon-man with Camille's scimitar seemed to need. He charged even closer, hooking the scimitar into the god's chest and yanking himself upward before Kalfou could swipe him off like a gnat.

Wind, air, earth, and fire hit the god in the face again.

The god roared as Cole-Strada hooked an arm around his neck, drew back the scimitar, and rammed the sharp hook of the blade directly into his wide, bellowing mouth.

The ear-crushing crack and shock wave of elemental energy shifting out of this plane of existence drove Camille back to the pavement. More hot air slammed into her as Kalfou made his escape from the alley, pushing her down until her ears, her face, her head, her whole body throbbed from the pressure. She had no strength left, not even enough to lift her head off the heated asphalt. Her vision flickered and her eyes closed. She fought the darkness, but she felt it closing in around her, slipping over her and shutting her away from the world.

Strong arms took hold of her and seemed to pull her back from oblivion, back into the smoldering, smoking and eerie-silent alley.

"I've got you," said that deep, entrancing voice she hadn't been able to stop thinking about since she first heard it, the night of the golden light.

Camille felt more muscles pressing against her face, her aching arm and shoulder. A carved chest, singed and bruised but still perfect. The demon-man's grip was firm but so gentle and comforting. "Be still, beautiful. You're pretty banged up."

"Don't move, you crazy-ass bastard." That was Dio, with wind screaming through every word she spoke. "I don't know what kind of mindfuck you're trying to pull, but we're done with it, and we're done with you."

Camille winced at the crash of thunder even though her eyes were closed.

Bela's voice sounded just as deadly. "Don't even twitch, Strada."

"I won't hurt her," Cole-Strada said. Camille couldn't see his face and she was glad, because she couldn't take another ounce of pain.

"Let go of her right now, nice and slow. No sudden moves or we'll cut you to pieces." Andy's command was matter-of-fact, and the forceful push of water energy touched Camille's essence, cooling her down and giving her some measure of comfort.

"Think," said the demon-man. "If I were really Strada, could I get this close to the dinar? I'm John Cole. Camille helped me take this body the last time you fought the Rakshasa."

Seconds seemed to tick by.

Earth and air and water energy twined into Camille, giving her strength, but not enough to struggle for her freedom, especially when she wasn't sure she wanted to.

"Let her go," Dio said again, but this time Camille didn't hear any thunder.

"I'm taking her back to the brownstone, to the infirmary room I know you've got in your basement." John Cole—because that's who Camille was hearing—sounded calm and determined. It was him. She was tired of fighting her own confusion and disbelief, and right that second she didn't care what it cost her. She wanted it to be him, and that was the reality until someone convinced her otherwise.

"After you take care of her," he said, holding her a little closer, "put me in whatever kind of elemental bindings you want until you summon your Mothers to examine me. They'll confirm what I'm telling you, but I'm not letting Camille go until I'm sure she's safe."

Don't let me go, she wanted to say. *Not now. Not ever.*

Okay, yeah, she had lost whatever was left of her mind.

The last thing she heard before she finally slipped into an involuntary healing trance was Andy's low, whispered, "Fuuuuck me," and that, at least, seemed somewhere close to sane.

11

John led the way to the brownstone, cradling Camille as he powered forward, paying close attention to her breathing. Even. Steady. He thought she was stable, but she was pale and it seemed she weighed no more than a feather. Her auburn hair touched her cheeks, highlighting the lack of color in her pretty face and making her seem tired and fragile. Too much stress. Not enough time to rest and eat. He'd be making sure that changed as soon as she felt better.

"You might want to slow down," Andy called out to him as he reached the steps of the brownstone, but John couldn't think past getting Camille inside, where she'd be safe and her quad could help her heal. He hit the first step—

And a big, mean fist of stupid clubbed him right between the eyes.

His muscles went wobbly and his jaw clamped into place. Strada's essence howled like a psychotic parasite, wriggling in his head until John wanted to retch up every burger he'd sucked down for the last two weeks. All of his energy went to keeping his grip on Camille—and not puking.

He stayed on his feet, pulling Camille against him like an anchor, and shook his head to clear his senses.

He'd been to this brownstone before, been inside it for weeks when he lived in Duncan Sharp's head. He knew the Sibyls protected themselves from paranormal attacks with elemental locks. The locks hadn't affected him when he was nothing but a powerless, hitchhiking spirit, but with leftover demon essence in his head—shit.

"Good job, tiger-man." Andy's water energy splashed against his back, pushing him up a step. "You know, I really don't talk just to hear my own voice. Next time I tell you to slow down, maybe you should listen."

"Sorry," he managed, grinding his teeth against the stabbing pains behind his eyes. He pulled Camille closer as Andy's water moved him another step, and another, cooling his back and neck as it splashed into him. Bela and Dio passed him on either side, and Bela opened the door. Dio went inside first, and a second or two later, the skull-crushing pressure eased. John stumbled through the door behind Bela, one hand gently over Camille's face to keep the sudden light from bothering her.

Andy slammed the door behind her, pushed past him and stormed through the entryway. She crossed the living room and didn't slow down until she reached the alcove near the swinging kitchen door. Weird yellow light played off the leather sofa and four leather chairs surrounding the gigantic wooden table that John remembered because it served double duty as the quad's communications platform. They used the platform to talk to the Motherhouses and other Sibyl groups, and occasionally to transport objects or people across long distances.

The sources of the glow, a dozen projective mirrors hanging on the walls of the recessed space, were quiet and dark except for strange, candle-like flickers that seemed to live in the glass—energy from ancient channels coursing across the earth. With his new, shared demon essence, John could sense the power in those channels. It pulled at his skin, as if daring him to come closer.

"Far enough," Bela said.

"I'll take her downstairs—" he started to say, but elemental shackles clanked as Dio slammed them closed around John's ankles. Immediately his senses dulled and his strength ebbed.

"Far enough," Bela repeated, steel in each word. Her eyes went hard as she reached for Camille.

Another set of elemental cuffs clamped hard around John's thighs, stinging his insides and deadening his senses almost as much as that first punch from the supernatural locks on the brownstone. He let Bela collect Camille from his arms, but only because he'd made a deal. His gut twisted like he was losing something precious, even though he realized somewhere deep in his mistrusting heart that these women knew how to take care of their own. Bela would die for Camille, just like he would. Of that, John was completely certain.

"I hate little suck-ass wannabes who summon Vodoun gods they can't control." Andy threw her blood-coated face mask on the nearest leather chair, then opened the kitchen door for Bela. "And why is it always me who gets totally and completely splatted with ritual blood when all the wind starts blowing? Chickens, pigs—it's a damned conspiracy."

John leaned forward, watching Camille as Bela carried her away from him, until the door swung shut and blocked Camille, Bela, and Andy from his view.

The room felt suddenly cold and empty—and a little breezy. Wind chimes rang, random and discordant, and John's spongy focus squeezed and shifted. He realized that Dio was still with him, moving in front of him, pulling at his right hand to fit it into a set of elemental cuffs. He lifted both arms to make her job easier. "Will I get a neck collar and chain, too?"

"Don't crack jokes, asshole." She slammed the right cuff down and locked it. "I've got a big collar if we need one, and I'm sure I could find a leash."

John felt his lips twitch as he held back a smile.

"Duncan was right. You're the real hard-ass of this operation, aren't you? Every unit has one."

Dio didn't answer him, but dark lightning seemed to flash across her eyes. Yeah, that was her role, no doubt about it, but he didn't get much of a sense that she liked it.

"Back when I was in Duncan's head, he asked you to kill him if he ever got out of control and tried to hurt Bela," John said, figuring she'd remember that little exchange.

"Fuck off." Dio kept her unforgiving gaze on the last cuff she was fastening, making sure he was about as mobile as a cooked Christmas turkey right before carving.

John knew that saying anything else would be pushing his luck, but he also knew that winning the right to work with Camille and keep her safe involved scoring a few points with the other women in her quad. Herding cats would be too tame a metaphor for that prospect. Herding porcupines might be more to the point. Porcupines with serious attitudes, giant fangs and claws, and deadly elemental power—not to mention swords, throwing knives, dart pistols, and who knew what else.

"What if I ask you to make that same deal with me now, about Camille?" John kept his eyes level and his chin up, and he felt a surge of triumph even though Dio banged the last cuff shut and let his arms fall so fast and hard he almost flew ass over teakettle into the communications platform. With his legs locked together, he didn't have much balance.

Dio stood a foot from him, glaring like she wanted to slug him right in the face. "I don't make deals with demons, and you don't even know Camille."

John hopped until he found his center again, never breaking eye contact. "I've touched Camille's soul and she's touched mine."

"You're a delusional dickhead." Dio pushed him

backward with both hands, and this time he did slam into the platform, sitting down hard to keep from pitching sideways.

"Call the Mothers, then." He kept right on looking at Dio, trying to challenge her without getting himself killed. "They'll examine me and tell you the truth."

Dio studied him in total silence for a moment, then shook her head. "Our quad doesn't do much business with the Mothers unless we have to. We have other ways of finding things out."

An unwelcome wave of surprise swept through John, and he had a sense of all his carefully laid plans crumbling as he watched an unfriendly smile spread across Dio's face.

He shifted on the table to sit up as straight as he could. "What other ways?"

Her smile turned positively predatory, and she leaned in close to make her point. "If you think I'm a hard-ass, demon-man, just wait till you meet our friends."

Huge.

Camille sensed it before she saw it, a moving, burning wall of death. She hefted her scimitar as the demon burst out of the little building in Van Cortlandt Park.

"Damnit!" Bette screamed. "Too big!"

She tried to shoot the thing with her crossbow, but it came on too fast. Moving. Rippling. Shifting. The sulfur stench of it made Camille's eyes water. The Asmodai was tall, then short; wide, then flat. Camille saw its face and she wanted to shriek. Flat, badly shaped clay. Utterly inhuman, with eyes like small burning pits from hell.

She swung her scimitar hard, but it caught the blade in its not-human hands. It ripped her sword straight out of her grip and hacked Bette shoulder to hip. Then it threw down the blade, knocked Bette to the ground with the force of its elemental power, and turned on Camille. . . .

"Wake up."

She heard the voice. Woke. Fell asleep again, and this time dreamed a little bit better.

At least, she thought she was dreaming, because as far as she knew, sharks didn't swim through the brownstone's living room. But in her dream, the whole space was filled with crystalline water, and big, gray, toothy shapes swept back and forth and back and forth around a piece of live bait chained to the ceiling.

She didn't like sharks.

They reminded her too much of Asmodai, with their dead, elementally loaded eyes, or maybe the girls she'd grown up fighting, or the Mothers—all rolled into one nasty package.

"It's time to wake up, Camille."

Oh, great. There was a shark in her bedroom, too. A little one with white skin, weird gold bracelets on its arm, and scars on its face where one of its eyes was supposed to be.

"Wake up," the little shark commanded again.

Camille tried to shake her head, but it made her brain hurt, so she stopped. "I can't wake up. I still need to heal. Bela told me to."

Before she went to swim with the sharks in the upstairs living room.

Camille had no idea why she felt like talking to the shark in her bedroom, but her mouth kept moving. "This used to be her room, you know, but she asked me for mine upstairs, so she and her husband could have more space." She yawned, becoming more and more aware of a dull, throbbing ache between her eyes. "Most fire Sibyls can't stand to live in basements, but it doesn't bother me. Bela lets me use her lab down the hall, too—and I haven't blown anything up. This month, at least. Most fire Sibyls can't be in labs, either."

The little shark hovered beside her bed, beginning to

look a little worried, though it was hard to read worry on a shark face. "You're not like most fire Sibyls. I thought you knew that by now."

Great. A sarcastic shark. Just what the world needed. Camille definitely didn't feel like arguing with a smart-mouthed fish, so she said, "Yeah. I know. The Mothers wanted to throw me out of the Sisterhood when I was a kid."

At this, the little shark fanned its tail and swept back, its toothy mouth opened in a mockery of surprise. "Throw you—? You thought—" The shark interrupted itself by laughing, and it couldn't seem to stop for a few seconds. Finally, giving off billowing wreaths of bubbles, it managed to choke out, "They wouldn't have dared."

Camille narrowed her eyes to get a better look at the shark, wondering what the hell that was supposed to mean, but the water in the bedroom seemed to be receding. She could see the walls now, with their cream-colored paint and forest-green trim. The dark greens of her furniture came into view, and the two posts at the end of her full-sized bed. The bedclothes, cream to match the walls, were rumpled around her bare legs, and she realized she was wearing one of her green silk tank tops with matching underwear—silk PJs in all forms and fashions were a guilty pleasure she indulged. The pajama set was pretty dry, but her sheets were damp and the dinar against her chest under her tank seemed to be stuck to her skin from all the moisture she'd shed in the healing trance.

She had a lot of lamps for a relatively small room—both table and floor lamps—and they were all switched on at the softest settings. Above her head, fastened to the ceiling, six small sets of copper wind chimes danced and tinkled, responding to elemental energy but not communicating any clear messages from other Sibyls, or warning of dangerous paranormal energy. The pictures on her walls, an oil rendering of Motherhouse Ireland, a pastel of Motherhouse Greece, a pen-and-ink sketch of rambling, ancient Motherhouse Russia, and a watercolor of the newly finished Motherhouse Kérkira, had all been created by Dio, who was an amazing artist. Dio had framed them all in tasteful wood, stained green to match the room's trim and Camille's furniture.

Camille glanced at her desk in the far corner—small, neatly organized, stacked with pieces of metal and library texts about metallurgy. Nothing out of order. Everything seemed in pretty good shape, so why was she dreaming about a—

"There, that's better," said a hoarse, crackly female voice.

Shark . . .

Camille turned to her left to find the little woman perched on the chair that went with Camille's desk. She must have pulled it over to Camille's bedside.

"Ona." Camille no longer found Ona's scarred face and bald head difficult to look at, and her green tunic and breeches fit her so loosely she almost looked like she was wearing Mothers' robes. Camille realized she was glad Mother Keara and other Sibyls had seen Ona at the remembrance ceremony, or she might be convinced she was dealing with yet another ghost in her life. "How did you get here? Did someone call you and fire up the projective mirrors?"

Ona's smile was kind, but her words came out firm and definite. "I don't need anyone to open channels for me, Camille, and I don't have to be summoned to know I'm needed."

Camille knew that was all the information she'd be getting on that subject. Ona's blunt style unsettled her, but she was almost starting to like it. Maybe even envy it.

Right about then, she had a slow, disorganized memory of a whole bunch of pig blood, a big Vodoun god eating people—and the night's battle came back to her in full. Camille groaned as she sat up and rubbed both sides of her head.

Then the next memory hit her, and this had a much bigger punch.

He's here.

The thought pounded at her, making her heart beat faster.

He's right upstairs.

Her body got warm all over, and she felt like five big pieces of Connemara marble had been lifted off her head now that the confusion had ended. All the old arguments she'd been having with herself about whether or not Strada was demon or human now seemed distant and pointless. The man who had saved her, who had held her and brought her home to heal—human. No question in her mind. She never should have doubted herself so much, or punished herself so recklessly.

Hadn't Ona told her to do what felt right?

Well, it felt right that the thing upstairs wasn't a thing at all. He was human, and he was a man, a *good-looking* man named John Cole.

Ona was watching her as if she could read each thought and emotion. Camille didn't doubt that Ona had gifts she hadn't begun to understand, but that didn't bother her as much as Ona's sudden, sad frown.

"Your man, he's been a part of many terrible things," Ona said. "I think they haunt him."

Camille twitched under her sheets. "He's not my man. I just helped him out once a while back."

My man. Interesting thought.

Camille cleared her throat. "I heard he spent most of his life fighting demons. Bela's husband, Duncan, told us that John Cole gave up his military career and his priesthood to track and kill the Rakshasa because he felt responsible for them being set loose on the world again."

Ona's next words flowed out like a pronouncement,

one of those things Mothers say that Sibyls don't get to argue with, except Ona kept telling Camille she wasn't a Mother at all.

Yeah, right.

"He is responsible for the demons being loose, but only in part." Ona's frown deepened. "He's wise enough to see that, and I think you are, too." She leaned toward Camille and gestured to the ceiling directly above Camille's head. "But this next bit, I don't think—I know. The universe often sends us the weapons we need just in time for us to need them. To defeat the Rakshasa, the Sibyls need John Cole's help, and the help of those he can bring to the table. Don't let anything happen to him."

If Camille had needed any confirmation of her own perceptions, Ona's opinion was more than enough for her. "Are the Mothers here to see John—or Strada, whoever the hell they think he is? Maybe we can save them some time and him a lot of discomfort."

"That's why I was trying to wake you." Ona slid out of her chair and brushed creases out of her tunic and breeches as she spoke. "Your quad didn't summon any Mothers save for Andy Myles, who is of course a Mother in her own right, however inexperienced—and already in residence here. Like you and me, your friends seem to have an aversion to involving the Mothers in their affairs if they have other methods of finding out what they need to know."

Camille felt herself go stiff. "What other methods?"

Ona sighed as if she really didn't want to say what she had to say—which in and of itself was frightening. "Maggie Cregan and her infernal sword."

Camille let that sink in as the chimes above her head began a slow, coordinated dirge. The coin around her neck tingled, then started to burn through the sweat on her chest. Her breathing got tight, and restless heat bubbled up from her legs to her chest to her face. She looked at the ceiling of her room, and in her mind, the living room above it filled up with sharks all over again.

"Oh, shit," she muttered, then shoved back her covers, pushed herself to her feet, and stumbled toward the bedroom door.

(12)

This had been his idea, right?

Well, it was a bad idea.

No, no. *Bad idea* didn't quite cover it.

Rotten stupid idea was more to the point.

John shifted on the communications platform, but changing position only made his shoulders nearly pop out of their sockets because his arms had been raised high and tight over his head, his elemental cuffs fastened to a hook on the ceiling.

A frigging meat hook anchored in a wooden support beam.

How had he managed to miss that little decorative detail when he visited this place in Duncan Sharp's head last year? The stupid thing looked even more menacing, reflected in all the weird magic mirrors hanging on the walls around the platform. Some of them were smoking so heavily John expected the pointy, pale face of one of those Disney witches to appear, demanding to know if he was the fairest in all the land.

Well, he was sure as hell the best-trussed.

Chains had been looped through metal rings on the outside of his ankle cuffs, pulled tight and secured to the bottom of the table. As for the fire burning in the small lead-lined lip of the platform—that shit was hot enough to cook what was left of his T-shirt and make his jeans smolder. He knew there was earth energy in that blazing lip, and air, and water—one big extra-powerful additional elemental lock to hold him in place.

"The energy's strange," Bela said in a tone like she

was talking about something on a microscope slide instead of a chained-up guy who could hear every word she was saying. She was standing right in front of him in her battle leathers, with her black hair pulled back and her dark eyes fixed on his midsection instead of his face. Around her neck, barely visible above the pulled-down zipper of her leather jumpsuit, was a copper charm, a crescent moon, that seemed to have a power all its own.

Dio was on Bela's right, and Andy had the spot on her left. They had their own crescent moon charms, Dio's a bright silver and Andy's a darker shade, like iron. Yeah, definitely energy coming from those things, though John had trouble figuring out what it was. Something shady and kind of disturbing, almost like the charms had some kind of potential that wasn't being realized. Dio wasn't smiling anymore, and her wispy blond hair made her look soft and gentle. What a total crock. Even Andy, the redheaded cop turned water Sibyl, seemed halfway ready to cut him open and find out if he really had ribs and blood and a heart on the inside.

Despite the danger from Bela, Dio, and Andy with their strange necklaces, it was the three other women in the room who really concerned John.

John had banked on the quad calling the Mothers to examine him. He had gotten to know a lot about them, especially Mother Keara from Ireland, when he lived in Duncan's head. He knew what to expect from them, and though Elana believed some of them might have issues with Camille, John knew that most Mothers were tough as hell but rational, fair, and powerful.

For the three Sibyls who had arrived a few minutes ago, *rational* and *fair* might not be part of their vocabulary. The East Ranger group seemed like wildcards to him, nomads with no fixed territory, used to living harder than other Sibyl fighting groups. They were standing behind Bela's group, battle leathers zipped, arms folded, just staring at him, and he could tell they definitely didn't see him as human.

The earth Sibyl in the group—Bela called her Sheila—had the blackest hair and eyes he had ever seen. The air Sibyl was Karin. She was shorter and stockier than other air Sibyls he'd seen, but her sandy brown hair and blue eyes made her look like the fairest fighter in this Ranger bunch.

The fire Sibyl, though—she was a piece of work.

That one with the redder-than-red hair and freaky-colored jade eyes, John didn't think he wanted much to do with her. Maggie Cregan looked like a woman who'd enjoy lots of yelling and screaming. She probably carried a spare ball gag in her pocket, and for some reason her sword was making Strada's essence crawl around in John's brain and snort like a tripped-out mole.

John studied the sword as best he could in his whip-me-now pose.

Short hilt. Massive blade tucked into its leather sheath. There was something about it, some energy that shouldn't be there, and it bothered him. A lot.

He could sense all that with Strada's remnant abilities, and he'd really upped his agility and hand-to-hand fighting skills thanks to Ben and his boys—but when it came to using his demon energy to shatter elemental cuffs and get himself out of this fetching BDSM get-up, John didn't have a clue how to do it. The cuffs made him feel tired and foggy and stupid, and maybe for now that was safer than trying to pull any big escape.

But what would happen if these women hurt him badly enough that he tapped out? Could Strada take over then and do real damage?

John didn't think the chains and locks could hold a Rakshasa Eldest in tiger form.

Well, that settles it. No tapping out.

He thought about Camille downstairs, unconscious and needing quiet, peaceful time to heal, and his insides burned. He didn't like to imagine her helpless and alone. She was going to get what she needed no matter what these women tried to pull.

In his time in Duncan's head, John had learned about Curson demons—the half-breeds. They kept their demon essences under control with a talisman, usually a piece of jewelry. As long as it was on their person, they had control of the demon aspect they carried inside them, end of story. He wished like hell he had some way to bell Strada with a talisman, wrap some piece of gold around his hateful energy and know that as long as John had it, Strada couldn't do jack shit.

"Her ancestors were executioners," Dio said, and John realized he was still staring at Maggie Cregan and her weapon. "They all used that sword."

"Some hanged the condemned," Maggie corrected with a smile much meaner than Dio's, "but even they needed a backup weapon." She drew the sword slowly, almost reverently, like touching it required some sort of negotiation with the energy it carried. "No piece of metal in history has ever been tempered with so much blood and pain. After a while, the blade took on a life of its own, so to speak."

The sword had markings on it, runes maybe, but when the metal started to glow from the fire energy Maggie was feeding it, John could make out what those runes really were.

People.

Dying people.

One was getting strung up. One beheaded. One drawn and quartered.

There were a lot more. Seemingly more every second. John really didn't want to examine all of them, especially the guy who looked like he was being flayed, but the hotter the sword got, the clearer those godawful pictures became.

And then they started moving.

Energy boiled off the sword and blasted across John's new supernatural instincts, scraping him inside and out.

Sandstorm . . .

Heat and all, blinding and choking until he barely caught a whole breath.

This was like the desert. This was like the war.

This was not good.

John gripped the chains above his cuffs. His eyes watered from the abrasive heat. He saw the Sibyls in prism, moving into a circle around the table, Maggie front and center with that sick sword. The flames on the table jumped higher. All he could smell was sulfur and hot air, burning against his mouth and nose.

More energy swelled through the room. Lots of it. Earth, air, fire, and water, pulled toward the Sibyls, flowing out from the Sibyls, changing and shifting until the flexing waves of power blotted out the details of the room. The world around John got five-day-bender blurry, and John couldn't make out who was who or who was where. They shifted past him in brief glimpses, red or yellow or black for their hair, a dash of leather, a flash of silver, and they kept moving. Even in his teen years, John had never had a trip like this.

Wolfpack. Wolfpack moving. Challenging the cat inside him. The sword blazed and the things on its blade writhed. John felt them demanding and needing and dreaming like living things.

They craved blood.

Not good, not good, not good.

Strada screeched like a demon banshee, and John was sure the sound belched out of his ears. He tried to stop it, couldn't, and Strada's essence pulled against his like a seam tearing at its threads

"Don't do this," John said, and he didn't like how harsh and hollow his voice sounded.

Maggie. Right in front of him. Her smile got meaner and stranger, and John's fuddled brain picked out other faces etched on top of hers, like she had turned into her sword. She moved the red-hot blade through the air, making the flames arc higher. "Don't do what?"

"Don't bring that thing close to me." John's vision shifted again. Shades and colors and murmurs and whispers and sounds and hints and smells and textures surged through his awareness. Too vivid. Too strong.

Fuck. What is this—super cat senses now? Christ. If he really had gotten himself bitten by a radioactive spider and started spitting big, sticky webs, it would have been easier than this. The ends of his fingers burned like claws wanted to explode out of his skin. His skin crawled like fur was trying to find a foothold. His teeth itched from the inside, like they were growing. His words jumbled in his mind; more to the point, they wouldn't come forward, like something was holding them back.

John jerked against the chains above his head and shoved back against Strada's energy with everything he had.

"That sword's not safe," he snarled at the women, way too tiger.

They were nothing but a blur—then, Andy. Andy in front, with her hand on the charm around her neck. "No shit the sword's dangerous," she said, and he had to figure she was still talking and not running or drawing down on him because she had no idea he was about to go all hairy and psychotic. "We agreed to examine you, not follow the Geneva Conventions. Now tell us—where are the Rakshasa hiding?"

Prickles of energy ran across his skin, watery yet sizzling, with a pressure-like power that seemed to drive him backward as Strada tried to come forward.

"I don't know." John rattled his chains again, using the pressure and pain of the cuffs cutting into his wrists to hold his focus. "These chains aren't strong enough."

This time he directed his words at the blond blur of movement that had to be Dio. Please, for the love of God, she had to hear what he was saying and understand. "Get the Mothers before you do it—whatever you're doing."

What the hell?

Whose voice was that? Not his, but it was him talking, him saying, "Get the Mothers to hold back this bastard in my head!"

Maggie Cregan spun into his view and laughed out loud. Her rune-covered sword blasted flames in every direction, and the wind chimes around the room started to ring in a weird pattern, like a marching step.

Funeral. Funeral march.

"We're not planning to hold you back, Strada," Maggie told him. "If you get out of line, we'll just kill you. I'll ask you again—where are your furry friends? What are they up to?"

"Kill me if you have to," John told Dio in Strada's voice. "I don't know where the demons are. When I find them, I'll call you."

He had an urge to let loose with a roar, a rattling, paralyzing sound so low it would break bones and snap trees and bounce off mountains. He could feel the dangerous noise building inside him, and it took every fraction of strength he possessed to hold it back.

Questions fired at him from every direction now, different voices, different intensities. More energy touched him and poked him and prodded him and shoved him, air and earth and more water, too much, all of it, suffocating his self-will and giving Strada too much of an opening.

"How did you really get that body?"

"Why are you so focused on Camille?"

"Why haven't you showed yourself before now?"

He couldn't tell who was talking. He felt like the elemental power in the room was trying to compel him to answer, that the circling was part of some bad-ass hypnosis, but it wasn't working, Christ, no, and the energy was even worse, stripping him down, tearing all the human off him. He couldn't say a word without losing what little control he had left. He couldn't tell them what they wanted to know, not this way, not here or now, or—

If I give in to this roar, I'll be gone.

They'll be gone.

He made himself imagine the room before all the weirdness started, with its leather furniture and its table and its smoky mirrors and sets of chimes. He made himself see it covered in gore. A battlefield. A bloodbath. Just without the sand and the rocks and hardware from the war.

Hold it together. Hold it. Hold it tight.

Dio stopped moving, breaking that blur of leather and Sibyl and pulsing elemental energy. John barely found the wits to stare at her face, to see the concern edge out her usual anger and distance.

"If I grow fur—" All snarl now. Could they even understand him? "If I grow fur, do it. Kill me fast."

Dio took her hand off the charm around her neck and gave him the once-over. Bela and Andy came up beside her and did the same thing.

"I don't think he can answer," Dio said. "Something's not right."

"Agreed," Bela said. Scientific. In charge. She had commander written all over her. If she was in John's unit, he would have put her up for a promotion, even if it meant losing her.

John couldn't see Maggie and the other two for now, just the Sibyls he knew, the Sibyls he wished knew him enough to realize he was about to explode like a pipe bomb made out of tiger-demon.

Dio. The hard-ass. She would stop him.

Bela. Married to Duncan. Duncan was part demon now, thanks to the Rakshasa attack. Was she seeing how hard he was fighting?

John's vision tapped out for a second, giving him darkness, like he was looking at the inside of his own skull.

No!

He burst forward again.

Andy. Andy was there. Two of the Curson demons working as detectives for the Occult Crimes Unit were her best friends. She had to get this.

Strada—the goat-fucker—seemed to be pounding on the inside of his head with a sledgehammer.

"Hurry, goddamnit," he growled at the three Sibyls closest to him, not able to temper his language even with all the women in the room. "I've got him. Whatever else you have to do, do it now. Right now."

Maggie Cregan flamed into view on his right, coming at him with that sword like she'd been looking forward to cutting somebody for weeks. Sheila and Karin followed her but didn't try to slow her down.

"Be careful." Bela held up both hands. "Be as gentle as you can be until you know what he really is."

Andy didn't say anything, but she looked like she was thinking about knocking the sword out of Maggie's hands.

It was Dio who blocked Maggie's path and faced off with her, and the blast of wind energy that put out the sword's flames cooled John's skin just enough for him to catch his breath and drop-kick Strada's essence a few more paces backward in his consciousness.

"Don't dick around," Dio told Maggie. "And don't do anything you don't have to do."

Maggie gave Dio a major frown. "Hey, you called me, remember? If you want the Mothers, I can open the channels for you if Camille's still out of it."

Bela, Andy, and Dio shook their heads at the same time.

Dio jerked a thumb over her shoulder toward John. "You can find out what we need to know. All I'm saying is, don't take chances, and don't be an ass. He's as much as saying Strada's in there with him, and it's obvious the demon's giving him a fight."

"Then why are we just questioning him and sampling his essence?" Sheila asked Bela. "If he's got Rakshasa in him, we should put him down."

Bela's sharp look might have killed a lesser Sibyl, and Sheila seemed to realize what she'd said. Then she appeared to remember whom she was talking to, or maybe whom and *what* Bela had married. "Oh. I—well. Never mind."

"Smooth," Andy said to Sheila. "Want to add a knee and butt cheek to that foot you just crammed in your mouth?"

The kitchen door swung open before Sheila could answer.

As John's divided mind grappled for a hold on what was happening, someone pushed through the wall of leather bodysuits in front of him. He felt a new shock of energy, fresher, different, more familiar—and the flames on the communications platform died away to reveal Camille, ethereal with her long auburn hair brushing across her freckled cheeks and shoulders.

Strada pushed to get at her.

John shoved right back at the demon, so hard the energy drained out of his knees and legs, leaving him dangling by the cuffs and chains.

Strada roared, but John held on inside himself, staring at Camille.

No. Fucking. Way.

New energy rose inside him, hotter and angrier, like he'd borrowed it directly from the fire Sibyl he intended to keep safe, no matter what. Screw Strada. The Rakshasa wasn't getting near Camille, not now, not ever, not if John had to die right here on this meat hook to keep it from happening.

"Be careful, honey," Bela said to Camille. "I'm not sure whom we're dealing with."

"I am," Camille said, but John barely heard the words because he was throwing breath and heartbeat and blood flow and absolutely everything else he had into containing the demon sharing his essence.

I'll kill you, he told Strada. *I'll find some way.*

The demon answered him with a shriek of absolute fury.

(13)

Long minutes seemed to tick by, but John knew it was only seconds. He had Strada now. He'd taken back the advantage, blocked the demon's advance, and left the bastard snarling in the blackest, farthest corner of his mind.

Camille gazed up at him, taking in the chains and cuffs and smoke and mirrors and God only knew what else.

John hoped he hadn't grown big tiger ears and a tail while he'd been distracted.

For a few seconds the room blurred out of John's awareness again, and he saw nothing but the woman he couldn't stop thinking about. Her unusual green-blue eyes drew his focus like rare jewels or secret sunlit pools hidden on some tropical island. She had on a little green silk number with matching bottoms so short they barely peeked out beneath the tank. The dinar around her neck hung below the shirt, making a circular outline just above the swell of her breasts. His cat senses, still on high, took in the sweet scent of lilies mingled with perspiration and some kind of lotion and seemingly everything female in the universe.

She was enough to make him do anything, give up anything—

Or she would have been if he hadn't been hanging from a meat hook trying like hell to be sure a Rakshasa didn't crawl out of his skin. Literally. But Strada didn't seem to be close at all now. Down for the count. Had the dinar around Camille's neck repelled Strada's remnant essence?

John wondered, but didn't think that was it.

It's her. It's being close to her. That makes everything else a nonissue, doesn't it?

Camille looked angry and tired, fragile and perfect all at the same time. John wanted to pick her up and hold her and keep her safe forever. Her expression mixed weariness and lingering pain from her injuries with a fury so deep and explosive John was surprised she wasn't letting off steam and trailing sparks like Maggie, but that didn't seem to be Camille's style.

"You shouldn't be here," Bela said to Camille, just about the same time Andy came out with "You need to be resting."

Dio didn't make any comments, but when Camille turned on Maggie Cregan, the wiry blond air Sibyl got the hell out of the way. Energy flowed and crackled around the alcove, making the mirrors rattle against the wall. John could have sworn he heard—that he *felt*—distant roaring, not human or animal or demon, but fire itself, the kind of deadly, endless flowing fire that lived in the center of the earth.

"Shit," somebody whispered. It sounded like Andy.

The two fire Sibyls went face-to-face with less than an arm's length separating them, and Camille didn't seem the least bit intimidated by the taller woman or her bizarre killing blade. Camille glanced at the sword, then glared at Maggie like she wanted to say a lot of things, maybe a lot of loud things. John waited for her to speak in the voice of that center-earth fire that seemed to be rattling the floor as it tried to burst through the planet's crust.

Instead, Camille seemed to channel every ounce of that power until her voice came out in cold, measured, and lethal tones. "If you cut him with that sword, I'll kill you."

Maggie's face tensed from surprise, and she gave ground. Just a step, but John read it as her version of total surrender. The thunder under the earth faded, as if a rising volcano under New York City had changed its mind about erupting.

For a moment, six pairs of eyes in the room lost focus, but the seventh pair, Camille's beautiful aquamarine ones, moved away from Maggie and fixed directly on John's face without the slightest hint of distraction. The amount of steel in that stare, the depth of fire he saw and sensed—John thought about all the men he had ever commanded, and he realized he'd take this woman by his side just as fast, any day, any battle, no matter what kind of hurt was coming down around them.

Warrior.

The whole fragile thing, that was just her shell, gorgeous as it was. There was absolutely nothing breakable underneath.

He realized that in some strange, primal way, she had just staked a claim on him, a claim all her sister Sibyls seemed to recognize and be inclined to respect, at least for now. John was impressed by that, and fine with it, and stupid-teenage-boy grateful she thought he was worth the risk.

"It's okay," he told her, feeling the strength of his own control over Strada growing more solid than iron and rock.

Everything's fine now that you're here.

That much he kept to himself, but he had a sense that she knew, that she had heard the words he didn't say, somewhere down deep in her heart. As long as John was looking at Camille, Strada didn't have a prayer in hell of taking him over.

"Let them do this," John said, relieved to hear his own voice speaking the words his brain threw forward. "Let me show them what I really am."

I won't let you down. Not now. Not ever.

Camille came back to stand in front of him, the air of dangerousness around her beginning to dissipate—though not completely. "There are risks with her sword. Once it tastes you, it'll know you forever. It can track you and hunt you, and it'll seek you in battle. Any chance it gets, it'll cut you again. She controls it, but not completely."

John had a lot of questions about that blade, but now wasn't the time to ask them. "I'm not planning to fight in any battles against her sword, or against the Sibyls."

"The Mothers' judgments can come fast and harsh," Dio said, moving in next to Camille. "And without a lot of discussion—but their tests would definitely be safer."

Bela came closer, too, and Andy, while Maggie and her two friends kept some distance. Camille's fighting group now seemed to be willing to let him choose between Maggie and her creepy little metal friend and summoning the Mothers, like he'd asked them to do in the first place. The Mothers none of these Sibyls seemed to really like or want in their safe space, except when they had no other choice.

John couldn't really shrug because of the chains and cuffs and meat hook, but he gave his answer in relaxed, casual tones, mostly to put Camille at ease. "Safer isn't always better or faster. Let's get on with it."

Everybody in the room seemed to wait for Camille's consent, and she gave it by turning away from John and moving out of her quad's way.

Dio, Andy, and Bela eased back into position around the big wooden table while Camille faced Maggie again, this time with more space between them. Maggie's fighting group stayed close to her, and John thought they looked ready to jump between the two fire Sibyls, just in case.

Probably not a bad idea.

This time, though, Camille didn't seem cocked and

ready to go off. She gestured to the sword Maggie still gripped like it might get away from her. "Be careful."

Maggie's nod was quick and confident.

Camille turned away from the group and went to sit on the leather sofa at the edge of the alcove, and Maggie's group spread out to complete the circle around the table. Elemental energy flowed around the circle, and once more flames erupted from the little lead-lined trough at the very edge of the platform. This time the blaze seemed powerful but subdued.

Nobody tried to hypnotize him or ask him any questions. Maggie didn't do all her threatening and dancing around, either. She just relit her sword and waited until the freakshow on the blade started moving. Then she came forward, reached over the flames at the edge of the table, and slid the sharp edge against his side, just below his waist.

He felt the metal bite into him.

Teeth.

But when he'd seen the blade, the edges were smooth. It was just a sword. He didn't need to get dramatic.

The damned thing's biting me like a vampire.

He felt it draw some of his blood, slowly, carefully, like it was tasting him. When he looked down, he didn't see the pointed teeth he expected, but the scene was gruesome enough. The runic pictures on the blade moved and pulsed and strained toward the blood flowing out of his side.

John watched, disgusted, as Maggie pulled the sword back, blasted his small wound with a jet of heat to seal it, and peered into the fire on her sword.

A red ribbon of fluid spread across the burning metal, sinking into each etching and hollow, alight but somehow untouched by the heat. The figures seemed to squirm with ecstasy at the taste of his blood. He'd have liked to pull a Lord of the Rings and haul that weapon to some mountain of ultimate doom and pitch it in just to be sure the bastard melted down to atoms and molecules.

The chimes above John's head whispered and tinkled from the traces of energy flickering through the room, some from the seven Sibyls, some from dark, smoking mirrors on the wall, a bit escaping containment from the lip of the platform—and the rest from the sword, though it seemed to be settling down now that it had—

What, been fed?

Maggie studied the designs on the blade like some old Irish witch reading entrails, and after a few more seconds, she said, "Spirit of a man, ghost of a demon. Well, not really a ghost. More like a shadow or a shade, a remnant essence with some energy."

The flames on the blade went out. She reached into her pocket, pulled out a cloth, and wiped the metal down, and a moment later the executioner's sword was sheathed.

"So he is what he claims to be." Bela wasn't really asking a question. Her dark eyes seemed relieved, and John would have bet his life that she was thinking of Duncan, and how Duncan would feel when he learned John was alive and in some ways okay. That would be a bitch of a conversation, no doubt, but John couldn't think about that now.

"Can the remnant essence of Strada control him?" Dio asked, sparing John a quick glance.

"Yes, if he allows it." Maggie rested her palm on the sword's hilt, and she looked nervous now, or maybe self-conscious. "Or if he's impaired somehow."

Andy's green eyes narrowed. "How impaired? Like, drunk or stoned?"

"More like enraged or cold-cocked—or, like we figured out with other types of demons, exposed to too much projective energy."

All the women in Camille's group raised the hands to

their crescent moon charms they were wearing, and Camille touched her dinar. John made the connection, understanding that somehow the dinar and the necklaces allowed these Sibyls to make use of this kind of energy, which he vaguely remembered from his time in Duncan's head. The mirrors on the wall—they used the same kind of energy.

"Projective energy can strip paranormals down to their nonhuman essence," Camille said, and John knew the explanation was for his benefit.

Maggie still had a grip on the hilt, and all the bravado was gone from her face. Worry lines softened her features, and when she spoke, she sounded scared and pissed—and somehow a little awed as she once more faced Camille, who stood even though she seemed too tired to get to her feet.

"You're in there, too," Maggie said. "In him, in his blood. I can't explain it. It's like you touched his essence—their essence—somehow."

John took in the words, but he couldn't quite sort through them beyond the fact that Maggie was verifying the connection he felt to Camille. Camille seemed to process this part, too, and her shoulders sagged.

Was that relief? His gut went double tight on the spot. Regret?

Keep it together, Cole.

"How did you join with two other souls?" Maggie asked Camille, a hint of judgment creeping into the question. "How is that even possible? What the hell did you do?"

The deep, deep fire in Camille's eyes flashed just enough to make Maggie lift her chin and tug at her sword like she was thinking about defending herself.

"I did what I had to do." Camille's tone invited argument, and Maggie seemed like she wanted to take the bait, but she didn't.

Camille still had a too-even, too-steady expression that made John worry she would suddenly draw a tiny derringer and blast Maggie right in the mouth, scary sword and all. Maybe Maggie was worried about the same thing, because she stopped pushing her luck and kept her mouth firmly closed.

John wasn't sure what kind of feud these women had, but he sensed it ran hot and nasty—yet they were willing to put it aside for the sake of their purpose. That was evident in the way they turned away from each other and let the conflict flow out of them like a dark, troubled breath.

Then, as if to punctuate the whole situation, a tiny woman came out of the kitchen and into the room—or, more to the point, she just appeared by the kitchen doorway like she'd been standing there all along.

John's first thought was *Sibyl Mother,* which was strange, given her scars and bald head and the way she was dressed—tunic and breeches instead of color-coded robes.

His second thought was *Oh, shit,* because Strada snapped awake in his mind, coming to full roaring alert. With Camille so close, John had no trouble containing the demon, but what he sensed from the essence lodged in his brain—whoa.

Another feud, this one a blood feud, right to the death.

Elana's warning to him, about the fire Sibyl Mothers coming for Camille, about Strada reacting negatively to them—it rang through his mind, but this woman wasn't sneaking around or spying on anybody. She was just standing there looking at him, and sometimes at Andy, with obvious discomfort on her scarred face. No matter how hard he tried, he couldn't see this little creature as a huge threat.

The demon in his head obviously disagreed.

The Sibyls in the room, save for Camille, seemed nervous with her, too. They drew away from the little figure, treating her like she might be slightly radioactive.

"Ona," Camille said, holding out her hand. To the others, she said, "This is Ona," like that explained everything. "She's come to visit from Motherhouse Ireland to work with me for a while."

Ona came forward and took Camille's fingers in her own, and now even Maggie looked afraid.

Okay.

If the executioners' spawn was scared of this one, maybe he should worry after all. But John found he didn't feel anything like that. His instincts acknowledged this Ona in much the same way as he had naturally been comfortable with Elana. Generals were generals, and John had dealt with enough of them that he respected their roles and whatever they'd gone through to reach that rank and position of command.

Plus Strada's essence hated Ona and seemed absolutely petrified of her, and John liked that a lot.

The East Ranger group said a few quick goodbyes, and Bela thanked them for coming over to help.

"No problem," Sheila told her as the three women headed for the door, almost like they were fleeing Ona and Camille. Sheila's tone was light, but with a please-don't-call-again-soon undertone John didn't think anybody could miss.

Fine by him. He'd just as soon not deal with the East Ranger group in the near future either, unless they were fighting together to behead Rakshasa.

"We need to tell the Mothers about him and spread the word before somebody kills him by accident," Camille said as the front door slammed shut behind the East Ranger air Sibyl. "Get him off the platform."

"Where are we going to keep him?" Dio asked, coming closer to John and Camille and Ona, but keeping her eyes on the strange little woman.

"We aren't keeping him unless the Mothers give that order," Bela said. She was staring at Ona, too. "He is who he says he is. We don't have any right to hold him."

"I can't—fuck!" Andy exploded out of her silence, jarring the room's stillness with a frenetic blur of motion and spraying cooling raindrops as she stormed around the table. "We can't just assume he's an ally. Y'all put every other demon mix we've worked with through a lot more testing than this."

"He kicked a Vodoun god's ass on our behalf," Dio reminded her. "Probably spared you another couple of facefuls of pig blood."

"Screw off," Andy snarled at Dio, but Bela's expression said she was agreeing with Andy even though Ona was still creeping her out in a major way.

"He's an ally." Camille kept hold of Ona's fingers, and with her free hand, she helped Bela absorb and return Andy's renegade water. Then Camille just looked at Dio, Andy, and Bela like she was waiting for them to get the hell on with getting him down already.

Obviously, none of them was used to her taking such an assertive role.

John wondered what kind of trouble that would cause, and how much of it had to do with him.

Camille's attitude seemed to do the trick, though, because while Andy grumbled to herself, she stopped fussing. The other two didn't seem like the fuss-in-your-face type. John figured Bela would sneak up from behind with a dagger to the throat, and Dio, hell, nobody would see her coming.

"You and Maggie," Bela said to Camille. "And you and—and John here. And Ona. And how you're feeling right now. We need to talk about all of this."

"I know." Camille's eyes shifted back to John's, and he felt her gaze like a touch. A slap. A rake of fingernails down his back. Whatever. He didn't care, as long as he could look at her, too.

Andy laughed, then groaned. "Oh, Christ, I'm not up for some huge exposé, even if the dirty parts are too hot for prime time. I need, like, five more baths to get the pig blood out from under my nails, and then I need some sleep."

"Later, then," Bela said, her black eyes boring into Camille. "After we rest and check in with other patrols and the OCU to see if there was any Rakshasa activity tonight."

Camille nodded without returning Bela's gaze. She was still staring at John, her expression a wild mix of power and curiosity and something else—intrigue? Fear? He didn't want her afraid of him. John knew he had a lot to learn in order to understand her, and a lot to do to teach her to trust him—and he wanted to take every lesson seriously.

"You staying?" she asked, and her question made everything in the room go away again, everything except her pretty face and the way her lips parted just enough for him to imagine running his thumb across the warm, damp skin.

He wasn't sure he could form words, but he managed, "If that's what you want."

Camille studied him from meat hook to ankle cuff. Another touch, this one slower and more deliberate, demanding every bit of his self-control not to let his body react to her right there in front of everybody. He could tell from the hot burn in her eyes that she knew she was in charge where he was concerned, that she had him in the kind of cuffs and chains a real man with real feelings never escaped.

Hell, he didn't even think he wanted to.

An excruciating second or two later, she said, "You can use my room."

John dug his fingers into the chains binding him to the meat hook. God, he hoped she'd be in it.

"Don't" was all Camille said to her sister Sibyls, who didn't seem to be inclined to argue with her about him again—at least not yet.

(14)

Camille kept it together in front of the Mothers.

Barely.

She helped her quad give a full report, but the second the old biddies winked out of the mirrors, she slammed the communications channels shut with a fast dance and jumped off the platform. Before anybody could say boo to her, she stormed out of the living room, almost tripping over the chains and cuffs Dio had pulled off John Cole when she turned him loose.

Nobody was stupid enough to follow Camille, thank the Goddess. Besides, their neighbor Mrs. Knight was banging on the front door to find out what the hell was going on thanks to all the smoke and fire and elemental energy flying around. Dio and Andy and Bela would be busy dealing with her for a while.

A few seconds later, Camille stood alone in the kitchen, listening to the swinging door bounce open and closed behind her, open and closed, open and closed, until it lost momentum.

She tried to breathe.

Too little. Too quiet. Too weak.

Right.

Well, she was making some big, noisy, powerful waves now, and she didn't think anybody liked it.

The Mothers sure as hell weren't happy about this new Rakshasa-human hybrid or, more to the point, that the dangerous mix of human and demon named John Cole preserved Strada's essence. Even better, the whole mess had been created by a Sibyl.

Bela, Dio, and Andy seemed a million miles away from her right now, even though they were with Ona in the living room just a few feet away. Camille knew it was her own fault that they suddenly felt so distant. She hadn't told them everything about last year before it all came spilling out. She hadn't told them much about her childhood and her fights with other fire Sibyls like Maggie, and she hadn't ever mentioned Ona, had she?

She'd barely told them anything about herself. Her real self. The Camille under all the littleness, quietness, and weakness.

How many secrets had she been keeping? She had thought it was just the one about Strada and John Cole and what had happened in the alley, but even that felt like dozens of part truths and unspoken opinions all rolled into one.

We need to talk, Bela had said.

Was that shorthand for *I've had enough of your bullshit and surprises*?

Probably.

"What have I done?" Camille asked the question out loud and hated the words, because she'd been asking herself the same thing over and over for a year, since the night John Cole "died."

She kept trying to breathe without her chest crushing in on itself.

Maybe Ona was keeping Bela and Andy and Dio entertained with tales of underground Motherhouse Ireland and Camille's amazing, thrilling career as a punching bag for the older training classes until Ona fought her battles for her and put a stop to all the teasing. Great. That would so help everybody trust her judgment and fighting prowess, right?

And down the steps from the kitchen, in the bedroom on the right, John Cole, the really-really-not-dead guy, the flesh-and-blood handsome man she couldn't forget about even for a second, was probably already stretching out to rest from his nasty encounter with the executioner's sword. Camille had a few scars from that frigging sword herself, because wounds from psychotically possessed blades didn't heal so well.

John was probably on her bed. Or maybe he was washing off, naked and steamy and covered in lather. In her shower. Giving him her room had been a brilliant idea. Really stellar. From dead soldier to ghost to demon-man to what—houseguest with benefits? Gorgeous, squeezable potential bed warmer with just that teensy problem of a Rakshasa demon hanging out in his brain?

"Stop it." Camille winced as her words made an unbearable clatter in the kitchen's quiet. Her neck was so tight she thought her head might shatter if she tried to move.

Ve aren't in the habit of making our own demons, Mother Yana from Russia had announced after Camille gave her part of the report. The Mother's brown robes fell loose against her ancient, gnarled limbs, and she reminded Camille of a tiny little hanging tree.

Mother Anemone from Greece had been a little more conciliatory: *Sibyl experiments of such magnitude can be dangerous at best.*

What, like Camille had planned to yank a spirit out of a dying guy and stuff it in a demon's body?

It's that infernal piece of jewelry, Mother Keara had reminded her, pointing to the dinar, which the Mothers had never officially approved for use. *A Sibyl shouldn't be needin' a piece of funny metal to fight.*

Fuck you, you fire-breathing old dragon hag. That's what Camille had been thinking, but she didn't say it. Her silence had been almost as disrespectful.

The Mothers also hadn't approved of the unique projective metal charms Camille had painstakingly constructed for the rest of her quad to help them fight Rakshasa last year, or the fact that Camille and her quad used projective elemental energy instead of more traditional—and respected—Sibyl talents.

When she didn't take off the dinar or defend the fact that the "funny metal" also just happened to repel Rakshasa demons—the only thing her charms couldn't do—she had as much told the Mothers she didn't care what they thought. Bela and Dio and Andy had done the same, leaving their charms in place.

Camille's breathing finally did slow down, though she was still hot enough to throw flames though the roof.

The whole thing with the projective coin and charms, that was the crux of it. The Mothers thought sentient talents were barely an inch above useless. It was so obvious that they didn't want anything to do with what Camille was exploring, yet they still seemed hesitant to outright forbid Camille, Bela, Andy, and Dio to develop their projective gifts. They were settling for *Look at all the damage you caused this time—wouldn't you rather fight like a* real *Sibyl?*

Like she was five years old and they wanted her to have an aha moment and promise to be more careful and never, ever do it again. Her, and maybe her whole quad.

Nobody was going for it.

Mother Keara always pissed her off most of all, but at least the old witch had gotten a start when she noticed Ona hanging out beside the leather sofa. Ona, who seemed so wonderful to Camille but so terrifying to everybody else.

Camille sighed.

Her anger burned out of her completely, replaced by a devil's brew of fear and doubt.

Really, I have to ask it again: What have I done?

Well, for one thing, she had gone and picked a brand-new fight with Maggie Cregan, and over a man, no less. The last thing Camille had ever wanted to do was start all the old childhood wars over again, least of all with Maggie, who had come to be a pretty good friend, at least in battle.

She can screw off, too, the angry-kid part of Camille's mind snarled. *She always has been a bitch. She and that sword truly deserve each other.*

True enough, but not productive. They were adults now, and Camille had to remember that, no matter what else happened.

She moved toward the steps to the basement, acknowledging that on top of everything else she'd probably freaked out her quad by being so angry, confrontational, and crazy-sounding with Maggie when they'd never seen that side of her personality. Yep, she'd probably done a fine job of confusing, confounding, and worrying the three women who cared most about her, and now she was running away downstairs to Bela's lab before she had to talk to any of them about it. They loved her enough to let her do it, of course. And of course, that just made Camille feel worse.

Don't forget Ona, her mind whispered as she slipped out of the kitchen.

Oh, yeah. There was that, too. She'd also just brought a strange fire Sibyl into the mix. A really old one who had a mysterious talent for scaring the shit out of everybody she met, not to mention the legends that Ona had done something horrible in her distant past. Camille had never asked her about that. Not that she'd answer, of course.

Camille headed down the stairs, not sure if Ona would follow her or just materialize in the lab later. She really wanted to understand how Ona did that, but she could ask Ona questions until she turned purple from the effort and never get any information. Ona was a lesson in patience. The old woman would share her secrets when she was good and ready, but not before.

Not looking at the bedroom, not looking at the bedroom . . .

Doing her best to keep her mind on anything but what was behind that door, she made it past temptation with a burst of speed, relieved and disappointed at the same time, and she was almost to the lab when she heard the soft whoosh of the door opening behind her.

The quiet but powerful sound of male footsteps followed shortly afterward, coming a short distance, then stopping.

Waiting.

Camille stopped, too, every inch of her skin prickling with warmth and excitement.

He was standing in the hall. Had to be. She sensed him like a dark field of power, magnetic and dangerous, pulling her toward its center.

"Thank you for your help upstairs." John Cole's voice hit that low register that doubled the prickles on her skin.

Camille didn't turn around, but she wanted to—no, no, she didn't. She couldn't. She was busy running away, and she never stopped when she was running.

Did she?

"You're, ah, welcome," she got out, though she had no idea how she'd made herself talk.

Silence opened in the dimly lit basement hallway, and Camille wished John would keep talking so he wouldn't notice her fast, shallow breathing.

He obliged. "Any word on the Rakshasa tonight?"

Good. Something normal and easy. "Sibyl patrols came up empty." Camille felt a little stupid talking with her back to the man, but she couldn't quite make herself turn around yet. "The OCU reported some increased criminal activity near the docks—mostly merchandise movement from the newer Balkan gangs. Nothing supernatural that they could find."

"It would be like Tarek to hook himself up with organized crime." John's cadence was unmistakably military or law enforcement now, straightforward and certain. "Strada was trying to do something like that before he got distracted with torturing and murdering women. We should look into the Balkan groups a little deeper, maybe see if there's been an unusual number of high-level hits."

His voice gave Camille tingles everywhere, even though he was talking shop. He seemed to notice, or maybe he was just zeroing in on the fact she wouldn't turn around to face him.

"I know it was backward, touching souls before we even got to meet in person," he said, his voice dropping impossibly lower, until her skin hummed with each word. "What happened in the alley, it made us more familiar with each other than we should be."

That deep voice felt like fingers gently stroking the back of her neck. Camille swallowed, but her throat was so dry she almost coughed. The man got right to the point, didn't he? Well, she was a fire Sibyl. She wasn't bad at getting to the point, either.

"I don't know you, John." She relaxed a little as she spoke. The truth had a way of doing that, easing tension even in the strangest circumstances. "No matter what happened in that alley, I really don't know you at all."

"Yes, you do. And I get that it makes you uncomfortable."

Camille wanted to double her fists, turn around, and sock him so hard in the gut that he couldn't catch his breath for an hour or two.

Yes, you do. . . .

She'd heard that before, and it was true, damn him, even though it wasn't, in that confusing reality that had existed between them since she—

Created him?

Saved him?

That was confusing, too, but none of it made *him* uncomfortable. She could tell. *Bastard.* If she could have made fire, she'd have turned around and blistered his ass just so he'd feel as jumpy as she did.

There were other ways to set fires, though. Plenty of them.

Camille wheeled to face John Cole.

He was standing just outside her bedroom door, just like she had imagined he would be—but he looked even better than she had dreamed. A single lamp glowed inside the room, spilling soft yellow light into the hallway to highlight the lean, tanned muscle of his bare chest. His jeans looked damp where he'd probably mopped off battle grime and the soot from his questioning upstairs. The denim hugged his tapered waist and powerful thighs in ways that made Camille want to press herself against every inch. His black hair, longer in the front than the back, shorter on the sides, curled toward his shoulders with the moisture from his shower. Touchable and soft, no doubt. Enough to run her fingers through. Enough to pull when he bit her neck or held her tight against all that hard muscle.

The heat in his deep green eyes made her aware of the thin layer of silk covering her own body. The soft fabric rubbed against her tight nipples and clung to her belly and hips. Her legs felt bare and exposed.

John's gaze let her know he'd like to expose everything else, maybe peel that silk off her with his teeth. He didn't even try to hide the desire on his face.

Camille didn't know whether to be furious or flattered or more intrigued, but that was her brain talking. Her body was excited, pure and simple, no questions asked. The distance between them suddenly seemed obscenely wrong, and she went straight toward him, not too fast, not too slow, and the truth of getting closer to him made more tension flow away from her in warm, soothing waves.

Even though Camille was no stranger to men, she was strange to this man, and he was strange to her, but as she got close to him, she felt that stirring, comfortable rightness that had rattled her each time she'd been near him.

John waited for her, reached for her, and she let him pull her close, let him wrap his heavy, powerful arms around her and hold her against the carved ridges of his chest. The dinar around her neck felt warm between them, vibrating ever so slightly, like the metal was trying to join to both of them at the same time.

He smelled like the plain, clean soap she kept in her bathroom to use when scented body wash just didn't feel right. Hints of his spicy aftershave were faint, showered and scrubbed away, but delicious as she stood on her toes and pressed first one cheek against his neck, then the other. She slid her fingers across his pecs to his shoulders, then to his stubbled cheeks and higher, exploring, into his hair, yes, as soft as she'd thought it would be, still damp and cool from the shower. Her lips moved upward like she had touched him a thousand times, like she knew just how high she'd have to lift herself to reach him as he bent to meet her.

She kissed him, and the first touch, damp skin on damp skin, mouth on mouth, set loose a fire inside her like Camille had never felt in her life.

He pulled her closer, held her even tighter, murmuring his pleasure into her mouth as his tongue teased her bottom lip. So soft, its own kind of silk, and she let him in, lip to lip, tongue to tongue now, moving with each other like they had always known this particular dance. He tasted like his scent, spicy and clean. Just right. They were perfect. Matched despite the major difference in height, in size. The swell of emotion caught Camille off guard, relief and happiness and excitement and warmth and wanting—Goddess, yes, the wanting, so unforgiving and immediate she wouldn't have cared if he'd slipped a hand between her legs to find the warmth and wetness waiting for him. His body was ready for hers, too. She could feel the proof hard against her belly, moving as she moved.

I can have him. I can have him right now.

Yes.

But—

She shivered in his embrace, letting the kiss deepen, letting herself fall further into the crazy waves of feeling and needing, until she stopped them, until she pulled back and sank to her heels, face against his chest, pressing both palms against the rock of his biceps.

"I *don't* know you," Camille whispered, barely aware of herself as a separate being from him. It was like a part of her was trying to pull away from her awareness to enter him and wrap around whatever he had inside, good or bad, right or wrong.

"You know more about what and who I really am than anyone on the planet." John's low, sexy voice did nothing to help her find her mental footing again.

"Not good enough. I need a lot more than that." She pushed against him with her palms, but not with any force. She was just trying to keep herself whole and sane, which he seemed to understand.

The pressure of his embrace never changed, and he sounded honest and sincere when he said, "Ask me anything, beautiful. I'll answer."

Of all the things he could have offered, that scared her worse than anything. Her pulse raced, fear mixing with excitement and fascination.

Time to run.

But she didn't want to run.

Oh, yes, she did.

No, yes, no, yes. Always the same contradiction with him.

A thousand questions wound up in her head. *Where did you grow up? What kinds of grades did you get in school? List of girlfriends . . . list of secrets . . .*

She wanted every detail and nuance, but right now she just wanted—needed—to run away. Not forever. Just long enough to breathe.

"I need—" she began, but couldn't finish. She stayed where she was, in his arms, and almost wished he'd press the issue, maybe pick her up and carry her into her bedroom and let her give him a complete and detailed tour of her bed.

"Time," he finished for her. No hint of disappointment. More like resignation, or maybe just acceptance. "You need time. You need proof. You need your chance to ask all those questions you dreamed up a second ago."

He still had a Southern accent, not an outright drawl, but it was strong, and just as intoxicating as the rest of him. "I'll give you all of that and more. Whatever you want and need." His green eyes burned like he was trying to reach inside her, pass through her and touch her essence all over again. "Then I'm going to kiss you everywhere. I'm going to touch you everywhere. I'm going to make love to you in ways you can't even imagine."

Heat flooded her chest, her breasts, and lower, covering her like she'd finally set herself on fire like every other fire Sibyl in the universe could do. She was ready for him. She didn't even know him, not even a little bit, but she could see herself spread out beneath him, legs wide, taking him deep and hard and never wanting to stop.

Help me . . .

But there was no help for her. There never had been. Camille felt lost even though she was only a few steps outside her own bedroom.

John let her go before she had to face the prospect of pulling away from him. The way he was looking at her almost made her melt right back into him and start kissing him, and if she did that, she'd forget all the reasons why she shouldn't. A guy like this, soldier by trade, cop at heart, so big and powerful—things could get out of hand fast if she let them.

"We'll see." She moved away from him, thinking she definitely would see—see if he meant what he said.

Just as soon as she found her nerve.

Which wouldn't be tonight.

When she got far enough toward the lab door to collect her wits and make sure she wasn't about to rip her own clothes off and let him have whatever he wanted, she gave him a good, stern stare. "Just so we're clear, you don't have any claim on me, John Cole."

He smiled at her, handsome and absolutely devilish. She caught a glimmer of her own fire in the green depths of his eyes as he said, "Yes, I do."

Then he ran away before she could, going into *her* bedroom and closing *her* out with a quick push of the door.

Asshole.

Camille was getting ready to yell it, winding up, and—

"That man's a smart one," said Ona from behind her.

Camille startled so badly she almost shrieked out loud. She spun around to find Ona standing right outside the lab door, and she pointed a finger in the old woman's face. "Don't *do* that, okay? Quit sneaking up on me."

"You'll have to get up early in the morning to outstrip him." Ona's smile was as devilish as John's, maybe twice again, plus a half. "But I think you already know that. Now come to the lab. I've made you some tea."

No fair. With her quad upstairs, John in the bedroom, and Ona standing in the now open door of the lab, gesturing for her to follow, where was Camille supposed to run away and hide?

She had a flash of memory from childhood, from the day she met Ona.

That was the day everything changed.

So what was today, then?

The same, her mind informed her. *Just like the day Bette died, and the day Bela came to get you at Mother-house Ireland, and the alley a year ago, and the night John spoke to you in Central Park, and—*

"Okay," Camille said out loud, to make her brain shut up.

Ona's smile got brighter and happier, or maybe just more mischievous. Camille couldn't tell, and she figured it was probably better if she didn't know.

Bela hadn't given in to Camille's begging to repaint the big laboratory with the small infirmary/treatment room in the far corner, so the entire space still radiated earth Sibyl calmness with its soft shades of sand and brown everywhere. The morning after John Cole came to the brownstone, Camille was sort of glad about that. The sedate colors helped soothe her jangly nerves.

Camille had been able to convince Bela to rearrange some of the machinery, though, so she didn't get sleepy every time she walked in the door. There were six lab tables in the room, with counters and sinks on every wall and a couple of rolling chairs that went with each work area. On the tables closest to the door, Camille had positioned the biogenetic analyzing equipment and other machines used for crime scene analysis, largest to smallest. On the next two tables, the ones with the readiest access to the treatment room, she kept the medical stock— centrifuges, tabletop X-ray, covered surgical trays, and the like. On the back two tables and all across the countered sink, she had her stuff—the machines she used most often, even if technically everything still belonged to Bela.

There were shiny black metallurgical microscopes, an arc emission spectroscope, a big white-and-silver scanning electron microscopy and energy dispersive spectroscopy system, and just about anything else she needed to extract, examine, analyze, construct, and resurface ores and metals. Sibyl technology far outstripped what was available in the mundane world, so Camille's machines could do more in much less space—things that were only in the planning stages in traditional metallurgy. On the walls around her tables, she'd plastered colorful periodic tables, charts and graphs, and anything else to make the area less mind-numbingly drab.

Ona was definitely a unique addition to the space.

"He's still sleeping," Ona said from atop Camille's back table, where she sat cross-legged in her standard black tunic and breeches, seeming to meditate, but apparently seeing and hearing everything in the universe.

Camille was already dressed, jeans and sweater, but she couldn't do anything besides hover near the door and think about going down the hall. "He's not sleeping as soundly this morning as he did last night. I can sense it."

"Come here." Ona gestured for her, her rough, scarred hand moving through the still, cool air. "Calm yourself."

"I'm a fire Sibyl. I don't do calm."

"And I know better, because we're of a kind." Ona stopped beckoning and waved her hand in the air. "See? No smoke. No sparks. Only at the rarest moments do I actually make flame, and I can't predict that or control it."

"Thanks for reminding me." Camille stared at the bracelets on Ona's arms, the ones that didn't move, and finally had to know more. She stepped over to Ona and looked at them more closely.

Ona held out her arm.

Camille couldn't tell where the metal ended and Ona's flesh began. She touched the top bracelet with one finger—and realized the truth.

The metal was *part* of Ona's skin somehow. It had been imbedded, or sewn in, or lodged there. She glanced up at Ona, but Ona didn't say a thing. She just pulled away from Camille's touch and hung her head, obviously unwilling to discuss the bracelets for now.

Camille moved back between the door and the first table, a little freaked out, then doubly distracted because she sensed John's disquiet all over again. "I've got . . . experiments to do. We've got demons to hunt."

"You've been hunting for weeks and finding nothing," Ona said, and she vanished.

Camille startled, raising her hand to her chest, but she almost had a heart attack when Ona said from behind her, right in front of the lab door, "Fire making isn't everything, you know."

Camille turned around. Slowly. She'd been pretty sure about Ona moving in what looked like unnatural ways before, but now—damn.

Ona's expression was serious as she shook her damaged, bald head. "It's not unnatural, if that's what you're thinking. Not even supernatural. You can learn it."

"I'm—" Camille stopped herself despite the shock of hearing what Ona had just told her. She had almost said, *I'm not sure I want to,* but then she thought about fire making and battles and gaining an advantage, any advantage, no matter how bizarre it seemed. She had a duty to learn as much as she could about whatever she could, if it would help her quad.

Ona's ancient and crazy. What she's doing—who could possibly understand it, much less learn it?

"You can," Ona repeated, like she might be reading Camille's mind.

John's energy turned more restless, and Camille glanced at the lab door. "Okay. I'll try anything if it might be useful, and if it's not instantly fatal."

"Come over here." Ona pulled her toward the center of the lab, away from the door and tables and away from the temptation of slipping down the hall and into her bedroom to check on John. "You understand basic Sibyl communications, and better than most, I'd wager?"

Camille nodded. "First in my class to open the old channels, to be able to move objects without help, and even transport people. It only takes me a few seconds of dancing to sweep the energy into motion, to grind open the doorways and barriers." Her focus broke away from John and came fully to Ona. "At least in that respect, I've come to understand I'm a natural pestle."

Ona's good eye narrowed. "The channels are everywhere. Have you come to understand that?"

Camille had a rudimentary grasp of what Ona meant. She had studied the channel charts at Motherhouse Ireland until her eyes blurred, learning the crisscrossing patterns, trying to grasp the ways elemental energy flowed and the ways it got blocked. "I memorized as much as I could, and I can see the rest in my mind."

Ona shook her head. Closed her eyes. "No, no. Not from all the drawings. Too limited." She touched her chest. "From here. You can feel them if you try."

Crazy, crazy, crazy, Camille thought, but she obliged, mostly to give herself something to do. She rested her palm on her chest, feeling her heart beat steadily beneath it. The rhythm was almost as soothing as the calming paints, and she closed her eyes.

"Now," Ona said. "Try the dance."

Camille opened one eye. "But I'm not on a communications platform. This is just a basement floor."

"Platforms are tools for those with skills weaker than your own." Ona stopped talking, then muttered to herself and rubbed her head like she was chastising herself for not getting around to this lesson years ago. "You don't need them. Many do—but you don't."

Camille opened both eyes wide at this, then had to fight to keep her expression neutral even though she was listening to what amounted to heresy and maybe real madness, not just eccentricity. To humor Ona and to keep the peace, she held her hand over her heart and did a few tentative steps of the dance fire Sibyls used to grind open the old channels.

Of course, nothing happened.

Ona snorted and gave her a push from behind. "I didn't say play at it, girl. Do it. Do the dance."

Camille sighed. Keeping her hand in place, she moved her right foot north, south, east, west. Then her left foot north, south, east, and she stopped. It wasn't working because it felt wrong, doing this on the basement floor instead of the platform upstairs. What if she did unleash some energy here in the lab? That could be a bad scene. Mrs. Knight might bang on the front door until she knocked it off the hinges.

Ona was starting to give her a look.

"Maybe if I close my eyes again," Camille muttered.

This was met with a terse "Fine."

Maybe if I pretend I'm where I'm supposed to be . . .

North, south, east, west.

North, south, east, west.

She said the words to herself, like she hadn't needed to do since she was little, and with her eyes closed, her feet moved automatically. If she concentrated, really shut out reality, the lab's smooth stone floor could feel like the petrified platforms in the communications chamber of Motherhouse Ireland, worn from centuries of movement and dancing and elemental storms of energy.

West, east, south, north, west, east, south, north.

Camille's hand squeezed against her chest and she started to spin, once, twice, three times. Then she stopped short, her eyes flying open, her hand falling away from her chest, because the floor had—

What?

Rumbled?

Rippled?

She couldn't describe it.

She looked down, and the rock beneath her didn't seem completely solid. Then it did. Camille thought about the channels on the charts and diagrams. One connected with the platform upstairs, through all the main and minor projective mirrors, but there were no channels running underneath the brownstone, at least not right where she was standing.

Ona looked thrilled and disappointed and scared all at once. Her scarred hand trembled against her mouth, and Camille thought she might be smiling.

When Ona moved her fingers, she said, "That was fast, Camille. I didn't reach that level for centuries, but then, I had no teacher."

Camille's heart sank a little at that. So Ona was giving her wisdom it would probably take decades to master. Nothing that would help her this week or this month, and nothing that would help her with killing demons or protecting her quad.

"The channels are everywhere," Ona said. "More than what the charts say. More than what many remember or most know."

"If you say so." Camille glanced at the stone floor. She was willing to take Ona at her word on that part, since there was no real way for her to explore it right now. Nothing in her thought Ona was crazy now, and in fact, Camille was beginning to feel major determination to be patient and try to grasp whatever Ona was willing to teach her. Projective energy was so disregarded, there really wasn't anything in the fire Sibyl archives about how to use it, except for managing the mirrors. Dio had checked through the main archives, too, at Motherhouse Greece—not much there, either.

"Where there is fire, there are channels," Ona continued, sounding more excited with each word.

Camille kept her eyes on the floor. "There's fire everywhere, Ona. Ambient fire all around us."

"Exactly!" Ona clenched one small fist and pounded it in the air, like Camille really understood something. "Air Sibyls and earth Sibyls can travel through their elements, just as water Sibyls once did. Air Sibyls can even move with the speed of wind—but they cannot move with the speed that flames burn. Only fire opens the old channels. Only we can move that fast."

Camille walked slowly back toward the front of the lab. What Ona was saying was fascinating, but it felt out of reach. "If it's really that easy for fire Sibyls to zip all over the world, why don't they teach us that at the Motherhouse? Why all the platforms and mirrors and charts?"

Ona's excitement waned, then seem to drain completely. When Camille turned to face her, she watched her small features wilt for a moment before she picked herself up enough to say, "Because the Mothers gave that up, just as they gave us up."

"Us." Camille leaned against the first table, hoping Ona would give her more details.

"You and me and those like us." Ona rubbed her hands together as if warming them. "What we can do."

Camille got hold of the concept a little better. "So you're saying that when the Mothers bred away from pyrosentience and focused more on pyrogenesis, they surrendered some of their ability to open the old channels without . . ." She fished through her brain for the right word, and while she was thinking, her fingers drifted to the dinar around her neck. The dinar that, when she wished it to, magnified her elemental abilities.

"Without help," she said, feeling a dull, almost aching surprise. All of this lined up too well. Was it possible that platforms and projective mirrors weren't just assumed tools of the trade, but props Motherhouse Ireland had developed to shore up their deliberately weakened pyrosentient abilities?

Possible, and now she realized, probable.

Ona was telling her the truth: it really was possible to open the channels anywhere—for a Sibyl with strong pyrosentient skills.

"I can learn to do this," Camille whispered, hearing a slight buzzing sound in her head. Shock, no doubt. "I can do it if my pyrosentience is strong enough."

"It will take much practice. Endless practice." Ona rushed to a table and pulled over a tablet and pen. She began sketching different sorts of diagrams, very simple ones compared to the complex charts Motherhouse Ireland had required Camille to memorize. "We have to reteach you, retrain your thinking on the channels, because in truth they're infinite, and in being infinite, they become one."

Camille knew she was staring like an idiot again, not comprehending. This was striking her like theoretical math—it made a little sense, then just left her behind.

Ona held up her paper and pointed to the picture, which was of a stick figure with lines moving in all directions away from her. "One," Ona insisted. "Wherever you ask it to be."

Camille felt a strange urgency to this, a crawling along her instincts. She wished she had more of the prescience air Sibyls had. She had a sense of needing to know what was coming, how this would be important, but of course she couldn't do that. Not really.

She was just about to ask Ona why the Sibyl was the center of the drawing when a restless blast of energy from John made her teeth click together.

Ona felt it this time, Camille could tell, because she put her hands to the sides of her face and squeezed her eyes shut. "Perhaps," she said, her quivery voice more solid than usual, "you should go see about him after all."

"Looks like it got cooked . . ."

"Blackjack's been gone twenty minutes. It's time."

The Italian priests don't say a word, but they dispatch two of their ranks to check the bits and pieces of city still visible above the sands in the Valley of the Gods. The rest wait for John to lead them inside.

He has no idea why, or what they want, or what they're looking for, but it's not for him to ask questions or get answers in situations like this.

John gestures for the soldier in motion between the four outer corners of the temple to join them. The kid's blond, good-looking, and barely eighteen. He joined Recon last month and John can't even remember his name. Too many lately, coming and going—and not always in one piece.

Together, John and Golden Boy head through the crumbling arched entry. The kid's got his weapon ready, pointing it left and right, letting the muzzle lead them into the ancient structure. The stone beneath their feet looks so old and cracked and sand-covered that it mimics asphalt, or maybe concrete. The whole place smells dry and wasted, like a crypt that hasn't been tended in a hundred years.

Late-day sunlight punches into the structure in shafts through the open roof area, but shadows cling to the deeper spaces. Scorpions could live there. There are what, twenty or twenty-five different kinds in this region? At least three or four are poisonous. And there are spiders and rodents and snakes, and truly, God only knows what else.

"Something's gonna bite us," the kid mutters as he starts checking spaces.

"Probably," John says, checking corners himself.

"Don't get why we're dragging a bunch of priests through Afghan ruins, sir."

"I don't know."

"But you're a priest, sir."

"Contrary to popular belief, we're not all psychically connected." He leans over to the soldier like he's sharing a terrible secret. "I don't even speak Italian."

Golden Boy looks horrified.

They check the entry space pretty thoroughly. No hostiles. No scorpions, not that they can find, anyway. The priests, eight of them, file into the twenty-by-twenty entry space, which appears to be the first of two chambers in the temple, and completely ruined by weather, or maybe other things. Nothing in it but sand and broken, blackened rock, but they look at it. Touch it. Talk to one another. Make notes.

The kid watches them. "Looks like it's been bombed, doesn't it, sir?"

"It does, but I don't think bombs were around when this place got destroyed." *John notices a hint of spice—incense, probably from one of the priests' traveling clothes. The floral smell seems out of place in this stony skeleton of the past.*

Best John and the kid can tell, there's only one other room in the temple, and this one has stone doors with no handles. It also appears to have a roof—stone, too. Whoever made this place sealed it, and they intended it to stay sealed.

The oldest priest, who seems to be in charge of the Vatican contingent, gestures to the stone doors.

"Open, please," *he says.*

"We can't destroy local sites, sir," *the kid says to the priest, but when the priest doesn't look at him, Golden Boy says the rest to John.* "Especially not religious sites."

"Open, please," *says the priest again. John wonders if the guy knows any other English words. He probably does. Vatican priests usually speak several languages.*

John and the kid exchange looks.

"How far do we go?" *the kid wants to know.*

"Blackjack said to do what we have to do."

Golden Boy pulls out his combat knife and chips the aged stone. Weathered by the endless movement of sand

*and wind, it crumbles like hard dirt against the sharp-
ened blade. It takes some time, half an hour, maybe
more, but they kick and hack until they hollow out a
man-sized opening, just enough for one person to get
through.*

The kid goes first. John goes in right behind him.

*The sealed chamber looks darker than purgatory, and
the only light comes through the hacked hole. John and
Golden Boy use their flashlights to show a surprisingly
wide and deep expanse with an altar on the very far side
of the room. There's a pattern in the floor near the altar,
with something round in the center of the pattern.*

*John can't study that for long, because he's too fasci-
nated by what else his flashlight finds. He and the kid
illuminate dozens and dozens of metallic statues, filling
the room. To John, it looks like the terra-cotta soldier
pits from China. Looks like several hundred of the things,
side by side, jammed together. A few have human shapes,
but the rest are absolutely demonic.*

*Satan in tiger form. That's the best John can do to de-
scribe the things.*

"Creepy, sir."

"Yeah."

"Should you bless us or say a prayer or something?"

"They're statues, kid." But he does a quick blessing to
make Golden Boy feel better.

Seems to help.

*As the kid heads for the front altar, John lets the Vati-
can priests come through the opening in the stone doors.*

*They take one look at the cat statues caught in John's
flashlight beam, cross themselves, and start talking fre-
netically among themselves.*

Clearly, this is what they've come to see.

*John leads them to the first cat-Satan, and he has an
urge to pray over the thing like Golden Boy asked him
to, to neutralize it somehow even though it's a statue.*

"Sir?" The kid's hollering at John through all the priest chatter and statues, using his beam to gesture across the pattern on the floor in front of the altar. "Did you see this? Looks like a necklace."

"Leave it," John tells him.

He glances at the kid.

The kid's not leaving it.

John's gaze shifts to the priests studying the cat statue. Back to the kid. He's inside that design on the floor now, and John gets a bad feeling. Superstitious. Sinful, really, by the letter of his religion.

"Leave it be," he tells Golden Boy, hearing his Southern drawl deepen because he's nervous. He hates that.

"I think it's a coin." The kid bends down.

Instinct kicks John's ass and he leaps away from the priests, leaving them in darkness, charging toward the kid. The priests call out in surprise and maybe anger.

John shouts at the kid, who seems to be trancing out as he keeps bending down, down, toward the center of that pattern.

The kid picks up the necklace, steps back, and raises his light to examine it—and his boot crunches against stone outside the circles and runes etched into the rock.

John gets to him. Grabs the necklace. Starts to hurl it back into the design where his gut tells him it has to stay—

The flashlights wink out.

John holds up in midthrow, gripping the cold metallic chain of that necklace.

"We're in a desert in the daytime." John's talking out loud, way beyond nervous now, heading toward freaked out and ready to take the kid's knife off him and get ready to fight. "How is this thing cold?"

The ground shivers and the stone cracks, like the walls and ceiling want to fall in, or maybe explode out, sending shrapnel all over the Valley of the Gods.

"Sir?" The kid sounds terrified.

John thinks the priests are praying. He's holding that weird necklace in one hand and fumbling for his own crucifix with the other because the room smells fertile and fresh all of a sudden. Darker than ever. And the air keeps getting thicker. A dark stench rolls over them, and they cough.

Rot? Ammonia?

What is that disgusting stink?

John's not sure of anything, but he doesn't think they're alone in the chamber anymore.

Then, behind the kid, something moves.

It starts to growl.

"Sir, I thi—"

A hard rustle of motion.

John reaches out in the dark. Golden Boy's gone. He hears growls and shouts, then chewing sounds.

John clings to the necklace and backs up, hoping he'll hit wall and not anything else.

One of the priests starts to scream.

Energy brushed over John, hot and strong and jarring. His eyes flew open.

The energy touched him again, softer this time, almost like lips and nails running across his bare chest and arms.

He sat up in the strange bed, confused as hell, mouth open, eyes wide. His whole body itched and burned, and it was hard to see even though he sensed lights were on all around him. His nose was expecting ammonia and sand and the stench of blood and entrails, but he couldn't smell anything. His ears were expecting laughter, terrible and psychotic and demonic in every sense of the word, but he didn't hear anything except his own breathing.

His teeth felt too big.

Fuck.

His head pounded like his brain was trying to crack against his skull. "Are you back with me now?" a woman's voice asked, and then John smelled the lilies.

"No." His voice came out guttural, not totally his. "Get out. Get away from me."

Fear for Camille blasted his senses clean, and he could see the room he was sitting in. Cream-colored paint with some kind of green trim. The furniture was green, too. Artwork on the walls—and he was sitting on very feminine silk sheets. His side gave a dull ache where . . . a sword had cut him.

A very weird sword.

A few seconds later, he pulled far enough out of his dream-flashback to remember coming down to this room—and to remember kissing Camille the night before.

She was standing at the bedroom door watching him, her arms folded across a bulky green sweater that covered her from her neck to the hips of her jeans. Everything about her looked so soft that John instantly wanted to touch her, but that thought cleared out pretty fast when he realized what had just happened. He'd had one of his dreams again. He'd gotten stressed like he always did, only this time Strada had almost gotten him.

"It may not be the best idea for me to stay here." He scrubbed a hand through his hair to get it out of his eyes. "I almost—just now I—"

"You were dreaming about the war." Camille unfolded her arms, and he realized she was holding a packet of papers. "I could sense it. It seemed like a good idea to wake you, but I didn't want to come too close or do anything too abrupt. I just turned on the lights and gave you a little elemental punch."

Her expression was wary but not fearful. John was about to tell her to leave again, but he was feeling more normal by the second. Sweaty and pissed off, but normal.

Camille showing up, that had given him strength and fire to fight Strada in a moment of weakness. He couldn't deny that.

"I should get out of here," he muttered, staring down at the sheets. "That was—look, I'm sorry. I shouldn't have let my guard down."

"You have to sleep and you can't help what you dream, especially with the memories you have." Her pretty eyes held his when he looked up at her. "I think the real problem would come if you were alone with nobody to wake you when that happens. You could kill a lot of innocent people before you came back to yourself."

John swallowed even though he felt like he had rocks in his throat. "I haven't had a dream like that since I got this body. I thought they were done." He started to shove the sheets off him to burn some of his annoyance, then remembered he was naked and decided against it. "Maybe I didn't think at all."

Camille's understanding smile gentled him even from across the room. "My bad dreams never go away. They just take brief vacations. Too brief." Her eyes wandered down from his face to his chest, and lower, to where the sheet rested around his waist. "Don't punish yourself for being a good soldier."

Something like embarrassment rose up inside him, and the strange feeling drove him to say, "You're not responsible for me. It's the other way around."

Not embarrassment. Not really. What am I feeling?

His frigging cock knew what *it* was feeling, and if she didn't stop staring at his package through the sheet, she was about to see more of it than she bargained for. He could already feel her breasts in his hands, taste her nipples in his mouth.

Good job, John. That kind of thinking, it's really going to help you give her time. You've been here, what, a day?

"In this house, we're all responsible for each other," Camille said. "It won't work any other way." She was still smiling, just a little, and still giving him that look.

I want her in my arms. I want her staring up at me while I rock her world—and mine. Shit, shit, shit, there's not a lot of sheet here.

He needed to stop. He needed to get up out of this bed and leave the brownstone, right now.

Camille shook her head, the smile finally fading away. "I know that look, and I really do get your reasoning, but I think you're wrong."

"What look?" That came out like a grumble. John heard it and got irritated with himself. His eyes darted from Camille to the walls, the paintings hanging neatly centered in all the right spaces. He couldn't process what was in the frames, but they distracted him enough to ease the misery stiffening between his legs.

"The I'm-about-to-run look," Camille said. "I'm good at running, too, so trust me, I know the signs."

Vulnerable. Is that how I'm feeling? Fuck. That's as bad as these sheets. This woman does funny things to me. John managed to quit looking at the walls, but he couldn't do much about feeling like a helpless teenager in Camille's presence.

"I'm not running away," he said. "I'm thinking about keeping you safe."

Her smile came back, and this time her aquamarine eyes seemed to tease him. "How about you trust me to take care of that and you just watch your own ass? Not that you can't look at mine now and then, if you want to."

Oh, I'll do a lot more than look at that ass, and soon, beautiful.

John grabbed a pillow and pulled it across his lap. He felt like his mental age had just dropped from seventeen to fourteen. Damnit, he had more control over the demon in his head than over his body parts. Something about that was jacked.

Camille raised the packet of papers she'd been holding on to, then laid it on a chair near the door. "Present from Dio—which, by the way, I wouldn't take lightly. She doesn't waste time, so if she's making you lists of demons and paranormal practitioners the New York City fighting groups have encountered, she thinks you're reasonably okay and worth teaching. Air Sibyls are big on their lists and packets and archival info."

John felt a flicker of surprise that Dio would leave him anything that didn't have wires and tick as it counted down to zero. "I learned some about all the different demons when I was in Duncan's head, but I'll memorize that packet in a big hurry."

"Good." Camille backed toward the door gracefully, obviously intending to leave—but not in any way that suggested fleeing.

He didn't want her to go.

He wanted her to stay so much his common sense tried to desert him and let him start begging.

Let me look at you for five more minutes. . .

"These sheets are girly," he said instead, just to have something to say.

Camille's gaze moved across the pillow, then up again, seeming to take in every muscle on his chest. "They look good on you."

She hesitated for a second, then added, "I'll try not to run if you don't. But you might want to get up soon. Duncan's home and I think he's coming down here to kick your ass."

And then she just left him, sitting there wrapped in silk sheets with a lily-scented pillow covering his unbelievably painful erection and a Demon Identification 101 packet sitting on the chair waiting for his attention. John watched the door close and listened to her pad down the hall. He heard the swish and click of the lab door opening, then closing, and he spent some time staring at the painted ceiling over his head ... which looked kind of feminine, too. This place was a million miles away from military barracks and tents, and a big change from the dives and hotels and apartments he'd blown through during his black ops years, or even the flat he'd taken in Harlem after his rebirth in this body.

Welcome to your new life.

Who knew it would be so frilly?

He had to admit, though, if he ended up with the girl actually in the girly room with him, that wouldn't be so bad. It would be good. Better than good. He was sure of that.

Duncan ...

The thought nudged into his brain.

Duncan's home. ...

John got out of the girly bed in one huge hurry then. Christ! Where was his head? He probably didn't have much time. He put his jeans on too fast, hopping into the legs, almost fell over, got his act together, and pulled his shirt over his head.

The door banged open, and two people walked into the bedroom at a pretty good clip. One was Bela, wearing a pair of brown slacks and a cream-colored shirt that highlighted her dark, exotic good looks and her very worried expression.

As for the other—

"Duncan," John said as he finished pulling down his shirt, grateful in spite of the circumstances to see his one and only lifelong friend healthy and presumably happy with his beautiful new wife at his side.

Duncan Sharp looked much as John remembered from their younger days—big but a little scrawny, close-cut brown hair, and spooky blue eyes. He had on his usual, jeans and an army-green T-shirt, so typical and familiar that John couldn't help smiling.

Duncan wasn't smiling.

He stopped next to the dark-haired beauty he'd married, staring at John, no doubt trying to take in the whole Strada-body thing. He must have been warned or he'd already be shooting. As it was, John glanced at Duncan's shirt and then his ankles, checking for holster bulges as he carefully came around the bed to say hello to his friend.

Duncan didn't wait for any greetings. He strode toward John with a fierce tension John recognized from their service days—but not in time to duck the punch Duncan threw.

Duncan's knuckles connected with John's jaw hard enough to stagger him and make him see a burst of blinking white stars. His ass thumped into the bathroom door, and he used the wood paneling and doorknob to hold himself upright. A few knickknacks toppled off a dresser, clattering as they bounced against the drawers and floor.

Bela didn't try to get in the way, and Camille didn't scream and come running down the hall from the lab to break up the fight. John sort of liked that. Camille knew what was probably happening, and she was more than capable of interfering if she decided to, but she knew some things had to work themselves out.

John rubbed his jaw reflexively, wondering if any teeth were loose. Okay, okay, he sort of wished Camille would scream and coming running down the hall, but that was sexist macho asshole thinking, and a pathetic, weak-minded excuse to get to put his arms around her again.

Don't be a dick, John.

"You piece of shit," Duncan snarled, advancing as John skirted the bed, keeping the frilly sheets between them. "I thought you were dead. I thought you were dead and I thought it was *my* fault."

John pointed a finger in Duncan's face. "It wasn't like I could jog up and say howdy. You would have shot me—and watch your mouth in front of the lady."

"Screw you. Bela and her quad know how to swear better than both of us." Duncan really wanted to throw a few more right hooks, John could tell, but he kept moving around the bed, jumping across it to the other side so Duncan couldn't reach him easily. He really didn't want to have to hit back. "You could have called. You could have dropped me a note."

"Ah, honey, it's so sweet you missed me." John blew a kiss at Duncan and thought he heard Bela snicker.

Duncan tried to scramble over the bed after him, but Bela grabbed him by the belt loops and hauled him back to the floor on the opposite side from John.

"All right, boys," she said. "No more breaking shit in Camille's bedroom. If you really need to slug it out, we'll go to the alley behind the house."

Duncan was still glaring across the bed at John, but Bela's touch obviously stilled the beast inside him, literally and figuratively. A patch of golden-orange fur with black stripes had rippled up on Duncan's face and neck, but as he stood next to his wife, the fur gradually receded. John winced, but otherwise kept his reaction to himself.

I should have done better protecting him. I shouldn't have let the Rakshasa get to him.

He thought about Camille, about possibly failing her like that, and it choked him up. What the hell was happening to him? It wasn't enough he'd turned part demon and started sleeping on frilly sheets—now he was getting misty because his best friend wanted to punch his teeth down his throat?

All because of a woman. Not just a woman. A Sibyl, though John was beginning to think she was a witch, too. Whatever kind of man he had been when he wore his first body, that man truly was dead—but the change had nothing to do with taking over a demon's skin. John knew it had everything to do with his soul touching Camille's, with meeting her again and speaking to her. He just couldn't be that cold, distant nothing-but-a-soldier thing anymore, not with her in the same house. Not knowing she was even on the same planet.

So what was he now?

Who the hell knew? He sure didn't.

I'm hers. I hope to God she'll decide she's mine after we both figure out who I am.

"I'm sorry," he told Duncan around the big irritating, embarrassing lump in his throat. "About the demons attacking you. About sucking you into all this last year."

Duncan's expression hardened again. "What about for leaving me in the desert before that? Just walking away after that temple disaster without so much as a 'Kiss my ass, buddy'?"

"What happened in the Valley of the Gods was classified. I couldn't say anything." John held Duncan's angry gaze, then felt himself relenting, holding up both hands in surrender. The room around them smelled like lilies and women and here and now and today, not then. No need to keep *then* so alive. "Yeah, yeah. I could have called. I could have dropped you a note to let you know everything was okay. I was wrong not to do that."

Duncan's mouth twitched at one corner. Not a smile, but not another windup for a tell-off, either. "Better."

John's gaze shifted to Bela and he lowered his hands. "I'm glad you're in his life. He deserves somebody like you."

Bela acknowledged this with a nod.

"And back when I was in Duncan's head, I never—you know." John coughed to give himself a second to pick the next words. "Got any cheap thrills, or anything."

Bela flushed, but she laughed.

"No," Duncan said, red highlights hitting both cheeks as he spoke. "No way. Just because you make nice with my wife doesn't mean we're finished with this."

John raised his hands again, palms out. "Whatever you say."

"Don't do that." Duncan jammed his fingers through his hair and looked twice as pissed.

John had to work not to grin, but he pulled it off by counting the pictures on Camille's walls. "Do what?"

"That whole whatever-you-say crap." Duncan's frown was severe, but more normal now. Irritated instead of furious. "You always won fights like that when we were growing up."

John shrugged. "Maybe I just didn't want to fight with you. Maybe I don't want to fight with you now."

Now Duncan's frown got a little more serious, and sad, too. "This is past fistfights in the fields, John." He looked away. "This isn't some little-kid bullshit."

The sadness showing on Duncan's face crept over to John, but really, he already felt it. The time for teasing and yelling and blustering was over, finished. "I know."

Duncan took a few seconds to compose himself, and he glanced at Bela more than once while he pulled his thoughts together. At last, when he was ready, he faced John straight on again, and his voice was steady and quiet when he spoke. "If you run out on me again, no matter what the reason, we're done."

John felt each word like a different kind of punch in the jaw. The kind that got his attention, made a permanent impression. He and Duncan had swapped a lot of licks and insults, but neither one had ever threatened the other with the end of their friendship.

Which meant this was no threat.

What was that old gospel song they'd been swapping back and forth when he was in Duncan's head?

Can't hide, sinner . . .

Yeah, that was it.

And John knew it was true.

"Got it," he said, because he did understand, and after everything he had put Duncan through, there wasn't really anything else he could say.

The two of them stayed quiet for a minute or so, and John felt all the anger seep out of Camille's bedroom. The space went back to its soothing tones and silky bedsheets, its neatly arranged art and furniture. Definitely nothing John or Duncan would ever put together, much less choose as the stage to play out what might prove to be the most important—and final—act of their friendship.

Bela seemed to judge it safe to give them a moment or two, because she picked up the stuff that had fallen off the dressers, put it back in place, and stepped out of the bedroom. John noticed she didn't go upstairs, though. Staying close, just in case. Poor woman was obviously used to refereeing.

"Why are you here?" Duncan asked as soon as Bela closed the door behind her. "I mean, right here, in this brownstone, right now."

John's response came reflexively. "I'm here to kill Rakshasa."

"And?"

John let out a breath.

Duncan was still his best friend. No matter how much time passed, no matter how much distance grew, nothing would ever change that. If he couldn't tell this man the truth, then there was no hope for him.

"A year ago, I would have said that was it. That I'm here to eradicate demons." John touched his temple. "Including the one in my brain, when he's the only one left."

Duncan worked that out faster than John would have liked, judging by the frown and wary expression. "And now?"

"Now—" John glanced at the door, imagining the hall, the door to the lab, and Camille hard at work over whatever was in that room. "Now I've got other things on my mind."

Duncan glanced around the bedroom as if he might just now be taking in the details, the nuances that had changed since Camille claimed and renovated the room. She was everywhere down here, like a tangible presence drifting through the air between them. More than anything, Duncan seemed to be processing John's willingness to stay in the brownstone, in the bedroom, when community living really wasn't his style. Duncan might also be remembering John's time as a ghost in his head, when John thought Camille was a special kind of hot.

"Why are you here, John?" Duncan asked again, this time more slowly, staring at John with the spooky blue eyes John had known since he first remembered anything about life.

"I think I came here to marry Camille." He couldn't quite believe he'd said that, but he didn't back away from it. "I don't know what else to say. She feels like my future. She feels like . . . everything. If she decides she likes me. And if I don't turn out to be a psychotic killer demon. And if none of you have to behead me."

There. That was it. Pretty much in a package, tied up with a bow. If it wasn't enough for Duncan, John didn't know what else he could offer.

"Okay." Duncan rubbed his hand across his short brown hair again, not too fast or hard this time. More like the habit John remembered.

"Just okay?" John gave Duncan a sideways look, because he knew there had to be more.

"I have faith in Camille." Duncan's grin came on slow and sly, not open or relaxed yet, but John would take whatever he could get. "She'll kick your balls up through your ribs if that's what you need."

"Great. Thanks.". John refused to let his hand twitch over his groin. He had no doubt that if a Sibyl planted her foot in his nuts, he'd know he'd been kicked.

"You, ah, need some sparring rounds to get in shape?" Duncan's grin was starting to spread across his face.

John shook his head. "Not today, thanks. Some Bengals are helping me out. I'm due there in a little bit."

Duncan didn't react to this, and John knew he wouldn't, and that he'd keep his mouth shut about it since Duncan had gotten some help from the Bengals himself in the early days after his transition to half demon. "When you're done with them, come by the townhouse on the Upper East Side, and go a round or two with me and my new friends. Creed, Nick, and Jake—the Lowell brothers—they're demons, too, and they can teach you a lot about self-control if you're willing to learn."

John matched Duncan's grin, feeling more relief as time went by without broken furniture and cracked jaws. "I could probably pick up some tips from you, too."

It was Duncan's turn to shrug. "We'll see."

After Duncan left, John got ready to head out to his training session with the Bengals and to pick up some clean clothes from his place. He collected Dio's demon packet, glanced at a few pages, then folded it and tucked it under his arm for later review. Just before he left the room, he took some things out of his pockets, like his zillion-year-old dirty rabbit's foot, his lucky quarter, and his mother's battered engagement ring—the few treasures he'd gotten Duncan to rescue from his personal effects before they buried his old body and what little he had on him when the Rakshasa cut him to pieces last year.

For good measure, he pulled off his watch, and he put it all on the nightstand, right where Camille would see the stuff if she checked inside the bedroom after he left.

"Here you go, beautiful," he said out loud, his voice calmer than he thought it would be. "So you'll know I'm not running away. Have to come back for this stuff, don't I? Among a lot of other things."

(16)

Camille tugged at the string of her sweatshirt hood as she tried to get comfortable on her end of the big leather sofa, and she wished she had a pillow to hold. Everybody else had pillows, one from each of the three leather chairs her quad was sitting in, positioned around the communications platform. That was fitting, since this felt kind of like an inquisition—and the swirling, smoking, dark projective mirrors on the walls weren't doing anything to lighten the mood.

"Are you in love with him?"

It was Andy who asked the question, but Camille could tell they all wanted to know. Her quad had given her exactly twenty-four hours before they invaded the lab and made Camille come upstairs. Duncan had split for OCU headquarters, and Bela had politely asked Ona to remain behind in the lab. Ona had said she wouldn't come "until it was her turn," whatever that meant. John was still off on whatever errands he was running, but Camille had seen what he left behind on the bedside table. An unwritten message.

Okay, you win. I'm not running—for now.

It took some effort, but Camille finally settled herself down enough to start talking—and to lead off with the most truthful answer she could give. "I have no idea if I'm in love with John—and don't tell me I do know, or I'll have to hit somebody. I've really only known him for a day or so."

Bela's intake and exhale were the only sounds that followed, and Camille felt unnaturally aware of the mix of light perfumes blending with the tang of air and water and earth energy. Everything seemed to be swirling together, inside her head and outside, too.

"All of that stuff about love or not love can be confusing at first," Bela said, a little too slowly and very gently, obviously drawing on her own experience of falling in love with her husband under weird, pressured circumstances. She rubbed the right knee of her faded work jeans, and Camille wondered if Bela even knew she was doing that. Her football jersey, just as worn as the jeans, was already frayed along the bottom hem, where Bela picked at it when she was nervous.

Andy never seemed to get nervous. She gave her opinion in a completely not-gentle rush. "Confusing, my ass. It's fucked up, that's what it is. Every time I've ever fallen in love, it's been nothing but a nightmare, and this—this *thing* you've got going with demon-man, I think it's dangerous, Camille."

She didn't say *too* dangerous, which Camille took as a positive sign even though she knew that was desperate. She was also glad nobody was asking her how long she'd been thinking about him, or how many times she'd had contact with him, because those answers could get her in some serious trouble with her quad.

"I'm okay with it." Dio was sitting sideways in her leather chair with both legs over the arm closest to Camille, and she bounced her white tennis shoe and slightly mud-stained jeans cuff with each word. "With him, I mean—unless he hurts you. Then I'll help behead him and we'll all feel better." She hesitated, then added, "And just so you all know, when John first showed up, he tried to get me to make the same deal Duncan did— that whole if-I-start-to-hurt-her-you-kill-me thing. And I'm not doing it."

"What are you, the group executioner?" Bela shook her head at Dio. "Why does everybody ask you to kill them?"

"Because she's the meanest bitch in the house," Andy suggested.

Dio hit Andy with her pillow, rumpling the black NYPD sweatshirt Andy always wore with her jeans.

"No?" Andy's smile would have been contagious if Camille hadn't been feeling so nervous about all of this. "Okay, then. We'll settle for this: Dio has a murderous nature that shows through now and again." Then, before Dio could hit her again or come up with some smartass remark, Andy went back at Camille. "I'm not okay with John. Not yet. I don't know if I'm speaking from new Sibyl instincts or good old-fashioned cop instincts, but you better be listening. There's something under the surface with that man. Something dark."

"Um, yeah." Dio snickered. "A not-quite-killed Rakshasa demon. Is that dark enough to suit everybody? And since when did you go all old-maid careful on us, Andy?"

Andy wasn't having any of that crap, and this time she shook her finger at Dio when she talked. "Don't judge this guy by Duncan or the Lowell brothers or any other part-human demons we know. John Cole is something new and we need to treat him that way." She glanced at her own pointing finger, frowned seemingly at herself, and bounced her hand on her pillow because she pulled it down so fast. "You people should have seen what the Sibyls who used to live here put my ex-partner Creed through before they accepted him as okay."

"And one of them married him." Bela wasn't snickering because her husband, Duncan, had faced a similar gauntlet of tests and procedures from the Mothers before he was declared safe for human consumption. So to speak.

"Whatever," Andy grumbled. "Just because we know good half-demons doesn't mean they're all good. I think Strada's essence may turn out to be more powerful than we understand. He could hurt you, Camille."

"Point taken." Camille kept the fingers of both hands locked together so she wouldn't fidget like a first-year adept. "It's a risk, and it's one I'm willing to take whether you want me to or not, but I'd rather have—"

She broke off, not sure what word to choose. Judging by the protective, suspicious look on Andy's face, it wouldn't really matter anyway. With the biggest brooding projective mirror over her red hair and serious frown, Andy looked almost like a fire Sibyl Mother ready to pass judgment.

"It's not that I'm not taking you seriously, Andy." Camille couldn't help herself. She fidgeted, then stared down at her hands to keep herself from trying too hard or crying or clamming up because she was intimidated by Andy's disapproval. "It's just that I'm not sure I can slow down my emotions, even if I know I should. I started off by touching his soul—literally. We're working backward from there, but how am I supposed to undo what that felt like?"

Nobody said anything, and when Camille made herself raise her chin again, Bela, Dio, and Andy wore almost matching expressions of worry, but also understanding. Above their heads, the chimes tinkled as the energy in the room flowed through them.

"When you put it like that, it's hard to keep giving you shit," Andy admitted. "So what do you want, our blessing or something?"

Blessing. That was a good word. Camille looked at Andy and waited.

"Oh, hell." Andy raised her hand and did a fast, idiotic mash-up of painting a rune in the air with two fingers. "Consider yourself blessed. If you wind up eaten, don't come bitching to me."

Camille quit squeezing her own fingers to death. "Will you all give him a chance? Seriously?"

"He's ex-military with a lot of experience, and yeah,

okay, he kicked a god's ass for us, like you all keep reminding me." Andy folded her arms like she didn't really want to be saying all of that, but Camille knew better. Andy gave credit where credit was due. "Maybe he'll prove he's worth something in the long run."

Dio's overly relaxed posture never changed, but she piped up with, "I still want to know where we're going to keep him. Not literally, like your bedroom and stuff, Camille, but during patrols and Sibyl business."

"He's got skills and he's the expert on Rakshasa." Bela always sat straight in her chair during meetings, but that didn't translate into personality stiffness, thank the Goddess. "I say we take him."

Andy's mouth came open. "We have no idea what'll happen when we come across an actual Rakshasa demon. What if Strada knows his own and comes straight to the front and takes over?"

"Running into Rakshasa won't be a problem," Camille reminded them, going back to fidgeting with her fingers. "It's already happened. The night—well, one of the nights I was out hunting alone. When you came to rescue me in the alley. We were on Tarek's trail, only I thought it was Strada's."

"Let's give him a try at least," Bela said to Andy, more a request than she needed to make it, since she was the quad's mortar. "We need all the help we can get against these things, and with what John knows, we might finally get the upper hand."

Andy seemed to consider this, and she finally gave in with a shrug. "I've fought with demons before, I guess, and newer, weirder ones than him. Okay, yeah. Let's see what happens. If he freaks, we'll all be there to deal with it."

Deal with it . . .

Camille shivered, but Bela was already moving on to

the next topic. "And you and Maggie, Camille. What's with the two of you?"

Camille leaned back against the leather cushion. "Old battles—and I'm so sorry I brought them into the present. She and I used to slug it out when we were little. All the other adepts at Motherhouse Ireland had issues with the fact I couldn't make fire. I won't let it get in the way again."

"Oh, let it get in the way," Dio said, probably because she'd gotten her own ration of shit from air Sibyl adepts and Mothers over her sort-of-illegal weather-making abilities. "If she gets too far out of line, we'll help you kick her ass."

"Tempting." Camille sighed. "But no. We don't need to fight with other Sibyls. I promised myself I'd leave all that crap between the stone walls of the Motherhouse when Alisa claimed me, and I did. I made the same vow to myself when Bela gave me a second chance."

"I didn't know you had such a temper," Andy said. "Kind of makes me feel better, since all the rest of the fire Sibyls I've known have been first-class bitches. Loveable, but, well, flammable."

"Goes with the territory." Bela gestured to the wall behind them, where the projective mirror that opened on Motherhouse Ireland smoked and swirled with more vigor than all the rest. "Working with such an unstable element. But Camille, if you're really pissed off inside, why don't you show it?"

Camille felt her words go cold like all the flames inside her had just fizzled away. She did an in-depth study of her knuckles, tried to find the words, and came up absolutely empty.

Damn, damn, damn.

This was important, so of course she was whiffing out like she always did when she tried to light her blade in battle. When nothing came out of her open mouth, she finally closed it and shook her head, tears blurring the image of her own clenched fingers.

For a few seconds, the room went as quiet as the endless warrens under Motherhouse Ireland, only Camille felt like she didn't know all these new stone corridors and blind corners in her life by heart.

Out of place.

Out of my element—in all possible ways.

"You consider yourself a liability already," Bela said. "You hold in your anger to keep from making more trouble for us."

Camille gulped back a sob. How did she *do* that? Were all earth Sibyls born psychic? She knew she should look at Bela, but right that second, she would have put the effort required to pull that off on par with willing herself to implode.

Bela's hands closed over hers, warming up the cold parts as Camille stared straight down at the floor. "You probably did the same with Alisa and Bette—kept everything to yourself so you wouldn't bother them."

Camille was crying too hard to answer her.

"You're no more a liability than the rest of us." Dio's bouncing foot made a *whoosh-whoosh* noise against the well-conditioned leather. "We've all got our shit, but we kick ass anyway, right?"

Right.

Camille wanted to say it, but the words still weren't there. It was getting time to go. Downstairs. Out the front door. Anywhere. Not for long, maybe just a few minutes. She had to—

"You being here with us"—Bela gave her fingers a squeeze—"that's not contingent on how much trouble you do or don't cause."

Camille's lips trembled, and her words left her again,

because yes, this was almost as important as the last thing. Maybe . . . maybe more important.

My staying here—what is it contingent on?

She remembered the awful feeling she'd gotten after her mother died, that time when Maggie's crowd threatened her with the Mothers putting her out. It was something like this, mixed with a kid's terror—a fear, it seemed, that had never really left her.

Bela's voice broke through the fear like the first hint of sunlight after darkness. "I didn't take you on a trial basis, Camille. I chose you because you were right for me and right for us. Nothing changes that. This commitment is for keeps unless you choose to break it and run away."

She really is reading my mind. Not that I'm such a big mystery.

"This is home now," Camille finally managed to mumble, right about the same time she made herself quit counting the lines and little hairs on her fingers and Bela's, too.

"Glad to hear it." Bela's smile came through as even more sunlight, and she turned Camille's hands loose.

"Oh, goody." Andy was smiling now, hinting that she might say something worthy of another pillow hit. "So now you'll make more trouble? Fire Sibyl trouble's always so much fun."

"John Cole might be plenty of trouble," Camille said, not feeling nearly as defensive and terrified.

Dio rolled her eyes. "So was Duncan."

"What are you going to do if Motherhouse Ireland pulls that whole if-you-get-with-him-we'll-kick-you-out shit?" Andy asked. "They've done that before when fire Sibyls showed an interest in loving half demons. Remember Cynda and Nick?"

Rage blasted upward from Camille's toes, heating her so completely she felt something hard cracking down

the middle inside her—or was it something hard forming, growing in new ways? She glared above Andy's
head at the projective mirror linked to the valley outside Connemara. "They *so* don't need to go there with
me."

Bela raised her hands to her cheeks in mock horror,
then looked a little stunned.

"You're, um, smoking." Dio gestured to the fog gath-
ering around them.

Camille glanced down at her elbows.

Son of a bitch.

She was letting off steam.

Literally.

No flames broke into life along her shoulders or arms,
and the smoke didn't last long, but still, it had been
there, and not in the depths of some life-or-death battle
or because she'd used the dinar to magnify her abilities.

The surprise lingered even as Dio plunged ahead. "So,
who is this Ona character? She's not even in the
Archives of the Mothers."

"She's not a Mother." Camille was still looking at her
elbows, at where the smoke had been, amazed that she
had actually seen it. Despite the leftover haze, the alcove
seemed so much brighter all of a sudden, like it was
fresh and full of new energy.

"Ona has to be a Mother," Andy said. "She's—well,
she's really, really old."

Camille scooched around on the couch until she got
her legs up under her, relaxing as much as she could now
that the worst had passed. "She may be the oldest Sibyl
alive, but she's always refused to take the title or duties
of Mother."

Bela's eyebrows came together. "Why?"

"No idea," Camille said. "She just sort of appeared in
my life when I was younger, showed up in a tunnel one
day and spoke to me. Later, she made the older girls

knock off pounding on me, but I don't even know why she did that."

"Maybe because it was the right thing." Bela's fingers curled into fists, and she smacked one of those fists against her knees. "Damnit, the other Mothers should have taken care of that for you."

"They thought all the conflict might, you know, spark me or something." Camille shrugged even though the gesture felt a little too casual for how much all that had pissed her off and wounded her when she was a kid. "They thought it might make me tougher."

"Or run you off," Dio said.

Andy was shaking her head. "I still don't get why she's not a Mother."

"Because when I was your age, I learned I didn't have the constitution for it. Nor did I deserve the honor, then or now."

Ona's voice made them all jump. Camille and Bella and Dio had to turn to see her where she was standing, in her usual black breeches and matching tunic, right in front of the swinging kitchen door. The swinging door wasn't moving.

Andy, however, had been staring straight at Ona when she did whatever it was Ona did with the channels.

"How do you *do* that?" Andy pointed toward the hardwood at Ona's feet, which still had a sort of puddly look, though it was drying up fast. "I swear I saw you this time. You came through the floor."

Ona's tone and expression stayed unreadable, except for the slightest twitch of her mouth as she averted her gaze from Andy's. If Camille hadn't known better, she'd have thought Andy's presence startled Ona or bothered her.

"Your eyes deceived you," Ona said, and now Camille knew she *was* bothered. Ona never deferred to anyone for any reason, but her tone sounded absolutely submissive.

"They did not." Andy's face flushed, and one of her hands clenched into a fist.

"You saw what you saw," Ona told her, still not looking her straight in the face. Her words were confrontational, but her voice was literally shaking. "Your interpretation wasn't correct."

And Ona was gone. Back through the floor, or into thin air, or whatever the hell she did. Camille had been looking at her intently, paying attention, and she still had no idea where Ona went.

Andy jumped to her feet like she was about to stalk down to the lab.

"Give it up." Camille waved Andy back to her seat. "She could be back in Ireland—and she's always like that with questions. That's why I don't know much about her. She only tells me what she wants to, when she wants to."

"What do the other fire Sibyl Mothers say about her?" Bela asked, still gazing at the spot where Ona had been.

"Not much." Camille watched as the hardwood went back to looking like hardwood again. "To stay away from her. That she's trouble. I think they're scared of her, especially Mother Keara."

Bela, who was very close to Mother Keara in an adversarial love-your-best-enemy sort of way, grinned when she heard this. "Then I think I like Ona. She can stay."

Laughter popped out before Camille could hold it back. "Good, because if you wanted her out of here, I couldn't do anything about it."

Gradually Bela shifted her full attention back to Camille, and when she did, she asked, "Are we finished with secrets?"

Camille swallowed, relieved that her words didn't take a quick hike again. "I think so."

"We need to be," Bela said without changing her expression from its usual calm kindness. "I'm to the point where I need your word on that."

"You have it." Camille lifted her hand like she was pledging to the flag. "I promise I'm not holding anything else back. Nothing I'm aware of, anyway."

Bela accepted this, then looked briefly worried. "And you trust us enough to tell us if anything else comes up?"

"Yes. I promise."

"Good," Andy muttered. "Because I can't take much more of this serious meeting crap. It gets on my nerves."

The chimes above her head gave a soft ring, then a harder, jangling warning.

Camille's heart surged, and she was on her feet with everyone else before she fully registered the message. "Friendlies. OCU. Nick sent the message, but he's not coming. He's meeting an informant in Central Park. It's Saul Brent and—"

She stopped, feeling flickers of surprise. "And Jack Blackmore."

"Oh, that's wonderful." Andy flopped back down in the leather chair under the Motherhouse Ireland mirror. "Just what I need to make my fucking day. Another meeting, and with the world's biggest puckered asshole."

"Come on, Andy," Dio said as she took her seat again, too. "Tell us what you really think."

Bela looked tense, but she went to answer the door as Camille once more took up residence on the end of the couch closest to Dio.

"If she starts a tidal wave," Dio whispered to Camille, "lend me whatever energy you can and I'll try to keep him from breaking any bones."

Camille nodded and snuck a peek at Andy, who was rubbing her eyes with her thumb and forefinger like she was warding off a migraine.

With Blackmore and Andy in the same space, even after a year of separation, rogue waves were a distinct possibility. The two had only known each other a few weeks before Blackmore went on sabbatical at the Motherhouses—but it was a few weeks too many.

The first man through the door was Saul Brent, wearing jeans and a Giants jacket like he usually did. He was so frigging tall he had to duck to get inside, and his long brown ponytail was loose and flyaway from the cold fall breezes. Saul looked a lot rougher than his older brother, Cal, thanks to years working undercover in narcotics. Cal was clean-cut, polished, and professional, while Saul had gorgeous brown eyes full of humor—and a lot of tattoos. The ones Camille had seen were way sexy, and she was willing to bet he had more under his clothes. She had always liked the tribal markings on his hands, and she could just make out the top of the Greek cross on his neck.

"I should get more tattoos," she said out loud, mostly to break the tension, but also because she thought it might suit her, that it might help her break out of the mold she had set for herself so long ago when she started failing at Motherhouse Ireland. "Maybe a Celtic knot—or what about a Greek cross like Saul's?"

"Do the barbed-wire armband," Andy said, pointedly keeping her attention off the doorway. "I dare you."

Jack Blackmore came in after Saul, and Bela closed the door behind him. Camille studied him from top to bottom. Coal black hair, nearly black eyes—yep. Not much different there. He was also wearing "the suit," as Andy called it, a dark ensemble that could have escaped from the set of *Men in Black*.

Doesn't that just scream Fed? Andy had been fond of asking last year, usually followed by her favorite epithet, Flaming Bunch of Idiots, even though Blackmore wasn't really FBI.

Right now, Andy just flicked her gaze toward Blackmore, looked briefly at the ceiling, and went back to staring at Camille.

Blackmore, however, let his gaze linger on Andy.

Camille twitched on the sofa.

Poor guy was probably weighing the odds that he'd get back out of the brownstone without having to go to the emergency room.

Yeah. Good luck with that, big guy. Or maybe I should say, big mouth.

She almost greeted with Blackmore with *I'm so surprised nobody in Ireland killed you,* but Bela's nervous expression made Camille hold her tongue.

Even Dio looked squirmy and uncomfortable, totally out of character.

Camille tensed, waiting for Blackmore to instantly say or do something stupid to piss Andy off, which he could usually manage in a few seconds.

He cleared his throat, nodded to all of them, Andy included, and addressed himself to Bela. "Duncan told me to get over here, but he wouldn't tell me why. Said I had to hear it—and see it—for myself."

Bela nodded. "Nice to see you," she said to Saul, but she didn't offer Blackmore the same courtesy. She just gestured to the end of the sofa where Camille wasn't sitting. Both men eased their tall frames onto the leather cushions, Saul closest to Camille—and Blackmore without arguing or bitching about not having time.

Dio's right eyebrow lifted as she glanced at Camille.

Camille shrugged.

Maybe Blackmore's time with the Mothers had taught him some manners. Camille found herself wondering how many wolf bites, burn scars, and wind-related shrapnel injuries he had taken. She was pretty sure Blackmore hadn't dared show up on the beaches at Motherhouse Kérkira this last summer to aggravate Andy. The fact that he was still alive was pretty much proof of that.

Bela didn't wait for any uncomfortable silences to extend themselves, or give Blackmore too much of a chance to step in muck right away. She explained quickly and succinctly about John Cole's spirit surviving the events in the alley a year ago, and the fact that Camille had inadvertently helped him take another body. "We don't feel certain of everything yet, so we're watching, and John's allowing that. If something goes wrong, I think we're all ready."

Camille's entire essence ached at the sound of this, but she kept her mouth shut.

Nothing bad will happen. He's not really a demon hybrid. It's not the same. And it wasn't—yet it was.

Contradictions. Camille held back a sigh. That pretty much defined John, didn't it?

"Whose body did you give him?" Jack Blackmore asked Camille, and she was surprised by the undisguised happiness in his dark eyes. The scowl he usually wore had faded away, too, leaving a handsome, almost relaxed-looking and eager man waiting for an answer.

Saul Brent was smiling, too. Camille didn't think Saul really knew John, but Saul knew Duncan—and all the OCU officers were always glad to gain a powerful new fighter.

Camille hated to complicate things by spilling this next part, but truth was truth. "John got Strada's body. Well, his human-form body."

Blackmore's expression became more troubled even though he seemed to be trying to keep himself in some sort of Zen state. "The Rakshasa leader. You . . . put John in demon skin?"

Camille kept herself from glaring at Blackmore, but it was a near miss. "It wasn't like I had a choice. This was an accident. Happenstance. Strada's body was there, so that's the body John got."

"And Strada?" Saul asked. "What happened to his insides? His . . . spirit, or whatever a demon has?"

Camille's hand moved to her heart. "We call it

essence. Strada's dead, but his essence isn't. Not completely." She did her best to explain about the remnant energy, finishing with, "As far as we can tell, as long as John's not exposed to extreme projective energy or knocked out or impaired in some other complete way like that, he'll keep control."

Blackmore's eager happiness had definitely been tuned down a few notches, and that scowl Camille remembered so well was trying to sneak back across his face. "So he could turn demon. He could lose control and let that monster loose."

"As could any of the demon hybrids allied with the OCU." Bela's voice remained icy calm, but her eyes communicated mistrust of this man, who'd once tried to take Duncan Sharp to a laboratory to more or less study him to death. "My husband has a monster inside him, too, but he does pretty well with it, don't you think?"

Blackmore seemed to consider this, and Camille figured he was thinking about Duncan, and maybe also the three Lowell brothers—two part demon and one full-blooded—not to mention all the other creatures who had cast their lots with the NYPD's Occult Crimes Unit. Similar alliances and partnerships had formed all over the world with different paranormal crime units during the years the Sibyls spent defeating the Legion cult. Now the Dark Crescent Sisterhood had thrown down against the Rakshasa, and anybody who could help in that fight was welcome.

"New enemies," Andy said to Blackmore without the roaring force of water behind her words. "New allies. That's how it goes in any war."

"I think the Rakshasa might be trying to build alliances of their own," John said from the front door, and everybody turned to stare at him.

Camille's eyes darted to the chimes over the table—the chimes that hadn't given the slightest ring when he approached. They hadn't even heard him opening the door. He was wearing a clean pair of jeans and an army-green sweatshirt, and he was carrying the demon packet Dio had written up for him. The pages already looked crinkled and well read. In his other hand he had what looked like a big gym bag.

Camille realized he probably had bags here and there in different cities—bus terminals, safe-deposit boxes, other hiding places, maybe even rented rooms or apartments that might still be his, technically, if the rent or payments had been made. As long as he had the keys, nobody would ask any questions. In his previous life, John had never known when he'd have to leave or where he'd have to go—or how fast.

Both Blackmore and Saul gaped at the image of Strada standing so close to them. Camille knew how disconcerting that could be, but she realized she had already stopped seeing the demon and started seeing only John. There were differences in the body from when Strada used it—subtle but definite. The posture. The facial expression. The energy around him, especially. This man standing before them, he was John Cole, and though he bore a strong resemblance to the former demon leader, he was becoming his own person again, inside and out.

It was Blackmore who got hold of himself first, responding to John's comment about the demons seeking allies. "You talking about the crime lords?"

"The Balkans, the Russians, the Irish, the Vietnamese or Chinese—or somebody completely under our radar." John slid his bag against a wall, laid his papers on top, and came through the living room. He skirted the chairs and communications platform and sat on the arm of the big leather sofa, as close to Camille as he could get without touching her. Then he folded his arms and openly studied the man who had been his commander for years.

The heat from John's body seemed like a force to Camille, distracting her and soothing her at the same time. She was glad he was in the room. Relieved, even. Something about his presence made her feel so much more supported and so much less alone.

"I was thinking the same." Blackmore's tone shifted, and he focused on John more completely, like he might be seeing through to the real John, just like Camille thought she had been doing. "Tarek won't use Strada's methods, at least not in the same way. I half expected him to show back up with troops and guns blazing, but he's going low-profile."

"Gotta be collecting help," Saul agreed, pressing one thumb into the tribal tattoos on the back of his hand. "The kind of help that doesn't answer want ads."

John stepped into his old Rakshasa-hunting role so smoothly Camille barely realized he was doing it. "Tarek's probably busy making a truckload of Created to help him, too. So, you working some angle, Blackjack? What's the plan?"

Blackmore almost started talking again, then shook his head, looked at his feet, and looked back at John. "Fuck, this is weird. I feel like I should shoot you."

John's grin came fast and natural. "I've felt like shooting you for years, so I guess that makes us even."

Blackmore's mouth crooked into a smile. "Nice bruise. Did Sharp kick your ass?"

John touched the dark spot already fading from his cheek. "Better than cutting off my head, right?"

"So far," Blackmore said, "but don't push your luck with us. With any of us."

John glanced at Camille, and she made sure to shift her weight against his leg. A little contact never hurt anything, and it might make him feel better. If he'd been in the room when her quad was grilling her—hell, she might have tried to get in his lap.

"I'll handle myself," John said, though Camille would have put money on the fact that he wasn't nearly as relaxed about that as he was trying to sound. "We were talking plans and angles to get at the Rakshasa?"

Saul started to say something, but Blackmore raised his hand. "You've got no official status in this city, John, even through our old special ops channels."

"Then give me one." John didn't seem the least bit distressed by this, like it was just a small hurdle Blackmore needed to remove before they could jump to the real issues.

"That'd be a lot easier if you weren't dead." Blackmore's voice stayed very, very calm, but Camille could tell he was trying to get reality across to John. "You have no legal identity, and I can't just pull one out of my ass."

"Yes, you can, and I know it." John tapped his cheek with one finger. "The face is different, but this is me, Blackjack. I'm not asking for anything you haven't done a hundred times. A thousand. Find me an official name and social, and don't take too long. If I'm working, I expect a paycheck."

Saul and Dio both laughed at the same time, looked at each other, and laughed harder. Dio covered her mouth with her hand.

Bela kept a passive expression, but Andy's eyes danced with the same mirth Camille felt. If she'd known it was this easy to play serious cards with the famous "Blackjack" Blackmore, she'd have tried this approach when he first showed up on the scene last year.

"Busted," Andy said, not very much under her breath.

Blackmore glanced in her direction, and a splash of color touched the top of his high cheekbones. It struck Camille that he was trying really, really hard not to tick Andy off, her more than any of the rest of them. The mirrors on the wall behind Andy swirled from the increasing energy in the room, but the clouds in the glass didn't look dark or foreboding. Whatever Andy was feeling, it was closer to neutral—or maybe light, like she was laughing at the man inside, at least as hard as Dio and Saul had laughed on the outside.

"It'll probably be through some OCU slush funds," Blackmore said, not looking at anyone in particular now, but keeping his eyes off the mirrors and even the chimes above the communications table. "I don't think I can sail this one past the Pentagon, not when they paid to put you in the ground months ago."

When Camille looked up at John, he was grinning. "Fine by me. Money's money, and demons are demons. It doesn't really matter who's paying me. I'll kill Rakshasa just the same."

If John cared that his military career was essentially over, he didn't show it, at least not that Camille could see. Circumstances had forced him to abandon his chosen profession before, more than once. Maybe he was used to it?

"For now, we'll make you . . . how does official advisor sound?" Blackmore seemed to be trying to be sincere, and Camille could tell John knew the man well enough to know that.

"Fine," John said.

Dio coughed to strangle another fit of laughter, but she just had to say, "If you don't consider the fact that some of our OCU and Sibyl advisors have wings and fangs."

John's warmth spilled through Camille as he pressed his thigh closer to her shoulder, getting really comfortable on the arm of the couch beside her. "As long as I get creds, a permit to carry, and you pay advisors with dollars and cents instead of raw steak or some other stupid crap, I'm in."

"No raw steak." Blackmore made like he was taking notes, and Camille restrained herself from pulling a fake faint. She'd never seen the man joke before—at all. She wouldn't have bet a nickel that he was even capable of it.

This time John's grin transformed his whole face. "And don't get me any stupid names, either."

To this, Blackmore said nothing, but his dark eyes seemed to dance with possibilities. He gestured to Saul, who unloaded a couple of big folded papers from inside his Giants jacket. As Saul spread maps of the city across the communications platform, Blackmore explained, "This is what we've put together so far."

Camille leaned in to get a better look at the papers, and so did Bela, Dio, and Andy. The maps had been marked with colored grids. Most of the grids had been labeled, and Camille read the names over each of the main sections.

"Foucci, Divac, Seneca, Sekulovich."

Dio ran a French-manicured nail over a few other sections, shaded gray, but they had been named, too. "Fitzsimmons, McBride, and Gordon to the north, and to the south, De Luca, Bianchi, and Tenace."

There were more, longer names, difficult to pronounce, though Camille thought they might be Russian.

"Irish and Italians." Saul pointed to the sections Dio had touched. "And over here, we've got the Russians and their territories, but really, the Russians claim everything is theirs. They're all bad, but not our worst problem right now. These boys"—he tapped the colored sections with the Balkan names—"they're a whole new kind of ruthless."

Blackmore scooted the map closer to him and oriented it so Camille, Bela, Andy, and Dio could easily view all the areas. "The NYPD's been tracking movement on the four main Balkan groups with the FBI. Mostly standard merchandising—drugs, human trafficking, counterfeit electronics, weaponry. Last week this group"—he put his index finger on the green section, marked *Foucci—*

"did a one-eighty. Temporarily froze a lot of merchandise movements, brought in heavy-hitter higher-ups from overseas, and had some major conferences with all their cells and factions. The NYPD thinks they lost their major player in the States."

"All they found was part of a leg bone near the docks," Saul said. "Forensics aren't back yet, but preliminary testing indicates everything matches up to Ioannis Foucci, and none of our guys on the ground have been able to make the old man."

"The leg bone was chewed," Blackmore added, sitting back on the couch. "According to the ME, some kind of large animal. My money's on tiger."

"Eating crime lords." John let out a low whistle, and his hand drifted down to touch Camille's shoulder. "That's one way to make a lot of friends—and enemies. So which of our three competitors hired him?"

Saul shook his head. "That's where we're coming up short."

"I don't think we can assume it's one of these three other Balkan families." Bela got comfortable in her own chair again. "I was just a boarder at Motherhouse Russia. I grew up around here, and I can tell you when these crime lords start shooting it out, there's no telling who might put guns in the fight—even bit players trying to get up the ladder. We could be looking at some unknowns, or maybe even the older groups—the Italians, the Irish. I don't know much about the Russians."

Blackmore focused on Bela, studiously keeping his gaze away from Andy. "I grew up in Jersey, and you're right. We don't think it's the Russians because they just go in with overwhelming force and mow everybody down, after they break all their bones for show. As for the rest of these larger groups, it's been business as usual for them, and the FBI doesn't think they're in good positions to start a war with the Balkans right now."

"These guys are loose cannons, not playing by the rules," Saul said, massaging the tattoos on his hand as if touching them gave him strength or focus. "When the older mobs hit them, it'll be all-out attacks and for keeps, no little penny-ante assassination stuff—and that's only if they think they can win."

"The NYPD and the FBI think they can't." Blackmore's tone darkened. "The Balkans are stronger than the Irish and Italians put together right now, at least in New York City."

It was obvious to Camille that Jack Blackmore had a particular hatred for the traditional mobs, even if he was keeping it pretty tight to the vest. The edge in his voice was easy to hear, and the way his eyes smoldered as they passed over the Italian sector especially—that said a lot.

"We're sending a team here tomorrow night to do a little recon after we check it out by daylight." Blackmore jerked his thumb toward the Divac section, gazing up at John, then looking at Bela. "Want to be that team?"

"You're on," John said, then backed off with a quick nod to Bela. "If, ah, everyone's in agreement."

The excitement and relief in John's voice registered instantly with Camille. This was familiar territory to him. Safe ground. He had to be more than thrilled to get back to normal operations, or what had served as normal for him since all his wars began. She kept her body pressed into his, still casual, not that apparent unless somebody really studied how they were sitting. She appreciated the contact, but a less generous part of her mind started wondering if this would be what she'd have if she matched up with John—strategy meetings and quick contacts as they constantly planned their attack on the next enemy.

He could worry about the same thing where you're concerned, idiot.

She wanted to smack herself in the forehead for putting the cart so far in front of the horse it wasn't even funny.

"We're in," Bela said. "At least it's a place to start."

Camille shared John's relief at her agreement, and she separated herself from him to head to the weapons closet and make sure all the gear was in order. Andy got to her feet, too, stretching to get herself limber for her afternoon workout.

Dio pointed at her. "That's Sibyl for 'Strategy session over, boys.' "

John and Saul and Blackmore nearly hurt themselves standing up so fast.

"No pig blood," Andy said, sounding psychotically cheerful as she flopped into an ungraceful, unbalanced downward-dog position beside her leather chair. "I'm so there."

Blackmore gave her a questioning look, but Saul waved him off. "Voodoo stuff. They got attacked by a god the other night."

"Oh. Right." Blackmore didn't seem to be able to take his eyes off Andy. "Karfour."

"Kalfou," Andy corrected, standing up straight again. "But you were close."

She didn't say she was impressed, but Camille could tell she was.

After Blackmore and Saul left, John came over to the weapons closet, but his eyes kept moving back to the front door. "Jack," he said as Camille pulled out their cache of swords. "He's—he seems a lot different than I remember. Did you give him a personality transplant while I wasn't around?"

"Not really." Camille lifted a blade and measured it against John's stance. Too short. "Well, he spent a lot of time with the Mothers, so maybe that helped after all. I can't put my finger on it, but he seems . . . better."

Dio walked by on her way to the stairs. "I think it's just that his demeanor doesn't scream 'arrogant asshole' quite as loud as it did last year."

Bela went in the other direction, heading for the kitchen, probably on her way downstairs to spend a little time in the lab she was now sharing with Camille to make some elementally treated bullets for John's Glock. "What impresses me is that he was here for almost half an hour, and Andy didn't try to drown him one single time."

"Fuck all of you," Andy said from her slightly pretzel-like yoga position beneath the Motherhouse Ireland mirror. "I may kill him yet. Just not today."

Camille gave John a look and whispered her real interpretation of Blackmore's visit. "Maybe there's hope for the world after all."

"I'll buy that," he whispered back, coming close enough that she wanted to touch him, and would have if she hadn't been balancing three swords to measure against John's height. "But let's see what jackass new name and identity he tries to saddle me with before we go too far."

She woke him the next morning, sitting on the edge of his bed, perched there like a delicate, tiny bird, just looking at him.

John thought he'd never experienced anything quite as sweet as opening his eyes to find Camille next to him in the bed, any bed, even if she hadn't spent the night with him. The sight of her in her clingy white silk babydoll pajamas, gazing at him with those tropical blue-green eyes, made his blood rush. Her auburn hair looked wild and uncombed, a riot of dark red shades spilling over her shoulders and brushing her cream-colored cheeks. Her freckles seemed like the same shade of red-brown, and John wanted to touch each one, count each one, and memorize its location.

Her arm was . . . dusty.

He reached up and brushed grit off her elbow and gave her a questioning look.

"I've been practicing some stuff about dances and channels and the rock—never mind." She wiped off her other elbow even though it wasn't dusty. "Anyway, since we're doing everything backward, I thought you should see me in the morning before I shower and get myself fixed up." She pointed a slightly dusty finger at her hair. "Scary enough for you?"

John adjusted the sheets, aware of the feminine softness of the silk, and more than aware that Camille had slept in them before she loaned him her room. They smelled like her, like lilies and woman. He wanted more of that. More of everything.

"Come closer," he told her, moving toward her just enough to get her attention. The huskiness in his voice was obvious to him, and he figured she noticed it, too. "Another few inches, and I'll show you just how terrified I am."

Her smile made him ache.

She didn't move toward him, but he saw in her eyes that she wanted to.

That made him ache worse.

If he reached out, he'd be touching her. If she reached out, her hand would hit him midbelly, just above the sheet covering the fact he slept naked.

He had to shift his weight on the bed to make his erection less obvious.

Camille looked away from him at the pictures on her walls—buildings John assumed had to be the Mother-houses, drawn or painted by a pretty good artist.

"Why did you become a priest?" she asked.

The question brought him out of his desire-laden haze, though not completely, because the answer was easy enough. "I wanted to help people."

He could have guessed her next question, but she asked it before he could do it for her. "Why did you give it up?"

"Same reason." John wished she would look at him again, not so he could gauge her reaction and adjust his answers, but so he could see those eyes, see what she might be feeling about what he was saying. About him. "I couldn't go after the demons with the church breathing down my neck. They had no problem with me being a military chaplain, but demon hunter probably wouldn't have gone over well."

Camille finished studying the pictures on her wall and gave him a fast, shy glance before she stared down at the tiny patch of cream-colored sheet between them. "Do you miss being with the church?"

"No."

Her quick, twitching frown made him worry that she didn't believe him, or that she thought he was being callous, so he tried to explain himself a little better. "Do I miss the peace and ceremony and prayer and the helping-people part? Yes, sometimes. But do I miss the demands and the restrictions and the limitations? No."

Camille nodded. And waited.

Was she working up to another question about his time in the service of the church? If so, he had a good guess what this one might be, too—or at least what she needed to know.

"I'm not one of those angst-ridden ex-priests you read about in books or magazines, and I don't get tempted to go back to that way of life. The way I see it, even though the circumstances sucked, I got a do-over about that choice, which is a good thing, because I made it when I was too young. Leaving the clergy was the right thing for me and the church, too. It was the right thing for everybody."

Camille seemed to be listening to every word, and not just what he said but how he said it. She could probably read more into his answer than he could begin to guess, but that didn't bother John. Whatever she needed to know or wanted to know, whatever she wanted from him, period, he'd give it to her.

She's trying to weigh who I really am against who she thought I'd be, he realized. He wondered how he was faring in that equation.

She didn't seem inclined to let him ask.

"I was born in Motherhouse Ireland," she said, combing through all that long hair with her fingers. "My mother got killed when I was eight, and I sucked as an adept. Never developed the fire talents the Mothers wanted, and what I could do—pyrosentience—they thought was stupid. The mortar of my first fighting group took me on anyway, and I would have died to save her if

I had the chance. The same for our air Sibyl, Bette. She got killed by an Asmodai in Van Cortlandt Park, and there was nothing I could do to save her, either. Losing them nearly drove me crazy. Maybe it did. I still haven't decided." She finished with her hair and pushed it behind her ears. "That's what I have nightmares about. Asmodai. Fire Asmodai."

Okay. So, this is what we're doing now—I talk, then she talks. An exchange.

And it was his turn.

Fine.

He could do this.

"Only child, straight-A nerd in school, but too big for anybody to kick my ass over it. Duncan and I grew up in fields and woods, drinking Coke and eating Moon Pies. It went with the territory." John watched Camille, alert for any sign of reaction, but she wasn't judging or evaluating now. Just listening. "Duncan was like my brother, and he was the best, because most kids didn't want anything to do with my family. We were Catholic, and in Georgia, Catholicism was something like devil worship as far as most religions were concerned. Duncan lived with us the last few years we were in high school because his parents died. When he went to the University of Georgia, I headed for St. John Vianney College Seminary, in Miami. Then came the war, and Duncan and I joined up together. I have nightmares about stuff I saw in the war, and about the Valley of the Gods in the mountains near Kabul. That's where a soldier I was with accidentally released the Rakshasa. What happened next—not pretty."

Her soft, caring smile felt like a blessing. "There. Easy so far, right?"

"No." John knew he was grinning back at her, and it made him feel like a teenager talking to the prettiest girl in school. "But doable."

She stretched out her arm and touched his face, running four of her fingers along his jaw, then his chin. He felt the contact everywhere at once, and stayed completely bound by her eyes. "You're used to doing everything alone, John."

"You should talk."

"Touché." Camille smiled at him again, and John had to move his hand down to cover the tent in the silk sheet around his waist. He couldn't stop his physical reaction to her, didn't want to, but he didn't want her to think that was everything. He didn't want her to believe that all he was seeing was how she looked, or all he was imagining was how he wanted to touch her, and where, and for how long.

Every bit of that was happening—but this, this was so much more for him. He hadn't imagined he could get this deep emotionally with any woman, much less before he ever got to make love to her.

"What do you think of me?" Camille murmured, as if she had heard every thought whirling through his mind.

John stared into those amazing eyes, wondering how it would feel to rock her underneath him, to see her gazing up at him with all the love and heat and passion he hoped he could give her.

I'm in so much trouble here, there aren't any words.

"What do I think of you?" He breathed her scent like a drug. "That's a big question, beautiful."

Her hand moved into his hair like she was sampling him, getting a basic feel for everything about him—or trying to see if her stray dog might bite her after all. "We got off to a strange start, John, more intimate than sex in some ways, so I think it's important for us to get rid of myths and fantasies and start dealing with reality."

It was taking all he had not to get lost in her touch. So slight, but so powerful. "Do you ever waste any words?"

"No. I don't." She gave his hair a soft tug. "As a rule,

no fire Sibyl does. If talking and communicating scare you to death, you might as well walk away now."

How could such a tiny little package carry such a big punch? "That sounded like a challenge."

Another smile. Another tug on his hair. She had to be trying to kill him.

"Definitely," she said.

"I don't walk away from challenges." He held her gaze. "Ever."

"We'll see."

John knew he had a question to answer, so he answered it without censoring himself, letting the words come as they would. "I think you're perfect—but not in some idealistic way. I think you might be perfect for me."

Her gaze didn't waiver, but her lips parted, and he could almost taste her tongue in his mouth.

"I think you're beautiful," he said, more a hoarse whisper than anything, because he was so far gone. "That's no secret. I think you're honest and direct and kind-hearted, and smarter than most people even know. Brilliant, even. I also think you're wounded and unsure of yourself, and stronger than *you* know."

Camille looked disconcerted, like he might have surprised her. Finally. Well, good, because he'd surprised himself, getting all of that out. He wasn't sure he'd strung that many sentences together in a personal situation for what, years? Ever?

Her parted lips finally started moving, at least enough to say, "Was that an audition?"

"It's the truth. It's what I think so far, but I want to find out a lot more. I want to know everything about you. I want to know every taste. Every scent. Every whisper-soft inch of your skin. I want to lose myself in you."

Her cheeks colored the prettiest red, making her freckles stand out and beg to be kissed.

"What do you want, Camille?"

"I don't know," she said, but her eyes had gone misty and wide, and he wanted his mouth on hers so badly he felt the fire in his chest, his fingers, his arms, just like she'd used her elemental energy to burn him. "Not yet. But I plan to figure it out. And figure you out."

John cleared his throat, mostly to test his voice. "Fair enough."

She moved her hand away from his face, and John wanted to catch her fingers and kiss them just to keep the contact.

"I feel like I'm responsible for all this," she said. Her fingers drifted to the already scarred-over gash in his side, the one made by Maggie Cregan's sword. "And this. For everything. For you still being here and having this body. Do you resent that?"

"Absolutely not. You didn't do it on purpose—and I wouldn't resent it even if you did. I got new skin and a fresh chance, Strada's out of commission, and I can help wipe out the Rakshasa. Everybody wins."

This time he got a frown instead of a smile, and he had a sense they were finally getting to the center of what was most on her mind. His gut tightened on instinct, because whatever this was, he'd better have the right answer, or this beautiful thing might die before it ever had a chance to bloom.

"And what happens after that, John?"

The tension in his gut got worse. "After what?"

"After all the Rakshasa are dead." Camille's gaze turned piercing, and John wondered if she could use her pyrosentience without him knowing it. "After your war is finally over. What then?"

John thought his gut might split in two. He hadn't expected that question, not even a little bit. "After," he echoed, because he had considered that, and he vaguely remembered that his plan had been to kill all the demons, then off himself and take Strada with him into the great beyond for good and all.

Then he'd spent time around Camille, and now . . .

Now that seemed like a pretty shitty plan.

But after?

Could he even believe there would be an after? A time when he wasn't at war?

"Don't even pretend you know what you're going to do, or what you'll want when this is over. You have no idea what *after*'s going to look like, because you've been at war forever." She moved closer to him, so close that he really felt her heat now, sensed her fire, and wanted every spark and flame. "I'm saying that because I know. I understand. What I think about you—I think you're a good soldier and a good man with no idea what life is like outside of a firefight. We're not so different in how we've lived, or how we'll have to live."

The softness in her voice and eyes unwound him inside and left him without anything to say at all. John swallowed, trying to regroup, trying to take in the truth that she really did understand, that she and her fellow Sibyls had known endless battles, endless wars. They were always fighting, always watching their backs.

He had just charged in among them, doing his thing, intent on his mission of protecting her and killing demons in the meantime, because—what? He thought Camille and her quad needed him?

They were happy to have his help, but they didn't need him.

He had no idea what to do with that.

She had gotten to the heart of his life—of him and the biggest part of his attitude toward life—that fast, and it made him feel disoriented and uncertain.

John didn't do uncertain.

He looked away from her, and when he looked back, she leaned over and pressed her lips against his.

The jolt of touching her almost sucked his self-control to nothing. He gripped her forearm, holding on as he tasted her lips, her tongue, as he felt the soft brush of her breath across his face. Every muscle in his body strained to get closer to her, but he made himself be still, made himself take what she offered. Her skin heated his palm, his fingers. She still smelled like lilies, now with a dash of silk sheets.

Camille found his hand with hers and moved it off her arm, over, over until his palm brushed her hard nipple. Shock fired from his fingers straight to his cock. Back and forth she moved his hand, letting him feel her through that barely there silk shirt.

Then she let him go and he cupped her breast, squeezing as she moaned into his mouth, kissing and pulling back.

"I have to touch you," he murmured, touching her lips with his as he spoke. "I have to feel you."

She didn't stop him when he slid his hand down to her waist, then up, inside the pajama top until he was caressing her breast, pinching the soft, pebbled nub, again, again—damn, she was just watching his fingers move on her nipple, lips parted, eyes heavy, and that turned him on beyond belief. Her whisper-sigh of pleasure made him harder even though he hadn't thought that was possible.

A second later, she had him, gripping him through the sheets, stroking his whole length.

"You're going to feel so good," she murmured as he tried to keep his sanity and not blow everything like a kid on his first date. She squeezed his erection as he rolled her nipple between his thumb and forefinger, one then the other, and this time, they both groaned into the kiss. He didn't want it to end, didn't want her to move away from him, let him go, let his hand slip from under her shirt. He wanted to keep going even though he already felt her pulling away.

He turned her loose, but he kept looking at her, watching as she stood and gave him a full, mouth-watering view of her bare legs and the curve of her hip in those short silk pajamas. Not teasing, not in a bad way, not on purpose, just taking it all in pieces, going slow and sane. He knew that, even if he wanted to be insane. Her nipples made hard knots against the soft-looking white fabric of her pajama top. They'd be hard in his mouth, too, and he'd use his tongue to make her moan until she didn't think she could take another second. Maybe she'd catch them both on fire. Maybe they'd burn up the bed, the room, the house—John really didn't care.

"You're going to be trouble, aren't you?" Her voice was so quiet and low he could hear her needing him, and he wanted to fill her up, fill her up here, now, until he convinced her she could never have enough.

"Absolutely."

That smile—he really could look at it all day, every day.

"Get up soon," she said. "Bela wants you to go to the park and train with us before we go out tonight. I think I found the right sword for your height and weight, and Bela's been busy making you some of our special demon-killer bullets. Oh, and Blackmore called."

John closed his eyes. *Here it comes.* "So, what's my new name, beautiful?"

Camille giggled, then covered her mouth.

It was all John could do to hold back a groan. "It's bad."

"Johann Kohl." She smiled at him. "See? Not awful. He said he'll Americanize it on all your final documents. John Cole. You're all set as you, just a different social security number and a different history by the records.

You can't run for president, but otherwise, same name, new man."

"That's not far off, I guess." John wasn't talking about the name, but he figured Camille knew that. She blew him a kiss, and a second or two later she was gone, leaving him with a major case of the aches and a strong need for an icy shower.

Johann Kohl, soon to be John Cole all over again, took that shower, and he did it without a single gripe in his head.

(18)

Two weeks after John got his official new name, Camille realized she wasn't running away. She was just . . . well, hiding.

The lab was the best place to stay away from John, and Camille knew that if she didn't keep a little distance, there'd be no more waiting. They had been talking every morning before the day got started, before the world got cluttered with other people's input—and she could still feel his hands on her breasts from this morning's little chat. Her lips wanted his all over again, and the rest of her just burned. A slow, sizzling sensation in all the right places.

But a few conversations just weren't enough—not that she hadn't had some quick relationships and in-and-out-of-bed experiences. She just didn't want this to be like that. She didn't want a one-night stand with John. She didn't know what she wanted.

Yes, I do.

"Shut up," she mumbled to herself as she cleaned off a lab counter.

She couldn't know. Not yet.

Yes, I do.

What to do with one tiny, mysterious old fire Sibyl during all of this angst—well, that was a puzzle, but Ona pretty much did whatever she wanted to do any-how. She was especially good at fiddling with whatever captured her attention.

"When I was younger, Sibyl labs were more basic," she said. She twisted knobs on a microscope Camille had taught her to use last week, then had to pull a stool over to look through the barrel. "Even then, the earth Sibyls didn't want us near their experiments. You're very fortunate."

"Bela doesn't stay in the lab like most earth Sibyls. We're all a little different. As Sibyls, I mean." She gestured to the ceiling and walls. "I don't feel closed in down here, and I like the cool air and the way everything smells so—clean."

"Metallic." Ona moved down to the next microscope as Camille pulled out her wooden box full of projective charms, the ones that hadn't worked as well. She wanted to do a fault analysis, find the weak spots, and manufacture new sets, in case other fighting groups wanted to try them.

"I've always liked the scent of copper myself." Ona rattled the microscope she was examining. "Elemental energy cleans so much more thoroughly than human bleaches—does much less damage to surfaces, too, I'd guess."

"It does, yes." Camille was listening, but only partially, as she handled her charms. The metal ticked together at the edges, almost a crystalline sound, and that soothed her a lot more than Bela's bland walls.

"Your trips to the docks these last ten nights haven't been productive." Ona rattled the microscope she was looking into again, and this time, she gave a little grunt of approval.

Camille looked up from her charms, surprised. "We haven't found anything all week. Not with traditional searches and observation, or with our sentient searches, either."

Had Ona been at the OCU briefings at the townhouse headquarters up by the Reservoir? Camille didn't remember her anywhere in the wood-paneled conference room during any of their patrol reports. Last night the place had been jammed with dozens of tired Sibyls and irritated, frustrated OCU officers—and some demons, the good kind. But no Ona. She had to have been spying in other ways Camille hadn't considered yet.

Ona kept her good eye glued to the microscope. "Your bedside conversations with your man—those are going better?"

Nosy little sneak. Camille glared at Ona, but of course Ona couldn't see that with her only good eye busy on the barrel. "They're going just fine."

Especially the kissing and making-out parts.

Ona obviously wasn't finished with her questions, and she kept her attention on the microscope. "And John Cole, has he acquitted himself well in his training sessions and patrols with your group so far?"

"He's already memorized Dio's demon list and how to kill each one of them, and he's meshing okay with Duncan and with our usual liaison, Nick Lowell. From what I can tell, he's a crack shot and an excellent close-quarters fighter—and he's holding his own up at the townhouse with some of the demons and half demons." Camille gave up on working the charms for the moment and set the wooden box down on the counter beside her. "Good with short blades, but the broadsword is still pretty strange to him."

Ona sniffed like she approved. "His body has abilities he doesn't understand as yet. He's afraid of them because he doesn't know how close the demon will come when he uses them." She finally stood from the microscope, but her words had given Camille a chill up her spine.

Someone walking on my grave . . .

She couldn't help remembering the blank, dangerous expression on John's face when she'd used nudges of elemental energy to rescue him from his war nightmare the first morning he had been at the brownstone. Strada had been right there, not in control, but definitely present in the room.

"Maybe John should be afraid," Camille said. "Maybe he's right not to use those skills if they're so dangerous."

Ona came over to Camille's table, shaking her head as she moved. "I'm of two minds about that issue. You may be right—and great evil could come of power raging out of control." She glanced at the ceiling, like she might be thinking about the mirrors upstairs and the Mother-houses, or maybe the other Sibyls in the brownstone. "Great evil *does* come from power raging out of control." She raised her right hand like she was balancing out her thought, and Camille saw those bracelets again, metal melded into skin. "Yet from that very evil, perhaps good rises."

Camille worked on this in her own head but couldn't quite get to the no-frills version of the meaning.

"Tell me what you're thinking, Camille." Ona's voice had an unusual gentleness to it, and the monotone sounds blended with the cream-and-sand walls until Camille didn't feel guarded, even though she probably should have. "Tell me the truth and hold nothing back, or we won't be able to work together."

"I'm thinking you're so ancient you've forgotten how to talk without riddling," Camille said, deciding to take Ona up on her instructions and censor nothing, even if it wasn't particularly respectful.

Ona gaped at her for a second, then coughed and made a choking noise. Her face and bald head turned redder than Camille's hair, and she leaned forward, propped herself on the sink counter, and wheezed.

Camille stood rooted, convinced this was the big one, that Ona was about to fall out on her and never get up again. Her own pulse hammered in her ears, and then she couldn't breathe right, either.

Unbelievable. I killed her!

Camille started toward her, but Ona rose, and Camille realized the old woman was laughing her ass off. Each giggle came after a wheeze, like Ona hadn't laughed without abandon in years, maybe decades—or longer. "That was perfect," she choked out, wheezing again. "I want more of that from you, Camille. I've always wanted to see more of that spirit." Her laughter slowly died away. "One day very soon, I fear, you'll need it more than ever."

Camille gripped the basin of the sink and stared at Ona. Since the old woman wasn't really dying, maybe Camille should just kill her. She'd probably earn a medal from the Mothers. "You know, I've been practicing every day, trying to open channels without platforms and projective mirrors, and the best I've done is trip a few times and stick my arm down in the floor before it goes solid or closes up or does whatever it does. I'm beginning to think I suck at that, too. You must have some abilities I don't. I think it's time you started telling me more yourself."

"I think it's time I started telling you more about you." Ona wasn't smiling at all now. In fact, she looked a little nervous. "Better than that, I should show you, because truth be told, that's why I came here. And this," she added, pointing to Camille's wooden box of charms, "would be the best place of all to start."

Camille suppressed an urge to grab her box and hug her charms to her chest. She had worked pretty hard on those things, and even though they weren't perfect, they could be salvaged or melted down for use at some later date.

Breathe. Don't be stupid. Those are just pieces of metal, not pets. They can be reforged if she does something weird to them.

It took some effort, but Camille allowed Ona to look in the box. "Tell me, how did you figure out these energy patterns? How did you form the intent of these metal pieces?"

Camille's fingers moved to the bulge in her sweater. "I used the dinar. It enhances projective energy, so I thought I could capture some of those qualities."

Ona rested her fingertips on the charms, just touching, not stirring. "Smart. The coin does what you want, so you modeled your charms after its properties."

Camille gestured to the box. "These charms fell short, but the ones I gave my quad work fairly well."

Ona picked up a few of the bits of metal and let them trickle through her fingers like tiny coins. The look on her face poked at Camille's emotions, because it was loving, or maybe longing. Camille felt guilty for wanting to guard the charms herself, and more than curious about the fact that Ona seemed as respectful of the metal as she was.

"It's been a long time since I handled metals with so few imperfections," Ona said, her admiration ringing in each word. "The design is slightly unbalanced on most of these, just a fraction of imperfection in one axis, east to west—but even with that fault, they would have been impressive if you hadn't used artificial heat to purify them."

Camille glanced at the nearest gas spigot. "You know I don't make fire very well."

"I'm not talking about making fire." Ona released the charms in her palm and let them clink back into the wooden box. "I'm talking about using it, using what the earth gives you."

Camille tried to sort that out but couldn't. "Stop riddling. Tell me plainly what you mean."

Ona got down from her stool, frowning, and for a time she didn't say anything. She kept opening and closing her good eye like she was searching for something in her own mind, but she didn't seem to be able to find it.

"Words can be hard, Camille. The names and terms for what I've seen and even some of what I know how to do—those are long lost, even to me."

Camille thought about herself upstairs, how she couldn't form the syllables to say what she needed to say to her quad when the emotions got too strong. Did Ona really not remember the terms, or had something happened that made it too hard for her to say them out loud?

Ona kept trying for another few moments, but at last, she shook her head. "I can't call them to mind, but I can show you my meaning if you'll accept that as enough."

"Of course I will." Camille scooted the box of charms back from the counter's edge. "Maybe we'll find our own words and names for things—or perhaps you'll remember it in the doing."

Ona considered this but didn't respond. She slipped her hand into the wooden box and, without looking, lifted out a charm that gleamed in the laboratory lights.

"What's this one?"

"Copper."

Ona placed the charm on the lab table beside the box and went after another bit of metal. "And this one?"

Camille smelled the flat tang of the substance even without touching it and said, "Iron."

Ona set the iron charm next to the copper piece, then pushed the whole box to the left, away from them. When she had everything positioned as she wished, she turned her back to the table holding the charms, then stretched out her hand.

Camille stared, trying not to worry that Ona really had gone soft in the mind, but—wait. Something felt different in the air. She smelled . . . smoke. Yes, that was it. She smelled it, but she didn't see any. Was the scent coming from outside, somehow?

Not possible, since the lab was sealed, mostly to protect Mrs. Knight and the rest of the block from noxious fumes and minor lab accidents and explosions.

The smoke smell got stronger, but Camille couldn't see anything other than Ona standing with her hand outstretched. She was so still there wasn't even a flutter in her fingers.

Ona closed her eyes.

A second later, a rush of energy sucked out Camille's breath like she'd been suddenly stuffed into a vacuum.

Light seemed to leap into Ona's hand—streaks of it, shooting straight up and landing directly in her now up-turned palm.

Camille's vision blurred as she staggered forward from the hot, fiery impact, and she had to catch herself on the edge of the table.

What the hell?

No flames—but I smell fire. I feel it everywhere.

Then the energy stopped suddenly, like somebody had snuffed out a match, and Camille gasped for air. The stone floor in front of Ona had that puddle-like look Camille had seen before, always in relation to Ona. The stone grew solid again, and Camille blinked to clear her watering eyes.

When she looked at Ona, Ona was pointing to something.

Two more charms lay on the lab table. They were the exact same shape and size of the iron and copper pieces she had created last year, and, she presumed, they shared all the same projective properties. She reached out with her pyrosentient skills, touching the new charms with her fire energy.

"They're perfect," Camille whispered. "No impurities. No imperfections at all. It's like you shaped them directly from their molten ore, like you took them straight out of the earth."

Ona nodded.

Camille remained enraptured by the charms for another few seconds, then realized the meaning of Ona's answer. "You . . . took them straight out of the earth?"

"I did," Ona said.

"How?" Camille had to fight her urge to grab Ona and hold on tight until she got every bit of this information, until she understood enough to use it herself. "How did you do that?"

Ona glanced at the charms, showing the same longing Camille had seen earlier, but she made no move to touch them. "I asked the fire to give them to me."

Camille glanced all around the room again, convinced one of the machines had to be on, or that she'd missed a tiny blaze Ona had been using somewhere. "What fire?"

"All the fire." Ona said. "It was the fire under the earth's surface that possessed what I needed, so that's the fire that answered when I called. In small measure, you can learn to shield yourself from the exchange of energy so that it doesn't leave you fighting for consciousness for days. In larger measure—" Ona hesitated. "Well, there are no shields large enough for some things."

Camille absolutely couldn't believe what she was hearing. "But how could you possibly communicate with the fire like that?"

Ona frowned. "Ancient channels of communication cross this earth like termite tunnels. They're everywhere. You use the mirrors upstairs, so you know that, Camille."

"But—"

"Those communication channels aren't just for objects and the stray live transport and to throw words back and forth." Ona opened her hands and arms like she was beseeching Camille to understand. "Even if they were just for talking, though, anything with energy has a voice, doesn't it? If you can just—"

"Learn its language," Camille parroted back, the line

so deeply ingrained from her training years that she couldn't have stopped herself from saying it even if she'd wanted to. *Everything with energy has a voice, if you can just learn its language.* A sense of amazement traveled through her, warm and slow, as new meanings for that old axiom opened in her mind. "You *talked* to the fire."

"We talk to fire all the time. Our existence is an endless conversation with everything that burns." Ona's hand lifted toward the charms she made, then lowered to her side again. "That's the truth of us, Camille. The truth of fire Sibyls."

Camille didn't know what to say. The possibilities Ona had just opened for her were enough to cloud her awareness completely, and then Ona asked, "Have you heard it?"

The question sounded wistful, like Ona might be re-membering a lover, or maybe a terrible, all-consuming addiction.

"Have I heard what?" Camille murmured.

"The fire." A little impatience now. Ona's words seemed rushed. "Has the fire spoken to you? When you use your pyrosentience, when you're deeply connected to your el-ement and drawing the flames into your essence, have you heard the roar?"

Camille stood dumbfounded and still for a thump of her own heart, because she *had* heard that before. She had thought she imagined it, or that it was an artifact of the power she was using, something like her own mind's reaction to holding so much fire inside her. Even thinking about it gave her a fresh round of shivers. She had never heard a sound so deep, so endless. It took her away from the real world sometimes. It was . . . almost addictive.

How could it possibly be real?

Yet when Bela had used projective earth energy, and when Dio had used her ventsentience, and even when Andy had made her limited, fearful effort at aquasentience—

hadn't Camille heard them all speak with the voice of their element, with the force of their elemental talent blasting through every word?

It wasn't just a metaphor or an altered perception. When I've heard that, it's been real. The energy has really been there. Right there. Waiting for us to use it.

"If you can hear it, it will come when you call," Ona said. "It will give you all the energy you ask for, and anything else it possesses, like this liquid metal. You just have to ask."

It . . . the fire?

The fire of the world. Camille slowly, slowly grasped that she didn't have to create fire at all. There was plenty to be had, everywhere, all the time. A dizzy madness tried to seize her as she grappled with this idea. She could see herself swimming through great molten pools, plunging into endless rivers and seas of moving fire. Sweet Goddess. She had to shut her eyes to catch hold of her sanity, and when she did, she saw an image of Ona on her eyelids. Ona, small and bald, metal fused into one arm, and so terribly scarred.

Camille opened her eyes and focused on the old woman. Focused on the scars. All the damage—damage from heat and flames that shouldn't have been possible, since Ona was a fire Sibyl.

"It will come when I call," Camille repeated, inventorying all the pain Ona must have suffered when she got those scars. "How much fire are we talking about here?"

"All of it," Ona whispered, her voice so quiet and tremulous Camille wasn't sure she'd really heard that. "If you want." She took a rattling, pained breath. "Or if you make a terrible mistake with consequences you can't begin to imagine."

Tears streamed from one of Ona's eyes, and Camille

realized the tear duct must have been burned from the other eye. She couldn't stand to see anyone hurt like that, so she did the only thing she knew to do, which was reach out. If she could hold Ona, if she could truly understand, maybe she could share Ona's pain and make it less.

For a moment, Ona seemed shocked that someone was trying to touch her. She allowed the embrace, tentatively reached up to return it, then pushed Camille away, shaking her head.

"No," she rasped, looking at the floor and shaking her head. "That's not something you want to do, I promise you."

"Camille?" Andy's voice rang down the hall. "I made some sandwiches if you guys want some. Pistachio paste and salami. And don't say it's gross until you taste it."

Ona looked stricken at the thought of somebody else approaching, and her good eye widened and lost its focus.

Camille knew what Ona was getting ready to do next because she'd done it so many times herself. "Please, wait. Stay. Whatever's hurting you so much, we can work it out."

"Some pains have no balm." Ona's words seemed to flicker across the air, but she was already gone, leaving nothing behind but a ripple in the floor.

Camille just stood there, uncertain, everything inside her a mix and a jumble. An amazing door had been opened—yet slammed shut again before she could even step through it.

The fire.

The fire of the world.

How could her ancestors have walked away from such a connection, such a powerful tool and weapon as speaking fire's language and calling it through them?

The roar of it, the power . . . She couldn't imagine how much she could accomplish if she truly used her abilities like Ona did.

But what had happened to her?

Camille's mind roved over that question, and when she touched on it, she remembered when she herself had drawn fire at the level Ona described. Whenever she'd heard fire speak to her in its volcanic growl—those had to be the times, and each of those times she'd been afraid. Each of those times she'd paid a price, so weak afterward she couldn't even function for a time.

It wasn't just that, though. It was . . . something else.

A sense of enormousness from the energy. A sense of risk.

How much fire are we talking about here?

All of it.

Camille's pulse went fluttery.

Ona hadn't been speaking in hyperbole or metaphor. She'd meant that literally, didn't she? Camille had been too absorbed to realize it, but— *Oh, Goddess.*

Her hands started shaking, and that dry tightness she hated claimed her throat before she could swallow to stop it from happening.

All of it, she mouthed, trying to grasp that, trying to imagine what that would be like, what could happen if she really did do something like that, tap into the world's fire and just let it blast through her, intensified and magnified—

"You okay?"

Bela's voice made Camille jump. She spun toward the sound, and there was Bela, standing beside the first table in her jeans and an NYPD sweatshirt. Her dark hair was pulled back, emphasizing the worry in her wide, dark eyes.

"I—I don't know." Camille immediately stared at the projective charm she had made Bela. Instinct overwhelmed her, and she wanted to snatch it off Bela's neck. It felt unsafe now, just thinking about everything Ona had said.

Could Bela call all the earth energy in the world and break the planet in half? And what about Dio and the wind, Andy and the oceans and seas? Just the thought of so much contact with fire had made Camille half drunk and fuzzy, so much so that she hadn't registered all of Ona's words, or the meaning of them.

Camille's chest got tight, then tighter.

What if the same thing happened to her quad?

Nobody should have charms to enhance their sentient talents. What had she been thinking when she made them? Camille wanted to go to Dio and Andy and demand theirs, and the dinar—shit. Would it melt if she had Bela tunnel to the earth's core, and they dropped it into all the pools and rivers and seas of fire-rock that had been roaring to Camille whenever she had been stupid enough—no, *arrogant* enough—to listen?

Camille's breath got faster and shallower. She couldn't stop looking at Bela's charm. "I'm not sure, but I don't think you should use that anymore." She pointed to the crescent pendant. "I don't think any of us should use anything to magnify our projective abilities."

Bela covered up her charm almost protectively, and Camille knew she wouldn't be surrendering it anytime soon. "Why?"

"I'm not sure about that, either." Camille chewed at her bottom lip, wanting to scream because her words were burning up in her mind before she could speak them clearly. "I just—feel it. That maybe . . . maybe the Mothers have been right, that the energy's too unpredictable and dangerous."

And maybe I've felt all the fire in the world, waiting to come at my call.

God, what could have happened . . .

Bela was staring at her like she was coming unhinged, and maybe she was. "Did something frighten you, Camille?"

A strange laugh burst out of Camille, one she couldn't quite control. "Fuck, yes. Ona did."

Bela came through the lab toward her, and the two of them sat down in rolling chairs by the back table and sink. Camille explained as best she could what Ona had done with the metals, what she'd shown Camille, and what she'd said. When Camille was finished, Bela looked rattled.

"She couldn't have been serious," Bela said, but Camille heard the doubt in Bela's voice. Maybe Bela had been hearing her own roaring, the voice of the earth, tempting her to do something beyond devastating.

"I think she was." Camille tried to keep her voice steady, but she heard the tremor in her words.

Bela usually picked up on stuff like that, but not today. She was too tied up in trying to think it through and find a solution, like most mortars tended to do. "Dio's been scouring the Motherhouse Greece archives about projective energy again, and there's nothing much, and sure as hell nothing like this. Are you sure Ona's not just shilling for the Mothers, trying to freak us out?"

Camille shook her head. "No way. I think she'd put out her one good eye before she did anything the Mothers wanted her to do. I think the problem is, the information is too old. The archives may not have anything about true and full uses of sentient talents, since the Sibyls have been breeding away from them since the Dark Crescent Sisterhood has existed as a formal organization."

This made Bela swear for a few seconds, close her eyes, and press her hands against her cheeks like she was trying to keep her skull in one piece. "Can you get Ona to come back?"

"Not if she doesn't want to." Camille glanced at the

spot where Ona had disappeared. "Whatever happened way back when, it scarred her insides as badly as her outsides, or maybe worse. Even showing me such a little bit and trying to discuss it made her run like hell. It may be a while before we see her again, if we do."

Bela's eyes roved over Camille's periodic tables, lingering on each color like they had meditative properties. "Then how can we find out?"

Camille didn't think she needed more information. She was sure of what her instincts were telling her, but before she could ask Bela and Dio and Andy to give up their charms, she knew she should offer them more proof.

But how could she? Who could—

Wait a minute.

Camille put her hand on Bela's wrist. "Maybe, if she's willing, Dio could ask Jake Lowell and the Astaroth demons?"

Bela looked thoughtful. "That's right. They have vestigial memories—and Merilee Lowell's always talking about the archives her husband and his kind have in that place that's not really in this plane of existence."

"Dio might not be able to go there, but Jake or his friends could have a look for us."

Bela patted Camille's hand and seemed very, very relieved. "I'll ask her. And the reason I came down here was to tell you tonight's trip to the docks is off. Riana's group is going to take our patrol so we can get some extra sleep." Bela glanced over her shoulder in the general direction of Camille's bedroom. "Thought you might appreciate some . . . um, spare time."

(19)

John felt like the luckiest man in the universe, out on a real date with this more-than-real woman. He couldn't even remember the last time he'd put on dress clothes, even if he couldn't quite do the suit. Camille had chosen a hot little winter-white number with killer cleavage. It hugged her just right, and she'd let all that auburn hair fall loose across her shoulders, chest, and back.

He'd hailed a cab for them, even though he really wanted to strut up and down Broadway with her on his arm, showing her off to anybody who'd look—and plenty would have. When they got out at 43 West Sixty-fifth, he felt almost underdressed in his black slacks and sport jacket, but then, that would always be an issue with Camille, wouldn't it? She could make a pair of jeans and a sweater look like runway fashion, in his opinion.

As it was, they opted for Chinese and he went upscale, taking her to Shun Lee West at Lincoln Center. Nothing screamed *You're worth it, baby*, like alabaster monkeys at the bar and giant golden dragons in the gold, white, and black dining area. The place was packed, but John paid heavy for a corner table, which afforded them a tiny bit of privacy.

"Ginger and lemon," she said when he escorted her to the table, his arm linked through hers, just like he wanted to do. "Mmmmm. I *love* Chinese food."

That alone was enough to convince John that they were basically compatible. He'd never gotten on with people who weren't up for a midnight egg roll run.

After they were seated, he couldn't stop himself from

staring at her, and she stared right back at him. The table was small, but it seemed too large, holding them apart with its whiter-than-white linens.

"It's been a long time since I've been on a date, beautiful." He just couldn't quit looking at her. "I can't remember the last time."

"All work and no play makes John a dull boy." Camille played with the edge of her napkin.

John shook his head once, slowly. "Ah, that's Jack. Makes Jack a dull boy, and yes, actually, he is. But you said we're not talking about Jack Blackmore or demons or anything to do with work, right?"

"Right." A smile. He never wanted it to go away.

"Good."

"So," she said, nervous tension adding tight lines to her pretty face.

John understood her hesitance. With work off the table, he had no idea what to talk about, either. Except maybe how much he wanted to make love to her, and how beautiful her eyes were, and the fact he really liked it when she left her hair down.

"You know, I really haven't done much but work myself." Camille finally broke eye contact and moved her napkin to her lap. "Not since the first time I left the Motherhouse and started fighting. I can carry on a mean conversation about oiling swords, making explosives, refining and casting metal—not, um, very feminine, is it?"

"It's perfect." John handled his own napkin, but he kept his eyes on her like she might vanish if he looked away. "Especially the explosives part. Nitroaromatics or plastics?"

Camille's pretty smile took on a wicked edge John liked equally well. "Plastics are better for mission work, but myself, I go for lead azide. I can keep it stable with elemental containment long enough to blow something to Mars—just not very long. I can't transport it very far."

She likes to blow shit up. I really think I'm in love with this woman.

The waiter came. John ordered spring rolls, dumplings, wontons, and baby littleneck clams with black bean sauce, and Camille said, "Hungry?"

He was about to explain that he hadn't had really good Chinese in about as long as it had been since he had a date when she added, "Because if you are, you really should order something for yourself, too."

At that point, John relaxed on a whole new level, ordered more appetizers, and told the waiter they would choose a main course after they finished.

When the waiter brought the appetizers, they dug in, and John couldn't keep himself from feeding her a few bites of spring roll. She let him, her aquamarine eyes dazzling against the gold-and-white backdrop.

"It's nice to go out with a woman who's not afraid to eat," he murmured, trying not to get overly caught up in the petal-soft touch of her lips on his fingers.

She polished off the last bite of spring roll without a blush or cough, then went searching for a sparerib. "It's nice to go out with a guy who doesn't look at me funny when I do."

"Not that I wish you had, but . . . why is it that you haven't been dating? Half the men in New York City would be showing up at your door with flowers if you'd let them."

Camille gestured to the wasteland of devastated appetizers between them. "I'm expensive. They're afraid I'll eat myself short and fat and wrinkled like Mother Keara."

He waited her out.

She realized what he was doing and rolled her eyes. "Okay, okay. I haven't been dating because I was afraid that would cause too many complications. My quad has been struggling to keep rhythm with each other, and New York City is still down a lot of Sibyls. We've got a lot on us, and I didn't want to add more."

John watched her carefully, searching for any sign he was missing part of her message, then decided just to ask her outright. "Am I some of that *more*? More stress? Be honest."

"Yes and no." She took a sip of her water, then let the glass slide slowly to the table as she held his gaze. "You're an amazing fighter and a good man." Then she realized what he might really be asking, and she answered that, too, reaching out to brush his hair across his forehead. "You're not a burden on our unit, John, and I can't imagine you ever would be. You're . . . another change. A risk. But I think you're a good one."

That answer made him unreasonably happy, but he didn't want to start grinning at everything like some stupid little boy. It was hard with her, though. She brought out the grins. "How do your girls feel about me as a risk?"

Camille fiddled with the last sparerib like she was counting. "One yes vote so far, and two maybes. And don't ask me to name names."

Better than three fuck-no's, at least. "What can I do to make it easier?"

"You don't have to do anything except be patient with me." She smiled, but the look in her eyes suggested she was serious. John could figure that. What did Camille do that required patience? He hadn't seen anything.

He realized that in the past, that kind of comment from a woman would have made him nervous. Coming from her, it just intrigued him.

"I'll be patient," he said, making it a promise.

She pointed her sparerib bone at his nose. "And don't start acting like a macho asshole."

John considered this, then conceded it with a shrug.

"I'll let Jack handle that job. He's good at the whole asshole thing."

Camille finally surrendered her sparerib bone, and the plate between them was completely empty except for the nonedibles. "I'm the one who has been adding more stress to the quad, not you. That fit I threw with Maggie—then bringing Ona into the mix."

She looked troubled, then deeply worried, and John was about to ask her what was wrong when the waiter came back again. The guy stared at their plates like they were both animals, but he cleaned up the mess and took their order without so much as a crosswise look. John let him get about three steps from the table before he locked eyes with Camille and said, "Okay, talk. That look's worrying me."

She looked away from him, then down at her hands. "It's about work."

Thank God. "Okay."

After a long, long, long pause, Camille said, "I'm not a typical fire Sibyl."

"Yeah, I got that much when I was living in Duncan's head. So? You've found other ways to fight." The restaurant seemed to be growing more distant now, the whites a little less bright, the tangy scents a little more dull. The universe was drilling down to Camille in John's head, and he was just fine with that.

Camille pulled her napkin out of her lap and twisted one of the edges, keeping her focus on the cloth. "None of us has the normal, expected talents Sibyls are supposed to have, except maybe Andy, and she's so new to everything, she doesn't even know what she can do and neither do we."

John thought about this, and offered what observation he could make. "You're all getting better at that different sort of stuff you do. The dinar, the charms—you're working it out."

"That's just it." She put the napkin down and raised her eyes to his, and he figured they were getting to it now. "I've been thinking of the charms like plastics or dynamite. Things I do that normal fire Sibyls don't. Things to make me stronger. Explosive, yeah, but pretty stable and safe if you know what you're doing. But John, those charms I made for Bela and Dio and Andy, what if they're not stable, even with careful use? What if they're lead azide—or worse?"

The food came, and the waiter placed it in front of them with a broad smile, waiting until John nodded for him to leave. He wanted to shove the guy away, but he could tell from the look on Camille's face that it was too late. The thread had been broken, at least for the moment, and her attention was captured completely by her food. She looked like a little kid sitting down to a Christmas feast, and he thought that was pretty cute.

John had gone for the Beijing duck, which was strong in a just-right way, even if it bugged him a little that the duck's head came cooked along with everything else, bill and all. He'd gotten used to stuff like that overseas. Camille had steered Cantonese and ordered the Grand Marnier prawns with honey walnuts—which, thank God, didn't get served with the little bobbling eye stalks or anything. Even John had his limits.

For a few minutes they chowed, and then she started picking at her broccoli and the rich, dark nuts, the rose on her plate brushing the light, soft skin of her hand. Whatever it was she was trying to say involving the atypical abilities and the lead azide metaphor, it was pretty important to her, he could tell.

"Imagine if you had some guys who were great soldiers," she said, "maybe the strongest soldiers in the unit, except they couldn't shoot as well as everybody else."

John scooted his duck head out of his direct line of sight. "Okay, yeah, I'm following you."

"You make them special guns that do the targeting for them, and the guns work. They really work." She looked up at him and smiled, and he thought this part of the story was real, maybe exactly what had happened, only with energy charms instead of other hardware. "All of a sudden they're not only just as good as everybody else, they're better. They even get to try the guns out in a few battles, and they kick ass and take names and make a gigantic difference."

She stopped. Waited. He didn't look at the duck head, and he added up her meaning, summarizing an old commander's words. "By giving them the special guns, you made them relevant."

Her expression brightened. "Relevant. Yes. Good word. *Great* word." She put down her fork. "Then in a practice session, one of the guns malfunctions, and you realize those weapons could go bad in a firefight and shoot everyone in a ten-mile radius, friend or foe. What do you do next?"

John felt the weight of the scenario, and he could imagine it in so many different ways: as a soldier himself, and as a commander, and as a man who had struggled for many years to find his own relevance. "It sucks, but you don't have a lot of choices. You have to retire the guns and go back to the drawing board on the design."

She winced, and her frown made his chest hurt. "What if the technology's faulty at base? What if it's lead azide and can't be stabilized no matter what you do?"

John's heart sank for Camille. "Then you have to take the guns away forever."

"And make the men, make my quad, who they used to be. Who we all used to be. The less-thans. The ones who struggle, who can't be as good as everybody else." She hesitated, spreading her fingers out on either side of her plate. "When I do that, I make us irrelevant again."

John's training and experience kicked in, and he spoke to her like an officer. "That's up to the squad. To its leader, its cohesion, and its initiative and ideas. Lack of skill in one area doesn't make any group a failure—hell, look at how strong your group was even before you made those charms."

Camille gazed at him for a few seconds, then nodded. "I hear that, and I'm sure you're right. Maybe the truth of this is, I feel like a bitch because I opened a door and now I might have to slam it closed. Even though I know it's the right thing, the safest thing, I don't want to do it. I don't want to go back to being . . . broken."

John couldn't quite believe he'd heard that. "There's nothing about you that's broken. Not a thing."

She closed her eyes. "Please don't tell me how everybody has different strengths and weaknesses. That's just bullshit."

"It's not, but I won't." He waited for her to look at him again, and he made sure to think through the next words pretty carefully. "That thing you do with the fire—how you explore objects and track things with your energy, and how you can pull fire through you to do stuff like you did when you gave me this body—don't you think that's important? There's got to be a reason you have that skill, and there's got to be a way to use it safely."

Camille finally went back to eating, a few little bites, and then she came up with, "If pyrosentience was so important, the fire Sibyl Mothers wouldn't have bred for stronger pyrogenesis instead. They think it's pretty useless and as unstable as any primary explosive."

"Maybe they don't think it's useless." John finally surrendered and put his napkin over the duck head. "Maybe it scares the hell out of them."

"You're an optimist."

"Never thought anybody would say that to me." He

knew he was grinning now, and he was starting not to worry about it. "You have a strange effect on me, beautiful."

"Yeah, well, that's mutual."

"Is it?"

"Yes."

God, he loved her straightforward answers. If she'd been the kind of woman to play coy, he'd have worked through it, but he was glad he didn't have to.

He lowered his voice just enough to be sure nobody else could hear them. "When I make love to you, will you light me on fire?"

"I'm not that kind of girl."

Why did she sound sad when she said that? So much about her he needed to learn. He hoped she gave him time to figure everything out. For now, he settled for something simple and relatively safe. "You want dessert?"

"Yes." She put down her fork again, and this time she put her napkin on her plate. "But not here."

John stood up so fast his chair went flying. It took him a second to realize he probably looked like an idiot for that and for waving for the waiter—and really, he didn't even care.

(20)

She liked walking with him. She liked talking with him. A cab would have been faster, but this light, slow stroll—it was its own kind of foreplay.

Camille had never felt so alive and powerful, hand in hand with John, buildings towering all around them, the city moving, moving, and them drifting through the nighttime lights and whirlwind chaos like they were the only people on the planet. He looked only at her, smiled just to her, talked to nobody but her, and she felt like everything to him. To this man who had been in her life for such a short time. This man with a wild, raging demon in his mind.

John was a risk. The perfect risk.

Camille really, really, really liked kissing him, even on the sidewalk with cars and buses and cabs whizzing by so fast the cold drafts made her hair blow. "You taste like duck and green tea with a hint of wonton," she told him after the third time he pulled her to him and pressed his lips against hers. "I could eat you up."

The next kiss came naturally, and the one after that, and the one after that, and all the while they were making progress toward the brownstone, not too fast, not too slow—just right. Camille thought she might be able to kiss this man forever, nipping his lips, brushing his tongue with hers, loving the way he moved his mouth, then found the line of her jaw, her ear. Not insistent. Not overbearing or way out of line. Just . . . teasing. Letting her know what she could have, whenever she wanted it.

They needed to get home soon. Still five or six blocks

away, though. Maybe the cab wouldn't have been such a bad idea.

When she put some space between them, he let her, though he kept stroking her arm as they walked. The contact kept her relaxed in some ways and increasingly tense in others. It was getting hard to think about words and walking and not running into lampposts.

Another kiss. Just one more. It wasn't enough anymore, but Camille found herself pulling back yet again after just a taste, staring at him and letting him stare at her.

Was it possible that they were running out of words?

Lots of ways to communicate . . .

The heat between them felt like the flames in her heart, the fire she could never quite make, and she wanted to touch it, hold it, let it wrap her in a never-ending inferno.

"Home now?" he asked, his voice husky. "As fast as we can get there?"

"Yes."

They made it about half a block farther before the mark on Camille's forearm heated up at the same time the dinar she had tucked in her underwear went off like some kind of ancient, perverted vibrator.

She startled, slapping her free hand against her hip, feeling the message hurtle through both sources, except it wasn't a targeted communication. No. Her tattoo's elemental paints and the dinar's projective metal were reacting to elemental energy, and very powerful stuff. It had struck Camille like a targeted bolt, like a shot across the bow.

Like a warning.

John let go of her hand and looked around. His nostrils flared like he was catching a strange scent. "Something's off. Wrong. Do you—"

He broke off when he saw her reaching under her dress and fishing out the dinar. She slipped the chain over her head and let the coin fall against her cleavage, then rammed her hand in her bra to get hold of her small dagger and one of the throwing knives Dio had loaned her. People moved past them on the sidewalk, so she kept the blades palmed and out of sight as best she could.

"Are you armed?" she asked John, heart racing, looking left, then right, homing in on the direction they needed to go to follow the energy trace.

"Always." He tipped his hand toward his left leg, where she saw the bulge of a holster under his slacks.

She gestured toward a side street. "This way. Go beside me. With just two of us, that's the best way to approach an elemental threat. I'll use my energy to shield you from an energy attack."

John didn't make a single macho bullshit argument against that, and she added up points in his favor for it. He fell in beside her as she used her tattoo to send a quick message home along with one to OCU headquarters asking for Sibyl and officer support. Then she led John in the direction of the disturbance—though she had a sense he'd be able to find it himself if she gave him a little time to search. He was still sniffing the air, using some of Strada's leftover superior senses.

Camille couldn't see the trace from that energy pulse, but she could feel it prickling across her skin like a thousand straight pins. Her pyrosentient talent, unenhanced, crackled at full mast. Her instincts and the ambient fire in the air led them to a brownstone, not as fancy as the one where they lived, but nice, with ten steps up, long narrow windows, and, weirdly, black curtains.

She reached out with her senses and searched the space in front of and immediately surrounding the brownstone. Nothing. All clean, so this was isolated to the building in front of them.

"You picking up any of those elemental locks?" John asked. "I don't want to get cold-cocked when I step on the stairs."

"No barriers that I can sense, but there should be." Camille checked one more time, but she still didn't pick up any protections. "What hit us, that was a lot of energy, well managed—and I think it got thrown at us on purpose. I'm sure whoever did it has the capacity to make elemental barriers."

"So . . . maybe they want us to come in?"

As Camille stared at the brownstone, one of the black curtains slid slowly to the side. The movement brought her pulse pounding into her ears. "John?"

He got closer. "I see her."

Female. Early twenties. Slight features, almost, like an Irish fae, one of the Seelie court. Blond hair, blue eyes. The girl was so pale Camille wondered if she had seen the sun in the last ten years.

"Hostage?" he asked, bending slowly toward his holster.

"No assumptions. She could grow wings and fangs and knock down half the building—and I'm thinking she might, because I don't sense . . . anything. Not even any life energy. You? What do those cat senses tell you?"

John made a face without taking his eyes off the building or the girl in the window. "The place smells like a gas leak. Like rotten eggs."

A shadow passed behind the girl.

She mouthed, "Help me—"

And she disappeared so fast Camille thought she might have been yanked out of the window.

John drew his Glock.

Camille palmed her dagger.

John nodded, and the two of them ran up the stairs.

John knocked and told a great big lie. "NYPD. Open the door."

Nothing.

He grimaced at Camille. "Backup?"

Her heartbeat and breathing had gone steady, and her

thoughts felt clear and focused, like the tip of a knife. "Ten minutes, give or take."

Somebody inside the brownstone screamed. The sound gripped Camille's insides, making her breath come sharp and fast.

John reared back to give the door a kick, but Camille shook her head. "Move. Get out of my way."

He immediately stepped to the side as she put one hand on the dinar and the other on the door. Second nature now, after all her practice. She pulled at the fire energy around her, brought it into herself, then blasted it back out with all the force of her fear and worry for the girl inside the house.

A huge fist of fire energy bashed against the door and blew it off its hinges. The wood cracked as it smashed against the stairs to the right of the foyer, and the boards smoked and smoldered.

Didn't even make my knees wobble. I'm getting better at this.

"Better than plastics," John told her as he went in, weapon ready. "Gotta love a woman who makes shit explode."

"Yeah, yeah. Just shoot the bad guys." She was right behind him, dagger raised.

From the foyer, he said, "Nothing."

Camille followed him, then split left where he went right. She opened doors, or knocked them down. Main room empty. "Clear," she said. Her heart was thumping against her ribs.

Where was the girl?

John, from what looked like the formal dining room, echoed with a quick "Clear."

He eased down the hall, weapon ready to fire. Camille pitched streamlined fire energy north, south, east, and west, searching for life or abnormal signatures.

Nothing. That made no sense at all.

They hit the stairs next, with John leading. She kept second position, because that's where she worked best when she only had little blades.

When they reached the landing, a weak life sign caught Camille's attention. "Left. Second door."

They took positions on either side of the door, and this time Camille let John kick it in. They spilled inside what looked like a bedroom with twin beds and a small two-seater couch.

Camille heard herself breathing hard. She was pumped for anything.

The girl was sitting on the couch, just staring at them. She didn't seem injured or distressed. She seemed to be waiting for them, and something in her bright blue eyes, in the way her mouth was set as she stared at the two of them, made Camille feel like the girl really was waiting for *them* specifically.

But why didn't the girl feel more alive? The signal Camille was sensing—the girl might as well have been a housecat or a parakeet.

"You're not worth much as warriors," the girl said, and her voice was flat and quiet but creepily eager. "I would have been dead if somebody wanted to hurt me."

"Who are you?" Camille asked.

The girl kept studying her like she was a lab specimen. "Why can't you make fire like the others? And where are your leathers? Oh, wait. I get it. A date? How . . . sweet."

To John, the girl said, "I told them you were back, but nobody believed me."

Footsteps clattered in the downstairs hallway. Camille reached toward the sound with her energy. No life signature. Nothing at all.

"Not one of ours, John."

The footsteps ran back to the stairs and started up.

John leveled his weapon at the bedroom door just as a

blond man topped the stairs and hurled himself into the room.

The girl waved her hand and Camille's dagger tore out of her fingers and buried itself in a wall across the room. John's Glock flew out of his hands and smashed against the same wall, firing wild and taking a chunk out of the door next to the man's head.

"What the hell?" John tried to go for his gun, but the girl kept her hand up. Camille felt a dense crawl of power, mingled elements, indistinct but enough to hold a human. Enough to hold a lot of humans.

What is that? What is she?

Camille could move enough to get a good fix on the guy. He had on jeans and a black sweatshirt, and he was wearing a necklace that looked like a long, hooked tooth.

The energy from that necklace was wrong.

"What the hell are you doing, Becca?" The man's voice sounded gruff. Angry, but not panicked.

"Showing you." The girl pointed to John. "What do you say now?"

The blond whirled to look at John and stepped back. His jaw seemed to loosen. "You—how—"

"I'm not who you think I am," John started to say, but the girl raised her other hand and he stopped making coherent sounds. Then John's eyes bulged. He grabbed the sides of his head, his mouth came open, and he let out a long, guttural yell of pain.

Camille's heart crushed inward. She lunged toward John, but she couldn't move outside of a tiny square. The dark, twisted energy all around her felt like ten-foot sheets of metal.

No. No!

John's fingers were growing.

His teeth extended.

White fur bristled from his cheeks and neck.

His eyes, furious, agonized—she couldn't stand it.

Camille swore and grabbed the dinar with both hands. She jerked fire, a lot of it, power and flames and heat, and she blasted it against the energy trying to contain her. The two energies met with a thunder crack—and the dark energy shattered.

The girl on the couch screeched like she'd been punched in the gut.

Camille threw herself at the man instead of the girl, acting on instinct, ripping that tooth necklace away from his neck. The second she touched it, the bleak, suffocating energy that plastered against her skin, her face, her mind almost made her vomit. It was so dark and twisted. Not Rakshasa. Almost worse. No, definitely worse.

And then it vanished.

The girl lowered her hand and fingered her own necklace. A tooth, just like the one Camille held. The girl looked furious, but she didn't show a hint of fear.

Camille squeezed the big tooth tight in her hand. *Whatever power's coming off this thing, it's blocking her.*

The blond man came toward Camille. From the corner of Camille's eye, she saw John regaining control, but still feigning like he was shifting into a demon. He was easing toward his Glock, which had landed about five feet from the man, who was now completely focused on Camille.

John reached the firearm.

"You shouldn't take what's not yours, honey." The man held out his hand, wiggling his fingers for the necklace—and John snatched the gun from the floor and clubbed him in the head so hard with the pistol grip the guy went staggering straight out of the room. Camille heard the thump and bang of him hitting the stairs and heading down the hard way.

The girl shrieked and her hands raised again, but Camille held up the tooth and whatever energy the girl had pitched at them ricocheted. It knocked her back to the sofa and she sat there gagging and glaring and still trying—something.

Some kind of projective energy this time.

The second it touched her, Camille knew what the energy was, but it was perverted, and didn't have a solid base in any one of the four elements. The tooth dispersed it.

"Knock it off," Camille told her, getting a grip on her dinar to see what she could do to contain this—this whatever she was. "I won't hurt you if you stop."

"Tiger," John told her, shaking his head and rubbing his neck. "Not her. The necklaces. They're made out of Rakshasa teeth. I think they're queering what I can sense about this place, about them."

The girl pointed both hands at the floor and blasted more energy through her fingertips.

Camille sent a shot of elemental energy back at her, and that's when the floor dissolved.

She and John fell so fast, Camille didn't even hear her own scream. Down. Straight down. Into pitch-darkness.

She hit the ground on her feet, letting her knees give to absorb the impact. The tooth necklace was still gripped in her right hand, and she managed to get out Dio's throwing knife with her left as she got her balance and coughed from the stench.

Of sulfur.

"Basement," John called. He had landed even better than she did, standing straight up in the middle of the room, but Camille couldn't answer him. Her words wouldn't work. Her brain wouldn't work, or her heart, or her breathing.

This couldn't be a nightmare, but it was. It was her nightmare, right here and now.

They were hulking behind John in the shadows. Three of them. Huge. Biggest she had ever seen. Giant, shifting clay-like faces gaped at her, maws open. Eyes like hell pits glared through the darkness. Blue and green fire dribbled out of their open mouths, out of their ears, out of their noses.

Asmodai, she tried to yell before it happened again, before the killing machines stole another precious life from her.

Nothing came out.

Damnit!

"Asmodai," she croaked, raising Dio's throwing knife in her shaking hand and trying to aim it. "Fire Asmodai, behind you!"

(21)

Asmodai.

John processed the word as he jumped toward Camille.

Legion demons. Made out of elements. Targeted with trash or other personal possessions. The things Camille had nightmares about.

John reached her in two leaps. If he'd had a human body, he probably would have broken both ankles in the initial fall, but thanks to Strada's abilities and Ben's training, he had landed like a pro, and now he had no problem putting himself between Camille and the monsters he hadn't gotten a good look at yet.

When he did, they made his gut churn.

Mountainous. Amorphous. Wearing human clothing, but that shifted and blended, unstable, like somebody kept erasing and redrawing it. Features and gender—those changed, too. Fire came out of every opening, and they stank something godawful. His eyes watered. Rotten eggs. Rotten eggs blown up and left in the sun.

Camille had pulled out one of Dio's throwing knives. The nearest Asmodai grabbed for her, but she dodged and hurled the wicked blade straight at the demon. The thing belched fire all over her, and the dagger went wide of its target.

The flames didn't hurt Camille, though her dress burned to nothing in three seconds flat.

"Step back," he said, and she did, and John put two rounds in the big bastard's head. He didn't waste time with the other two, drilling the next one three times in the chest, and catching the last one right between its shifting, ugly eyes.

A bomb went off in the basement then, or something like it.

Camille grabbed John and plastered herself against his chest, wrapping her arms around his neck as triple-strong waves of green, infected fire crackled and growled over both of them. John realized she was shielding him from demon fallout, or whatever he was supposed to call the release of perverted energy when Asmodai bit the dust.

Hair burned—his hair, at the tips. And his jacket and slacks smoked as she patted out what was left of the flames.

A lot of yelling kicked up outside, and John heard the distinct tones and rhythms of a police unit making entry and checking rooms upstairs. Two seconds later, three women in leather came crashing into the basement, weapons drawn. Two had on zipped face masks. The third, Maggie Cregan, landed front and center, with that big executioner's sword flaming over her head. It lurched in her hands, pointing first at John, then at Camille, then back to John. It wanted to come for him—for them—but Maggie controlled it.

Barely.

John realized Camille was shaking all over, soot-streaked and wide-eyed and naked except for the smoldering threads of her once-beautiful dress. He holstered his weapon and yanked off his jacket, and she let him slip it over her arms and fasten it like some weird-looking giant cloak.

"It's okay. We got this." He squeezed her forearm to bring her back to the here and now. "We did it."

Her eyes cleared a fraction, enough for her to focus on him, and she said, "You did it." Her expression reflected relief and misery at the same time.

"I'd have been cooked without you. Literally." He wouldn't back down on that or let her minimize it. "This was a team operation."

"Clear!" Maggie called up through the ruined basement ceiling. The stairs behind her had been burned down to the studs, too, and above their heads, a hole gaped in the floor leading to the kitchen at the back of the house, and higher, to the bedroom where the girl had been.

On the ground-level floor, four men in NYPD riot gear peered down at them. Maggie and the two other East Ranger fighters gave them a thumbs-up.

"If you find a blond-headed girl or blond-headed man, surround them and call for Sibyl backup," Camille shouted. "Do *not* attempt approach."

"Understood," said one of the officers, who got on his radio to spread the word.

Camille's expression was flat and unreadable as she turned away from John to face Maggie. The flame light from Maggie's sword played off her auburn hair, and the strange lighting made the other two members of the East Ranger group on her left and right seem to flicker in and out of existence.

"Fire Asmodai," Camille reported. "Three of them."

"Asmodai," Maggie said, sounding incredulous. The flames on her sword went out, and she sheathed the monstrous thing. John kept an eye on it anyway, because he sensed it wanting to tear out of its leather prison and get another bite of him.

Sheila Gray pulled off her face mask and kicked a pile of stinking, smoking ash. "I never wanted to see another one of these bastards."

"Are you sure they were Asmodai?" Karin Maros asked as she pulled off her mask, letting her brown hair free. John didn't think she was questioning Camille the way Maggie had done. It was more like she was hoping

Camille would take it back so she wouldn't have to add the demons to her crap-to-worry-about list.

A small commotion ensued upstairs. John thought about drawing his Glock, but right about then, he heard Dio tell somebody, "Back off before I blow you to Jersey."

"Camille?" Bela dropped into the basement between the East Ranger group and where Camille and John were standing. She ran to Camille, catching her up in her arms and holding on tight. "You okay?"

"I'm fine." Camille's voice came out muffled by Bela's leather-clad shoulder. "But how the hell did you get here so fast?"

Dio dropped down next, and the East Ranger group backed up a step to give her room. "We flew," she said as Bela turned Camille loose. "Andy's outside puking. She says she's never riding a fucking tornado again."

"That was risky," Karin said. "Making funnels in town where everyone could see."

Dio's glare was clearly visible in the low lighting. "Back off. When it's one of yours, let's see what you do."

Karin held up both hands. "Okay, okay."

"And, uh, thanks for getting here." Dio directed that to all three of them, giving them each a nod.

"No problem." Maggie had her hand on the hilt of her sword, and John could tell she was trying to keep the thing under control. "Hey!" she called to the OCU officers trundling above them. "Can we get some rope down here?"

By the time John had given his report to the OCU officers in charge and helped mark off the scene, Camille was long gone, back to the brownstone.

He was glad.

She was healthy and safe, probably needed a shower

and some rest. What she didn't need, he was now deeply certain, was him.

He stood in the ruins of the house near the kitchen, staring around as OCU crime scene techs catalogued and measured everything worth attention. Three OCU officers in NYPD uniforms formed a line outside, keeping the scene secure, though nobody on the street seemed to have any interest in coming inside. This would probably be passed off as a water heater explosion or some other understandable disaster—and people would let that happen, because way down inside, they understood that not knowing was better than knowing.

John got that. He really did, especially now.

Duncan and two big dark-headed men were still giving some instructions, moving around and pointing at burn marks and broken furniture. Creed and Nick Lowell were the big guys, twins and officers, and Curson demons who had learned to contain their supernatural aspects. They had been giving John a few lessons—not that he'd learned much, judging by tonight's near disaster.

"You squared away?" Nick, the brother with shorter hair, came over to where John was—what? Investigating? Killing time because he didn't want to go back to the brownstone and face what he needed to face?

"I'm fine." John forced a smile. "This wasn't my first demon fight. Unless Blackjack starts some shit about me not being official yet, it's all good."

"Blackmore won't say anything," Nick assured him. "Guy's a lot more mellow since he got back from the Motherhouses."

Duncan and Creed joined them. Creed was shaking his head as he studied the big-ass hole in the floors. "The girl who did this—what's your take?"

"Never encountered anything like her." John looked away from the brothers as he spoke, feeling something like shame over what the little witch had been able to do to him. "The energy she used, it was powerful. Reminded me of the stuff that comes out of those mirrors the Sibyls use to communicate."

And it nearly stripped me down to nothing but demon in five seconds flat.

He had thought he was better than that. Stronger. Safer. But maybe he'd never been all that safe and in control. Maybe he'd just been arrogant, refusing to recognize what a huge risk he posed to Camille.

Nick gave a low grumble. "Too powerful for a human pushing the elements around. I have an idea who she was. I think that was Rebecca Kincaid, and the man who showed up had to be Samuel Griffen, her half-brother."

John recognized the names at a lot of levels—the papers Dio had printed for him, his memories from living in Duncan's head, and Strada's own recall. He focused on Nick. "Griffen's the sorcerer who runs the Coven, which helps the Rakshasa. You had to fight him and his people last year, when you first took on Strada and his boys."

"When we hunted for them and didn't find any hint of them, my wife swore they couldn't be completely human, not if they were evading the Sibyls so completely." Duncan frowned at the devastated trap-house. "I think all the Sibyls believe that."

"She wasn't human," John said. "Powerful as hell, but I can't tell you much more. I haven't learned enough about all this body's extra talents to get much deeper than surface smells and appearances, basic energy sensing and stuff."

He rubbed his hand across the back of his neck as the brothers exchanged glances. As if by some preordained agreement, Creed and Duncan headed off to speak to one of the techs while Nick stayed behind and studied John.

"You doing all right with Camille? I know this whole

fire Sibyl thing can be a little daunting." Nick's grin was friendly. "Nobody knows that better than me. I'm still amazed I survived dating Cynda, but she was more than worth it."

"Camille's great. She's everything any man could want, and more." John almost groaned saying that out loud, but it also felt good to put it into words to somebody else. "That's the problem, see? I'm not a man. Not anymore. I got a teeth-kicking reminder of that tonight."

Nick paused, looking thoughtful. "Whatever that girl did, she almost changed you against your will. You felt like you were going to lose control."

John wanted to punch something, like a wall, but he held himself back because this was a paranormal crime scene. Big fist holes in the wall wouldn't help anything. "Yeah. That's about the size of it."

"We've all been there, my brothers and me, and Duncan, too." Nick took on a faint golden glow, and John's instincts sensed the Curson presence lurking inside him. "We know how that feels, and it sucks."

"So, what, you overcame it, Duncan overcame it, and so can I?" John really wanted to hit something now, maybe Nick instead of a wall. He'd shift, John would shift, and John would probably lose the fight. Suicide by demon. New concept.

"I don't know if you can get past it or not," Nick said, at least being honest. "That'll depend on you and how bad you want to conquer it. When you decide, let me know, but for now, I am going to tell you one thing, even though it's probably out of line."

John's fists ached from clenching, and when he answered, the word came out more like a growl. "What?"

"Go home." Nick pointed toward the brownstone.

John's clenched jaw went loose from surprise. "Are you nuts? I can't. Not after—"

"Go home to Camille." Nick's expression was earnest and his gaze didn't waver. "The two of you, you'll figure it out, but you need to do it together."

John didn't answer. Nothing that he wanted to say would have been friendly. The battered house seemed to creak all around them, stinking like rotten eggs each time a breeze blew. The sounds of officers walking and talking in the background seemed muffled and distant.

Nick leaned in a little closer, crowding John enough to make him pull back. "She's a fire Sibyl. Powerful, brilliant—and loyal to her last breath. Go home, John, or you'll regret it the rest of your life, but the worst part is, so will she."

22

Camille paced the lab, beyond glad Ona hadn't shown back up and that her quad had the good sense to give her space right now. The tiger tooth necklace she had taken from the scene of the demolished house had been placed in the smallest elemental stasis chamber on Bela's tables for Bela to tackle later, when she'd had some rest. For now, though, the space belonged to Camille.

The cool, antiseptic darkness of the basement was what she needed, what she had to have, to keep from collapsing in on herself.

Asmodai. Fucking Asmodai, of all things. And that girl, what the hell was she? The smell of sulfur was still stuck in Camille's nose even after a long, hot shower.

And John wasn't home yet.

Camille knew it would take time, him giving his statement and walking Creed and Nick through everything that went down, but he should have been home. Camille shivered in her green cotton sweats. Comfort clothes, for all the good they were doing.

Dawn was creeping toward the brownstone. She could feel its brightness even though she couldn't see it down here underground.

Was John staying away because of what the girl had done, almost forcing him to shift to demon form? Had that rattled his confidence?

Maybe it was me. Maybe he finally understood that I'm as much a liability as an asset in a fight, and he doesn't know what to do with that.

Camille hated the reality that she was still damaged.

After all these years and the new fighting group and all the work she'd done, she was still so broken inside that she'd frozen when she saw Asmodai. She hadn't even gotten off a good shot with the throwing knife. And—almost as bad—she hadn't been able to tell Maggie Cregan to stuff it up her ass when Maggie doubted her report on the demons.

"Of course he's not coming back," she said out loud, just to make herself acknowledge reality. Complications on top of complications on top of—oh, hell.

He wasn't coming back.

She leaned against a corner of a lab table, folded her arms, and let her head droop. Good thing she wasn't a typical fire Sibyl, or this whole place would be burned to bits right now, probably exploded, with Mrs. Knight's place and everything within a mile going up in one giant fireball.

A soft sound traveled down the hallway outside the lab. The opening and shutting of a door.

Camille's heart rate jumped.

No. She had imagined that. Heard what she wanted to hear.

But a minute or two later came the whispering rush of a shower running.

She tried to swallow, but all she could do was stand there and hug herself. It seemed like a million years ago, that night in the alley when she'd first seen John Cole in the flesh, and a hundred years ago since she'd met him again in person. The date, so perfect until it just wasn't. That was years ago, too, wasn't it?

Tears clouded her vision, blurring the dark, shadowy lab. She listened to the water splashing softly in the distance.

Was it John?

It had to be John.

Who else would go into her room and use her shower?

She listened for longer, and longer still, not knowing whether to feel elated or completely freaked. Why weren't Bela and Dio and Andy coming down to tell her he was home?

Because they were probably sleeping off the shock of the distress call and of Asmodai coming back on their radar. Or they were staying the hell out of her private business. Her quad could be so nosy and sticky in some ways, but they were all very good at giving space when space was needed. That was probably why their brownstone was still standing.

How long had he been in the shower now? Minutes. Felt like hours. She should wait and let him finish, see if he wanted to come down the hall and talk to her. She should give him space and time to decide what he wanted, without any pressure. That would be the thoughtful approach, wouldn't it?

More running away, just without all the arm pumping and sweating.

What would it be like to run *toward* something, just once in her life?

Camille chewed at her bottom lip, pulled between her life so far, her opinion of herself, her thousand doubts—and all that could be if she stopped letting all of that hold her back.

But he hadn't come straight to her. He'd gone to another room, closed the door, gotten in the shower. Maybe he needed—

Ah, screw it.

She was out of the lab and down the hall in seconds, her own footfalls echoing in her ears. She hesitated at the door, breathing in the swirling scents of soap and water. She thought about knocking, then just turned the knob and went inside.

One lamp was on, bathing the room in a soft, warm yellow light. John was standing just outside the bathroom door with one of her big green towels wrapped around his waist. He was using a smaller towel to dry his hair.

He lowered the towel and stared at her.

She stared right back at him.

It was no secret how handsome he was. She'd seen him shirtless during their morning chats, covered in nothing but a sheet, but somehow, standing there with so little on, he was even more gorgeous. Her fingers tingled from wanting to touch the damp, glistening muscles of his chest and his big arms, from wanting to stroke the ridge of the scar where Maggie's sword had taken its taste. The way his wet hair tumbled into his eyes—no words. She felt like she could eat that towel straight off his waist.

His eyes, so green and deep, burned with the passion she felt, and she knew in an instant how much he wanted her. He'd never tried to hold that back. Why had she doubted him? Why had she doubted herself?

"I had a big speech about what happened at the house," he said, his voice thick, like he was barely holding himself back. "I'm not safe, beautiful. You understand that now, right?"

Camille went toward him and he threw down the small towel and raised his hands—whether to embrace her or push her away, she couldn't tell, but she kept coming.

"I'm dangerous," he whispered, putting his hands on her shoulders.

Camille put her hands on his fingers and squeezed. "Don't run away from me, John."

She saw him go to war with himself, felt the heat rising through her as he fought his battle and lost—or won. Flames ignited deep in her belly, hotter than hot. Was she smoking like a normal fire Sibyl now?

He pulled her to him rough and hard, crushing his lips against hers, taking her completely and filling her mouth with his minty, male taste. She met his tongue, thrust for thrust, winding her arms around his neck and pressing herself into the firm, warm ridges of his muscles. Camille couldn't breathe anymore, didn't even care about breathing. She just wanted him, more of him, all of him.

He kissed her deeper, working his fingers through her hair, holding her head closer, possessing her until she had to take what she wanted, too. She slid her hands from his neck, down across his pecs, raking with her nails, lower, lower, until she grabbed the towel and tore it off him.

He was unzipping her sweatshirt, pushing it aside. The room's cool air swept across her bare breasts just before he cupped them, just before she wrapped both hands around his stiff, pulsing length. He felt perfect. Hard and thick and ready.

He pinched both of her nipples and she tore away from their kiss, moaning, trying to get air. She bit his chin reflexively, then his neck.

"So beautiful." He rubbed her nipples in his fingers, around and around, then groaned as she squeezed him.

Camille's insides caught fire. She really was losing it for John, in all the right ways. Her sweatpants sparked, then burned away in a quick rush of smoke and flame, almost as fast as her shirt hanging off her arms. Naked now, except for the dinar hanging around her neck. It took every bit of her will to pull the energy back and put out the fires before she burned down the bedroom.

"Who's dangerous?" she murmured in John's ear, stroking him, fingering each glorious inch of him from the damp tip to the soft sack that made him groan when she touched it. "Who's the killer in this room?"

Fire. She'd never known it like this before, so close, all over. It flickered off her skin in bursts, in fast little waves. Was she burning them? Did he care?

He had her by the waist, then by the ass, lifting her, pressing her bare center against his erection.

The contact made her want to scream. It made her

want to open wide and take him in and never, ever let him go. Camille held on to his neck, locked her legs around his waist and gripped him, moving herself along his hard length.

"More," she heard herself saying. "More now." A husky sound, barely controlled. When she looked into his eyes, she saw feral desire. Tenderness. She saw everything.

He carried her toward the bed, walking like she weighed nothing, moving like he didn't care about the fire, the smoke, the burning. She kept trying to pull the energy back, but fire spilled out of her like he was calling it straight from her depths. He was touching the dinar as he touched her, and Camille saw the flames dance over him like the coin was shielding him from her power, and maybe it was. She hoped something was, because she couldn't help herself.

"I love how you feel." He sat her on the edge of the bed and knelt between her legs, brushing his rough hands across her belly. "Is there anything we should do, protection-wise?"

"I'm immune to diseases," she whispered, hoarse from excitement. "Pregnant by choice only. We're good to go, so *go*."

John bent down and kissed between her legs, and thrills shot through her, heating her skin more, making her tilt her head back and lean to meet him as he rose and caught one of her nipples in his teeth.

Camille cried out, need and want blended together. She was helpless to stop the sound. Crazy feelings sizzled in her body, and she grabbed the sides of his head and held on tight.

He pushed the chain and dinar out of the way and nibbled one nipple, then the other. Then he took them again, longer, slower, biting harder until she arched her back higher and moaned, pulling his hair tight with both hands. He nuzzled the sensitized skin with his lips, nuzzling her whole breast, sending fresh shocks of pleasure rippling through her center and making her throb, throb. Goddess, she needed him *now*.

When he moved lower, pushing her up on the bed and widening her legs, she could smell her own arousal.

"That's it." He kissed the insides of her thighs. "I told you a long time ago, I like it hot."

"Quit teasing me or I'll burn down the house." The words came out in a rush, barely audible, but the wicked roar of fire crept into each syllable.

His laughter rumbled across her sex, and that drove her twice as crazy. Then he moved his tongue inside and tasted, really tasted, and she screamed again, shaking from the perfect torture. She needed more relief than he was giving her. Part of her mind realized she was pulling his hair, then pushing his head down, down, harder. She moved against his mouth, and he let her do the work, teasing, flicking his tongue up and down over her swollen center.

He slipped two fingers into her wet channel, and Camille rocked, moaning from the connection, from the joining.

"Yes," he murmured. "Show me, beautiful. Let me know what you want."

Camille clenched tight around him, but he slid his fingers out, and she thought about fire and burning him up—then his tongue found her center and she couldn't make a sound or even a spark.

He teased with his mouth, with his thumb, moving his fingers into her and out of her, into her and out of her. Sweat coated her entire body and nothing was left in the world except John and what he was doing between her legs. Pleasure spun through the heat inside Camille, building, burning, closing in, but he backed off *again*, leaving her hanging, kissing her thighs, letting his fingers go still in her depths.

"Not yet." His voice was as much a tease as anything else, a vibrating rumble that seemed to touch her everywhere at once.

Camille pulled his hair again, and he swept his tongue along her folds. Just right. Just enough to make her yelp. She wanted to kill him. Camille wasn't a squirmer, she wasn't a screamer, but she was doing both with him already, and he hadn't come close to giving her the satisfaction she wanted.

"Please," she heard herself saying, not really believing she was starting to beg, but what the hell.

He slipped his fingers out of her again, grabbed her hips, and pulled her to his face. His growl of male pleasure gave her fresh, hot shivers. He wasn't just tasting anymore, he was moving his tongue hard and fast, just where she wanted, just where she needed. Camille shot toward the brink, bucking against his mouth, moaning—and he stopped.

Waited.

She clamped her eyes closed and called him names.

He laughed at her. "I'm enjoying this, beautiful. I want it to last forever."

The sheets were on fire. Camille let go of John's hair long enough to absorb the flames and pat out the embers.

Then he was kissing her again, her thighs, and inside. He had her so worked up she couldn't stand it, but he made her stand it, pulling her sensitive flesh into his mouth, then letting it go, again, again, and she was building again, building, building—

Everything inside Camille flared, yellow-hot, white-hot. The climax took her over, claimed her, flattened her, and she cried out low and loud. Fire burned through her mind, her senses. Everything pounded. Everything throbbed. Even the dinar seemed to get hot, melding into her skin

And his fingers were inside her, pumping, pumping, pushing her higher, so hard and fast she didn't even have a chance to grab the sheets and hold on. Her second orgasm blew through her, wild and hard, and she shrieked and almost crushed his head with her knees.

Aftershocks like big fiery earthquakes shook her inside and out, but he wasn't stopping. John was moving his body up, pushing her onto the bed. He pressed his hard cock into her belly, his gaze more fire, green fire, flaming into her awareness as she gripped his shoulders.

"Too much, beautiful? Are *you* ready to run?"

"Never." Just a rasp. Camille had no idea how she'd gotten the word out. *Have I lost my mind?*

His mouth came down on hers, so soft, yet so powerful. She smelled herself on him. Something new. So intimate. Camille didn't usually let herself get so close, much less absolutely lose her mind, but John wasn't giving her many choices.

He moved her legs with his until she was wide open, waiting for him.

Camille gasped as he pressed into her opening, stretching her, showing her how he'd fill her with his thickness. His gaze held her as tight as any embrace, and she felt the sweet warmth of his breath on her face.

"You're big," she murmured, squeezing his arms, digging in with her fingers to anchor herself, to keep herself from burning away to nothing.

"Too much?" he asked again, only this time, he wasn't teasing.

She answered by lifting herself, taking an inch, then another, and groaning from the absolute joy and satisfaction of finally feeling him inside her.

He went slow, easy, moving himself into her depths, and Camille had to close her eyes. Deep. Full. Wonderful.

"Just right," she whispered, loving how careful and

tender he was, how strong and deliberate. With gentle, measured thrusts, he rocked into her, rocked her body, rocked her senses in every possible way.

She felt herself relaxing, taking more, wanting even more, and then she was begging again. "Don't stop. Don't ever stop."

John picked up speed, and when she opened her eyes, he was staring down at her, adoring her. She felt like the center of the universe. He was sure as hell the center of hers.

"Made for me," he growled, teeth clenched. He was holding himself back. He was waiting for her.

No way she could have another orgasm—but she felt it building, rising, threatening to blow any second. She wasn't sure she'd be sane when it finished, and she really, really, really didn't care.

23

She screamed when her climax hit her, and John couldn't hold himself back another second. He exploded inside her, going as deep as her body allowed, reveling in her moans and the way she thrashed and scratched at him, the way she set the sheets on fire.

Instinct made him reach out to the flames with some of his own energy, and to his surprise, the fire went out. Didn't even burn him.

Her walls gripped his cock, squeezing, squeezing, until he had nothing left, but he already wanted to go again. He wanted to keep pleasing her all day, all night, as long as she'd let him.

"Enough," she was whispering, her beautiful eyes closed, her gorgeous face slack from exhaustion. A fine sheet of perspiration made her glisten in the room's soft lighting, and she seemed magical in his arms, otherworldly, like something he should hold forever to keep her from disappearing.

"Is my weight too much for you?" he murmured in her ear, kissing away the sweet, damp strands of hair and smelling that delicious lily scent.

She pulled him down to her, holding on, still clenching now and again. "You're perfect. Don't move."

He lay there on his elbows, keeping some of his bulk off her slight frame. He knew she wasn't fragile, but she felt so delicate to him that he had to honor that. Her eyes stayed closed as he kissed her cheeks, her eyelids, her nose. A lot of freckles. Light, barely visible—they were hard to find in places, but he searched with care and diligence.

Soon, too soon, he felt her even breathing, and he knew she was asleep. Before he gave in to his own exhaustion and accidentally crushed her, he eased himself out of her warm depths and wrapped her in his arms. She arched her back, moving her ass against his spent cock. He kissed her neck and shoulders, finally burying his face in her hair and falling into oblivion, wondering how long he should wait before he told her he loved her.

John dreamed in fits and starts, bouncing from the war to demons to Bengals to training sessions with Duncan and the guys at OCU headquarters. They used a basement with gym equipment and stone floors and stone walls, and he thought that might be a good place to take Camille, especially if she kept getting better at the fire-making thing. Stone wasn't flammable.

The next John knew in his dream, Camille was there in the big stone basement with him. She had his cock in her slender, graceful fingers, stroking, stroking, like she was trying to—

Wake me up.

He opened his eyes, and Camille's bed and bedroom came into focus. Cream-colored sheets with a few scorch marks, rumpled and shoved around. Calm, soothing walls with the Motherhouse artwork. And she was—

Down at his waist, her long auburn hair spread across the covers and his belly, running her palm up and down his throbbing erection.

John came fully awake in every possible way.

Her warm breath covered his length along with her fingers, giving him hints, and damn, he was already tight all over.

"You *are* big," she murmured, her breath an exotic vibration along his shaft.

John ran his fingers through her silky hair, holding his breath and letting it out slow to keep himself regulated. "You're too beautiful for words."

Slowly, sweetly, almost teasing, she slipped him into her mouth, running her tongue around the head.

He groaned, then had to bite down on the inside of his mouth to keep from shoving himself all the way into that delicious, hot warmth.

She tested again, taking him a little deeper, using her tongue all along the sensitive underside. His cock bucked from the stimulation, and Camille took all of him then. Her mouth hit him like wet fire. Nothing shy. Nothing tentative.

His fists clenched in her hair and he had to let out his groans, let his body move with her as she stroked with her hand, her mouth, pulling him in and out of paradise. When he looked down at her, she was stretched across the bed naked, the curve of her firm ass rising as her legs crossed at the ankles. Her toes stretched and wiggled like she was thoroughly enjoying herself.

John was more than enjoying it. He was hostage. Completely captivated. He'd had plenty of experience, but nothing like her, so light but so powerful and intense. He gave her control and didn't want to do anything else. Sweet God, that tongue—

His hips started to move. Sweat broke out along his shoulders, his back, and she kept sliding up and down on him, taking him in completely, then sliding him out again, hand and mouth, hand and mouth.

"Can't hold it much longer," he told her to warn her in case she wanted to ease up and finish with her hands, but she didn't slow down. She went faster, a little harder, and purred her satisfaction.

The vibration drove him right over the top.

John's body jerked and knotted, and he shouted with his release. She didn't let him go, didn't back off, taking every bit he could give her and making his pleasure last until he was completely spent. He lay back on the pillows—more like collapsed—wiped out from the incredible sensations, still running her soft hair through his fingers.

"You're incredible," he said, not able to get his voice louder than a cracked whisper.

Camille kept touching him, softer and slower, letting every last bit of energy play out of him before she let go. Then she moved herself up along his body, warming him an inch at a time.

"I was thinking the same thing about you," she murmured, her breath hot against his belly. "Incredible."

Her lips eased up to his chest, then she slid her nails across his nipples, sending tiny electric shocks through every muscle he had. John stood the subtle torture as long as he could, then pulled her into his arms and cradled her under his chin. For a time, they didn't speak, because no words seemed necessary. John thought he could lie there forever, demons and the world's needs be damned.

It was Camille who broke the silence gently. "Thanks for coming home. I was afraid you wouldn't."

John held her closer and closed his eyes as he kissed the top of her head. "I debated hitting the road. After what that girl did to me and how easily she did it, I don't feel like I have as much control over Strada as I thought I did."

"I don't know any way to defend against the energy that girl used to attack you, except maybe the paranormal technology in that tiger tooth necklace we retrieved—if Bela can analyze it, and if we can turn the energy and make it stable." She ran her nails over his chest again, giving him those shock-tingles. "I'd say that's a long shot."

John didn't hold out much hope for that, either. Anything created by Rakshasa and sorcerers couldn't be good. "Might give us more insight into why we haven't been able to find any trace of the Rakshasa, if Tarek has his boys using those pendants."

Camille's nails drummed across his skin. "But how

would they extend the protection to entire buildings? Unless you think the Rakshasa just have Eldest in town and they aren't building hordes of Created they would need to hide."

"Maybe not here," John said. "Maybe they're keeping the little kitties salted away somewhere, with one of their new criminal element allies."

She went quiet, maybe thinking, maybe realizing they had just made love for the first time and now were talking about hunting demons instead of what to do next in the relationship.

John thought about that for a second and realized he was totally okay with it. Hell, he had *dreamed* about being able to be so relaxed with a woman at other times in his life. Did they have to analyze every little thing?

This thing with Camille, it was different in every way. It was just . . . happening as it happened.

"When you're not working out with the guys at OCU headquarters, where do you go?" she asked, trailing her fingers under his chin in small, relaxed circles.

"Sometimes to my apartment, or to the park to run." John caught her hand in his, rubbed her knuckles, debated half-truths, and decided honesty was the best option, even if it carried some risks. "Sometimes I train with some other fighters."

"The Bengals. The ones who helped Duncan?" Camille slid off him and rose beside him, her aquamarine eyes bright with interest. "Mrs. Knight explained about that when we first learned about the Bengals, though she didn't give any specifics. Are they good?"

John gazed at her, realizing she'd been hoping for this answer when she asked the question—though he had no idea why. "They're the best warriors I've ever taken on."

She chewed her bottom lip for a second, probably not trying to look adorable, but succeeding anyway. "The next time you're headed there, can I go with you?"

That caught him completely unprepared. His breath slowed and he almost pulled away from her, but he made himself be still and think.

Come on. She has no idea the weight of what she's asking. Just be straight with her.

The best he could offer was "I don't know."

She looked down at the bed, clearly disappointed. "I understand how secret everything has to be. I'll be happy if you just ask—you know, whoever's in charge. If that's okay."

God, he hated seeing her disappointed in any way, even over this. "If I knew what was on your mind, it might be easier to make the request."

Camille kept her eyes on the sheets. "They know techniques I don't know, so I could learn from watching, or they could teach me. I want to keep getting stronger every way I can, especially since I'm being careful with projective energy."

John pointed to the burn holes all around them on the sheets. "It's not like you don't have the ability to make fire. You burned plenty when we got hot enough, beautiful."

He could see her frowning even though she wasn't looking at him. "If I were a re— I mean, a normal fire Sibyl, I really would have scorched the place."

Ouch.

John was pretty sure she'd almost said *If I were a real fire Sibyl*. He reached out and stroked her cheek with his fingers.

No way he could stand her seeing herself as inferior to anyone, for any reason. Her analogy came back to him then, the one she'd used at the restaurant about good soldiers who couldn't shoot as well as the rest of their squad.

John had worked with men like that before, and he knew from experience that nothing he could say would make those soldiers feel any better about themselves. He just had to teach the guys the tricks of the trade. He had to help them learn to shoot straighter.

Camille's fire, that was a whole different ball game. He had no idea how to help her tap into that skill, but if fighting better was what she wanted, he could do something about that, couldn't he?

John mentally went over his agreement with Elana about not revealing the Bengals to anyone who didn't already know about their existence. Well, Camille knew. Her sister Sibyl, the mortar of her fighting quad, was married to a Bengal. That qualified.

Showing her the hideout in the Old Croton Aqueduct, that might be dicey, but Elana had taken a special interest in Camille. She had wanted Camille safe, so maybe she'd accept a visit. If she wasn't inclined to be hospitable, Camille might get the sparring she was looking for—only not the way she intended.

"Next time I'm due there, you're with me," he said, tousling her hair. "And if I were you, I'd wear something with padding—and bring that big pocketknife. For now, though, we need to get up and eat. Patrol comes early, doesn't it?"

But she started kissing him again, and he was pretty sure they'd be grabbing one of Andy's weird sandwiches on the way out the door.

24

If Camille had kept a diary, she might have been writing something like this:

Endless weeks of dock watching with zip to show for it: about as much fun as picking flies off a horse's ass.

Raspberry, pecan, and cheddar sandwiches on pumpernickel made by Andy: good for a few burps with interesting flavors.

Nonstop pre-patrol sex: perfect.

"It still feels weird," John murmured to her, "doing this with other people again."

Camille shivered from the dark, dank cold, then shifted on her haunches and glanced at him, gratified that he was still just as handsome as he was five minutes ago. The OCU body armor Blackmore and his buddies had loaned him the first night he went out with the Sibyls fit him like a sleek black glove, even though he griped that he'd gotten out of the habit of body armor when he fought demons. Kevlar didn't help much against prehistoric-sized claws and teeth. Neither did battle leathers, but Camille had them on anyway.

John was crouched beside her in the shadows on her right, while Bela and Andy, both in full battle gear sans face masks, knelt on her left. Dio was somewhere in the night, guarding them from behind and above. They were on dock duty *again*, hidden from the world by two rock retaining walls and a big blue trash bin. Elsewhere in the city, the North Manhattan triad was busy canvassing for any hint of Rebecca or Samuel Griffen, or Tarek's alternative human identity of Corst Brevin. Every other available patrol was managing the usual—Vodoun rituals out of control, renegade Pagan practitioners and other types of troublemakers, people selling real paranormal charms or artifacts (whether they knew it or not), kids with some elemental ability making mischief, and the hundreds of frauds and phonies who liked to play at supernatural talents to con people out of their money.

Camille never thought she'd miss fortune-teller sweeps, but at the moment, chasing a bunch of idiots down a back alley while they frantically shed Tarot cards and crystal balls actually seemed appealing. At least all the running might keep her warm.

John's breath rose in steady, feathery plumes as he took his turn studying the nearby dock with night vision binoculars that had special Sibyl-added glass that would illuminate demon trace in addition to normal infrared heat signatures. Now that he'd been on patrol with them enough times, he was starting to get the hang of the lenses.

"Flecks of red," he said. "Living creatures, probably mice or rats—and some trace paranormal plumes, minor, either old or weak."

The cold night air smelled like the water, but she didn't catch any whiffs of cat piss or even the stench of a random dead body, though the occasional icy breeze across the trash bin was a little hard to take. She knew she needed to stay on full alert, but each night they came out and found nothing, it was getting harder to feel anything but increasing irritation—and the slow deadening of hypothermia.

John coughed when he got his own faceful of chilled trash bin stench. "Sorry," he whispered. "Demon super-scent ability, pretty easy to use, but not something I'd recommend. I bet Spider-Man didn't have this much trouble getting used to his radioactive spider powers."

He handed the binoculars to Camille.

"I bet Spidey slammed into buildings and broke his dick ten or twelve times," Andy muttered. "That just wouldn't be appropriate to put in comic books. Anything, Camille?"

A minute or two later, Camille sighed. "Nothing but rats. Probably suffering from frostbite on their little rat feet."

When she was sure the lenses wouldn't tell her anything more, Camille lowered the binoculars and raised her hand over the dinar, letting her fingers hover above the circle the coin made in her bodysuit, but she didn't unzip the leathers to touch it. She was getting to the point where she didn't have to make direct contact to send out her energy. What little bit Ona had taught her made it that much easier.

Camille had noticed that Bela wasn't touching her copper charm as much, either. Maybe projective talents got stronger with use. That, or Camille had scared the bejesus out of her with their conversation in the lab.

After a minute or so, Andy gave up on her probes. "Nada. All these nights in a row with no pig blood thrown in my face—I shouldn't be bitching, but this whole dock-search thing has been a giant bust so far."

"Are we calling it?" Camille asked Bela.

"Yeah, we're done." Bela gave a hand signal to a nearby rooftop to bring Dio down. "We'll check off another bunch of grid sections and move on tomorrow night. Right now we need to make a pass through the southern part of Central Park before we head in for the night."

Andy's groan probably carried into New Jersey. "If there's any voodoo shit going on, John can handle it. I'm keeping my blood-free streak going, damnit."

"Agreed." Bela watched as Andy stowed the binoculars in a pack around her waist, then winked at Camille before she gave John a quick glance and smile. "You kicked ass with a god before, John. Think you could do it again if we run into another pissed-off victim of a summoning gone wrong?"

John gave Camille his best sly look. "I'll try, if she'll loan me her scimitar."

"Not happening." Camille reached out and rattled the hilt of the broadsword he was carrying. "You've got your own blade, and you're decent with it now. Use it in good health. Besides, nobody summons *loas* in Central Park."

"Stick to the gun," Andy told John. "Your Glock has a sweet grip and nothing works better than elementally treated bullets in most circumstances."

"I like Camille's sword better," John tried again, and Camille realized he was hoping he was needling her at least a little bit.

"Fuck off," she said, just to make his night.

His grin definitely made hers.

Bela ignored them both, pointed in the general direction of Central Park, and said, "Move out."

Camille started walking, and John fell in beside her. She was surprised he could follow Bela's lead so easily, especially after all his years of working alone and rogue, off any grid or chart or accountability ledger. It seemed so . . . normal, having him there with them.

"I'm glad I'm with Sibyls and not a bunch of swaggering dicks trying to one-up the next guy," he said, like he was following her line of thinking. "That kind of banter's comfortable, but it can get old."

Camille didn't think working with John would get old anytime soon, and she was glad he was loosening up on the whole swearing-around-women thing.

"As an added bonus, in quieter moments, I get to look at you," he went on, keeping eyes forward, a grin still playing at the lips she wanted to kiss even right now, when she absolutely couldn't. "Any idea how gorgeous you are with that little athletic body in those battle leathers?"

"Behave, John," Camille said as she led the way toward Twelfth Avenue, hoping he wouldn't behave, but knowing he would because they were on point. Bela was close behind them, with Andy next in line and Dio far to the rear, holding perspective on the whole area, ready to strike from a distance if something attacked. So far, Camille wasn't sensing any paranormal energy out of the ordinary, but she stayed ready. John walked a little faster beside her.

"When I fought with my first group, there were a lot more Sibyls in New York City," Camille said as they crossed through traffic. "We covered set territories, with rotating patrols so nobody got dog-ass tired like this."

"You lost a lot of fighters." John touched her elbow as she cleared the far curb. "Must have hurt like hell."

"Everybody took hits during the Legion war," Camille agreed, leaving off the reality that she and the other members of her quad had suffered some of the most brutal losses of all.

"The bad guys never seem to lose as much as the good guys." The pain that crossed John's face made Camille hurt, but she wasn't arrogant enough to think she could fix it. She knew better. Her own wars had taught her that much. "Maybe we can help each other avoid more losses."

"Thanks," she said.

"No, thank *you*, Camille."

"For what?" She glanced at him again, surprised to see the expression on his face.

She turned her attention back to the sidewalk, moving fast along the route, making sure nobody looked at them too long. Just a bunch of actors in leather, playing a scene, right?

"Thanks for not trying to give me a load of stuff about how everything gets better with time," he said.

"It never gets better," she admitted. "My mother, my first triad, everybody I've lost—they're still living with me, haunting me in their own way. So, no. It never gets better. It just gets further away."

"Yeah." John's gaze stayed on the sidewalk. "That's my take on it so far."

It took a while, but they got to Central Park with no incidents. Camille knew by heart the route they'd walk, leaving the upper sections to other fighting groups who had been scheduled for those areas with their OCU partners. Nick Lowell was this group's official officer liaison, but in his absence, Saul Brent or one of the Lowell brothers usually worked with them. For now, Blackjack was letting John do the honors, even though there was no way he'd be allowed to join the OCU officially, at least not yet, Johann Kohl identity or not.

The park was a startling change from the streets, even this time of night when the roads weren't that crowded. Silence descended quickly as they moved across the grass. She didn't hear any chorus of crickets or frogs because it was too cold for them now, but the trees still had a few leaves to whisper against one another, and branches creaked in the easy breeze. Scents shifted from concrete, asphalt, exhaust, and late-night restaurant cooking to damp earth and the fertile smell of the fallen leaves trying to return themselves to nature.

John followed Camille toward the nearest group of trees in the park, and he seemed strong and fast-moving under the bright fall stars. Her breath rose in soft plumes in the semi-darkness, and she was glad for her enhanced Sibyl vision.

"These cat eyes, they're not bad," John said, referring to the enhanced vision Strada's remnant powers allowed him to enjoy, however inconsistent it might be. "I could be an improved asset to Blackjack with these new abilities—so thank God my 'untimely demise' ended my official commission with Blackjack's shadow ops group. I'm dead to the military now."

Camille searched through the darkness, seeing nothing, feeling nothing in terms of paranormal energy. "Are you glad to have your choices back?"

"I can do whatever I want: move to Paris, hang out on some Bermuda beach—or maybe put down roots in New York City." John frowned. "But I'm probably being too pushy, right?"

Camille didn't want to let herself dream like that. Truth was, no matter what John said, she figured he'd go where the demons went, or wherever they showed up once they disappeared from here. No matter which body he lived in, the Rakshasa had been his responsibility, and they still were. Nothing had changed with that, not that she could tell.

But she said, "Not too pushy. If you are, I'll let you know."

"With the scimitar? Or can you be gentle?"

Camille laughed and pushed deeper into the trees. John followed, Bela and Andy flanking him.

Everything's changed, the quietest and most certain part of her mind informed her as she listened to him clearing brush behind her. *You'll never walk away from him if he doesn't walk away from you. Be honest with yourself at least.* Then again, maybe she wasn't quite ready for that yet.

Just then some sort of ripple passed over Camille. Subtle.

But it was elemental energy, and it was out of place.

She slowed her pace, then stopped and held up one

hand. Her other hand dropped to the hilt of her scimitar. John drew his Glock before the Sibyls reacted, but Andy got him by the elbow.

"Not yet," she murmured. "It could be nothing. I'm not picking up anything, and neither is Bela. Sometimes kids with elemental talent jack around with Wiccan rituals and let off trace energy. Camille's sensitive. She picks up everything. Let her check."

Camille let her energy flow, searching, poking around nearby hiding places. Bela came up beside her and Camille saw her eyelids twitch just before she sensed her elemental energy flowing outward, into the earth. She was looking for what Camille had detected. A touch of wind let her know that Dio was taking her own sample of the nearby air.

"I'm not good at doing that yet," Andy told John. "It's risky when I put my energy into water or pull the water into me, so I only do it when I have to."

"Risky . . . like, geyser risky?" John asked. "Or world-ending tidal wave risky?"

"Somewhere in between. Can you do anything?"

"I don't know," John answered. "The stuff this body and my senses can do, I don't really know the limits, or where the danger zone would be."

Camille could imagine Andy's grin. "Welcome to the bump-on-a-log club, then."

She had to shut them out after that, because she caught a taste of the energy just about the same time Bela found it.

"North," Bela said. "It's out of our area. Riana's triad is already on it. Seems pretty minor. Good. I need to get home and get on analyzing that necklace, anyway."

Relief claimed Camille.

As bored as she had been earlier, she was cold and tired, and she wanted to go home.

"Thank the Goddess," Andy said. "Let's get the hell out of here."

They started for the brownstone, but before they got halfway to the fence, a mind-rattling bolt of fire blasted into Camille's tattoo. She pulled up short, heart racing as she stared down at the mark and read the energy message as it ricocheted though her mind.

Trouble . . .

All help . . .

Demons . . .

All help . . .

"North," she shouted. "North now!"

25

John felt . . . something.

A tingle across his brain. A stutter across his heart. Almost like somebody had just fired an energy arrow straight through him, and outward, onward, into the whole city. The sensation made his pulse beat faster.

In the time it took him to think about that, Camille yelled, "North! North now!" and the Sibyls ran away from him so fast they were nothing but black blurs in the night.

"Shit!" He took off after them, and he had to pound grass and dirt to keep up with them as they swarmed north toward—

Whatever was happening.

And something was.

John felt it for sure now, strong and biting and dark against his senses. He smelled it, too. Rotten and strong and wrong for the city night.

The women ran like hell and kept running, farther and farther, toward the Reservoir, then past it, all the way to the North Meadow. John pushed his legs to the limit, finally keeping pace, drawing down inside himself to better work this new body, to find his new stride and maximize the abilities that came naturally to him.

Seconds later, he saw dust roiling through the night. Battle screams sounded out of the thick cloud, echoing into winds that slashed dirt off ball fields and pathways. Flames roared as the ground shook under his feet. The rattling almost tripped John, but the Sibyls never slowed down.

Camille's scimitar flashed in the moonlight seconds before she plunged into the dust cloud and out of sight. Bela and Andy, weapons ready, leaped into the fray behind her.

John swore and charged after all of them.

The ball field dirt hit him like a grit tornado, scouring his face and arms. He tried to use his new senses, or at least his old ones, to figure out what the hell they were fighting against. He saw big Frankenstein-like shapes, a lot of them, human but not human, swiping left and right at anything that moved. Demons, like the ones he and Camille had faced in that basement, only there were different kinds. Some of them had on suits. Some of them wore jeans. Some were naked and way beyond nasty, features shifting every second or two, all lumpy and unreal, like they only knew how to pretend to be people. And they stank, these things, bad enough to make his eyes water. Had to be about thirty of them, maybe more, and they had strong energy, elemental cores—but the energy felt wrong. Twisted.

"Asmodai!" Dio's voice carried to him through the fray, and a throwing knife whizzed past him and hit one of the big bastards right between the eyes. It crumpled into dust that blew away in the increasing winds.

John targeted the nearest Asmodai and pumped an elementally treated bullet into its chest, heart level, dead hit. It collapsed with a spray of sizzling water, dousing Camille. The water raised welts across her chin and forehead wherever it landed on her. She ignored it all and leaped high enough to hack off the head of another one of the things. This one turned into wind that hit John in the face like a whirling cloud of grave rot.

He coughed and choked it back up, feeling like his lungs were on fire. Jesus, these demons smelled like old death and puke.

Bela and Andy were working on a bigger creature, this

one spitting flames out of its eyes and ears. John sighted it but didn't have a clean shot. He couldn't help thinking the demon looked like a fresco of Satan come to earth. His old priest's instincts kicked in, and he wondered if holy water or prayers would have any effect—not that he'd be able to use weapons like that, since he'd walked away from his vows.

When Bela ran the demon through, she whirled and tackled Andy, shielding her as a wave of fire blasted outward, scorching everything it touched with sick-looking green heat.

What the hell?

John didn't have time to think.

Sibyls seemed to be everywhere at once, faces he recognized and some he didn't, just a blur of steel and arrows and flames and whirling stars and knives. Some human officers were there, too, some male, some female, all wearing goggles, targeting the big bastards and firing, firing, firing.

Good strategy.

Keeping Camille in view, John picked out ugly non-human heads and eyes and mouths high enough to shoot at without collateral damage, and he fed them bullets.

For every creature he took down, another stumbled into view.

Did these things breed on the spot or something?

Where were they coming from?

"Woods!" he heard somebody yell, as if to answer his question. A voice he knew from his time with Duncan.

Was her name Riana? Or maybe it was that group's air Sibyl, Merilee.

"Handlers, in the trees behind the field!"

Bela brushed past John, and he saw her raise a hand to the charm at her throat. She held up her sword, pointing it toward the trees. The energy that blasted out of her, targeted through that sword, nearly made him gut-sick, it was so harsh. He sensed more than heard earth tearing open with a crack and rumble in the distance.

Bela crumpled to her knees, and Camille threw herself in front of Bela, hacking at the knees of one of the big Asmodai. Another fire-spitter. Andy fired a dart at its head. Missed.

John popped it three times in its jowly cheek, then shouted when the blast of green fire rolled over Camille and Bela.

A wave of water from Andy splashed across them a split second later, putting out every last ember.

Camille was up before John reached her, leathers and hair smoking, face and hands blistered, screaming as she dared anything else to come near Bela, who was still on the ground, struggling to get back to her feet. Whatever Bela had done to those assholes in the trees, it had cost her. John grabbed her arm, pulled her to her feet, then used her sword to skewer a shambling demon-wreck charging her from behind. He shot it before it evaporated into stinking dirt, just for good measure.

When he shot the next fucker before it could reach Camille, turning it to wind, he had a moment to realize the demon numbers were finally going down. The Sibyls and the OCU were gaining an advantage. Maybe.

Bela sagged in his grip, and he realized she'd lost consciousness. He lifted her over his shoulder, keeping his Glock arm free to fire. Camille took his left to guard Bela.

"Got your back," Andy yelled, and a blast from her sidearm let him know she had stopped shooting darts and reverted to her old police standard. Good enough for these demon assholes. The creature she shot stumbled, then burst into a cloud of dirt.

The dust on the ball field started to settle.

John turned left, then right, searching. Sibyls had weapons at the ready. A lot of swords were on fire. OCU officers were staggering to their feet or searching for targets just like he was doing, but no more demons presented themselves to get Swiss-cheesed.

"I can't believe it!" somebody yelled. "How the hell did we get Asmodai again?"

Andy joined Camille and put her arm around Camille's shoulders.

It was then that John saw Camille's wide-eyed, tight-jawed stare and the way she was gripping her still-raised scimitar and shaking. The red burn marks across her face and hands were already fading, and when Andy let out some of her water energy, they seemed to fade faster.

Camille's expression didn't change, though. She seemed stuck. Frozen. She wasn't really here, at least not in mind or spirit, and he figured he knew what she was seeing in her mind, what she was thinking about: Bette, one of the women from her first fighting group.

She got killed by an Asmodai in Van Cortlandt, and there was nothing I could do to save her, either. Losing them nearly drove me crazy. Maybe it did. I still haven't decided. . . .

The sight of her so undone made his heart ache. If he hadn't been carrying Bela, he would have tried to talk her down, to hold her if she'd let him. He would have done something.

Stand down, soldier.

The thought drifted through his mind, along with an image of Blackjack pulling a rifle out of his hot, locked-up hands.

Valley of the Gods.

Everybody had been dead but him, and it had been Blackjack who'd come for him, Blackjack who'd almost gotten his ass blown off by a freaked-out priest who hadn't been able to save a single life but his own that day.

"Stand down," he murmured, and Camille glanced at him like she was keying on the sound of his voice.

"You're not crazy, just wounded in the heart. It'll get further away, even if it never gets better."

Her gaze softened, then her focus grew sharp and she seemed to realize he was carrying Bela.

"Breathing's regular, pulse is good, no blood." John rattled off all he knew like he was talking to a medic in the field, and he was glad to see Camille's features relax enough that he wasn't worried about her tapping out again. "I think she just got floored by whatever she did with her earth power."

"She tore the hell out of the demon handlers," Dio said, jogging up with two other air Sibyls. John recognized Merilee Alexander Lowell from the North Manhattan bunch and Karin Maros from the East Ranger group. "Yanked the ground out from under their feet and sent them straight to hell, best we can tell, then covered it all back up again nice and neat. It was a big hole. A huge one, and way deep, but she kept it small enough that she didn't disrupt anything major."

John wasn't totally sure, but that sounded hard to do—unleash a power that destructive but hold it to such a small, focused area.

"We found the ritual pattern for creating Asmodai burned into the ground in the woods," Merilee said, "plus the elemental tools and a bunch of trash they must have been using to target the bastards."

John shifted Bela's weight on his shoulder as a nearby OCU officer asked. "What exactly were those things again?"

"Man-made demons," Karin told him. "Asmodai. Check your reference manual. We've fought them before, back when the Sibyls were at war with a bunch of jerks who called themselves the Legion—same creatures who attacked at that brownstone a little while ago."

"And it's obvious all the secrets of demon making didn't die with the Legion," Andy said.

Merilee's frown seemed intense. "Or maybe some of the secret-keepers stayed alive. I'm heading out. We've got OCU wounded to get back to the townhouse, and headquarters needs to know about this. Is Bela okay?"

"Yeah, she'll be fine," Andy said. "We just need to get her to bed, then feed her pretty good when she wakes up."

"That was amazing, what she did." Karin gave Bela a reverent look. "But dangerous. I'm not sure she should take risks like that with projective energy."

Andy's smile turned a lot less friendly. "You'd rather she left the bastards up and moving to make more Asmodai? Next time I'll see what we can do."

As Andy finished talking, thunder rumbled in the clear sky overhead, and John sensed unusual energy. Not malicious, just strong as hell.

Karin frowned, and the expression didn't look right on her normally happy face.

John saw Merilee's cautious glance, first at Dio and then at Bela. She seemed okay with Andy, but Camille got another guarded look, then both air Sibyls took off to do whatever they needed to do.

"Y'all are popular," John said to Andy, who was steering Camille toward the brownstone.

"They can all fuck themselves," Andy said, still using that overly sweet voice. "I'll pay a porn producer to film it."

"Shut up before you give me nightmares," Dio muttered, stalking past them with energy literally crackling out of her elbows.

John remembered about Dio being able to make weather, about that being another Sibyl talent that no Sibyl really wanted to have, like this projective energy thing—but he hadn't known it meant she could shoot lightning from her elbows.

That was . . . amazing.

"People are always jealous of power," he said as Dio let it thunder two or three more times, probably just for the hell of it.

She sort of smiled at him when she finished, and so did Camille.

"Okay, troops," Andy said. "Let's move these tired asses home."

26

"Your Asmodai demons fought well," Tarek told Griffen as they sat at the isolated park picnic table far from the ambush site, using the dark for cover. Tarek's brown woolen suit and expensive full-length coat protected him from the worst of the cold, and it reinforced his human identity of Corst Brevin, though all his companions this night knew that persona to be a shell. The elementally treated tooth pendant around his neck had been reinforced, shielding his life signature from detection better than ever.

Seneca, seated beside Tarek, was dressed similarly, and he did not seem bothered by the fall chill, either. His dark hair remained slick atop his large head, and his breath issued in short, foggy bursts. Above them, stars glowed in a wide sky, making an impressive halo above distant buildings.

Griffen occupied the opposite bench at the table, and he wore only jeans and a dark sweatshirt. "Man-made demons are strong, as I told you they would be, and infinitely easier to direct and control than Created. Asmodai are suitable for mass attacks and diversions, and they work well as supplemental fighters. In the past, many groups have made the mistake of using them as primary foot soldiers. Definitely not smart enough or durable enough for that role."

Griffen's hood remained down and his sleeves were pushed up, revealing the odd twin-serpent tattoo that took up much of his left forearm, yet Griffen's pale skin had no flush from the chill air. Tarek found that a bit strange now that he knew more about human bodies, but he assumed the sorcerer had divined ways to protect himself from the cold, much as his clever charms crafted from the teeth of the Created protected Tarek and his other true brother in New York City, Aarif, from detection by the Sibyls or other sensitives. Griffen's half sister, Rebecca, much slighter than her brother, wore only a short-sleeved T-shirt with a rock concert slogan along with her jeans and tooth charm, but she frolicked in a nearby clearing, dancing to music only she could hear, as if the moonlight were truly the brightest, warmest sun.

"You lost good men in the demonstration tonight," Seneca said to Griffen. "Three of your trained sorcerers. For that, I'm sorry."

Griffen's shrug came too quickly. "They were expendable."

"I find that wasteful." Tarek found himself unable to curtail the sharpness in his tone. "You should be more cautious with talented people. Valuable time will be lost while you find and train new men."

Griffen shook his head. In the glow of city lights, stars, and the moon, his hair seemed more silver than blond. "Already in place. I started a second Coven at the same time I was rebuilding the first, and I've been training with them on quieter days. They continue to live in their previous homes, and they're still going to work, so they won't attract any attention. I can promote as many as I need, whenever I need them."

Tarek gave a gesture of dismissal, too quick, he knew, just like Griffen's shrug had been. Seneca would know that Tarek had had no idea about the under-Coven, not that a *culla* should be troubled with such menial workings—but still. He should have been aware, just like he should have had a better idea about the night's events and how they might play out once the battle started. The Sibyl who wrecked their plan to ambush, wear down, and slaughter several fighting groups at once, she was one of the witches who resided in the brownstone. They had special abilities, those four, and Tarek knew he had to deal with them sooner rather than later.

Griffen's winning smile was directed at Seneca this time. "Midlevel talent can always be replaced. Every game has to have its pawns, wouldn't you agree?"

Seneca grunted, and Tarek appreciated the fact that the man refused to answer. One *culla* to another, they had come to understand each other, as much as two such different beings could.

Tarek centered himself and focused on his Brevin identity, on Corst Brevin's gestures and tones, to keep himself calm and focused. "For our longer-range plans to be successful, Griffen, we must do more than harass and annoy the Sibyls. They must die, and in great number. We must set an example and find methods to share with our remaining true brothers in other locations."

Griffen's teeth flashed as he smiled yet again, though this grin had a wolfish, aggressive cast to it. "We're working up to that. If we add a few Created to the mix next time along with some of Seneca's men, and if we make sure our handlers can't be harmed, we can destroy as many Sibyls and OCU officers as choose to join our battle." Once more he shifted his gaze to Seneca, though with better deference this time, not making direct eye contact and keeping his tone respectful, if overly excited. "Even better, when we're set to carry out consolidation of your empire's power, teams of man-made demons and the Created could provide comprehensive initial assaults, not to mention distractions."

"A pleasing prospect," Seneca allowed, but only after he glanced at Tarek and received a nod.

"Not unless the Sibyls in the brownstone are neutralized first." Tarek gestured across the park to the structure he despised so very deeply. "They have more skills than the rest of the elemental witches. Or, rather, different skills that seem to prove more difficult for us to contend with, especially when we don't know the breadth and depth of those powers. Find out what they're doing, Griffen. And get rid of them."

Griffen's expression remained placid but for the briefest flicker in his blue eyes. "As you wish, *culla*. I'll make that my priority. I'll bring up the new Coven members, and we'll do some test battles with lesser groups, then go after the main targets within the month."

Tarek nodded. Much better. "Prepare carefully. The more I observe these women, the more I fear we are lacking much information about their talents."

Griffen slid from the bench seat, gave Tarek a half-hearted bow, then strode off toward a park exit. He motioned for his strange sibling to follow him, and she did so, still dancing lightly along like she could hear a sweet melody played only for her ears.

"He is eager," Tarek said as he watched Griffen and his sister depart. "Sometimes overly so, but he is talented and his Coven is quite powerful when they work together."

"His tattoo is of the old Legion cult that once tried to assume power across the world," Seneca said, gesturing to his left forearm. "This my men have told me after much research. The dye used to make it seems to have some enchantment, the way it moves around his skin."

Tarek nodded. "The tattoo is made of elementally treated metals—very rare, very difficult to create and control. Griffen did it himself, with the aid of his sibling."

"So he has had intimate contact with the Legion in the past?" Seneca looked interested, but Tarek sensed the deception and knew the man was uncomfortable. "They began well enough, but in the end, they were crazed. Cult-like. They did not follow . . . sound business practices."

"You're right in that Griffen had contact with the Legion in the past, but as foe, not ally," Tarek said to reassure his human partner. "His tattoo is more coincidence than a symbol of belonging. He saw it, admired it, and claimed it for his own. All of this information I took directly from his mind, so I know it to be truthful."

Seneca shifted his bulk on the bench, and as he had been on their first meeting, Tarek was struck by the hollowness in his clothing, hinting at more weight loss, though the man could spare many pounds as yet.

"Could Griffen have some method of deceiving you about what's in his mind and heart, my friend?"

Tarek was about to laugh and tell the old crime lord no, of course not, when his hand came to rest on the charm about his neck, the one that confused many with supernatural perception about his true origins. His denial died before he spoke it, and he let his human fingers drift back to a resting position on the table.

Seneca's frown was visible even with the barest hints of starlight finding their table. "My men have also told me that your Griffen and his odd sister took on some Sibyls themselves recently, in a brownstone they had packed with these . . . these Asmodai creatures. They fared poorly in the attempt."

Tarek maintained his even expression, but snarling broke out in his mind. The girl, Rebecca, had been insisting that Strada was not dead, or had returned from the dead, and was living with those most troublesome Sibyls. Tarek had seen the man in question, and the resemblance was stunning—but any fool could sense that Strada's energy was nowhere present in that human shell. It was nothing but a Sibyl trick, to throw them off stride.

Had Rebecca set out to prove her point?

Or was Griffen making trial attacks without informing Tarek of his failures?

It took Tarek a few moments, but he tamed his temper

enough to speak normally. "I have learned, Seneca, that nothing is impossible in this world, but I would say that if you fear Griffen is laboring for masters we do not know, it's improbable. Griffen has something he wants rom me, something perhaps only I or one of my true brothers can provide, and he works very hard to receive that reward."

This seemed to give Seneca some comfort, but once more he shifted, indicating that he had yet another difficult question. "And you're quite certain this man is ͞man, that he is what he says he is?"

"Yes." Tarek felt more confident in this response, though his ever-analyzing mind added, *Griffen's unusual half sister may be another matter, now that I consider it.*

Seneca remained silent for a time, then his shoulders relaxed and he seemed more at ease. He turned his head to make eye contact with Tarek, something he rarely did because he respected Tarek. Seneca only resorted to facing off when he posed the most important of queries, so Tarek was inclined to listen very carefully when Seneca said, "I suppose the truth of Griffen is neither here nor there, as the real issue is this, Tarek—or should I say, to keep in the habit, Mr. Brevin. Whatever Griffen may prove to be, can you and your true brother Aarif control him?"

Tarek took his time in answering so that he did not seem too defensive, or worse yet, desperate or untruthful, however perilously close to reality those characterizations might be. "Without question."

"I am old, and—as you have probably noted—I am sick." Seneca once more turned to face the darkness and the trees of Central Park. "I have much to do to secure my business operations for my sons, and not much time to do it. Most of our plans ride on the aid of your Griffen and his mysterious and powerful Coven. I hope for both our sakes that you are correct about being able to control him, else we will both regret it in ways we can't yet imagine."

Tarek swallowed his surge of anger at Seneca's boldness, because he had to admit the ailing man was correct in virtually every word he spoke. Because of that, he didn't abandon his agreement with Seneca and kill him on the spot. Instead, he said his goodbyes, then made his own exit from Central Park without looking back to be certain Seneca departed unmolested. Seneca had his own private security, separate from that hired and trained by the corporation Tarek had established under his Corst Brevin identity—and Seneca's armed forces were never far from him, even if they could not be readily discerned.

Tarek traveled in flame form tonight, moving with the fluid grace of fire. Burning across the New York City ground all the way back to his dwelling—it suited his mood. It also reduced his need for security forces like the one Seneca had developed.

If the Rakshasa were greater in number, or the Created could be more sustainable and stable, Tarek would use them to build his own impenetrable wall of weapons and power. But those were aims he could not achieve, not yet at least. Perhaps in the future, once the Sibyls had been defeated and the way cleared for the Rakshasa to move forward without competent opposition, such goals could be established and reached.

For now, Tarek had one goal outside of seeing to the destruction of the four Sibyls who resided in the brownstone, and that goal was surprising and new. He needed to speak to Aarif, and the two of them needed to establish contingency plans for managing Griffen and the Coven.

No ruler who loses sight of his most powerful subjects rules for long—that much Tarek had learned in the time before his imprisonment in the Valley of the Gods. His conversation with Seneca had been—how did humans say it? Ah, yes. A wake-up call.

Perhaps it was time to give Griffen a wake-up call of his own.

27

Occult Crimes Unit headquarters, sarcastically dubbed Headcase Quarters, was a little pretentious for Camille's tastes. She knew Sibyls and NYPD officers had to have a place to interact without public scrutiny, especially given the high number of demons wandering in or out at all hours, and sure, the Lowell brothers owned the place and let the OCU use it for free, but still. At night, the outdoor safety lights turned the place into a five-story showplace with lots of balconies, a black metal safety fence, and dual white entry staircases winding up to a brick landing with big white columns. There was even an eagle seal above the white front door.

Camille jostled through the door with John and Dio, heading for the emergency meeting. Andy had stayed behind at the brownstone to look after Bela. Camille was still aching from the fight, wearing yesterday's jeans and sweater, running on literally about an hour's sleep, and worrying about her quad—yeah, this was going to be fun.

Inside the townhouse, there was a massive basement gym, a ground floor with a kitchen, a great big conference room, and offices. The next two floors had private bedrooms, occupied by visiting demons and officers like Jack Blackmore, while the third floor had a few rooms but also a huge library. Everything was polished hardwood and expensive carpets and paintings, and it smelled like the wake room at Motherhouse Ireland. All polish and fresh linen and floral highlights to hide . . . well, better not to think about that.

High-end living overkill, even if it was being put to good use.

The conference room on the first floor, where the Sibyls and the OCU shared reports, had wood paneling and wooden blinds, a ton of chairs, and a blackboard and long table at the front. Despite the ample space, the room felt small and stuffy when they got inside.

"I hate it when it's so crowded," Dio grumbled under the low roar of officers and Sibyls rattling around and finding chairs. Camille was thankful she heard no thunder overhead. She didn't like being Dio's only babysitter, but she had to admit Dio was getting better at not losing her cool so often, even in large groups.

"Back with you in a few," John said, giving Camille's hand a squeeze before he peeled off to speak to Saul Brent, who was hunched over the main table with his brother, Cal.

Camille watched him go, hoping to have a second to enjoy watching him walk, but she was immediately besieged by Riana's triad.

Dio went stiff beside her, but she didn't say anything.

"How's Bela?" Riana asked, her dark eyes, dark hair, and vaguely Russian looks reminding Camille enough of Bela to make her chest hurt. Behind her, Cynda Flynn let off a steady cloud of smoke from her shoulders, and Merilee kept it dispersed with casual bursts of air energy from her fingertips. At least the smoke blocked out the thick scent of leather, wood polish, sword oil, cologne, and perfume collecting in the air.

"Tired, but fine." Camille ignored the little flames dancing along Cynda's arms, though she really didn't have issues with Cynda—and she adored Cynda's little girl, who was one of the lights of Andy's life. "Andy's with her. Where are the guys?"

"They're all with Blackmore getting ready for the

meeting," Cynda said, scooting her red hair out of her eyes. "The Brent brothers are still working the phones and secure e-mail with the rank and file, making sure everybody's been notified and checking in with other paranormal crime units across this country and everywhere else."

"That move Bela made in the meadow—kickass," Merilee said, and Camille knew she was waiting for more explanation. Earth Sibyls could shake limited patches of ground and move small amounts of earth without making lots of trouble for surrounding areas. The way-deep, very targeted hole Bela had dug was unusual, especially since everyone knew earthmoving wasn't Bela's big strength.

"Yeah. Desperation breeds invention." Camille smiled and gave Merilee nothing else. Dio, who had serious issues with Merilee and most other air Sibyls, wouldn't have said a word for love or money, so Merilee didn't bother to ask. That was good. Camille wasn't much in the mood for a tornado outburst.

Nick Lowell came through the conference room door, followed by his twin, Creed, and their brother, Jake. Jake Lowell was one of the few Astaroth demons comfortable keeping a consistent human form, and he really was a gorgeous, ethereal man, with his tall frame and startling blond hair and blue eyes. In his demon form, he had white hair, golden eyes, translucent pearl skin, great big fangs, claws, and a double set of huge leathery wings—but either way, human or demon, his presence tended to get everyone's attention. People started moving toward seats, getting out of his way, and barely paying any mind to the man behind him, Jack Blackmore, who for once had on jeans and a white shirt instead of his Flaming Bunch of Idiots suit. Camille made a mental note to tell Andy, then see if she fainted.

Riana and her group went to join their husbands, and John elbowed his way through the milling crowd, pressing his hand to the small of Camille's back when he got to her. His touch gave her unexpected strength, and she liked the fact he wasn't shy about putting his hands on her in public. Let everybody stare. Most of the people in the room probably had no idea what to do with John, and they most likely thought she was a freak anyway— not that she cared.

She caught John's hand and laced her fingers through his, and with her other hand she gently took Dio's wrist. "Come on. We better get seats."

They jostled around and sat, all leaning forward as one, straining to hear over the continuing noise as Blackmore said, "So, as everybody probably knows, we've got Asmodai again, and we've had two strikes using these demons within the last month, one small, one large-scale."

His dark eyes looked serious, and his too-handsome face seemed unusually pale. His black hair looked tousled, like he'd run his hand through it a hundred times in the last hour. Add that to the imposing figure of Jake Lowell standing next to him on his right like a silent blond thunderhead, and the effect was disconcerting. The twin Lowells on his left only added to the mood, as dark and big as Blackmore in build and coloring, and obviously just as concerned.

Camille felt her anxiety crank up a few notches. If she hadn't been so exhausted, she might actually have mustered some panic. She realized she was still holding hands with John and sort of holding hands with Dio, but she wasn't sorry. Let everybody else be hard-asses. She hated even hearing the word *Asmodai*, much less thinking about them or fighting them. If that made her chickenshit, then so be it.

"I've ordered an increase in production on our elementally locked bullets, and every OCU officer should carry elementally treated blades as backups," Blackmore continued. "Those of you who were on duty during the Legion conflict, share what you know. We'll have to reorganize patrols, because paranormal activity may go off the charts now that these bastards are back in play."

Sheila Gray from the East Ranger group asked, "Have any other cities reported Asmodai resurgence?"

Nick Lowell took that question. "Not as yet. Seems like this is an NYC exclusive for now." His gaze drifted to Camille and Dio, and Camille felt their liaison's concern like a leaden weight descending on her shoulders.

"Is there any evidence the Legion is making these demons?" That question came from Riana, analytical as always. "Did we recover anything to analyze to explore that?"

Jake Lowell fielded her question. "Asmodai were Legion creations, but the ritual can be performed by anyone with elemental talent. We have samples of dirt from the earth Asmodai, but no additional artifacts or talismans. Their handlers"—he gestured to the wooden floor beneath his feet—"burned up in the earth's core, as far as we know, so not much is left of them, either."

People who hadn't heard about Bela's primo hole digging muttered among themselves, but Camille ignored them. Dio pulled her hand free and sat back, arms folded, and Camille knew she was working on keeping her temper managed, because Dio hated it when anybody said anything about Bela. Well, about any of them. Dio was a little protective, in her own slightly psycho way. John gave her fingers a gentle squeeze, and when she glanced at him, his gorgeous green eyes told her, *We'll get through this.*

Camille wanted to believe him. She really did.

"Start watching your trash again, people," Creed Lowell said, his dark ponytail spread across one shoulder. "Discarded personal items and in-container food products are the most common ways of targeting Asmodai."

Blackmore took over again, stressing, "These demons are without human properties. Terminate on sight, but be careful about the blowback, especially from the fire Asmodai. Sibyls weather it pretty well, but the flameout can scar or kill humans who aren't wearing protective gear."

Camille watched everyone in the room get tenser, even Legion war veterans who knew this drill. She tried not to focus on everyone else's worries, since she had so many of her own, but it was hard not to. The briefing droned on for a time, but she hardly heard the details. More and more, she just wanted to be alone with John and sleep, not necessarily in that order, and not necessarily without intervening events.

She held back a sigh and closed her eyes for a few seconds. She had to find some way to really rest, to relax and focus and think. After what had happened in the meadow, it was obvious that this round with the Asmodai and the Rakshasa and whoever else might be involved was going to demand more of everybody. Moreover, Camille and her quad had something to offer in this war, something more than low-average elemental talents, good fighting skills, and excellent demon tracking. They had to get better with their projective talents, and Camille knew she was the one who had to help them all get better.

Yet Ona's words haunted her, about how dangerous their sentient gifts might be.

Were Ona's warnings overblown?

What *were* the real dangers, other than exhaustion to the point of falling out, or maybe even dying? Camille had to know, and apparently Ona was the only person on earth who could tell her.

"You still with me, beautiful?" John's sexy voice jerked her out of her obsessing, and she opened her eyes. The room felt even more stuffy, Blackmore was still talking, and she'd had about all she could take. She had to get out. Go. She didn't even know where.

She smiled at John so he wouldn't worry, then loosened her hand from his. "I'm fine, but I need some air."

To Dio she murmured, "Don't hurt anybody, okay? If the meeting ends, play nice and go home."

For once, Dio didn't crack back with anything. She eyed Camille like she could sense the jumpy agitation building in Camille's chest, and she just nodded.

Camille excused herself as quietly as possible, slipping through all the standing and sitting people until she made it to the door, then out into the hallway. She almost headed outside, but opted out of that because the meeting might let out and flood her with people all over again.

Instead, she walked across the hall to the door to the basement gym and headed down, into the earth and stone most fire Sibyls abhorred. The second she hit the stairs, the cool air started to relieve her and help her think, and she almost ran the rest of the way down, through the gym door and into the big, empty stone space. There was equipment spread everywhere, with weights and mats and balls and machines, but there was a lot of open space, too.

She had only switched on one light, so the space seemed candlelit, and that was just fine by her. She went to the middle of the room, and for a time she just sat on the soothing, cold stone, breathing in the earthy, rocky smell of the place. Hints of rubber and sweat, light shades of cleanser—the gym smelled alive and fertile, energized yet completely relaxed. She needed to match that combination, but it wasn't easy.

After a time centering herself, she said, "Ona?"

No idea why. Just hoping.

No answer.

"Ona, if you can hear me, I need to know more."
Tears collected in Camille's eyes. "I need to know everything, and I know you can tell me."

She waited.

Still nothing.

Of course there was nothing. Camille let her head roll
forward to her chest. Ona wasn't some ghost or invisi-
ble Astaroth lurking in the unseen shadows. If Camille
wanted to talk to her, she'd have to use communication
channels, but she definitely didn't want to go through
platforms and mirrors where everybody would know.
She need to talk to Ona the way Ona had tried to teach
her—the old way. Ona would probably say *the real way*.

Camille got up and took off her shoes, letting her bare
feet touch the stone. She tried to imagine communication channels, large and small, running everywhere all
around her. Ona's diagram had shown the channels
flowing away from the Sibyl, but Camille couldn't wrap
her consciousness around how that would work. She'd
have to rely on the older models.

She remembered what had worked in the lab the few
times she had been successful at getting some energy flowing, and she closed her eyes and got her feet moving. The
dance came easily enough this time, faster and faster,
flowing out of her like it did when she got on the platforms and worked the mirrors.

Camille put out her arms and started to spin, something
she didn't often have to do, but it built the fire energy
flowing out of her, agitated it, and helped it join the ambient energy in the room, in the rock, and seemingly
everywhere in the air. She imagined Ona hiding out in one
of the tunnels in Motherhouse Ireland, maybe even the
hollow little space where Camille first encountered her. In
her mind, she reached out to the fire in the channels she
imagined around her, and envisioned herself connected to

Ona. The dinar around her neck warmed her chest and hummed, like she was feeding it exactly what it liked.

Her left foot came down, and she sensed a flexing burst in the fire, a sensation like the actual channels grinding open, only not so violent and total. This opening was just enough, just right, and she thought maybe, maybe, she could send a word through, and her right foot came down—

On dirt instead of stone.

The air changed so abruptly Camille felt it like thunder in her belly, beating out her breath. She stopped spinning so fast she almost fell on her face, and when her hands touched the wall in front of her, she froze stock-still with absolute shock.

She wasn't in the townhouse gym in New York City anymore.

She knew exactly where she was, only she couldn't let herself believe it.

I know this place, her rational mind insisted. *I know every stone in this castle, better than I know my own reflection.*

She was in Motherhouse Ireland. She was down in the tunnels, in the exact spot where she had been standing the day she met Ona.

Oh. My. Goddess.

Her heart lurched into her throat and she covered her mouth to keep from screaming.

Energy radiated away from her and dissipated in the elemental protections coating every inch of the Motherhouse, and Camille felt the castle's immense bulk looming above her, a sentinel, a soldier in its own right. As her own energy cleared, she felt something fractured and tenuous coming from behind her, deeper in the tunnels, down in the dark.

When she was a child, the energy had terrified her, but

now she knew it. She couldn't say she understood it, but she at least knew what to call it.

"Ona," she said, but her only answer was soft, broken sobs.

Camille dusted her hands off on her jeans, still dizzy from where she was and how she'd gotten here, but she pulled herself together as fast as she could and headed into the blackness to find the person she'd come to talk to.

Ona was huddled on a cot in a room at the end of a hallway Camille had rarely traversed. A single candle lit the room, which smelled faintly of sage and the fresh bowl of stew Ona hadn't touched. Camille glanced at the room's rough ceiling, thinking of the adepts and Mothers above. Somebody was looking after Ona, just as they always looked after the infirm. She was one of the broken, but no, not really forgotten. Just tended to and left to find her own way back if she could.

When Camille saw Ona as she was, tiny and fetal, a rough woolen blanket pulled up so high only the top of her bald head peeked out, she was struck by memories of herself. She'd been in much the same shape after Bette and Alisa died. She had come back to the castle, to an old nun's cell just like this, and she'd done much of what Ona was doing. She had checked out. She had stayed checked out until Bela came to get her—but Camille didn't have any illusions that she could just reach out and claim Ona the way Bela had claimed her.

This woman was well and truly damaged.

Camille's heart hurt. She approached the cot quietly and settled on her knees beside it.

"I'm here," she told Ona in a soft voice, so she wouldn't startle her. "I came the way you taught me. Thank you."

Ona kept her face turned to the wall and didn't respond except with a strangled, shuddering sob.

Camille reached out and stroked her head, so aged that even the scars had gone smooth.

"Don't touch me," Ona rasped, though she didn't pull away. "You—you don't know what I've done."

"Tell me," Camille urged.

But Ona just cried and cried, and Camille sensed that her presence was disrupting whatever fragment of peace Ona had managed to claim since she fled the brownstone. She could feel Ona's fragility, feel her instability deep, deep inside, and she knew it all too well.

This is me, Camille thought. *If I don't learn, if I don't understand, if I start running away from what hurts me again, this is me*. She caressed Ona's head a little longer, wishing she had something to give her to help her, but coming up empty. *This is my future if I don't change it*.

"It's okay," Camille whispered, understanding at last that whatever answers awaited her, Ona likely wouldn't be supplying them. She had given Camille her gifts in what she'd already taught her and shown her, and she was finished; Camille had to let that be enough or hurt the old woman even more. "I won't ask you any more questions. If you ever want to come see me again—if you want to talk, or stay with me, or just be there—you're always welcome."

Ona pulled away from her, and Camille let her go. For a while, she just sat in the room saying nothing, hoping her presence made a difference.

28

Sometime later, Camille walked back to the place where she'd come into the Motherhouse, and this time it only took her a few spins to work up the state of mind, the right energy, and the right imagery to get herself home. She even stepped into the gym instead of falling in, and this time she didn't freak and almost start screaming.

Until she saw the big guy standing with his back to her, about two feet away.

Camille slammed her hand over her mouth, but about that fast she realized it was John, come hunting for her since she hadn't made it back to the meeting. His attention was riveted by the shoes she'd left behind when she took her little unscheduled transcontinental flight.

"Hey," she said. "Looking for me?"

He turned, his face going slack with surprise when he saw her. Camille let him fill her senses because he looked so good and smelled so good, and she knew when she touched him that all the jumbled thoughts and emotions she couldn't settle would ease—at least until she let him go. She could tell he wanted to talk, but she had to kiss him first, and once she had kissed him, she wouldn't want to talk at all.

John read her, understood without asking, and his arms took her in and shut her off from all the craziness outside the two of them. His lips moved on hers, gentle and demanding, yet giving—how could such a rough man feel so soft? Her whole being responded to him, tensing in all the right ways. He tasted hot and male with a whisper of mint, and she didn't want anything else in the world but more of that, more of him, more of them together.

I want him inside me. I want him deep, and I don't want him to stop.

The image was so stark and consuming she had to pull away for a breath, and she saw that his chest was heaving. So was hers. He studied her like he was counting freckles and making a chart, then like he was trying to find exactly the right words for what he wanted to say, or the exact route to her heart and the way to make it his forever.

"I've been thinking, beautiful, about what you asked me." He touched her face, keeping the distance between them even though she felt like he was sharing half her soul already. "About after. After this is over."

Camille's belly did a little flip. "Yeah?"

His fingers traced her cheek, from eye to chin and back again, sending delicious shocks all over her body.

"I don't have a lot of answers yet, but whatever after looks like, I want you in it."

Camille let that rush through her like prairie fire, warming all the dark corners inside her. She didn't say yes and she didn't say no, because she couldn't talk, but she could smile at him, and that seemed to be enough for the moment.

"Did I say too much?" he asked, sounding careful and earnest, not like he was about to pull away from her or act wounded.

"No," she whispered, loving the feel of his fingertips stroking her face. Her eyelids fluttered closed from the sensation, but she knew he was waiting for the rest of the answer, so she tried to give it to him.

"I . . . just want there to be an after." Tears suddenly rushed into her eyes, and she couldn't stop them. "John, I'm so stupid—I don't just want an after, I want *happily* ever after, for us, for all the people we love."

"It can happen." He kissed her like he was trying to convince her, and if anyone could make her believe, this was the man.

She raised her fingers to his chin, then slid them between their mouths so she could talk. "We both know how war works, John."

He pulled away a few inches and gave her an even deeper look. His voice dropped impossibly lower, getting impossibly sexier. "Happily ever after *can* happen."

His lips took hers again, cutting off her arguments, cutting off her worries. The world swirled away from her and she let it go, back to wanting nothing but him inside her, nothing but him for hours.

It was hard, but she let him turn her loose, and she waited while he locked the gym door and pulled over two thick mats for them to use.

It was a lot easier to let him undress her slow and easy, sliding her jeans over her hips, then hooking his fingers in her underwear and getting rid of them, too, all the while kissing her and telling her she was the most beautiful woman he had ever seen.

He raised her sweater over her head and discarded it, then stroked her sides until he brought chills across every inch of her body. "I could look at you for days," he murmured, kissing the hollow between her neck and chest as he unfastened her bra and finally, finally, she was naked, nothing on her body except the dinar. Excitement coursed through her, heating her like liquid fire, and she wanted his hands and mouth everywhere at the same time. Could there ever be anything more erotic than standing in the wide, cool basement, totally vulnerable to anything John wanted to do?

And he wasn't even undressed yet.

She rubbed herself against his jeans and sweatshirt, letting the rough fabric tease her breasts, her belly, her thighs as he cupped her ass and pulled her closer, kissing her with his entire body. When the coin around her neck made contact with him, it vibrated. She met his tongue, groaning already, knowing she had to have him soon or the want would kill her.

"I could touch you for days," he whispered. "Weeks."

Camille got more warm shivers from his edgy tone. She leaned back into his grip just enough to run her hands over her own nipples while he watched, his eyes going wide when she pinched. Before he could react, she moved her hand down to the damp red curls between her legs and touched herself there, too, making sure he could see.

"Come on," she said, surprised at the tease in her voice. "You told me you never walk away from challenges."

"Never." He grabbed her wrists and pulled her to the mat with him, holding her hands above her head as he settled on top of her. The sudden move caught her off guard and made her heart pound in the most delicious way as he stared at her, his eyes going dark and heavy with desire.

Captive . . .

"Can you take what I have to give?" he asked, sounding serious and five steps past dangerous.

His challenge right back to her—and his was better. She felt every word, in all the places that mattered. "Yes."

He moved his knee between her legs, hitting her sweet spot and making her moan.

"You sure about that, Camille?"

She couldn't breathe. How could she speak? He kept up the pressure, moving his knee back and forth, making her buck from the exquisite pressure, and she knew he wouldn't stop until she said something or exploded, whichever came first.

"Positive," she said, a rasp, not really a word at all.

John kept her hands trapped and kissed her so fiercely Camille thought she might never recover. His knee kept moving, his jeans sliding against her sex, rough and fast. Her pulse pounded and more warm shivers shook her. Already building. How was that possible?

"You're mine now," John said, and then his mouth claimed her so completely she couldn't argue.

He eased the pressure between her legs, refusing her any release as his lips traveled from her mouth to her jaw and lower, tracing and nibbling, letting his stubbled chin brush across her skin. She groaned at the fire of his teeth on her flesh, biting her neck, biting what ached, all the way down to her chest, to the top of her breasts. Her nipples throbbed, waiting, waiting, but he was taking his time.

"I asked for this, didn't I?" She said that through her teeth even though she tried to sound casual.

His only response was a laugh—and more waiting.

Camille twisted against his grip, pressing her breasts closer to his mouth, but John wouldn't let her free. Her breathing got faster and faster, and she tried again to push toward what she wanted.

John chuckled against her nipple, keeping his lips closed, and the vibration doubled the heat at Camille's center.

"Impatient, aren't we." He kissed the tip of her breast. She moaned from the contact, straining toward him, and mercy came. His mouth found her aching nipple and fastened on, sucking deeply. When his tongue raked against the tight, beaded flesh, Camille cried out, wishing he would touch her between her legs—or let her touch herself.

"I need you," she whispered, not even able to play games.

He heard her. She knew because he bit down harder on the nipple, driving her half insane.

Camille arched off the mat as he sucked her other nipple, then kissed every inch of her breasts, nipping and biting just to make her scream.

Begging seemed like a good idea, but Camille was way past words, way past caring about anything but John and what she wanted him to do. She begged him with her body, with every move she made, pleading with him to touch her where she craved.

Too wild, with her hands trapped like this, her body naked and at his mercy, and damn him, he took his time, kissing each inch of her at his leisure. His teeth, his tongue, his lips covered her belly, licking rises and hollows, nipping freckles and dimples. He even used the dinar, moving the steadily humming chain and coin back and forth across her breasts, doubling the heat that was already making her give off sparks.

"You still sure?" he murmured, teasing her lower curls with his mouth.

"Yes." She moved her wrists against his palms. If he let her go, she'd hit him. "Yes, yes!"

John turned her wrists loose, but before she could react, he pushed her legs open and sank three fingers knuckle-deep in her wet, pounding channel.

Camille lost it, thrashing as she climaxed almost instantly, sensations bursting through her like chain-reaction explosions. She raised her hips to meet his thrusts and grabbed for his hair, but he had already moved his head lower. A second later, he ran his tongue across her swollen center.

She jerked and groaned, trapped in a whole new way, captive to the skill of his hands, his mouth, and she hit the top again before she could even catch her breath from the first time. Everything in her body turned red-hot, sensitized, and she had to sit up.

He raised himself with her, settling on his knees, locking eyes with her as he used his free hand to pull her hips onto his thighs. He never stopped moving his fingers, pushing them deeper, keeping rhythm, making her suck air with each plunge.

"You win," she said between thrusts. " I have to have you. Now, John, please. Now."

And this time he didn't make her wait very long. He shifted her to the mat and came out of his clothes. In a matter of seconds he was back, positioning her beneath him, rubbing himself against her pulsing, ready opening.

So big. She knew that, but feeling him again—*damn.*

He went slow on the first stroke even though she was aroused, careful even at the height of excitement.

With a deep sigh of satisfaction, Camille lifted her hips to take him. "Yes, ah, Goddess, that's it." She wrapped her legs around him and held him for a moment, savoring how he filled her, trusting him with every sensation and emotion, and needing so much more. Then she let go of everything and opened her legs wide, taking every inch, trying to let him know how fast and how hard she wanted him.

John took her cue and plunged deep, as deep as she could stand, and she screamed in triumph. This was what she wanted, what she absolutely had to have. She felt herself catch fire inside, burning, burning, and all around them the smoke started to rise. The coin around her neck bounced and hummed, going still only when it touched both of them at the same time.

"More," she demanded. Camille couldn't get enough of him. She raised her hips and met him with force, and still he went deeper.

"More, please."

With a growl, he pumped into her, pulling her hips to meet him, again, again, again, making them one body, one need, until fire covered her skin and his skin, only the dinar saving him from going up in smoke.

This time when she reached the top, she flew like a phoenix, rising high, heading for the sun, then burning in perfect, soul-soothing flames all the way back down to earth again. She lay in his arms, letting her tears stream for a time. Release. Total relaxation. Absolute pleasure. He gave her everything, and then they shared it until neither of them had anything left at all.

It's definitely supposed to be this way, she thought. *I don't want anything else ever again.*

29

John never wanted to let her go.

He stayed inside her, feeling her heart beat, feeling his heart beat, as they breathed together, both coated in sweat and a decent amount of soot and ash. The whole basement smelled like sex and sweat and fire. It was hot as hell, but she was hotter. He'd never felt anything like that, but if he stayed where he was, he could swear he'd get hard all over again.

"You're unbelievable." He ran his lips around the edges of her ear, loving the way she shivered. Then he kissed her cheek and neck, sampling a few of the different kinds of softness she had to offer.

"And you want me again," she said, her smile intoxicating him as much as her voice, nothing but a deep, sexy purr as she wrapped her legs around him and started moving.

John made love to her, slowly this time, taking time with each rolling thrust. Her arms flopped away from him and her head tilted back. Her eyes were closed, her mouth open, totally without inhibition—and totally his.

There had never been anything better than this. There couldn't be anything better than her.

For a time afterward, he cradled her face-to-face on the mat, and they didn't speak. For all her communicating, Camille seemed comfortable with times that didn't require any words. He liked that. He liked everything about her.

Later, still face-to-face with him, she asked him about

the end of the meeting that she'd missed, and she kissed him between sentences as he gave the report.

"Blackmore talked a lot about what Bela did in the meadow, and how it helped, and how everybody needed to think of unique solutions to old problems. Jack always had a little bit of football coach in him."

Camille's expression was still relaxed. "Maybe that's what we need, though I have to be honest—I can't imagine Jack Blackmore as a rah-rah kind of guy."

John had been thinking through a few things he needed to ask Camille, and this seemed like as good a time as any, since they were on the subject. "What exactly did Bela do in the north meadow? Why did it hit her so hard?"

"It's part of her terrasentience. Bela's not strong with terrakinesis—earthmoving—so she uses the charm I made her to pump it up sometimes." The lines on Camille's face tightened at the mention of the charm. "With the charm, she channels her earth energy through her to do the heavy lifting. It's hard on us when we do projective stuff, all that energy pushing through us."

"I can imagine, but this fight against the demons, it'll take everything we've got and then some." He brushed her hair out of her face.

"I'm aware of that." She sounded a little tense. Worried? Or maybe slightly annoyed? He wondered if he'd been patronizing her. He had, hadn't he?

"Sorry," he said. "I really have to work on my pillow talk."

She laughed. "We don't have any pillows." Her laughter faded then, too quickly for John's tastes. "But, our lives are what they are. We could make shit up, or we could keep doing this—sharing what's really happening in our heads and hearts."

Those eyes. He could look into them until next year, at least. "You can be scary sometimes."

"I'm sure you're terrified." She picked those words, but John couldn't miss the fact that she had started looking away and fidgeting, like she was plotting a great escape any second.

"Are you afraid, beautiful?"

"Yes."

"Of me?"

"Yes. No. Not—not really."

"Put it in words. I can wait."

Camille closed her eyes. Opened them. Seemed surprised that he was still there. He didn't have a sense that she was trying to torture him or herself, only that she had deep hurts, deep fears that only a long time of loving and talking could put to rest.

"We've got patrol in a few hours," she said, her voice coming out in a husky rasp.

John acknowledged this by rubbing her arm some more, keeping her close, and not taking back his question. Waiting her out—it worked almost every time.

Her muscles got tighter than tight, and her breathing became shallow even though he was trying to comfort her. He was getting a sense she was close to her bolt point, that soon she just wouldn't be able to stay anymore if she didn't start talking to him about what was bothering her, what was hurting her.

"Don't go, beautiful." He wasn't begging or demanding. Just asking.

"I feel like I'm a complete coward. I know that's what I'm being, but I don't know how to be anything else." A second later, she added, "I don't want to be Ona, terrified and broken and alone."

John wasn't entirely sure what she meant with that last part, but the terrified and broken and alone part was easy enough to grasp, and hearing it made him hurt for her. "I'm right here." God, he couldn't stand it when he couldn't comfort her. Everything he was saying felt lame, but he had nothing else to offer but himself and the few phrases that came to him. "We're right here together."

The fear finally showed on her face, and he heard it in her voice, too. "What if you stay? What if you start meaning everything to me, and then I lose you, too?"

"I don't plan to lose you, Camille—and I don't plan to get lost." He kissed her, soft and easy, pulling back before he risked making her feel trapped. "Can we do any better than that?"

She tried to say something, but the words choked off. This was it.

When her famous fire Sibyl communication shut down, she was about to get up and run.

"Don't go," he said again.

For a few long seconds, he was sure she would pull away from him, scramble to her feet, grab her clothes, and disappear out the gym door. He thought he was ready for it even though he didn't know how he'd stand it, but what he really wasn't ready for was what happened next.

Camille seemed to go to war with herself, closing her eyes, opening them, swallowing a few times, and giving off thin lines of smoke from her shoulders. She shook in his loose embrace, but after a long, searching look into his eyes, she just stopped. Went still. She quit fighting—what? Him? Herself?

Then Camille settled back into John's arms, hugged his neck tightly . . . and stayed.

30

Tarek was no stranger to dark urges and emotions. Rage, hunger, and lust were as familiar to him as desert landscapes, the rising of the sun, the moon's cold glow, and the ridges of his fangs in tiger form. He was not, however, accustomed to joy, to pride, to the fierce sense of triumph he experienced when he entered the conference room of the Westchester mansion Seneca had made available for his personal use.

The room itself was simple in its splendor, with a golden chandelier illuminating framed pictures of ocean-going ships on dark paneling, hardwood floors, and a large oak table with twenty leather chairs. On any normal day, the space smelled of lemon and cotton from cleansers and rags. The carefully laid charms and elemental bindings Griffen had created and placed at its corners blocked all incoming energy, just as it shielded any energy within the house from detection—but tonight the air reeked of strength and power and new, expensive suits. Surely any passerby would know something wonderful was occurring within. How could the world remain unaware of what Tarek found so bone-stirringly magnificent?

The twenty chairs in the large room had been filled with heavily muscled human-looking men of all colorings and tastes in clothing. The walls behind the table were also crowded with men of similar height and weight. From Tarek's left, the youngest specimen came forward. This man, a boy in comparison to the rest, had an indistinct nationality, both by accent and features, though Tarek would have guessed Hispanic heritage.

The boy wore dark slacks, a white shirt, and leather shoes, and he looked like he'd escaped from a preparatory school only days ago.

"Aarif." Tarek put his hand on his true brother's shoulder, smiling in spite of the many challenges awaiting them this night, and perhaps many nights to come.

Aarif's eyes gleamed, a golden light burning in the dark depths. He seemed overwhelmed, unable to put his thoughts fully into words, but he spread out his arms. "*Culla.* Just . . . *look* at them."

Tarek could do little else. He smiled at the men around the table and standing against the walls, and they returned his pleased expression.

"My brothers," he said. "You have come. You have all come."

Since the moment of their release from their temple prison in the Valley of the Gods, the surviving Eldest had not been in the same location together. They had all been cultivating supporters and their own Created in locations scattered across the globe. That made the most sense for their long-term survival, but even with their precautions and separation, Rakshasa losses had been heavy at the hands of John Cole before he died, and now due to Sibyl interference.

These men, these true brothers, were all Tarek had left, and all he cared about. Each Rakshasa appeared skilled in maintaining human form, so each had followed Strada's last edict: to learn their enemy, to fit in, and to form alliances that would serve them. Each had answered their new *culla*'s call to put aside their individual triumphs and join him for the good of the pride.

Tarek moved to the head of the table, deeply touched when each head bowed in a gesture of submission. Then his true brothers met his eyes. Cool air bathed Tarek's face, issuing from the room's many vents, and he was grateful for the stark sensation. Otherwise, the sight of his real family might have left him speechless for some time.

"Separation no longer serves us," he told them, knowing they required explanation for his urgent demand that they come at once to New York City. "In large numbers, we cannot be defeated, even by an army of elemental witches whose ancestors harmed us in the past."

Naveed, the tallest around the table, had chosen brown skin and short brown hair, and he wore a standard American business suit that probably drew no undue attention in Boston, where he had been operating. He made gestures with his hands as he said, "At the height of our desert empire, these women were disorganized and only beginning to find their identity, yet they used old magicks to slaughter half our number and trap us for centuries in that accursed temple. Now that they call themselves Sibyls of the Dark Crescent Sisterhood instead of witches, wise women, and healers, now that they are greater in organization, numbers, and power—how can we hope to prevail?"

"These Sibyls do not wield the terrible and ultimate elemental powers of their ancestors," said Bakr, who would become *culla* upon Tarek's death. He had chosen lighter brown hair than Naveed, and his fawn-brown eyes and light coloring seemed fitting for his location in the Southern city of Atlanta. "Still, they are fierce and brutal in direct battles. We have found no certain solution to counter their attacks, though the protections you instructed us to create to hide our energy signatures have been very useful."

Tarek appreciated Bakr's honesty and rewarded it with openness of his own. "I believe our way forward is to band together and eliminate the Sibyls in each population center. When enough of their fighters lie dead in the streets and we have taken city after city, perhaps they will be interested in establishing a treaty. Until then, we must kill them without hesitation or mercy."

He watched his brothers carefully for any hint of dissent or disagreement, but he saw nothing of the sort. Fahaad, who had been leading their efforts in Houston, Texas, closed his blue eyes in obvious relief. His sunburned skin seemed to loosen at the edges as he grew more hopeful from Tarek's words.

"Why are we beginning here in New York?" Hasram asked, his flame-colored hair a match for his temperament. "Dalal and I have dealt the Sibyls in Los Angeles many crushing blows—they are nearly on the run. Should we not finish the job there before coming here?"

"For that matter, we could locate the dens and caves where they train their young and go after them at their source," Ramar suggested. His human form had dark hair, eyes, and skin like Tarek had chosen for himself, giving him a faintly Egyptian appearance.

"In due time," Tarek said. He allowed a moment of silence, studying each of his true brothers in the late-day sunlight sinking into the room's floor-to-ceiling windows. The setting sun gave the oak table a bloody cast, which seemed more than appropriate.

When Tarek was certain each one in the room was ready to listen to him, he revealed the truth of his request for their presence. "I have brought you to New York City first because I believe we face our greatest and most imminent threat here."

He gestured to Aarif, who flushed at the honor of addressing his true brothers as an equal. "We have reason to believe the leader of the rebellious Created who call themselves Bengals has located herself here, along with her amassed army," Aarif said, almost too eagerly. "I discovered their trace scent and ultimately their lair in some of my travels in the past two weeks."

Tarek saw lips curl and heard the rumbles of anger. The Bengals were thorns in the paw, but never a serious threat, save for their *culla*, a woman who had faced the Rakshasa in direct battle before—and aided in their near destruction.

"To eliminate that fiend and her ragged band of rebels would bring us all great satisfaction," he said, "and avenge the deaths of our many brothers in the Valley of the Gods."

There were nods, but also scowls and some uncertain expressions. Still, Aarif continued with confidence. "But there is another and even more urgent reason. The Dark Crescent Sisterhood has indeed abandoned the older powers that once devastated us in favor of skills that give them more immediate and controllable weapons in direct combat. Here in New York City, however, we have located a pocket of these witches who still have the old magicks of their ancestors."

This announcement caused some consternation and an outbreak of small discussions. The human-form Rakshasa against the back walls pushed forward to join in the talk around the table, and Tarek didn't feel any need to stop his true brothers until they once more grew ready to listen. After a minute or so, the swell of words subsided, and attention began to turn back to Tarek.

Shafeer, with his boyish American sand-colored hair and splash of freckles, became the one to state the obvious, his higher-pitched voice rising over the swells and lulls of his brothers' lingering conversations. "If the old magicks have survived, the Dark Crescent Sisterhood could defeat us again."

Tarek nodded. "If we leave these four alive to fight us."

Total silence took over then, extending as the Eldest stared at one another, Tarek, or the table in silent contemplation.

"Only four?" asked someone from the back of the room. "We're afraid of just four Sibyls?"

Bakr snarled, and for the first time since they gathered, Tarek caught a flash of fur, silver as starlight, along his heir's knuckles. "It took only four the first time. Your memory is short, Dubar."

Jabrail, who had elected to present himself with rich, dark skin to match his black hair, asked perhaps the most important question, for which Tarek had been waiting. "If they still have the strength to do so, why haven't the Sibyls made a definitive and coordinated move against us?"

Tarek nodded to Aarif, who once more plunged in with eagerness, filling the tense room with his forceful, youthful voice. "They seem uncertain. Hesitant. Tarek and I question if they fully understand their own abilities and how to employ them—which is why we must act with haste."

This time the murmurings and conversations were snuffed out like candle flames under a bell. In each set of eyes, blue, green, brown, black, or any shade in between, Tarek saw the unmistakable gleam of sudden optimism, along with hints of lust for the coming fight. The conference room now smelled of sweat and exertion—like cat and claw and fang and fur. Like Rakshasa. Tarek wanted to roar his solidarity with his true brothers, but it was not yet time for battle cries.

"We have all shared our experiences and reports," Aarif said. "We have all had our allies search and explore and report. I believe that without question, the four witches skulking here in Manhattan are the only women on earth other than the Bengal bitch who could do us lasting harm."

Bakr's toothy grin lifted Tarek's spirits even more. "What is your plan?"

Aarif spread his arms. "Sibyls with the old magicks aren't as effective in simple combat, so that's how we must engage them."

"I propose we draw them into a closed space with barriers too powerful for them to shatter." Tarek placed his hands on the table and leaned forward to be closer to his pride. "Then we meet them in force with our superior numbers and abilities, and we tear them to pieces."

Ramar's expression communicated approval, but he voiced the doubt he carried. "What would cause them to take such a risk, to pursue us into what will no doubt seem like an obvious trap?"

Tarek smiled, and this time he didn't try to stop his fangs from extending. "Bait."

Aarif, black fur showing along both hands, added, "With a strong enough lure, the Sibyls will come."

Now almost every face at the table, including those standing behind, radiated anticipation along with approval.

"Do you propose to capture one of the four and use her to draw her sisters?" Bakr asked.

"That has much merit," Tarek said, "but I believe I have determined an even better enticement. If I am correct, they will come for us with great numbers, perhaps their entire New York contingent, and their human law enforcement associates as well."

No one questioned him on this or asked him for more information, and Tarek knew he had his pride's total trust and support.

Hasram's hectic red coloring had settled, and he now seemed to be calculating his own portion of the battle plan. "How will we contend with the Sibyls who do not have the old magicks—the ones who *do* fight well in close combat?"

"We will leave their destruction to our allies," Aarif said, glancing at Tarek for approval, which Tarek gave with a nod. "The sorcerer and his Coven will defend against the demons and paranormals who fight with the Dark Crescent Sisterhood. Our human friend who so generously gifted us with this house, he and his many foot soldiers will meet the other Sibyls in battle, with Created for shields. Sibyls have no natural resistance to bullets."

Tarek strode to the wall opposite the room's floor-to-ceiling windows, and he opened two wooden panels to reveal a white board on which he had drawn a diagram of the location where he planned to carry out his ambitious plan.

When he looked back at his true brothers to gauge reactions, he saw fangs and claws and fur. He saw gleaming eyes and heard the untamed snorts of approval. The splendid scent of tiger filled his nose, and he felt his own fangs extending.

"I take it," he growled, almost overrun by his own elation, "that we're all in agreement."

The dwelling Seneca had provided offered four stories of luxurious rooms, baths, and relaxing areas, but the Eldest chose to congregate for a human-style meal, refreshments, and companionship in the ample walled backyard, beneath leafless trees and among the dead remnants of flowers and bushes. Tarek found the chilled air refreshing, and the stark landscape only fueled his desire for the upcoming battle. Their first move would be brutal indeed, and he savored even thinking of it—though he knew he had a small chore to perform, just to ensure that all went as he planned.

That chore presented itself in a matter of minutes, as Tarek knew it would.

Dressed in jeans and a black sweatshirt, Griffen came out the back door of the house, walking quickly into the barely illuminated night. "Tarek," he called, tension obvious in his voice. "Has Rebecca been here? I can't find—"

Griffen's breath streamed around his face in ragged, misty ribbons, and the scant moonlight caught the exact moment when he took in just who—and what—he was approaching. He came to a clumsy halt when the crowd of Eldest ceased conversation and turned as one to face him.

The sorcerer's usually arrogant expression faded, replaced by naked shock, then by a flat, neutral mask Tarek took for barely concealed terror.

Good.

Aarif's lips twitched, but he held back his mirth, and Tarek appreciated his youngest true brother for his restraint. He didn't want Griffen afforded the slightest measure of comfort or reassurance. The sorcerer had become complacent in his dealings with Tarek and Aarif, perhaps even thinking of himself as equal in stature and status. To come face-to-face with the full measure of Rakshasa power—the strain showed instantly in the dulling of his blue eyes and the rubbery loosening of his arms.

Tarek gestured to his brothers to resume their festivities, and he and Aarif took Griffen by both arms, helping him walk back to Seneca's mansion. Once they reached the massive kitchen with its polished stone countertops; its hanging racks of utensils, pots, and pans; and its steadily crackling fire on the hearth that also opened onto the main living area, Tarek let Aarif hold on to Griffen while he faced the sorcerer.

"You—you didn't tell me," Griffen said, still rattled, but having regained enough composure enough to try to meet Tarek's gaze. "I didn't know to expect ... company."

It took some doing, but Tarek calmed himself and chose his words with care and deliberation. "We haven't been honest or open with each other of late, have we, my friend?"

Griffen's eyes darted from Tarek to the back door and back to Tarek again. "I don't know what you mean."

It was a challenge to Tarek to keep his human form. Good practice, but difficult. "Did you truly believe I would allow you or your Coven to overshadow me?"

Griffen's mouth came open in mock outrage. "I'm not trying to—"

Aarif remained in human form but for his fully extended claws, which he raised to Griffen's throat with a none too gentle warning snarl.

Tarek lifted one finger to his lips, and Griffen fell silent, though his blue eyes now burned with an indignant rage.

When Tarek was certain he could speak without lunging at the sorcerer, he said, "It took me some time to understand that your brilliant charms to repel energy also repel my ability to track you and your sister, your thoughts, and your activities. I corrected that oversight some time ago."

Griffen's color turned pasty, though the rage didn't leave his eyes. Tarek could tell he wanted to ask Tarek how he'd made that correction, but common sense likely gave him the answer before he voiced the question.

"I didn't know about your encounter with the Sibyls until after it occurred," Tarek said, "but I know where you're keeping your Coven and I know the identity and location of each member of your under-Coven. I know all of your movements since the failed battle in Central Park, and I must say, I'm not pleased with the amount of contact you've had with the other Balkan families, or with the Russians or the Italians."

Griffen fidgeted in Aarif's grip. "I'm trying to build allies. Our human army. I thought that's what you wanted."

"You're trying to build *your* human army, held together by fear of *my* power." Tarek let out a low, hungry snarl. "You have forgotten who serves whom."

Somehow the sorcerer managed to go totally still and make his voice sound amazingly earnest. "I haven't betrayed you, *culla*."

"Not yet," Tarek growled. "And you will not have the chance."

Tarek nodded to Aarif, who released Griffen. Griffen rubbed his neck, clearly checking to see if Aarif had broken the skin on his throat.

Seneca is a wise man, Tarek thought, though he hated that his human ally had noticed so much that Tarek himself had missed.

Griffen had feigned such interest in becoming Created to ensure his immortality and his power over the dominating army Tarek would one day build to do his bidding, once he had proper control of the human population. Tonight, his fear of infection put a lie to everything Tarek had believed about the man. Tarek's lips curled away from his human teeth, and he longed to shift to tiger form and chew the human down to bones and gristle.

The sorcerer seemed to understand that he had given himself away, and his pale face went suddenly dark and sour. His fingers twitched like he might be considering drawing on some of his considerable elemental talents, but Tarek and his true brothers had worked some old magick of their own, making this kitchen and the wine cellar below it an elemental dead zone. Griffen would not be able to draw on his protections here.

Griffen glanced around, eyebrows pulling together as he realized his helplessness and his peril.

Oh, how Tarek longed to spill the sorcerer's entrails on the smooth, modern stone floor—but unfortunately, he needed what Griffen could do, at least for a short time in the future.

"Since you no longer desire to keep our original bargain, I have a new incentive for your cooperation." Tarek gestured to the door at the back of the kitchen that led down to the wine cellar.

When Griffen didn't move, Aarif walked to the cellar door and opened it. He gave Griffen a sarcastic bow, and gestured to the darkened stairs winding down to the cold chamber beneath the earth.

When Griffen made no attempt to walk to the door, Tarek gave him a warning growl. "Will you use your own legs, or shall I assist you?"

Griffen's eyes flared for a moment, his fingers curling to fists, but he made no response. After a few moments of breathing rapidly, he headed for Aarif, faced off with him for a moment, then turned and marched down the stairs. Aarif followed, and Tarek brought up the rear, fastening the cellar door behind them.

Before Tarek reached the final step, he heard Griffen cry out—a moment of high human emotion, true pain, and definite fury. He envied Aarif the pleasure of seeing Griffen's unguarded expression.

Tarek stepped onto the cellar's cobblestone floor, gratified to see the six Created he had selected for this duty facing him with silent dignity. They were each in full tiger form, golden eyes bright with intelligence and, thankfully, sanity. He had armed them with swords and rifles to complement their impressive fangs and claws, and once he and Aarif took Griffen from the cellar tonight, these loyal children would slaughter anyone who attempted to enter the space without Tarek's leave.

Tarek turned to his right, where rows of wine racks filled the wall in front of Aarif and Griffen. The bottles had been removed to make room for the elementally treated shackles. She had been placed in a semiconscious state using an injection of Rakshasa venom balanced with metal extracts, opiates, and elemental fluids to keep the venom temporarily inert. The shackles fixed her limp, unconscious body to the wooden racks at the wrists and ankles. A flat, band-shaped clamp held her head back to prevent her from leaning forward until she slowly suffocated. In a gesture of mercy, Tarek had left the girl clothed, and he had hooded her so her slack-faced drooling didn't offend him.

Still, Rebecca Kincaid was recognizable by her size and shape alone. Her slight frame seemed unnaturally small against the cuffs and chains.

Griffen didn't take his eyes from Rebecca, and his words left him in a harsh rush. "Let my sister go, or I'll kill you all."

Tarek allowed himself a chuckle at the sorcerer's expense, and the sound bounced through the little cellar. "If you had the power to do that, you would have acted by now. We both know you don't."

Griffen turned on Tarek so fast and fiercely that Tarek actually knew a moment's startled doubt, but he quickly read the mix of abject rage and helplessness on the sorcerer's face. He took a slow breath of the cellar's air, which still held a hint of wine bouquet from bottles that had been broken in the removal, then he held up his hand in a calming gesture. "She is unharmed and safe for now."

He explained about the stasis induced by the inert venom, and the simple injection it would take to activate that venom.

Griffen's gaze whipped to his sister, and Tarek knew the sorcerer wanted to run to her and rip her chains free of the wine racks. Aarif tensed, ready to stop him if it came to that, but Griffen held himself in check.

"When the four Sibyls who concern me are dead," Tarek said, "I'll administer an injection that dissolves the venom and return her to you undamaged."

Griffen took this in with another modicum of self-control, impressive for a human. Tarek knew better than to let him regain his emotional balance, so he moved closer to the sorcerer, violating the man's sense of safety in the ways he knew Griffen would despise the most.

"If you betray me or disappoint me in any way, she'll be turned and used as the Eldest see fit." Tarek knew his own smile was cruel now, as it had to be. "When we tire of her, she'll be put to death."

"We will not spare her any pain," Aarif said, gazing at the girl in a fashion that suggested he would very much like to have some time with Rebecca and inflict that pain himself. "Her suffering will be proportional to your failures."

Griffen went an unpleasant shade of purple, but his mouth remained firmly closed.

Tarek understood the sorcerer's feelings, though he felt no sympathy. Rebecca was Griffen's only real companion, a pride of one, but Griffen's pride nonetheless. If Tarek were in the sorcerer's position, he would do all he could to retrieve his kin and protect her from pain.

After many long, silent seconds, the sorcerer spoke through his teeth. "What do you want?"

The enraged submission in Griffen's tone pleased Tarek. Better. Things were already improving between them.

"I need your assistance in retrieving the lure I intend to use to hook the Sibyls, and when the Sibyls take the bait you will fight with us and help us to destroy the four witches with the old magicks."

Griffen let out air through his nose, loudly, almost a snort. "And after that?"

"Rebecca is yours again, we part ways, and you will be free to pursue your own desires and aims. And I—" Tarek leaned into Griffen's face, letting his claws extend before he put his hand on the back of Griffen's neck and pulled him forward until they touched at the forehead.

"I will be free of you. If you cross my path again in the future, I'll rip out your throat and feed your carcass to the Created."

He waited, his eyes inches from Griffen's gleaming blue orbs.

"I'll do it," the sorcerer said, though Tarek knew Griffen would rather bring the mansion down around them than agree to surrender whatever it was he had been plotting outside of Tarek's awareness. Whatever it was didn't matter in the least to Tarek, not now that he had regained control of the servant he had once counted as his most valuable tool in the Rakshasa's bid to regain their former glory and happiness.

Tarek let Griffen go. "Report to me daily by noon with reports of your Coven's progress and the preparation of the Created for battle, or your sister will meet her fate."

Griffen's single nod was so stiff Tarek thought it a wonder the man's neck didn't crack at its base.

The sorcerer spent a few long seconds studying his chained sister, then made his way up the steps and out of the wine cellar.

"Should I follow?" asked Aarif, who unbeknownst to Griffen had been the sorcerer's shadow since Tarek realized he needed more direct means of tracking the man's activities.

"No. It no longer matter whether or not he complies." Tarek patted Aarif on the shoulder, promising himself that he would never again lose sight of whom he could trust. "Either he reports to me and I see progress, or we kill the girl, slaughter his Covens, and have done with them."

"But the battle—" Aarif began.

"The Coven is important to our aims, yes, but we could succeed without them."

Aarif's bow was graceful. *"Culla."*

Tarek's heart swelled anew at his true brother's loyalty. They had come so far since the days of Strada's leadership, when Tarek had taken regular beatings for disagreeing with the older brother he now missed with a reasonable detachment.

"Come, brother." Tarek patted Aarif again. "Let us rejoin our family and enjoy this reunion. In the morning our work resumes."

Tarek turned for the stairs and climbed for the kitchen, hearing Aarif padding quietly in his wake. As Aarif closed the cellar door behind them, Tarek thought he heard a whimper from the chained girl below.

She was strong, that one, despite her appearance, to regain any sort of consciousness with the venom she'd received.

Tarek snarled as he left the door behind him and headed back toward the celebration in the mansion's walled backyard. It was a pity, really, that he was so certain Griffen would keep his part of their new bargain, because Aarif was right about Rebecca.

She would be an interesting conquest.

31

Camille had been nervous more times in her life than she could count, but this about took the cake. She had put on her best jeans, a loose-fitting black shirt, and a long leather overcoat to cover her scimitar. He was dressed in like fashion, carrying his broadsword—but he didn't have to deal with a blindfold.

"How does Central Park sound?" he asked as he walked her along, arm around her shoulder, holding her close to him so she could match his steps.

"Like it did five minutes ago, when you started turning me in circles."

"Listen." He stopped her, kissed her. They were two young lovers heading for a big surprise—part of which was true.

Camille kept her arms around John's neck and did as he suggested, taking in the laughter of children, the rattle of wind through branches that had shed their leaves, and the distant rush of traffic on the main roads. If she really paid attention, she could spend hours detailing each nuance and hint of a noise—Sibyl hearing was as acute as Sibyl vision, just not accurate over long distances.

John kissed her again, warming her lips and finding her tongue with his.

"Mmm." He tasted like mint again, this time from gum. She liked the sharper sensation, and it made the inside of her mouth tingle. "You're into this role-playing, aren't you?" she said against his rough cheek. "Maybe it's the blindfold. Are you into blindfolds, John?"

"Let me tie you up one day and you'll find out."

Goddess, that voice.

And the invitation made her insides tingle as much as her mouth.

"Come on," John said. "We've got a lot of ground to cover."

He took her hand again, pulling her along fast, making her laugh and stumble as she ran with him, trusting him more than she thought she could. Running blind. What a complete rush.

She knew he was taking her around and around, covering ground they had already covered, but she tried not to pay attention even though her Sibyl brain automatically traced the route and calculated their position and direction—steadily northeast. Sometime later, Camille estimated they were somewhere near 119th Street, and she had an idea where they were headed. Probably into the aqueduct, down into the earth, into one of the lost tunnels no longer in use under New York City.

She tried to keep her step light and her breathing normal, but she couldn't help remembering that the Legion used to manufacture Asmodai demons in those tunnels. The demon who'd killed Bette had ambushed them from one of the old aqueduct gatehouses.

Then and now. Two different time periods, two different realities. There are no Asmodai here.

"You okay, beautiful?" John's voice echoed against stone because they were inside now. "If this is making you nervous—"

"I'm fine. Just keep us going. I—I trust you."

He squeezed her arm and moved them ahead, just like she asked, taking a more direct route now, and Camille noticed the smells changing. City air shifted to something more stale. At first she picked up mold and rot, but that finally gave way to something more fertile. Old rock and moss. Her tenseness gave way at the familiarity, like the tunnels under Motherhouse Ireland. Maybe all stone places shared things in common. Camille had a flash of the channels of energy she had learned to work since she could first walk and talk. They were a lot like this—big, quiet, dark holes through the earth, through space and time. Passageways. There were so many, infinite directions, infinite possibilities. It would be like connecting every tunnel on the planet, hooking them all together. She could get anywhere if she just knew the way and held the destination firmly in her mind.

She stumbled from the image and the realization, from seeing communications channels in a new, simpler way. John steadied her, and before he could ask, she said, "Sorry. I was thinking about something too hard and not paying attention to my feet."

"I could carry you," he offered, talking close enough to her ear that chills rushed along her neck and shoulders.

"Don't tempt me, hot stuff."

From somewhere up ahead, Camille heard footsteps.

John slowed, and she immediately had trouble catching her breath.

Asmodai—

It's not Asmodai. Get over it.

The smell was all wrong for Asmodai.

Whatever was heading toward them, it had fur, and it walked with a measured, stealthy gait.

Cat, her nose told her. *Tiger. Rakshasa—but different.* It really did have to be different, because the dinar around her neck gave off little more than a faint buzz with an occasional tremble. That was interesting to her, since the coin reacted to Created, and biologically, as far as anyone knew, Bengals and Created were exactly the same creatures.

Cloth and leather scrubbed against stone. Weapons tapped in sheaths. Big weapons. The space around them seemed small and compressed, still a tunnel, not much room to maneuver. John's grip on her arm tightened, and she knew he was ready to pull off her blindfold if he needed to.

A few moments of silence ensued, then a very deep voice, more snarl than speech, said, "She is the one?"

"Yes," John said.

The other . . . man? Bengal? . . . made a noise like a long, slow sniff. Then they were moving again, walking at a fast pace seemingly straight toward the center of the earth.

When they stopped a minute or so later, a cool, steady breeze told Camille they had entered a much larger space, probably some sort of big chamber. Even though she sensed a lot of life around her, the place was so quiet she could almost hear the air stirring past her ears.

John pressed his hand against her back, encouraging her to lean over, so Camille bent at the waist, and her dinar came forward to dangle in the air below her neck. Somebody started loosening her blindfold, but she didn't think it was John.

When the cloth fell away from her face, Camille found herself almost nose to nose with a silver-haired woman in a silver gown. She had white eyes and strange scars, she smelled like rosewood, and she felt like a Mother, though Camille couldn't say which element dominated her energy signature.

Behind the woman, in a gigantic candlelit chamber, stood dozens of soldiers, silent and unmoving, dressed in jeans and T-shirts and armed with broadswords. Not anything like Sibyls, but an army all the same. Camille could tell they were elite fighters, well trained, the type that were always improving.

"Camille," the woman said, as if she had known Camille her whole life. "I'm Elana, *taza* of the Bengals." She touched the coin around Camille's neck as if in greeting, and the freaky little piece of jewelry seemed to purr like it knew her or something.

"The dinar repels Rakshasa and Created," Camille said. "But it doesn't repel you. Why?"

"It knows me." Elana touched the coin again and made it purr. "It's keyed to demon essence. Those of us who have learned to be more human than demon won't activate its protections."

It knows me.

Great. More riddles.

Camille resisted the urge to ask Elana if she had ever met anyone named Ona. Her energy was as powerful as Ona's, as limitless as any Mother's, yet different. This was a woman who could see without seeing, know without being told, and find the answers to the world's mysteries without ever whispering them to a soul.

Careful to be considerate and deliberate in all her movements, Camille stood.

"She asked to come," John said.

"So I assumed." Elana moved back and let Camille's blindfold drop to the chamber's stone floor. "You were right to bring her. I'm impressed that you've done so well with the Sibyls. You're a man of many talents, John Cole."

"I'm a man with a goal, Elana." He smiled back at her, and Camille noticed how much more softly he spoke to Elana, like she might be his grandmother. That was fitting. Elana felt scary and powerful, for sure, but yeah, also grandmotherly.

"Camille is a fine purpose," Elana said, bringing a fast rush of heat to Camille's cheeks.

John cleared his throat. "I meant killing Rakshasa."

"That's on your list, I have no doubt. I think, however, that it's been a while since you examined that list and checked the order of its items."

Elana let Camille take in the magnitude and extent of her fighting force, then gestured for them to disperse. When the room had emptied except for six huge fighters

Camille figured were her personal guards, Elana said, "I'm honored by your visit, Camille, but if you've come to ask us for our alliance in battle, I can't grant that request—though we remain friendly to and supportive of your aims."

Elana's assumption took Camille by surprise. "That's not my purpose, but if I might ask, why would you refuse a fighting agreement?"

"Like your own people, mine have seen too much of war." Elana gestured to her warrior guard. "Most of these, even my own guards, never asked for what befell them, and they battle only to protect their own and their freedom. That's all I can ask of them. We make no pact to defend the world."

Camille studied the stone-faced Bengal guards, not even able to guess at their ages, but she knew the fatigue she saw in their eyes. "I understand."

Elana watched Camille for a few moments, though Camille knew that interpretation was in her head, since Elana had no actual vision. "If alliance wasn't the purpose for this visit, why have you come?"

"I want to learn better fighting skills." Why did that sound so lame?

It was Elana's turn to be surprised, because she said, "You? Of all Sibyls, why on earth would you feel deficient?"

She must not know. Camille felt herself deflate. John had emphasized that Elana thought Camille was very important in the coming battle with the Rakshasa. "I'm not like my sister Sibyls. I can't make fire on command, not easily or consistently at least, and—"

"Of course you can't." Elana waved this off with some impatience. "One talent gives in favor of the other."

Camille stopped talking and she stopped trying to find the right words to plead her case. "Excuse me?"

"You're a elemental sentient, not a generator. As one

ability grows stronger, the other weakens, since they draw from the same source."

The simplicity and certainty of Elana's statement struck Camille like a slap, and her head snapped back. She found herself blinking, trying to grasp what Elana had said so easily, like this was something everyone had been taught in childhood, but confusion descended.

"You're losing me," John said. "Can I get a quick primer?"

"I'm wondering if I need one myself," Camille muttered.

Elana's expression moved from surprise to concern to anger. She made a motion to her guards, and they, too, cleared the chamber. As soon as they were completely alone, in barely controlled and shaky tones, Elana asked, "Why would you not know something so basic about your own abilities?"

Camille didn't know what to say to this. Finally she explained, "Sentient talents aren't given much value in the Motherhouses these days. There are no lessons about sentience, just basic definitions and explanations about how to use sentience in conjunction with pyrogenesis."

Elana's coloring darkened a shade. "I know the Sibyls chose to develop other skills, but they would have to expect some like yourself to be born with the full measure of older talents—especially when the universe understands the need."

Camille knew she should be respectful to John's friend, but she started pacing. "I think I'm the first in a long time with more than minimal pyrosentient talents."

"So there was no one to teach you? No one at all?" Elana seemed to need to sit down.

Camille glanced around but saw nothing. John had been looking around the chamber, too, and once he realized nothing was there, he offered Elana his arm to steady her.

Elana favored him with a smile, giving her scarred face a gentler, more serene appearance, though her flat, white eyes had gone wide, and that made her seem unusually distant. Camille imagined she saw distraction in those eyes, and new worry, confusion, and concern.

"So you're familiar with projective energy?" Camille asked. "You understand it?"

Elana's fingers curled against John's arm, and color rose in her scarred face. "I am, but until this moment, it wasn't something I thought I'd ever have to discuss in much detail again."

"I need to understand, Elana," John said. "I'm living in a houseful of women who use this stuff every day—and even they don't seem to fully know what they're doing." He stopped. Looked at Camille. "Sorry. I didn't mean for it to come out like that."

"It's true," Camille said. "All we know is what we've found in our archives—which isn't much—and what we've been able to teach ourselves."

Elana's complexion was too dark to turn pale, but her lips twitched toward frowning. She seemed to argue with herself for a nanosecond, then she gestured to a door in the chamber and led them to a smaller room with a stone table with seven stone chairs around it.

The first thing Camille noticed in the room was its smell. Elementally clean. Moist, well-kept stone—and all over the walls, paintings, only these paintings were maps. She moved closer to the nearest map and saw that mountains and other landmarks were raised and textured. She touched the tiny wooden and clay and plaster areas, noting the lines running from everything, faint but connected, like little threads tying the whole world together. Because of new structures left off the maps and old landmarks still visible, some of these works of art were old indeed. A few had jagged words painted in a few places, labeling them, and the center map, a wide desert landscape, had what looked like a child's pencil scrawl near the center, saying, *Heaven.*

The maps had been signed simply *Elana.*

Camille glanced at the woman as she took a seat at the stone table. Elana might have lost her eyes, but not her art. That said a lot for her determination.

John took the seat across from Elana, and after Camille had settled herself next to him, Elana said, "And now for your primer, John. I believe you're familiar with the more common Sibyl talents, such as elemental genesis."

She stretched out her hand, and a small blue flame popped up at the table's center. Camille wondered about Elana's ability to make flame, but many people with elemental talent could perform rudimentary skills and tasks with earth, air, fire, or water.

"Terminus is an additional talent, related to genesis." Elana once more extended her dark hand with its pink ribbon-like scars and motioned to Camille.

Camille held her hand over the flame and absorbed its energy, and it went out.

Elana re-created it a second later. "Kinesis, moving energy, follows much the same principle as terminus." She made a pushing motion with her hand, and the flame on the table arced to a new position like someone had smacked it with a bat. "Used with caution, on small amounts of energy, it's quite useful—but if a Sibyl attempts to move too large an amount, the consequences could be deadly.

"And that brings us to the fourth power, that of sentience, called such because Sibyls had no other way to describe the process of knowing the world through their element, or knowing their element so intimately, by pulling its energy through their essence and projecting it out again, enhanced in force and power by the magnitude of their elemental gift." Elana reached for the flames on the table, and they moved into her hand.

She turned her head away from John and Camille, opened her mouth—

And roared out a gout of flames easily ten times the size and heat of what she had taken in.

Camille sat straight up in her seat as it happened. *Okay, very strong elemental talent, especially if her base ability isn't fire.*

When Elana finished, she leaned forward against the table, and John had to catch her to keep her from slumping face-first on the rock.

"I have very little natural projective talent myself," Elana explained to John when she could speak again, extracting herself from his supporting arm and sitting erect once more. "But that's hardly the point. It doesn't take much of that ability to do tremendous damage—to the Sibyl, or to the world."

John let Elana rest for a second, then went straight back at it. "I don't get it. It's impressive and all, but why is that any more dangerous than the rest of the Sibyl skill set?"

Elana gave him a kind smile. "When a Sibyl uses projective energy, she's neither creating, absorbing, or moving power. She's merely pulling it through her, serving as a mirror, if you will, then projecting it."

Camille got that part, and so did John, because he said, "I understand. But why—"

"Don't you see, my boy?" Elana opened her palm, and the little blue flame came back, then disappeared, like it fell through her palm. "The Sibyl is only a conduit. The natural world is supplying the energy she's using."

Everything Ona had tried to tell Camille came blazing back to her, without all the riddling, without all the wondering this time. It hit her. Shit, did it hit her, and hard.

John was getting it at the same time. "Then . . . the energy they could use, it would be—"

"Limitless," Elana confirmed. "Without boundaries. An earth Sibyl might take down a mountain or a entire mountain range—or form one. An air Sibyl might alter the wind movement across the world and single-handedly destroy the planet's ecological balance. It was this talent that destroyed the water Sibyls long ago, when they were aplenty and kept their Motherhouse at Antilla."

"And fire Sibyls, when we use projective energy?" Camille couldn't help the childish catch in her voice.

Elana shuddered. "Fire Sibyls who manifest projective talents could ignite a village, a countryside, or a continent—but it doesn't stop there. The metals and ores of the earth, the substances that form the earth's molten, beating heart, they are full of fire. The most powerful fire known to those with elemental talents. That metal calls to fire Sibyls with projective inclinations; worse than that, it obeys them."

Camille had a sudden flash of volcanoes blasting out of the earth, of geysers of molten stone raining across North America. Something like that could cause earthquakes and tsunamis. Climate change. Any number of natural disasters. She was pretty sure she wasn't even thinking of everything that could go wrong.

"It's almost like a fire Sibyl using her projective ability somehow joins all the elemental talents together," Camille murmured, fists clenched, knuckles pressing into the stone table.

"She does, in a very primal way. She makes them communicate, though fire remains the base of it all." Elana turned to John. "Fire is very much like air and water, John. It's almost everywhere, in almost everything. The fire Sibyl with projective abilities can draw it into her, through her. With skill and training, much of what she does will seem like storybook magic."

"And the cost?" he asked. "Nothing's free, right? Everything's an exchange, so what's the cost—other than the disaster stuff?"

Elana moved her attention back to Camille. Even though John had asked the question, Camille realized Elana wanted her to hear this part above all else. "Most fire Sibyls with any projective ability die young, victims of their own success. The others have difficulty with emotional balance, because they're always blending their essence with a mercurial and unstable element. It costs them their life, and if not their life, then their health or their mind."

Camille knew she had to have realized that, at least on some level, since Ona had visited and tried to give her a few of the sentient basics. Yet to hear it summarized so clearly—it was still jarring.

John was tense now, fists on the table only inches from Camille's. "Life, health, sanity—are those absolutes? Does it always have to work that way?"

"Those are likelihoods," Elana said, more to Camille again. "I think it's criminal that your Mothers just ignored you. Left you to struggle with something so immense on your own. You could have died. You could die now if you ask too much of yourself, untrained as you are."

"Hold on a minute." John was shaking his head like he wanted to reject most of what he was hearing. "If this is so dangerous, why did the Mothers allow Camille to finish her training and join a fighting group at all?"

"I don't think they knew," Camille said. "I think they understood it could cause problems, that sentient talents had something to do with old catastrophes like Mother-house Antilla, but thanks to the breeding programs, sentient gifts are so rare nowadays that the Mothers don't really understand them anymore. The knowledge was lost."

And me with it.

Fury colored the tops of John's cheeks a deep red. "Maybe they do know," he said to Elana. "Maybe to the Mothers, Camille's like a neat, pretty atomic bomb. They know exactly what she can do and they're just waiting until they need her to set her off. That's why you asked me to be sure none of her own was watching her, isn't it?"

Camille felt everything inside her run hot, then frigid cold. "What?"

She glanced from John to Elana, expecting some kind of explanation, but all Elana said was, "I admit, I've considered that they do know, and yes, that's why I asked you to watch for that, John. The Rakshasa nearly defeated the Sibyls when they first walked the earth. Had it not been for women with projective talent, the Sibyls would not now exist, nor would the world as you know it."

"They know she's a weapon." John banged one fist against the table, but it was too solid to rattle. "They know that in the end, she may be their only hope, and they'll use her no matter what it costs her." He focused on Camille, his green eyes burning hot, more angry with every word. "That's not going to happen, beautiful. We'll find another way."

But Camille barely heard what he said.

So much made sense now, and it tore her in half that in Elana's blind eyes, she saw the things she'd never received from her own Mothers: understanding, acceptance, respect.

"If the time comes, John, you must understand— Camille will do what she believes she must," Elana said. "It's why she was born, it's how she was trained. It's why the universe blessed her with this talent."

John stood. "But the Mothers didn't teach her how to *use* this thing. She'll tear herself apart trying to do whatever has to be done to win the battles. She'll kill herself—all four of them, her quad, too. They'll all die trying to save everybody else using that kind of power."

Elana's hand lifted toward her scarred face like she was dreaming. Her fingers touched the scars with a familiarity that told Camille she didn't even realize she was doing it. "If Camille and her friends kill only themselves in their pursuits, John Cole, we will all count ourselves fortunate in the end."

Camille thought the top of John's head might come off, but she had to leave him to fend for himself a few seconds. Her eyes took in the maps, the beautiful maps, with their lines like Ona had drawn on the sketch she gave Camille.

"Who are you?" she asked Elana, because now she needed to know. "Who are you really?"

Elana hesitated, and for the first time all day, she seemed not to have a ready answer. "I died long ago, my dear, yet I live."

"You were a Sibyl." Camille was sure of it, though she had no real feel for what kind.

"I died, as I told you." Elana's placid expression got tense, but her words stayed calm. "Whatever I was died with me."

Gently, not forcing her to move at all, Camille turned over Elana's right forearm, which was so scarred the marks were hard to see—but they were there. Mortar, pestle, and broom around a dark crescent moon, joined by waves to symbolize water.

"You were a Sibyl," Camille said again. "And you were born before Motherhouse Antilla was destroyed. The wavy lines they added to our tattoos look different."

Elana looked down at the stone table, and Camille had no more doubts left. She let go of Elana's arm. "Can you teach me what I need to know?"

"Camille." John's voice sounded wary and tight.

"Don't make this an issue," Camille said, barely looking at him because she was so afraid Elana would find some way to disappear like Ona. "Don't make this make-or-break between us, John, or we'll break right here."

He was still standing beside his seat with his fists doubled. "You don't owe the Sibyls anything, not after what they did to you."

Camille finally took her eyes off Elana long enough to really look at him, to connect with him and try to make him understand. "None of my oaths is sworn to the Dark Crescent Sisterhood. My oaths are all to the weak, the helpless, all those who need my protection—and to my quad."

The color in his face deepened. "Please don't head in this direction. Please don't put yourself at risk like this."

"She just sighted my gun, John."

As she suspected, he had absolutely no comeback for this. He understood exactly what she meant, what she had to do, and why. The red drained out of his face and his hands relaxed, but misery rose into his normally bright eyes.

Please, she wanted to say, though she didn't really understand what she wanted from him. Support? Belief? Respect for her choices?

He would give her all those things, she was sure of it, and she wouldn't even have to plead. But how could she ask him to be okay with her setting herself on a course that likely would get her and a lot of other people killed?

That would be too much for anybody.

The pain on his face felt like knives in her own heart, and when he hung his head and walked out of the room, it hurt even more than she'd imagined it could.

Seconds went by, then minutes, and Camille knew John had taken his leave, not just of the room but of the aqueduct, and maybe of her, too.

"He's a strong man," Elana said, moving her hands on

the table until she found Camille's and held them. "He'll come to terms with his inability to save you, especially as you know better how to save yourself."

Camille made herself look away from the chamber door and gaze at Elana, who was sitting below the map marked *Heaven*. "Whether he does or not, this is something I have to do."

Elana's smile was kind, but sad, too. "I know."

32

John had been official for four days, had his temporary advisor's shield for three days, had been allowed
into report sessions at OCU headquarters for two days,
and had been going half out of his mind about Camille
for one day, the length of time she'd been gone.

He pushed his way into OCU headquarters to meet
the rest of her quad for their report even though they
had spent the time Camille had been gone glaring at him
and barely tolerating him on patrol. Camille had let them
know she was fine, that she had something to work out
and would be home very soon.

OCU officers and Sibyls milled in every available space
on the ground floor, discussing maps and charts, arguing
about strategies, and proposing options to improve their
search for Rakshasa strongholds. John wanted to be a
part of all that, but he couldn't focus on a bet right now.
He had told Bela that Camille was with the Bengals by
choice, trying to figure something out about her projective abilities—something that she could pass along to
them, something that might make a big difference in
battles even if he hated the risk it posed.

*And you're the one who took her to Elana. Good go-
ing, asshole.*

Duncan had to tell him more than once to lock his door
at night and guard his manhood, because Bela and Dio
and Andy thought John and Camille had been fighting.

And had they fought?

John banged open the conference room door.

No. They hadn't fought. Camille had made a choice,

decided on a course of action that would probably get her killed. No way that was okay. She was being unreasonable.

Or maybe, just maybe, you've got no idea what you're going to do if you lose her.

He sat down hard in the nearest chair, not really able to get a good lungful of air or figure out what the hell he was supposed to do next.

Shit.

War was easier than this.

The conference room door opened again, and in walked Bela in her battle leathers. She had a blank, distracted look on her face, like she was completely lost in thought and irritated by even having to be there. Andy came next, wearing leathers, too, and Dio was right behind her in her battle gear. The three of them sighted him like a target and frowned, but went around the other side of his row and sat beside him in the folding chairs, leaving one chair between him and the first one—Bela.

She sort of nodded at him, a combination *Hey* and *Fuck you very much, you bastard who hurt my friend.*

God, these women were different. They could be nine different kinds of pissed off at you but still deal with you like a human.

John had no idea what to do with them.

He was about to ask Bela what she was so tied up about, but the door opened again, and this time John's instincts prickled.

He turned to see who had come in just about the time he caught her light scent of lilies, this time mixed with the tang of fire.

"Camille." He stood so fast he turned his chair over. Crap. He'd done that in the restaurant, too, hadn't he?

I'm fifteen all over again any time I get around her, and there's nothing I can do about it.

Her quad was so busy ignoring him that they hadn't seen her yet.

The room was filling up fast with people as Camille came over to him and stopped in front of him, inches away. She looked . . . tired. Her pretty aquamarine eyes were sad and sunken, and she was pale. Thinner, maybe. He wanted to pick her up, carry her straight out of the conference room, and hold her all night.

"I'm sorry," he said just in case that would help anything.

She closed her eyes. Nodded. Opened her eyes. Looked like she was about to kiss him—and pandemonium broke loose because her quad realized she was standing there.

"Where the hell have you been?"

"Why? You left us again, and you're not supposed to do that!"

"I ought to blow you to Greece and back again."

It was all jumbled as they hugged her, but John could pretty much match statements to Sibyls. Camille hugged each one of them, and John's arms ached to hold her even though everybody was getting seated and he still hadn't picked up the chair he knocked over.

Up at the front of the room, Jack Blackmore and Duncan and all the brothers, both Lowell and Brent, stopped jawing. Blackmore turned around and whapped his hand on the long table.

Camille's quad sat down, and John grabbed his chair and parked his ass as close to Camille as he could get.

"I feel like we're running out of time, people, though to be honest, I can't put my finger on why." Blackmore started talking about new search grids, with the Lowell brothers tacking up charts on the board behind him.

John glanced at Camille, who had her mouth clamped in a straight line. Beside her, Bela was fidgeting like hell, and that was strange, because Bela was anything but the fidgeting type.

They couldn't go straight out on patrol after report,

not like this. Somebody would get their balls—or, ah, their ovaries?—blown off.

The rest of the meeting went by in a hot blur, with John hearing only part of what was said. When it was obvious Blackmore was heading into the wrap-up, he touched Camille on the arm.

She glanced up at him, taking his breath away for a second.

"We should talk, all of us, before we go out."

"Yeah." She gazed at him for a second, like she really wanted to talk to him alone but knew they had to wait.

The fact that she wanted that, though, some alone time with him, that felt like a week's nourishment and good sleep to John. The big-ass knot in his gut untied, and he thought maybe he could make it through the night without losing his mind.

Camille leaned over and said something to Bela, who gave an emphatic nod and made some gestures to Andy and Dio.

When the meeting broke up, John managed to get up without kicking over his chair again, and he made his way out of the conference room, doing his best to clear a path. He held open the door for Camille and her quad, then the five of them silently filed across the hall to the basement door and went down the steps. Five or six people were on machines working out, but John and Camille were able to pull exercise balls, a chair, and a stack of mats into an unoccupied corner.

John had barely gotten himself seated on a mat beside Camille's exercise ball when Andy turned loose and let fly. "Okay, spill it. What the fuck's going on and where the fuck have you been?"

"The Bengals have a leader who understands projective energy." Camille stopped, and John wondered if she was going to hold some stuff back to protect Elana and maybe get herself in trouble with her girls again.

Bela reacted first, letting out a long, slow sigh. "It's about time *somebody* showed up with a clue. Who is she?"

"She's . . . old." Camille rubbed her fingers together once, then twice, and refocused on her group. "Older than you're going to want to believe. She's given me permission to talk to you. To be completely honest."

John's attention snapped to a man walking across the gym, tall and blond, too smooth in his walk to be completely human. It was Jake Lowell, the Astaroth demon. As he got closer, John could almost see the word *trouble* blaring out of Jake's blue eyes. Jake came straight to them, not even stopping to greet anyone else.

Jake shook hands with John, saying, "Sorry to interrupt." His gaze shifted to Dio. "You asked me to look up some information in our archives, and I found something disturbing."

Andy managed a fairly dramatic groan.

Camille gestured to the only free mat left, right across from her. "Sit down. Let me go first, and if I miss anything, you fill in the details."

"Fuck me," Andy muttered. "I'm not liking any of this, and I haven't even heard it."

Dio's expression suggested she was in total agreement.

Bela was looking fidgety again. What the hell was with that?

Camille wasted no time getting back to business. "The Bengal leader, she was changed a long time ago, during the first war with the Rakshasa."

"No way," Dio said. "She'd have to be, what, a thousand years old?"

"Yes," Camille said. "Rakshasa and Created are immortal. But before she was Created, she was a Sibyl, and we have at least one in our number as old as she is."

Camille explained to the quad how Elana knew way more than most Sibyl Mothers, how she had built an amazing army of Bengals—and then what she knew about projective energy, how to use it, and how dangerous it was. Then she looked at Jake.

"That's exactly what I learned." Jake looked serene and relaxed sitting on his mat, but John could sense the frustration and concern coming off him. "Before the Dark Crescent Sisterhood was fully organized and formed, when the Motherhouses had just begun operation, many Sibyls had strong projective talents. They came into play in the first war with the Rakshasa, which was almost lost until—"

He broke off, looking at Camille.

"Until a quad with strong projective talents killed half of them and put the other half in elemental stasis using their projective talents." Camille touched her dinar. "The reason this coin has the power it does is because the projective quad made it, to keep the Rakshasa trapped in flame form."

"Why flame form?" Andy asked.

"They were trying to save themselves," Jake said. "They had realized if they continued fighting these women, they would all die. It's why so many of them survived what happened."

"What did the Sibyls do?" Bela asked, staring at Camille instead of Jake.

"They caught the demons in a projective trap." Camille looked down at her hands. John could tell she really didn't want to talk about this next part, that it was hurting her. He touched her shoulder, just gave it a squeeze, and she reached to cover his hand with hers.

"The fire Sibyl in the group pulled molten metal out of the earth and covered them," she said. "Encased them all. Half got pierced in the heart, beheaded, and incinerated all at the same time, so they died. It was a desperation move on the Sibyls' part—that or lose the battle and lose the world."

"How did she—" Bela began.

"Later for that part." Camille cleared her throat like she was about to say a lot more, but John saw she couldn't do it. He looked at Jake.

"There were consequences," Jake said.

"I hate it when people get vague." Andy rubbed droplets off her hand. "Spit it out. What consequences?"

Jake and Camille studied each other for a moment.

"Everyone was encased, including the fire Sibyl and her quad," Jake said. "Two died instantly. The other two were left maimed. And only half the Rakshasa died, so after they worked their way out of the molten metal, the two Sibyl survivors had to trap the remaining demons. That's how one of them got bitten and changed."

That made no sense to John at all, and he broke in with his own question. "Why didn't the Sibyls just kill the remaining Rakshasa?"

Camille looked away, but she was the one who answered him. "Perhaps at that moment they had lost their will to kill."

"There were more *consequences*, weren't there?" Andy asked, her pitch going up as she went unnaturally still.

Camille's gaze was fixed on Andy, and now her hands were shaking. "The molten ore came from where the earth could spare it, a volcanic chamber. The sudden loss of volume caused an earthquake, just like an eruption. That caused an elementally fueled tidal wave."

"The wave that destroyed Motherhouse Antilla and killed all the water Sibyls," Andy said. "Fucking wonderful."

Camille still looked like she was dreading something. John couldn't figure out what would be worse, but Andy slowly got off her exercise ball. She had a look on her face he'd never seen before. Bela and Dio reacted instantly, throwing up elemental barriers to contain her energy. Jake Lowell helped, and even Camille, as tired as she was, lifted her hands to help with keeping Andy's water contained.

Even with all that effort, sprinklers exploded and rained all over the gym. People working out on the other side of the basement started swearing, then seemed to realize there was serious Sibyl business going down. John had never seen people get the hell out of a room so fast in his life.

"Who was the fire Sibyl, Camille?" Andy's voice had gone deadly now. "Was she one of the survivors?"

Camille nodded, and then John knew.

Ona.

Andy worked it out almost as fast as he did, and her face turned redder than hot flames. "And you let her in our *house*?"

"I didn't know." Camille rocked on her exercise ball. "She didn't do it—"

"What are you going to say? It was an accident? She didn't do it on purpose?" Andy's wild red hair soaked in water from somewhere, dripping down her leathers. "Camille, she wiped out hundreds of people. She killed two of her own quad. It's because of her I'm stuck in this all alone, with no idea what I'm doing—"

Dio cut her off by jumping up in front of her, squaring off with Camille. "What kind of Sibyl is Elana?"

Camille looked even more nervous at this question. She chewed her bottom lip for a second, her gaze still locked on Andy.

"You're shitting me." Andy's knees seemed to go wobbly on her, and Dio had to get hold of her to keep her on her feet. "No, you're not serious." Andy covered her mouth. "Tell me you're serious, that she really is a water Sibyl?"

Camille opened her hands like somebody beseeching heaven. "You're not alone anymore. She agreed that once we've defeated the Rakshasa, she'll do what she can to help you, though she wants you to know she was just a year out of Motherhouse Antilla when this happened."

Andy started crying, sudden fast bursts of sobs, and Dio got an arm around her, giving her some support. John had to look away because Andy wasn't the crying sort of woman. This was gut-level desperation and panic and relief all balled into one big bunch of tears.

After a time, her whole quad got up and held her, and John and Jake sat back exchanging fish-out-of-water glances. John understood the depth of Andy's breakdown. He only had to deal with demon essence in his head, and he'd had lots of good help with that from the Bengals and all the OCU half demons and demons. Even Camille had been able to help him a little bit.

Andy—her ass had been hanging in the wind since the day she first started shoving water around. She had all these amazing specialized skills she was supposed to know and learn, and only vague descriptions in books that left her guessing. Even better, she was supposed to teach what she didn't really know to all the water Sibyls showing up at Motherhouse Kérkira.

"Okay, okay." She started pushing people back. "Get away from me or I'll never stop blubbering."

Jake Lowell glanced at the inch or so of water now coursing around the basement floor, then looked at John with something like relief that Andy might get the sprinklers under control in a few.

She wiped her face, then slowly shut off the flow to each spigot.

"They'll have to be repaired," she told Jake.

"I'll add it to the list."

John saw the look in Andy's eyes, and in Jake's. This was an old conversation between them, and a comfortable one.

"I haven't knocked out any walls," she said.

"You haven't," Jake agreed.

"I don't like the look on your face, Jake. There's still stuff you aren't telling us."

"I was waiting."

"For what?"

Jake shrugged. "A chance we could get through this without needing paddles and canoes."

Andy squeezed water out of her hair and made sure to drip some on Jake. "Fuck you, you scrawny winged Dracula."

Jake grinned at her, lots less demon, very human.

"Spill it," Andy said.

Jake slowly stopped smiling, and before he spoke, he looked positively grim. "I don't believe this information was completely lost to the Mothers. Nor is it lost on them that the universe tends to provide for its own needs. Much as when you manifested your talent, Andy, other, younger water Sibyls began to appear."

Dio had balanced herself so perfectly on the exercise ball that the rubber could have been bolted to the floor, but after Jake spoke, the whole ball started to shake. "What are you saying?"

Jake held up his hand and counted off. One. "Each Motherhouse had the birth of a Sibyl gifted with projective talents after centuries of only the most minor abilities in this respect." Two. "All of you were of similar age." Three. "Andy miraculously appeared with her abilities." Four. "She, too, was of similar age—"

"They knew we'd be needed," Dio said, coming off the exercise ball she'd been sitting on and walking to the stone wall beside her, her back to John and Jake and her quad. "That's why the Mothers let me fight."

The undertone in her statement made John angry and sad all over again.

That's why they let me fight . . . not because they thought I was worth anything.

"And why they let me be claimed," Camille said, with almost the same undertone.

"And they still didn't train you," John said, wishing he could call up the Sibyl Mothers and have some long . . . discussions.

"They didn't know how to train me," Camille said. "They still don't know how."

"They're probably scared shitless we'll wipe them out." Bela came off her ball and kicked it back toward the exercise equipment. "*I'm* scared shitless we will."

"We're weapons to use against unbeatable numbers and insurmountable power," Camille said. "We're—"

She left off again, gazing at her sister Sibyls, who didn't seem to be able to go where she needed them to go.

Jake said it for them, in his analytical Astaroth tones. "You are sacrifices for the greater good."

"Kinda like the self-destruct cycles on spaceships in all the sci-fi movies," Andy mused, looking up at the ceiling. "The doomsday device. They deploy us, knowing we'll scorch the earth and wreck the world, but some people will survive."

"That's my take on it," Camille said. "I was able to learn some basic barriers and self-protections from Elana, which I'll start teaching you tomorrow, but even with those, if we use projective energy at the level we'll need to use it, there's not a huge chance that we'll all walk away."

Ino faced them again, her anger evident in her expression and tone. "So when this all goes to hell in a handbasket, we're supposed to sacrifice ourselves to rescue these women who—who just put us aside?"

Bela paced, hitting puddles of water as she walked. "Not just them."

Andy's laugh was real and bittersweet at the same time. "Don't you all get it? We're supposed to save the world. That's why we're here. That's why we were made."

John watched the four women, hoping one of them would kick up more of an objection to this idea. Most of his hopes were pinned on Dio, who seemed to have the most anger, or Bela, who had Duncan to think about.

But really, he knew better.

They were Sibyls, no matter how their own had treated them, no matter what anybody else thought about them. When they'd taken their oaths to protect the weak and to fulfill their roles as mortar, pestle, broom, and flow of their fighting quad, they'd meant every word.

Bela raised her eyes to Jake.

"The time may come," she said, glancing at John, "where we'll have to count on you and your friends to make sure we can do what we have to do."

Fast, fast rage gripped John. He glared at Jake. "You don't have to worry about me. I'll have my sword and pistol out protecting them. I won't get in the way."

Not a single one of them looked like they believed him, especially not Jake, but at least Jake was nice enough to say, "Duncan may not be so cooperative."

"He will if you explain it to him." John knew he had to be as red as a damned beet, but he couldn't help it.

"He might try to do something stupid and heroic," Jake said.

"Yeah, well . . ." It was John's turn to look away, because his brain was whizzing through ten thousand ways to save their lives.

"This is all serious, and we have to deal with it," Bela said, "but we also have patrol."

"We probably don't have to worry about dying tonight." Andy gave one of the exercise balls a good kick and sent it spinning. "We haven't found shit-all on these assholes for weeks."

Bela fidgeted where she was standing, then finally spat out what must have been on her mind all evening. "We've got a better chance tonight. I cracked the elemental code on that tooth." She touched her pendant. "I modified my charm to help me detect muted energy, even at fairly low levels."

John felt a pleasant shock, then something he hadn't expected: anticipation.

"Well, let's go, then," Andy said. "Anything to get my mind off all the rest of this crap."

Bela looked at Jake again, and Jake started to change.

John hadn't ever seen the man in his demon form before. He had to see the transition.

Jake pulled off his shirt and dropped it on the mat where he was standing. His eyes shifted from blue to golden, and his lips pulled back to show large, pointed fangs, top and bottom, and a mouthful of sharp teeth. Claws curled out from his fingers. His skin went pearl white, and a few seconds later, a double pair of white, leathery wings unfurled from his back. He gave John a nod and a snarl, flapped those massive wings once, sending the exercise balls scooting and floating, and then popped out. Just vanished. Poof. Gone.

John didn't like that. He stared at the ceiling, the walls. Wherever the bastard had gone, he was probably getting help in case he had to snatch John and Duncan out of play in a battle when the women tried to do their thing.

Wonder if Rakshasa and Astaroth are an even match in one-on-one combat.

Because if Jake tried something like that, they just might get that question answered.

33

Camille walked down the dirty pavement with John and her quad, listening to the creak of her battle leathers in the cold night air. She was letting Bela take point with Andy because of Bela's modified charm, but also because she didn't think she had ever been so tired in her life. Dio had already fallen back to take sweep-up, but Camille usually had a sense of where she was. No such thing right now. She didn't even know what day it was—well, night, now.

The last few days had blurred together completely. The time she spent working with Elana had pushed her to her limits, taken her straight to the edge. She hadn't seen daylight the entire time she was underground, and even though she didn't have nearly the problem with enclosed spaces that most fire Sibyls did, it still had been a little much.

Everything in the New York City night seemed too loud, too bright, too everything—especially the stench at the docks when they finally stopped walking. They were right back where they had started weeks ago, staring into the darkness with treated lenses, swapping binoculars back and forth, but Bela had eyes free, her charm gripped in her hand as she studied the dock entrance.

"Can you do this, beautiful?" John's concern was evident in his tone, in the way his hand rested gently against her back.

She wanted to fold into him and let him carry her home. "I can make it. I have to. As soon as we find what we're looking for, I'll crash until we absolutely have to get up again."

"So we're agreed," Andy said, hanging the binoculars around her neck. "We find them tonight. We have the OCU stake them out, keep them under watch. We sleep, we eat, we learn barriers, and we go after them."

"Simple but elegant," Bela said. "I'm sure they've been watching us for days and weeks. Maybe we can return the favor. And I'm not seeing anything on this dock."

They moved on to the next dock, and the next. Camille held John's hand even though that was not proper patrol procedure, because she just didn't care. She had missed him so much, and the thought that there might be a rift between them made everything feel too hard.

When they came up empty at the fourth dock, she let herself look at him, and the handsome outline of his tanned face, and the way his dark hair spilled into his green eyes as he scouted for whatever he could see in the dark.

She really was in love with him. No question about that. It just didn't seem reasonable or rational to discuss that right now, and maybe not ever.

It figured that just when she'd finally worked out that she was probably supposed to die to save the world, at last she had something she really, really wanted to live for.

He must have felt her gazing at him, because he looked at her. His face shifted from focused and stern to soft and totally hers in a split second, and she knew he wanted to kiss her. He wanted to make love to her. The way he let her see that with no shame or hesitation took another little piece of Camille's heart.

"You better stop staring at me like that in public, beautiful." His voice was so quiet, pitched for only her to hear, and she loved the shivers it gave her.

"I'm tired," she said, squeezing his fingers, "but not that tired. Save some energy for me when we get home."

"Always."

"I think I've got something." Bela sounded uncertain, but the words brought Camille to full alert. She turned toward the mortar of her triad, who was slowly approaching the edge of the sixth dock.

"What does it look like?" Andy asked. "I'm not seeing any demon trace with the goggles."

Bela kept walking, stopping, then walking again. "It's not anything I can see. Their elemental charm disperses most traces. This is more a sense that something was here."

Camille joined Bela. She lifted her fingers to her dinar, then extended her other hand toward Bela's hand and the charm she was gripping in her palm. "Can I try to boost your awareness with some fire energy?"

Bela gave her a wary look, but Camille knew she was thinking about last year, when the four of them had managed to combine their sentient talents enough to track demons all over Manhattan. They'd had no idea how dangerous it was . . . but it worked.

"This is small potatoes," Camille told her. "I can control it."

Bela nodded, and Camille put her hand over Bela's. Carefully, keeping in place the rudimentary self-protections she had learned from Elana and doing what she could to extend those to Bela, Camille drew a measured amount of fire energy into her, through the dinar, and sent it back out again along her arm and down her hand, into Bela's skin and into the charm Bela was holding.

When her energy touched Bela's charm, Camille felt the impact in her teeth.

Bela sucked in a breath, blinked, and said, "Unbelievable."

Camille looked in the direction Bela was looking, and she could see it, too. Red demon trace. Yellow demon trace. Green demon trace. Stomped and restomped paths of elemental energy, hundreds and hundreds of them. Too many to count, too many to even begin to follow— but the strongest traces led off the docks and back into the city, in the general direction of Central Park. The air took on a whispering, sulfur-ammonia stench. Created. Eldest. Asmodai. Other things Camille couldn't even identify. The size and scope of it made the city seem distant and strange behind them, like there couldn't possibly be so many lives this close to such a massive amount of perverted energy and danger.

Camille let go of Bela's hand and stopped her pull on the fire energy.

If she was tired before, she was bone-deep exhausted now.

Bela let go of her charm and rubbed her eyes with her fingers. "That was a hell of a lot of trace. What have they been doing, importing demons and Created?"

"No idea," Camille said, "but it's not good."

"I'll call it in." John pulled his phone out of his pocket. "Jack and the guys will get in touch with the Port Authority, see who has been shipping in this area, and nail down which of our friendly neighborhood crime lords has hired himself some nasty, furry buddies."

"At least we'll know whom to kill," Andy said, maybe because she was really ready to kill something. Camille wasn't even sure Andy would be that discriminating at this point.

John stepped away from the Sibyls so his secure cell would have a prayer of working, and she heard him relaying in quick, terse sentences what they'd found.

"What do you think, Camille?" Bela asked. "The park? Farther north—or maybe west? With all that we just saw, they could be hiding out in Jersey."

"I know they've been concealing themselves, but the East and West Ranger groups have covered just about every inch of that territory while we've been watching the docks and hunting at night." Camille frowned, trying to decide if she was blowing that area off too easily. "They might be in Jersey, but not in the numbers those traces suggested."

"They've got a central location here in Manhattan," Andy said. "I feel that in my guts."

Camille checked her own instincts. "I'm with you on that."

Bela gave it some consideration, then pointed toward the center of the city. "Let's start where everything seems to start, then. The park."

"We'll focus on the stronger traces and where they go." Andy smiled. "That works for me, following the insects back to their nests, like good exterminators."

"They're on it," John said as he stuffed his phone back in his pocket. "Nick and Creed Lowell had already mapped this area out pretty well—this is one of Ari Seneca's high-activity areas. Blackmore's pulling together strike patrols to move in and check all of his known sites and listed properties."

Camille's heart stirred, giving her the tiniest flood of energy. After all this time, finally, some definite progress.

"We'll go in near Columbus Circle and walk the boundary," Bela said as they headed through Manhattan toward the park.

Camille couldn't help thinking it would be hard to get that close to home and not run to the brownstone to her quiet little room with its quiet little walls and paintings and tuck herself in for the rest of the night.

Just walk the park. Let John call in what you find— then *you can sleep.*

It seemed to take ten hours to get to the entrance, but Camille knew that was her fatigue talking. She walked beside Bela and made herself keep pace in case Bela needed her to enhance the charm again. John was right behind them with Andy, and now and then Camille caught the windy rush of Dio's energy. She was glad Dio had their back. Dio could be hard to tolerate in so many ways, but she was loyal, sharp, alert, and maybe the best fighter in the whole quad.

In the early throes of winter, Central Park's normal dirt and grass and smells seemed muted in favor of the limestone-copper scent of wet rocks and the fertile, loamy odor of rotting leaves. The darkness seemed a little darker, especially around the playground area. They skirted along the south entrance, turning at Grand Army Plaza and heading up toward the zoo. Now and then Bela glanced across the park in the general direction of the brownstone, and Camille wondered if she was tired, too, and thinking about meeting up with Duncan and cuddling until morning.

When they were about even with Wollman Rink, Bela finally stopped walking, glanced at Camille, then glanced west toward the brownstone again.

Camille felt the beat of her own pulse pick up all over again. "Are you getting something?"

Bela tilted her head. "I don't know."

Camille moved a little closer to Bela, fishing around with her own senses. "When did the feeling start?"

Bela gripped her charm. "Almost the minute we got into the park. I keep thinking it's more in my head since we're close to home, but really, what I'm sensing is that way." She pointed across the park toward Sixty-third and the brownstone.

Camille took hold of her dinar and offered her hand to Bela, and together they both looked in that direction.

"I don't see anything," Bela said, her mouth twisting in a frown of absolute frustration.

Camille saw nothing but the park, yet—

Something was there. Something so slight it might have been a moth's heartbeat—but it wasn't normal. Just the slightest bit out of place.

"I feel it," she told Bela. "I just can't tell where it's coming from."

Camille looked back at John and Andy. Both had hands on weapons, waiting.

She didn't see anything else but leafless trees and, farther, the city's buildings, windows glowing like thousands of stars.

Channels everywhere . . .

The world had so many different kinds of channels.

Camille looked down at the frosty ground.

Channels and tunnels.

Years ago, when she'd lost Bette, the Asmodai that killed her had come out of the earth in Van Cortlandt Park at the gatehouse—from yet another remnant of the Old Croton Aqueduct. She'd just spent days herself in chambers and tunnels related to the old waterworks.

"Maybe they're underground," Camille said, not adding, *Like the Bengals, just in a different place.* "Bela, can you sense any tunnels around here?"

Bela closed her eyes, and Camille felt the ripple of Bela's terrasentience move outward, then reach down, deeper than she went when she was just sampling soil for trace and footprints. The frustrated expression on her face increased, and lines formed on her forehead from the effort she was exerting.

A second or so later, her earth energy brushed past Camille as it returned, and Bela opened her eyes. "Something's down there, but it's muted, too."

Camille's insides twitched. The night seemed to get a lot darker and colder, and the buildings surrounding the park seemed that much taller and farther away. "Protected?"

"Pretty sure, yes." Bela frowned. "Not good."

Camille wondered if the Bengals had carved out large spaces and used some sort of muting charms and energy themselves. For now, she couldn't assume that.

"John," she said, "we think we're standing on tunnels with deliberately muted energy."

He immediately stepped back from Andy and got on the telephone again.

"Let's go toward the brownstone," Bela said, gesturing at the ice rink. "I still think there's something bigger in that direction."

"Something's off," John said. "OCU did initial hits on Seneca's main places, but they're all empty. People have been there—lots of people, it looks like—but the houses and warehouses are empty now. They won't know about demon trace until later, after you guys can get there."

"Let's head toward the house and whatever you're worried about," Andy said to Bela and Camille. "But don't push it. We seriously don't want to engage, not until we know what we're dealing with."

Evil, Camille thought as they moved out. That was the only word that came to her. They were dealing with evil, and it was under them and behind them and beside them, and she didn't know how long she'd have to teach her quad the boundaries they needed to know. The Rakshasa and their allies were planning something, and it felt huge, and it felt . . . soon.

"That's fucked up," Bela muttered, elbowing Camille as they went wide of the ice rink, which should have been deserted at this hour.

The place looked pretty crowded, both the bleachers and the ice.

"Men," Andy said. "Humans, it feels like."

"Yeah," Bela agreed. "A load of them. Why haven't the park police run them off?"

Camille studied the mass of people skulking around the rink. "Maybe it's some sort of planned meeting and they've got a permit."

John was a few steps back, using his cell again. "I don't think it's a party," he growled to whoever had answered at OCU. "Forty, maybe fifty guys in dark clothes. Yeah."

Camille sensed that some of the men at the rink were watching them pass by even though she and her quad were keeping to the shadows as best they could. Some murmuring broke out among the men. The tone sounded tense. Maybe a little surprised.

"Let's blow our asses out of here fast," Andy suggested, and they picked up speed, running now.

Camille crossed first into Heckscher Playground, trying to get through the open spaces as fast as she could.

"Anything?" she called back to Bela as they once more approached the waiting, welcoming cover of trees.

"Same," Bela called back. "Hints, but nothing solid."

Camille had one hand on her dinar, the other on her sword. Andy muttered softly to herself, and John jogged up closer to Camille.

A boy stepped out of the woods directly in front of her. She barely had time to process his dark, nondescript features, his astonished expression—and the unnatural light burning in his dark, demon eyes—before the dinar around her neck went off like a grenade against her chest, blasting her backward, blasting the boy backward. As she fell, Camille saw John stagger away a few steps, gripping the sides of his head, snarling, coughing, and swearing as he tried to fight off the human-stripping projective energy that flowed off the coin, completely out of Camille's control.

Camille hit the hard, cold ground and rolled back up, leaping between John, her quad, and the boy.

"Eldest!" she screamed—

And living hell on earth broke loose all around her.

Earth tore. Sulfur blasted into the air. The mindless

roar of Asmodai rose into the night and the boy staggered to his feet, calling forward what looked like a solid wall of armed, armored Created.

From behind Camille came the sound of gunshots. She blasted warnings and distress calls through her tattoo, felt her quad's terror shoot across her arm as they sent their own rudimentary messages.

The boy and his troops roared at Camille, but they couldn't move forward against the power of the dinar.

The boy's eyes blazed furiously. He was obviously surprised, not ready for the repellant power the dinar gave her. Camille yanked fire energy from every direction, extending the barrier, wrapping the elemental shield around the demons until she was pretty sure the Rakshasa couldn't advance or retreat, either. Bela ran up beside her and her earth energy flowed into Camille, steadying her. Some of Andy's cool water energy found her, and from farther away, Dio's powerful wind trickled in to give her more strength.

"Aarif," John said, and the boy's head whipped toward him.

Aarif's face showed a mix of rage and uncertainty.

He feels the demon inside me. He's sensing that I'm holding on to some bit or piece of Strada.

"Your trick does not impress me." He pointed at John. "However you came to wear that skin, you'll shed it when you die."

John didn't answer the kid because he was firing his Glock, not at the demon-boy, but behind Camille. She knew he was picking off hulking shadows as they charged toward them from seemingly every direction. The metallic reek of gunpowder drifted over Camille like a dark cloud.

"Stay close to me," she shouted to Bela and Andy. "I don't think the Rakshasa can touch us. Maybe not the Asmodai, either, but I don't know how long I can hold this."

Aarif roared again, drew a knife, and tried to throw it at Camille.

The protective barrier trapping him made his hand shake, made the blade fall useless on the ground. The Rakshasa Created were trying to raise what looked like Czech Vz. 58s, but they couldn't get them into firing position.

Eight hundred rounds per minute on full auto. We're so dead if I let them move.

Camille had them for now, though, ringing Aarif and the Created with a solid wall of projective energy, magnified and fueled by the dinar. She couldn't approach the demons any more than they could approach her, because the coin's repelling properties worked both ways.

But maybe she didn't have to get close.

The dinar felt so hot against Camille's skin that she was sure it would catch her own fire. Her battle leathers smoked and seared away from it, and her barrier got even stronger.

Something stung her leg. Bad.

She hopped, reaching down toward her calf, but her wall of energy held. The protections she had learned from Elana cut the drain on her from so much focused pyrosentience, or she'd already be passed out on the ground, letting everybody die around her.

"Can't do it forever." She kept her gaze directly on Aarif. "But I can do it for now, asshole, and help's coming."

Sirens cut through the night, lots of sirens, and Camille had a sense of Sibyl energy closing in on them from north, south, east, and west.

John fired and fired. Andy was shooting, too. Rotten earth pummeled against Camille and the shield she was holding. She limped each time she tried to adjust her position. Green fire spilled across her vision, and sulfurous wind battered her eyes and nose as Asmodai got torn apart.

"There's too many!" Andy shouted, but Sibyl battle cries echoed through Central Park, and from the corner of her eye Camille saw dark leather-clad shapes with flaming swords and shining blades and arrows and throwing knifes come blasting out of the trees around Heckscher Playground and the ball fields.

Fresh gunfire erupted. Camille felt a new sting, this time in her right arm, just above her elbow.

"What the hell?" John yelled. "Who's shooting now?"

Then more gunfire, and more.

"Automatic weapons!" Andy called. "The men from the rink—we're fucked."

Camille's throat went totally dry, but she couldn't do anything other than what she was doing.

"OCU," John shouted. "Flanking those assholes."

Andy again as she shot more demons. "Cole, who the hell are they? There, coming over the ice. Shit! More Rakshasa!"

Camille's heart stuttered, but John was yelling into his phone again. "Bengals. Bengals! Duncan, don't let the OCU take down the good guys. The Bengals are here!"

Then the world behind Camille dissolved into more shouting and shooting and snarling and sulfur and fire.

"Let them have the Asmodai and the shooters," Camille shouted to her quad. "We've got to deal with these demons, or nothing else will matter."

She was remembering what Elana told her, about how the original Rakshasa had been defeated, caught in a projective energy trap. Camille had no frigging idea how to make one, but she wondered what would happen if—

"John, can you cover us? Keep the Asmodai off our asses?"

"Nobody's touching your ass but me," he called back, and she heard the metallic jamming sound of him loading a fresh clip.

She shifted her attention to Bela, who was still standing next to her, silent and determined, feeding earth energy into the shield Camille held.

"Can you call Dio in?" Camille asked her.

"Done." Bela raised one arm and siphoned off a targeted blast of earth energy.

Less than a minute later, Camille heard Dio's check-in shout of "Here!" through all the gunfire and roaring and the cries of Sibyls cutting down whatever was after them. Keeping her back to the battle felt insane, but if an Eldest and all these Created made it into the mix, it might turn into a slaughter—and not of the bad guys.

"They're covered in armor," Andy said as she and Dio pulled in behind Camille and Bela. "How can we pierce their hearts, behead them, and burn them to ashes if they're made out of metal?"

"For now, we just need to surround them." Camille kept her eyes and body very still as she spoke. She spread out her arms to hold her shield, which was getting harder to do. The energy was draining her after all, because there were so many demons and because this was taking time. "I've got them roped off, but I think if we take positions along all four axes and join the flow of our energy, we might be able to do more than hold them."

Nobody questioned her.

Bela took off north. Andy went north, then west, and Dio ran south. John stayed at Camille's back, coming closer, but not too close, because the energy coming off her would strip him to Rakshasa in a second if it flowed over him. He fired and fired again, seemingly oblivious to the threat or fighting past it because he wouldn't leave her.

Camille tasted earth energy, then air, then water as her quad got into position, anchored themselves, and let loose with their sentient powers. Each of them had the charms Camille had made gripped tightly in their fists.

Camille didn't dare touch the dinar. It would burn her

fingers down to the knuckle. It was all she could do to soak up enough of its fire and heat to keep it from branding her and sizzling straight through her breast-bone.

They don't know barriers, she reminded herself as she gathered their energy and added it to the wall of power she had wrapped around Aarif and the Created. *Be careful. Careful . . .*

Aarif and his squad of armored monsters howled as Camille hooked in the last of the four elements. The boy didn't look furious anymore. He looked scared. Camille knew that whatever his plan had been, this wasn't the scenario he'd been aiming to achieve.

"Welcome to my world, asshole," she muttered. "Nothing ever goes as planned, does it?"

And she imagined the shield pulling tighter. She squeezed it in. Brought the energy toward her.

The Rakshasa Eldest howled, shattering the night, and all the kitties with him elbowed against the energy, hitting it with fists, helmets, the tips of guns that still wouldn't aim at Camille or her quad. They got a lot closer together, all the Rakshasa, and Camille kept the energy where it was and gave herself a moment to breathe.

She checked on her quad. All still standing. All still looking strong.

John blasted away with his Glock, and Camille was pretty sure that if she hadn't been wrapped in an energy shield, she'd be deaf by now. She couldn't hear the Sibyls anymore over the shouts and radios of the OCU as they got closer.

"Here we go," Camille said, and she pulled the shield around the Rakshasa tighter. Her arms stretched even wider but her fingers curled in, matching her thoughts. *Tighter. A little tighter. Yes.*

The cats scrambled on top of one another. Aarif

thrashed and howled where he stood, but he didn't seem to be able to move. He was shifting, though. Black fur. Fangs. Claws. All the human was falling away from him, and that was good, because killing a giant psychotic tiger was easier than taking down a wide-eyed teenage boy, illusion or not.

Camille really felt the drain now. Her right arm throbbed and shook in the air like it didn't want to stay stretched out, and her leg had stopped stinging and started aching. Her jaw clenched from the pain and effort, and her vision got a little wavy.

The next time she tightened her shield, the energy would make contact with the Rakshasa. She had no idea what would happen then, but she hoped it would be bad for them.

"John," she said in as even a voice as she could muster. "Are the Asmodai handled?"

"Down and out."

"And the shooters?"

"OCU's got them."

"Walk away from me. No, run."

"Camille—"

"I have no idea how far this is going to reach," she said, doing all she could to hold her focus. "Don't be anywhere near it unless you want to answer to 'Here, kitty-kitty' and eat Tender Vittles for the rest of your life."

Her only answer was John's footsteps as he hauled ass away from the trees, across the ball fields.

Good.

She felt better knowing he was out of range, or getting there fast.

Bela and Dio and Andy must have sensed that she was about to do something big, because they increased the flow of their energies into the shield around the Rakshasa.

Camille took a breath, imagining that shield as a big

dome or partial bubble. No, wait. More like a cylinder. A metal can, wrapping around the demons and extending up over their heads.

She centered herself and balanced her own weight as best she could, then brought her arms together, slowly, slowly, to guide her thoughts. The shield got smaller.

The roars from the Rakshasa turned into screaming bellows. Camille squinted at them, because it looked like their fur was starting to . . . fall off. Metal armor was melting. Weapons clattered as the tiger-demons banged into one another.

Were the demons melting, too?

Camille felt her strength waver for the first time, and knew she had to act. This was it. Now or never. Goddess help them all.

She squeezed her eyes shut, wrapped her mind all around the energy shield, and crushed the can.

Smashed it. Into demon. Into the ground. Tigers burst into flames or melted or evaporated or just disappeared.

Bela, Dio, and Andy stumbled forward from the sudden downward suck of energy.

Camille felt an odd pressure all over her. She heard a sound actually a lot like stomping an aluminum can into concrete.

A second went by.

Earth, fire, air, and water exploded like a bomb, blowing Camille off her feet and slamming her hard into the casing-littered dirt. Hot demon ash rained on her face as pain jammed through her wounded shoulder and leg. She hit her head so hard her tongue went numb and her eyes seemed to shake in her skull. She couldn't smell anything, taste anything, see anything, or hear anything. Then she couldn't feel anything. Not even pain.

Numb.

Flat and numb.

I'm dead, she thought. *I died.*

But . . . dead people didn't have thoughts.

She went out. Came back in.

Night in Central Park. She was lying in a cold field of bullet casings and Asmodai leftovers. She couldn't even get her face out of the stinking dirt.

Out again.

Bela. Dio. Andy . . .

And back.

Her senses were slowly, slowly coming back to her. She remembered Bela describing something like this last year, when the Rakshasa had caught them in a similar energy trap. Bela had, for a time, lost all five senses and thought she was the only one of their assault group left alive.

Camille knew how Bela must have felt. This deadening from projective energy blowback was brutal and disorienting.

She forced herself up on her elbows, then into a sitting position.

Hands grabbed her.

She turned in slow motion to see—

EMTs and OCU officers.

"That hurts." Camille tried to take her aching arm back from the guy, but he was dressing a wound right above her elbow.

"Be still," the medic said. "This one's through and through. Not sure about the leg."

And then she heard Andy. "Touch me again, fuckhead, and we'll see who needs transportation to a hospital."

Dio was bitching from somewhere, and Bela was telling them both to shut up, that she had one mother of a headache.

Thank the Goddess.

"John?" Camille called, uncertain, still too confused to get things straight. "John!"

All the hands pulling at her suddenly let go, and he

was there. He was with her, kneeling down, pulling her to him. He smelled like gunpowder and sweat and blood, but he was real, and he was here.

She grabbed his neck and held on despite the screaming protests from her right elbow.

"You got a bullet in that leg, I think." He kissed the top of her head. "Need to get you to a hospital—"

Camille cut him off by reaching down and locating the metal in her calf. She pulled on enough fire energy to heat it and draw it out, letting it sear the wound shut as it went. Glowing red and steaming with her blood, the bullet plopped onto the ground beside them.

"Handled," she grumbled, looking into his night-shadowed green eyes. "Now what the hell happened behind me while I couldn't watch?"

"I think I've told you this before," he said, pausing to kiss her cheek. "You're a little scary."

Then he told her about the battle—Asmodai from old Croton Aqueduct tunnels, handlers underground taken out by earth Sibyls crashing the tunnels down on their heads, Rakshasa Eldest and Created eliminated by Camille and her quad. The automatic gunfire had been from humans, Seneca's foot soldiers, most of them cut to ribbons by OCU half demons and Astaroths who could eat bullets for breakfast if they had a second to prepare for them. A few humans had been arrested, and they were being taken by the OCU for questioning at the front station on West Thirtieth, in the old Fourteenth Precinct station—the one that looked like a castle.

Camille wanted to be relieved that the fighting was done, that the threat had passed for the moment, but her mind was already working over details. Like, where was Tarek? Why wasn't he here—and Samuel Griffen and his sorcerers?

She knew they had surprised the Rakshasa before they

were totally ready to launch the attack. Maybe Tarek and the sorcerers just hadn't made it into position.

But they should have shown up at some point.

Seneca probably had more men, and that couldn't have been all the Created fighting for the Rakshasa, just a select few. Where were the rest?

And then there was the question she didn't want to ask. The question that made her want to pull away from John, lie back on the chilly dirt, and stare at the cold night sky.

"How many did we lose?"

John frowned. "I don't know yet. At least four OCU officers and an Astaroth—one of Jake's friends. And I'm sorry, but three Sibyls that I know of. They weren't expecting all the gunfire."

Camille closed her eyes at this, wanting to shut it out. *Not again. Please, don't let all the dying start again.* "Names?"

"I don't know." John brushed his fingers across her cheek and ear, pushing her hair out of her face and making her look at him. "I didn't recognize them, and two of them were really young."

"Probably newly chosen adepts," she said, feeling a crackle of grief down in her chest. "Probably fire Sibyls."

"The Bengals came." John sounded both understanding and concerned. "I want to find Ben and thank him— and ask him why."

A few moments later, the captain of Elana's personal guard found them, and his aristocratic features reflected no joy at the victory.

Camille struggled to sit upright, letting John help her as Ben approached. Bela, Dio, and Andy limped and hopped over to her, then sat on the ground beside her, watching the big Bengal stride across the open space while his Bengal fighters, at least thirty of them, milled in the distance behind him. They weren't quite forming ranks, but it looked like they wanted to. Nick, Creed, and Jake Lowell were with the Bengals, talking to them, no doubt to get information, but also to keep Sibyls or OCU officers from becoming confused and going after the warriors who couldn't quite get rid of all their tiger traits even in human form.

"Ben," John said, standing to shake hands as he reached them. "I don't know why Elana changed her mind about fighting with us, but I'm glad she did."

"She's been taken," Ben said. "She is hostage to the Rakshasa."

Camille felt her sore ribs throb as all the breath left her. John jerked like he'd been kicked in the gut, but it was Andy—Goddess. Andy's cry of dismay cut into Camille like a dozen fiery daggers.

"What?" Andy's horror was a tangible thing, and Camille wanted to cry for Elana, for herself—but so much more for Andy. "No. She can't—they're not—they can't have her!"

Camille couldn't even look in Andy's direction. She kept her gaze firmly fixed on Ben.

Ben's face remained placid, but Camille sensed his rage and shame like a steady stream of energy rushing out of him. "Tarek and his demons laid siege to our stronghold in the aqueduct. They had old magick makers with them—we weren't prepared for that aspect of the battle, so they drove us out."

"The Coven," Camille said, all the missing pieces of tonight's battle clicking into place.

"The rest of your army?" John asked.

Ben's shame increasing tenfold, he bowed his shoulders as he gripped the hilt of his sword. "Possibly alive and hostage, but more likely slaughtered."

"And you're sure they didn't kill Elana?" Camille asked, as much for Andy as herself.

"I'm positive," Ben said. "The strike was designed specifically to capture her."

John was already checking his Glock and ammunition. "Any idea where they've taken her?"

Ben shook his head. "They didn't take her anywhere. The Rakshasa are holding her in the aqueduct, in our own stronghold."

"So . . . this battle was a diversion." John holstered his weapon, and Camille could tell he was trying to get a fix on what he should do next. "They sucked all our attention here and hit you while we weren't looking. They let you go to be sure we got the message."

"Yes," Ben said.

"Do you think they're wanting to bargain?" John asked Ben, checking the hilt of his broadsword. "Some sort of horse trade?"

Ben frowned. "Rakshasa do not bargain."

"What do you think they want?" Camille asked, not able to come up with any logical answers herself.

Ben didn't hesitate. "You and your fighting group. If they couldn't kill you here, I think they hoped to capture one of you and hold you with Elana."

"They know we'll go after her." Camille suddenly felt like the devastation in the park all around her had been just a warm-up.

"They're counting on it," Ben said. "And they believe they can win."

34

John had never wanted to see the Sibyl Mothers again, much less share space with them, after he understood what they'd done to Camille and her quad. He especially didn't want to be around them now, when the demon in his head was giving him more trouble. From the moment he saw Aarif in the park, Strada had been more active—and when the kid went down, Jesus. John had thought the demon essence was going to blow right out of the side of his head.

He'd gotten it under control, but it was a close battle. Now he had to stare at people who pissed him off beyond reason, and that wasn't good. Three of the Mothers had been present at the OCU debriefing in the townhouse conference room, and now the same three were attending a private meeting between Jack Blackmore, Cal and Saul Brent, Ben, Camille's group, and John and Duncan. The meeting was also in the conference room, but the other OCU officers and Sibyls had been dismissed to rest and see to their wounds while the next strike was mapped out and discussed. The entire space smelled like strong coffee, which was brewing on a small counter at the very back of the room.

The Brent brothers and Jack had drawn the blinds to the hallway, locked the door, and taken command of the long table at the front of the room. The Mothers had seated themselves on the right side of the conference room, and John and Duncan stood with Camille, Bela, Dio, and Andy on the left side. Ben stayed close to John.

He had left his men outside on the ground floor, with OCU officers and Sibyls alike staring at them.

While Jack got ready to start talking and drawing up plans, John took his time glaring at Mother Keara, from Ireland. The blinds on the street side of the conference room were open, and morning sunlight sliced through the panes, lighting up every wrinkle and line on her ancient face. Even though she was, by sight, just a little old woman, John wanted to grab the ancient fire Sibyl and use all those ropes of gray hair to wrap her up in her green robes and pitch her straight out that window.

Mother Yana, from Russia, bothered him on Bela's behalf, but she didn't seem as hard to deal with as Mother Keara. Mother Yana was smaller than the other two and seemingly older, shriveled inside her brown robes. Her hair looked like an explosion of white threads nobody had bothered to comb in a century or so, and her face bore a spooky resemblance to the lined wolf's head on her hand-carved walking stick.

Mother Anemone, from Greece, wore her blue robes in a tailored fit, and her ash-blond hair had been swept back and piled on her head. She had probably been a looker when she was younger, and she seemed nicer than the other Mothers, but John had issues with her, too. He wanted to ask her what the hell she'd been thinking, leaving Dio all alone to figure out her powerful ventsentience, which he had learned often came with the weather-making she wasn't supposed to do.

Camille, who was standing right in front of him, seemed to sense his tension and leaned into him, capturing his attention. He wrapped his arms around her and kissed the back of her head. "How the hell are you still on your feet, beautiful?"

Her voice came back to him sounding beyond tired. "You're holding me up."

Duncan was doing pretty much the same thing with Bela, while Dio sat with her arms folded, her head ramrod straight, and her eyes closed. Andy was hovering close to Ben, and she was so stressed and agitated John could almost feel the frigid cold water from the sprinkler over his head. No doubt it would break soon.

Jack looked up. "We think the best way to go is a full assault, all possible entries, but Bela, I don't want your quad to be present."

Ben came to attention, and John's muscles tightened. He gripped Camille by both forearms and faced off with Jack and Cal Brent, who seemed to be the proponents on this one. "Hostages don't survive assaults."

"No way," Andy said, talking right over him and glaring at Jack. "They'll shoot Elana dead before we get two steps in the door. We negotiate. We buy time. We find a better plan."

Camille pulled out of John's grip. "There have to be other options. My quad and I, we could—"

"No," Mother Keara said firmly. "Like he said, you four won't be goin' on this raid. We won't be riskin' what you four can do. Not again."

Bela barked out a laugh, standing away from Duncan so she could get a good look at the fire Sibyl Mother. "Excuse me, old woman, but the four of us just wiped out a Rakshasa Eldest and a boatload of Created in Central Park while you were what—at home, picking your teeth?"

"Damn straight," Dio muttered. "And we lived through it, no thanks to any of you."

"Luck, perhaps," Mother Anemone said, her voice gentle, her eyes anywhere but on Dio. "Or perhaps the demons wanted you to survive."

"We could get Elana out," Camille said, but she stopped short of offering up how they'd do it. "We could go in and take her before your raid."

Camille's words seemed to give Ben some comfort, but

Cal Brent didn't have any mercy. "I think there's zero chance Elana survives this no matter which way we go. She's just bait, and when bait's been taken, it's discarded. The second any of the four of you sets foot in the aqueduct, she's toast." More directly to Andy and Ben, he said, "I'm sorry."

Ben lowered his head, but the sprinkler over John's head finally tore off and doused him as Andy glared at Cal. "Screw you with the 'I'm sorry.' Do you know what she is? The only water Sibyl in the world who's fully trained in all the old ways—not the half-ass hodgepodge training I got. She's not going to die like that. She's not going to die at all."

Camille swept her hand up and deflected the water from John's head. A second later, he felt a gust from Dio, drying him off and keeping the shower at bay until Andy got the leak under control.

"Elana isn't what you think she is," Mother Keara snapped back. "Don't be tellin' yerself you know everything about her. She's a danger to herself and everyone around her. And she can be cruel." The bitterness in the old woman's voice was startling.

Ben looked like he wanted to march over and challenge Mother Keara to a duel, but the little maniac's outward appearance of being a helpless old woman probably confused him. As it was, he stood his ground, as stiff as if somebody had starched him, and John could feel him seething.

Mother Anemone put a long-fingered hand on Mother Keara's shoulder, as if to persuade her to stop talking, and Mother Yana took over. "Vat she means is, Elana has as much knowledge as any Sibyl Mother. The likes of that in the hands of the likes of those—no. It cannot be. If ve cannot rescue Elana outright, it may be best that she perish before she's tortured to give up our secrets and who knows vat else."

"Possessing her is like holding all the information in our archives and having it for their personal use," Mother Anemone said. "She has enough elemental power to take down the city, and she's knowledgeable enough to com-promise every Sibyl fighting group and most of the Motherhouses, too."

"Do they have to be here?" John asked Jack, gesturing toward the Mothers. He didn't care how his question sounded or that Bela and, surprisingly, Camille flinched a little at his disrespect. "I don't see why they have a stake in this, Mothers or not. They haven't done anything to train the fighters who can beat the Rakshasa. It's Elana who's been helping Camille."

His words seemed to strike all three Mothers as painfully as any slap. Mother Anemone actually hung her head. Mother Yana looked away. Mother Keara started to smoke, fingering the edge of her fold-out chair like she might find some prize under the edges.

Jack Blackmore looked pretty miserable himself, but what he said next was pretty predictable. "You four are the target here, Bela, Camille, Dio, Andy—you specifically. That's obvious. The Rakshasa leader Tarek has done this to get you four to come to him, so my math gets pretty simple from there. You can't go anywhere near that aqueduct."

All four Sibyls started arguing at the same time, with Duncan, John, and even Ben stepping back from them.

"We have to try," Camille said.

"Stupidest thing I ever heard." That was Dio.

Andy was still relying on "Fuck you," but it was Bela who said, "Not your call, Blackmore, sorry. Elana's a Sibyl, so in the end it's Sibyl business."

"Which makes it our call," Mother Yana announced. "And we side with Captain Blackmore."

John's jaw clenched. They were old women. Old.

Women. Power or no, it wasn't okay for him to slug them or boot them out the door.

"We're simply not willing to sacrifice the four of you for Elana," Mother Anemone said, gentling things down like John was realizing most air Sibyls other than Dio tended to try to do. "She's had her time on earth. You're young and powerful, and much more valuable—"

She stopped, maybe understanding how hollow her words sounded to the four women standing like angry leather-clad statues in front of John.

"Valuable to whom?" Dio's expression fell somewhere between hurt and incredulous. "Sure as hell not to you. You discount us for our whole lives, and now you think you have some right to tell us when and where we're most valuable?"

John glanced at Duncan and Ben. Ben looked bewildered and distressed. Duncan's face reflected what John felt—anger and concern.

"You may be havin' issues with us," Mother Keara said, finally managing to look at Camille when she spoke. "I can't fault you for that, but we're still yer elders, and you still answer to us. We're tellin' you, let the OCU make this strike. If they can't reach Elana, let her die before she hurts anyone else or kills us all. If you can't abide that, we'll pull you all out of fightin', as you'll have proved yourselves no safer than she and hers were."

This time, none of the Sibyls said anything, not even Andy.

What the hell? John stood a little straighter himself, and his anger ratcheted up enough that the demon in his head thrashed around and made him wince.

No. No way. These old bitches were not finally managing to cow Camille and the rest—were they? That was an empty threat. It had to be.

And Blackmore and his "simple math." The simple

math was, Elana had hung herself out there for the Bengals, for John, for Camille, for all of them. Camille and her quad didn't owe the Mothers the time of day, but he felt like they did owe Elana something.

The rational part of his brain reminded him that he didn't want Camille in danger or hurt—her or any of her quad. But it disgusted him to see them let the Mothers win a round, for any reason, and it hurt him to think about Elana, who had given him nothing but kindness and wisdom and trust, trapped by a monster like Tarek with no help coming for her.

"Camille," he said, touching her arm.

She turned toward him, and the tears glistening in her eyes gave him a sinking feeling.

"We have to talk about this," she said. "The five of us—and not here."

The rumble of Strada moving in his head didn't escape him, but he couldn't help how pissed he was getting. "They're full of shit. They'd never throw you out."

"Leave it alone," Bela said through her teeth, keeping her gaze forward while Dio got up from her seat and Andy kept her eyes squeezed shut, probably to hold on to her temper.

"Let it go, buddy," Duncan echoed. "Let them figure it out. They always do."

The growling in John's head got a little worse. He tamped the demon back as best he could when he was really starting to want to kill something, and he swept his glare back to Jack. "It's not right, this assault. I won't be a part of it."

"Nor will I," Ben said. "My warriors and I will find our own solution. We'll go after her ourselves."

Jack considered this. "Then you better get there first."

John's neck twitched as Strada growled loudly in his brain. "Asshole," he muttered.

The Sibyls said nothing else, and Andy didn't attack

Jack with so much as a sprinkler head. The Mothers had gone quiet, too, obviously convinced they had made their point and won their battle.

Ben glanced once at John, his dark eyes troubled, angry, and worried, then made his way toward the conference room door. With a last quick glance at Camille standing there in her tearful silence, John followed Ben. If the Bengals were going to try to save Elana, he'd damned sure be with them.

Strada could keep up his snarl-and-howl routine. It didn't matter. They were going after the Rakshasa *culla* and whatever he wanted to throw at them, and maybe they'd be able to take the bastard down.

He'd made it a few steps into the hallway when the Sibyls spilled out the door behind him.

"John, please wait," Camille said, probably about to plead her case about how this was a big decision for her quad. Yeah, he got that, but he just didn't want to hear it, especially not with Strada giving him such a fight all of a sudden. "Let me explain what just happened in there."

He intended to tell her it was okay, that they'd talk later, but when he turned to face her, what came out of his mouth was, "I can't believe you'd listen to the Mothers after everything they did to you. And everything they *didn't* do for you."

"Until my quad found each other, the Mothers and the Sibyls were the only family we knew." The conflict on Camille's face made her feel like a stranger to him. "It isn't so easy to just walk away from everything that defines you—but we weren't listening to them. We were just keeping the peace until—"

Her words blurred in his mind, and his brain seized on the thing that pissed him off the most. John dug his thumb into his chest. "Ex-soldier. Ex-priest. Yeah, I do have a grip on having to walk away from what defines you to do what's right."

Camille just stared at him. "You're only hearing part of what I'm saying—literally. What's wrong, John?"

He wasn't sure, but he thought she was getting pissed. Well, too bad. In the end, right was right and loyalty was loyalty, and she shouldn't have had any conflict about this at all.

"The Mothers never helped you," he said. "They never even wanted any of you. Elana did."

Camille's breath hitched and the tears in her eyes got a little brighter. "You're making it simpler than it is."

"Sometimes things are just exactly what they seem to be, Camille. Elana's expendable to them. Just not to Ben. Not to me. Not to Andy. And I thought not to you."

"Of course she's not expendable to me!"

"Then why aren't you telling those women and Jack Blackmore exactly where to get off?"

Camille started talking, something about how she knew what had to be done and she and her quad would do it, but it wasn't worth starting an open war with the Mothers. They'd just take action and let the Mothers do or think whatever they chose—like always.

John's thoughts buzzed so loudly he didn't catch it all, and he really didn't think it was important. Something was breaking loose inside him, and he was afraid that when it finished fracturing, there wouldn't be anything left for him and for Camille. He didn't want her to die. He didn't even want her to get hurt. To tell the truth, he was a little relieved Blackmore was ordering them off this battle. Still, he didn't know if he could live with seeing them walk away from Elana in her time of need. He couldn't live with himself if he did that.

"We should let this go for now," he told Camille, meaning the argument, but he saw instantly that she took it for more than that—and he just let that misperception stand. "You need some rest, and Ben and I have work to do."

He and Ben started for the door again, but Camille said, "Something's wrong. Something's happening in your head and I'm not sure what it is. Don't go, John."

John hesitated. Doubted himself. He looked at the ceiling, doing what he could to keep Strada's growling to a minimum. "I'm not running away, Camille. It's not me who's running out on anybody."

To that, Camille said nothing at all.

He followed Ben out the front door. If Strada hadn't been kicking around so hard, he might have looked back, but he doubted that Camille had followed him outside.

35

Camille didn't know how she got down to the basement or why she wasn't sobbing her head off.

Too tired to waste that kind of energy.

Though she wasn't too tired to care.

The entire gym looked dull to her, even though she knew the stone floors were covered with colorful balls and mats.

The mats. Damn. She didn't want to think about John on the mats, the way they had made love down here with such total abandon.

That was starting to seem like another person, another Camille, a lifetime ago.

John's gone.

The thought tried to form, but Camille wouldn't let it. She breathed in the stone and sweat and vinyl scent of the gym as Andy, Bela, and Dio came into the room and Dio bolted the door behind them.

"Duncan's trying to make Blackmore see reason," Bela said. "Luck to him on that."

Camille let the words go into her mind, then let them roll right back out again. No room. For the first time in all her years of training and trying to overcome her fears and flaws, she was seriously considering walking away from the Dark Crescent Sisterhood, because she could not—would not—honor the Mothers' instructions not to go down to the aqueduct. The fact that her quad would be walking away with her made things easier, but no less monumental.

Why didn't John know that? Why had he ignored her when she told him outright?

"Am I mistaken," Bela asked, rubbing a scorch mark on her battle leathers just above her heart, "or did John and his friend Ben the Bengal just blow us off and leave?"

"He *left*?" Dio turned back to the gym door like she was considering going after him. Camille was pretty sure that would involve tornados, targeted lightning, and other unpleasant outcomes, so she spent the energy trying to explain.

"I think he got pissed when we stopped fighting the Mothers and said we needed to discuss things privately." Camille felt herself frowning but couldn't stop it. At least the tears were gone. They had dried up all of a sudden, and she felt no hint of needing to cry. Weird. "He didn't seem to get the fact that we just didn't want to draw swords right there in the conference room and have to fight our own. Something—something wasn't right with him."

Andy stared at Camille openmouthed. "He had to know we meant discussing what we were going to do about Elana, not whether or not we were listening to any of that hot air in there." She let her head fall back and stared at the ceiling. "Fuck those old bitches. I'm a Mother myself, for shit's sake. They can't pull me out of anything." She looked back at Camille. "John knew that, right?"

Camille wished there were some ritual other than sleep to suddenly make herself less exhausted. "He wasn't himself. Like I said, he wasn't listening."

"He didn't know," Dio said. "Damn him."

A moment or two later, Camille came clear on the truth of that. "He should have known. I know he cares about me, and I know he'd never doubt me, or us. Not in his right mind." Dread tingled in her belly, then spread upward in a cold wave. "Maybe Strada found a way to play with his mind or his emotions."

Andy banged her fist into her palm, and the sprinklers over the treadmill in the corner exploded and started raining all over the machine. She didn't even try to stop them. "Great. Just when we need him most—but we can't do anything about that right now. What's our next move?"

John's gone. He was really gone, and he might be in trouble she couldn't fix. Not yet. Not now. "Can you teach us those self-protections?" Bela asked, pacing now, like Bela always did when she was thinking hard.

"Not in a few minutes, or even a day." Camille wanted to sink down to the stone floor, bury her head in her hands, and maybe never even look up again. "It's complicated and it takes practice."

Dio was starting to stride back and forth, too, but she always kept a more frenetic pace than Bela. "Can you put it in a charm for us? Something we could use immediately?"

Camille gave this a thought for about two seconds. "Eventually, probably, but that would take weeks."

John's gone. I might be losing him to Strada.

And Elana. Poor Elana.

Camille looked around at her quad as they burst into excited maybe-this's and maybe-that's, eagerly debating possibilities, and all she could think was, *They'll be killed.*

She didn't just suspect that. She knew it for a fact. Whether it was instinct, the prescience she always wanted finally showing up, or whatever, she was certain at a level she couldn't deny that if Bela, Dio, and Andy tried to use projective energy like they had in the park but on a larger scale, they would die.

To honor her commitment to Bela and the rest about speaking her mind, she said. "You can't do this. You just can't. Aarif was young and probably less powerful than the older Eldest—and he only had a few Created. There may be hundreds guarding Elana. Trying to work at that level would tear you apart."

It may tear me *apart.*

"The whole energy trap thing did great." Andy looked at Camille like she was nuts. "It took the demons out and we walked away fine."

Camille gazed into Andy's face.

She had to save Elana for Andy, if for no other reason—and she had plenty of other reasons.

"John and the Bengals are about to go after Elana without any prayer of succeeding and without any backup," she told Bela, so that the earth Sibyl couldn't accuse of her of not being open, of keeping too many secrets. She really was much better about the whole secret thing now. Mostly. "John might not even be stable or able to keep control of himself. I have to help."

Andy and Dio kept bouncing ideas around, but Bela focused on Camille enough to ask, "Then how can we help?"

"Keep yourselves safe. If I screw this up, clean up the mess." Camille managed a smile to try to soften her words, but Andy and Dio had gone dead quiet. They were both listening now, giving her their total attention. The gym seemed insanely small even though Camille knew the space hadn't been shrinking when she wasn't paying attention.

Dio and Andy were crowding her, with Bela taking a position between them and the door like they thought Camille was going to make a sudden break for the basement door.

"I'm serious about you not being able to use projective energy without better protections." Camille looked at each of them, hoping like hell they believed her. "You have to learn them first."

"And you have to teach them to us." Andy sounded less than patient.

Dio was shaking her head, an almost amused smile on her face. "You can't just think we're going to let you walk out of here without us, Camille."

"Of course I don't think that." Camille smiled at Dio and loved her fiercely, like a best friend, like a sister. She loved each one of them like that.

She loved John just as much, in a whole different way, and he was already gone. Maybe these three she could save.

Ah. There were the tears. She had known they were in there somewhere.

"Sorry about this secret I kept," she told Bela. "It was just a little one. You can kill me over it later—I hope."

Bela's gaze leaped to the dinar showing through the burn marks in Camille's leathers, but Camille didn't need the dinar anymore, not for this. She didn't need anything at all.

Her quad watched in absolute confusion and then disbelief as Camille, tears streaming, took one step back, only one step, because a little space would make it safer for Dio, who was standing too close.

Then Camille opened her mind to the channels of energy flowing all over the earth, the tunnels, the ever-connecting tunnels, and she sank away from the quad, flowing off from the townhouse at the mind-blinding speed of fire.

36

John stumbled into Van Cortlandt Park behind Ben, with the Bengal fighters following.

Something was off in his head. Really off.

He was walking like he was drunk. Couldn't keep his balance. He hadn't taken any major hits in the battle, so what the hell was this about?

The Bengals were moving fast and quietly, sticking to less traveled routes to avoid the population. Most people who saw them would assume they were actors, models, reenactors, or just freaks in costumes. If John's head exploded, though, even disinterested passersby might get that something was up.

"Ben," he growled as they reached one of the secret entrances to the Old Croton Aqueduct, a small stone house, ten feet by ten feet at most, well hidden by evergreens and hearty shrubs even in early winter.

John more or less fell into the stone house and hit his knees. He didn't even feel the pain. At least it wasn't too dark inside, because sunlight crowded in from holes at the top of the walls. In the dark, he might just have passed out dead to the world.

Ben turned, saw John, and signaled his fighters to wait outside. Then Ben drew his broadsword. John didn't blame him.

"I think—I think he's taking me." John was fighting like hell to even talk. His vision had gone blurry, and Ben's heartbeat seemed too loud in the small stone space.

"How is that possible?" Ben circled John, holding his blade at the ready. "Why don't you fight?"

"Am." John threw his will into it. Tried to pretend Camille was right here with him, that he had to keep the demon bastard away from her. It bought him an inch. Maybe. His mind had to be on fire. His head had to be smoking. "He's been quiet for so long. He lulled me. He laid traps in my mind. Something—"

God, the pain between his eyes was unbelievable. Like the smell of Ben's blood. "Something set him off. Gave him strength."

"Aarif," Ben said. "Strada was always closest to his youngest true brother."

At the sound of Aarif's name, John felt a massive lurch in the center of his being and he almost blacked out. Falling forward, he put his hands on the ground, and saw the claws growing out of his fingertips. They looked like alien life-forms, long and curved and sharp.

Ben had to be right. Aarif was Strada's silver bullet like Camille was John's.

Ah, Christ. If John had watched Camille die, there would be no stopping him from going after whoever hurt her—and it was Camille who'd killed Aarif. No way could he let Strada get away with this. The Rakshasa would be on Camille in one second flat.

John tried to pick out the demon essence, tried to isolate it to push back, but it was everywhere. His heart thudded, dull and distant, but Ben's heartbeat got downright deafening. The blood in Ben's veins was starting to sing to John.

"No," he snarled, hearing Strada in his voice even as he fought. He looked up at Ben, desperate. "Sneaky this time. Got . . . got into my thoughts instead of just . . . jumping forward."

Ben kept circling, staying out of reach. John's arms itched. White fur rippled out near his left elbow.

Ben's voice drifted down to him from a hundred miles away. "Fight harder. I don't want to kill you, John."

"If . . . get up furry . . . do it." John stayed down, shaking his head back and forth like a rabid dog. He felt like a bunch of dogs or maybe a mule had stomped his brain.

Camille . . .

John held her image in his mind. What the fuck had he said to her at the townhouse? It had seemed so real and huge and important at the moment. Grain of truth, but Strada—Strada had already been there, and he'd built on John's emotions to take him away from his human talisman.

Camille . . .

Pain knifed into his joints, all the way to bone. His body was changing.

Camille . . .

And she was there, somehow just there in the stone house, standing beside him in her leathers, reaching down to take his arm and pull him to his feet.

Joy—then rage. Then—nothing.

37

"Do not touch him!"

Ben's shout was the first thing Camille heard after she came through the channels to John, because she didn't know where else to go, where else to start to save Elana.

It was almost the last thing she ever heard.

John burst off the ground, flinging her off him like some disgusting insect. She slammed against the nearest stone wall so hard she lost her wind and came up gasping, clawing at the stone, trying to get to her feet. At the same moment, John dodged Ben's sword and smashed his fist into Ben's face.

Ben stumbled and went down. The Bengals outside howled and started forward, but Ben waved them off. "Tidas. Take command. Retrieve Elana." He grabbed for his dropped sword. "Close that door. Lock us in. Now. Now!"

"Murdering bitch." John's low voice—but it wasn't really John's anymore.

Camille heard the door bang shut, heard the sound of debris being thrown against it to keep it fastened.

When she managed to lift her head, John was standing over her, fists doubled, eyes blazing.

Black eyes. Blacker than night itself.

Everything inside her froze over. She didn't feel pain or fatigue or even fear. Just vast, cold nothingness.

"Strada," she said, and the Rakshasa roared at her. He charged, and she launched herself to the other side of the house to stand beside Ben. A second later she had her scimitar drawn, but Goddess, how could she use it? This was John. This was the man she loved, trapped in that body somewhere behind a raging demon.

The ice inside Camille cracked an inch, then another. Everything in her body started to hurt and drag, most of all her heart. The tears came sudden and fast, half blinding her, and she swiped them out of her eyes with the back of one hand.

"Not this," she said out loud, though she didn't really know whom she was talking to. Her heart was beating so hard she wondered if she was about to go down facefirst on the rock floor and feed herself to the Rakshasa like John had once accused her of trying to do.

Strada came at her again, shifting more, shifting more, but still not enough for the dinar to repel him. Camille and Ben dodged away from him, split to opposite sides, catching the demon between them.

Both had position. Both had blades ready.

Neither could swing.

Strada laughed at them. "Weak fools."

The voice was definitely not John's now. Not even a hint of him seemed to be battling with Strada.

As for the demon, he was deciding between targets. He lunged for Ben first, but Ben knocked his huge claws aside with the broadsword and joined up with Camille again.

If she didn't cut him, she risked being killed—or turned herself. A Created with sentient talents—that couldn't happen.

Camille drew in what power she could, keeping her protections carefully in place, and fed that power into her scimitar.

"John," she said, trying one more time because her heart gave her no choice. "Don't go. Don't run away from me. I'm here. I'm staying right here."

Strada roared so loud Camille's ears buzzed.

He jumped for her, more demon than human now—

and the dinar's energy cracked like gunfire, hurling him hard against the far stone wall.

Strada struck the rock like he'd been fired out of a cannon, and Camille covered him with projective energy. She knew she was dooming John, stripping Strada down to nothing but demon, but it was either that or cut his head off. This would be terrible, but easier than that.

Strada thrashed, and the fur fell away from half his body.

Camille saw the ridged scar on John's side, made by Maggie's terrible sword.

"Whatever you're doing, don't stop," Ben told her, approaching the downed demon more closely, blade in front of him.

Camille could see more of John now, coming back into focus under Strada's essence. He was naked, sweating, kicking and thrashing, though his arms and head seemed to be pinned to the ground.

She glanced down at the dinar. Maybe her black-and-white thinking had been wrong. Maybe if two distinct energies occupied the same body, projective energy functioned as a phase changer instead of just stripping away all human aspects.

Or maybe that depended on the entities in the bodies.

"Camille." John groaned, and it was John, without claws now, without white fur—though he still had black eyes and didn't seem to be able to move from the waist up.

She got a little closer to him and didn't feel the shove of the dinar's energy trying to move her back.

"Take care," Ben warned, holding his sword tip at John's chest as Camille knelt beside John, just out of reach of his seemingly frozen right arm and hand.

"No . . . fool," John gasped.

Confused, Camille glanced up at Ben.

"I believe he means don't let Strada fool you," Ben

said. "This attack was motivated by the death of Aarif, and Strada was cunning and devious in his approach."

Aarif's name seemed to cause John physical pain, and for a moment Camille saw the shadow of fur and felt the nudge of the dinar. Seconds later it disappeared, and John turned his head toward her.

Green eyes. Beautiful green eyes.

"Love . . . you." He was struggling, trying to get his words out all at once. "In the townhouse—didn't mean it."

Camille wanted to touch him so badly she almost risked it, but the eyes shifted to black and the dinar held her away from John.

"Love you," John's voice said, a little more clearly this time, and the dinar's repelling ebbed.

"Can't live . . . like this." He clenched his jaw. His teeth. "Too strong for me now."

"He's asking us to kill him," Ben said, keeping his sword touching John's chest right above his beating heart.

John shook his head once, hard. Kept Camille's gaze. His green eyes flicked to the dinar. "Do it . . . fast."

And Camille understood.

He wanted her to kill him like he was Rakshasa—pierce his heart with elementally treated metal, behead him, then use the dinar to magnify her pyrogenesis and burn him to ashes.

The thought of that made her sick, then furious. "Not happening. I'm not losing you, and Strada's *not* going to win."

She grabbed the dinar, remembering the moment of golden light when she'd first seen John, the real John, free of his prison in Duncan Sharp's mind. That had been impossible, amazing—and they had done it together.

How could such a miracle come down to this—help a man regain his life, then kill him again?

No.

Her fingers tingled against the metal as blood thumped in her ears. She studied John's face, his beautiful eyes searching hers even as his chest started to jerk with each breath. Getting weaker.

He's losing the battle.

No!

She'd used the coin to help him once before. Maybe she could use it again. Camille tightened her grip on the metal as her rational mind argued with her heart. Too dangerous. Too insane.

But it was a chance.

As much as she didn't want to spend a second away from John, she turned and explained her idea to Ben as fast and simply as she could, adding, "It will probably kill him."

"Or you," Ben said. "The risk is too much."

"Greater than leaving him like this?" Camille settled the dinar into her left hand and closed her fingers around it. "I can take care of myself, but right now, Ben, you need to back away."

The man moved immediately, withdrawing his sword tip from John's chest and retreating to the barred door of the stone house.

John looked confused, then angry.

It was just Camille and John now. "I'll do it another way," she said, then felt his trusting look like a knife straight into her essence.

A darkness danced in the back of John's eyes now, an evil alien presence Camille knew she had to face, and right away. With the dinar in her hand, Strada couldn't touch her in his demon form, and she couldn't touch him either—though if he got a good amount of control over John, no doubt the bastard could still beat her to death or eat her.

"Not today," she whispered to that wicked gleam

threatening to overtake the gentle care in John's expression.

She tapped into her pyrosentience and reached out to pockets of nearby fire energy, finding a strong source not too far away. Yes. Just right. Enough without being too much. She opened herself to the fire, keeping her gaze fixed on John's, and she let the power build, let it build more, as she tried to remember every nuance of a year ago in that alley when she first saw John.

That night she had only moved a soul, just helped it transition from one place to another.

Now she was about to attack and try to destroy a soul.

Totally different. Maybe not even possible.

She let her right hand creep toward John's, and when they made contact, Camille felt it like an embrace, everywhere, all over her at the same time. "I love you," she told John.

"I love you," he said, obviously believing she was granting his request and preparing to tear him apart in some new, awful way he didn't even understand—but that was okay with him. He was just fine with believing she was about to kill him.

Goddess, she hoped he wasn't right.

Camille squeezed the dinar, squeezed John's hand, closed her eyes, and let the fire energy flow through her into him. She tried to find his channels, his body's tunnels, and her awareness flew through them just like she had flown through the pockets of energy under New York City.

This was John. And here was John. And all this energy was John. But that energy—she slowed her exploration, touching the perverted darkness, finding it, rooting it out, and going straight for it with everything she could bring to bear.

Die, she thought, willing her fire into Strada's darkness, opening herself into a conduit, sending the energy with no flames, but heat. So much heat!

John started to scream.

She smelled smoke. Burning flesh. The dinar sizzled against her hand, so hot, too hot, but she made herself hold tight, squeeze the coin tighter as the demon fought for its life.

"Die," she said aloud, then reverted to John's word. "Burn. Burn, you bastard, burn!"

She was burning. Her left arm had to be on fire. She tried to channel her power to relieve it, but she couldn't. The pain made her scream along with John, but she kept after the darkness inside him, lighting it up, lighting him up.

From deep beneath her, the world seemed to be talking to her, whispering at first, then growling at her, with her, as she imagined Strada turned to ashes and blowing away. Strada. Strada's energy. The demon's darkness. She imagined John whole and demon-free, green-eyed and healthy.

The ground shook as the fire below came closer. Closer.

Somebody was praying. Ben. A language Camille didn't even know.

So much smoke. So much heat. The sweet tang of liquid gold filled her senses, and she rushed on through John's essence, finding him, finding John, finding light and no darkness.

With a cry of triumph, Camille pulled back her fire power and let him go, collapsing backward. Sleep came so hard, so fast, she couldn't fight it.

My arm, she thought, wishing she could ease the agony. Then, *John. I have to see him. I have to know.*

And—

38

Somebody was weeping.

Camille came slowly back to herself and opened her eyes.

Smoke drifted across her field of vision.

Her left arm felt too strange for words, stiff and kind of crusty, but at least it wasn't burning anymore. She squinted at the angle of the light in the small space, coming through chinks in the rock high above her head. She'd been out, definitely, but not for long.

"John." She sat straight up, her battle leathers pulling at her shoulders from the sudden movement.

John was lying a little ways away from her, naked and pale and very, very still. Tiny tendrils of smoke rose from his elbows and knees, like his insides had been cooked to well done. His arms were folded unnaturally on his chest, and Camille realized Ben had done this.

Ben was on one knee beside John, tears on his smooth brown cheeks. He had his hand on John's hands, and his head was bowed.

Camille got dizzy, and numbness moved all through her body.

She stared at John.

He was breathing. He *was* breathing. She could see it.

She pushed herself to her hands and knees, and instantly realized the different sensation in her left hand. She looked down, and her mouth came open.

The dinar—it was gone. Melted. Poured into her skin in a pattern like the world's most intricate lace. The gold filigree wrapped from the tip of her middle finger across her palm, moving to the back of her hand to her wrist and all the way to her elbow. No human could have created lines so delicate and fragile, yet there they were, marking her forever just like the tattoo of the Dark Crescent Sisterhood on her right forearm.

Favoring her metal-infused arm, Camille crawled over to John. Yes, he was definitely breathing.

"Strada took his weapons in the change," Ben whispered. "A warrior should meet his maker with his sword, but that dung heap of a demon robbed him of that chance."

"He's still alive, Ben."

"This body is breathing. This body's heart is beating." Ben shook his head and more tears appeared on his face. "But there is nothing inside." His dark eyes found Camille's. "Check for yourself. Perhaps you're more sensitive than me."

Camille looked down at John, who seemed to be sleeping peacefully. She reached out with her awareness, tried to sense his human energy, his signature—something.

Anything.

She found nothing.

Her lips parted.

She tried again, going a little deeper, but the body seemed to have no life beyond its basic functions.

"Maybe he just needs time," she whispered to Ben, hoping to make that real just by saying it. She needed to believe that. She had to believe that instead of the other possibility—that she had burned John's soul away along with Strada's, sending both of them back to the universe in one brilliant, flaming burst of energy.

"He just needs time," she said again. "You stay with him, okay?"

No crying. No time for tears now. She could cry later if she really needed to. If she thought any further than that, she'd fall apart into gibberish and screaming, and whatever small chance Elana still had to make it out of the aqueduct would burn away to nothing.

Camille gave John one last, long glance.

He just needs . . .

On impulse, she leaned forward and touched her lips to his. The gold in her arm tingled, but John didn't wake like a sleeping prince recognizing the touch of his princess.

"Happily ever after," she whispered in his ear. "You made me believe. Now wake up and prove it can happen."

John's eyes remained closed, and his face stayed slack and vacant. She couldn't detect any hint of life's energy inside him, except for his beating heart.

"Where are you going?" Ben asked in a quiet, worried voice.

Camille didn't know how to explain it, so she just said, "Down. I'm going down to get Elana."

She bit back the terrible scream she wanted to turn loose, tried to ignore the wretched ache in her heart, and let herself fade into the earth's channels again.

39

Down.

It took only a moment, because Camille knew right where to go. To the map room with the little stone table. To the place where Elana had taken some sort of marker and, like a happy child, scrawled the word *Heaven* beside her favorite place in the world.

Left arm tingling like crazy, she rose out of the channel exactly in that room, and there was Elana sitting at the stone table. Her silvery hair and robes were smeared with grime and blood, but she herself seemed to be intact.

When Camille stepped free of the channel, Elana's white eyes turned straight to her, and Elana whispered, "Camille."

Instead of the relief Camille expected, Elana's whisper was absolutely horrified. "My dear," she said in the quietest voice Camille had ever heard, "go back where you came from right away. Hurry!"

"I came to get you out of here."

"That's not possible."

"The Occult Crimes Unit and the Sibyls are coming on a raid. If I don't get you to safety, Tarek will kill you the second the raid starts."

Elana looked like that was the worst news she had ever heard in her life. She put her finger to her lips and gestured toward the door. After a few seconds, Camille understood that the old woman wanted her to use her energy to explore what was in the big chamber outside the map room and beyond, in the tunnels.

Camille could sense the strange fuzzy-cotton energy of the muting charms deployed by the Rakshasa and Griffen's Coven, but she had to be inside the field. She had no trouble reaching out and finding—

Oh.

Oh, no.

Camille's chest got so tight she almost coughed and had to stuff her gold-laced fist in her mouth. The projective gold hummed against her lips, reacting to the massive quantity of demon energy standing only a few feet away from her.

After she had checked the tunnels in every direction, she staggered back to Elana, knelt beside the woman, and whispered into her ear, "How many Eldest are out there?"

"All," Elana said back. "All that still live, I believe, save for Tarek."

The surrounding tunnels were jammed with Created, and humans were scattered along the corridors as well, some elementally talented and some elementally quiet—but likely carrying Czech assault rifles.

The OCU and every Sibyl and good demon in New York City were about to get slaughtered.

Camille took Elana's hands and tried to move her into the channels below the aqueduct, but Elana didn't sink when Camille started to move down. She could tell immediately that transporting something more complex than clothing and weapons would take far more understanding and knowledge than she possessed.

"Go," Elana told her. "Warn them."

Camille nodded.

She turned Elana's hands loose, hating to leave her even for the minute this would take, and far off in the distance, Camille heard the first spits and barks of gunfire.

"Too late," Elana said, her voice shaking.

The door to Elana's room burst open, and a Rakshasa Eldest Camille didn't recognize came striding in, blade drawn to cut Elana down.

Camille didn't even have time to draw her sword. She raised her left hand on instinct and pulled on her fire energy, intending to hit him with a burst of flameless heat—but the metal in her hand crackled. Her arm jerked back so violently she felt like she'd fired a rifle, and a ball of blue-white fire hit the Eldest square in the face.

He bellowed and reeled out of the room, banging at the flames, which clung to him in ways no simple fire would ever do.

No time to think about it.

Camille grabbed Elana's hand and pulled her out of the room.

Dear Goddess. Rakshasa everywhere, looking at them. All of them Eldest. Every last one.

Camille held up her golden arm to see what would happen—and the metal of the dinar didn't let her down. With the slightest touch of fire energy, the gold sent out burst after burst of that sticky blue fire, driving the wall of Eldest back as they fought with singed fur and scorched eyes.

Camille was grateful for that, but heartsick that the coin's repelling properties had been lost. Without that, no way were they getting out of this chamber alive.

From far out in the tunnels, she heard screaming.

"They'll all be killed," Elana yelled. "Go to them. Go now and get your friends out of this aqueduct."

Camille couldn't make herself leave Elana, but she couldn't let the OCU and all the Sibyls die, either. Panic seized her, gripped her, and she snatched at fire energy, blasting and blasting, hitting all the Eldest like her fireballs were targeting themselves.

Probably were. Her hand was projective. It was mirroring her will.

They were fighting off the flames better by the second. How many of the bastards? Thirty? Thirty-five? More? She had no idea, but she kept pulling Elana toward one of the exits even though her rational mind told her she was heading toward a huge crowd of mobsters and Created.

The demons were less than five feet away from her now, battling through all the fire she threw. It wasn't even slowing them down, so she stopped using it.

A sword swiped at Camille, cutting her right arm from shoulder to elbow. Pain seared her senses, and she cried out and stopped running, thrusting Elana behind her, keeping her between the chamber wall and her own body.

The Eldest had gotten over their surprise. They had formed ranks. They even had frigging shields Camille assumed they'd robbed from the Bengal armory. There were black tigers and white tigers and tawny-colored demons. So many shades. So many claws and fangs.

She took another sword bite, this time on her left. Drawing her scimitar seemed pretty useless against such numbers, but she did it anyway. They were just toying with her right now, making sure she couldn't do anything else they didn't expect.

The Created out in the tunnels started to snarl and pummel against the doors.

It was probably time for the Eldest to go out and help them, but they hadn't counted on a breach from within. Too fucking bad.

Camille used her projective hand to light the scimitar just because she could. Seeing the blade burst into brilliant blue-white flames made her happy. Good. People should be happy when they die.

She swung the blade, but the first blow from the nearest Eldest tore it right out of her hand and left her fingers broken and limp.

These monsters were five times her size. It was like taking on a roomful of Vodoun gods.

Most of them were starting to laugh at her.

Camille held her broken, throbbing hand against her midsection. Outside the chamber, the screaming got worse. So much worse. She thought she could smell gunpowder and blood even through the mind-numbing ammonia.

She should have done what Elana told her to do and left the old woman behind to warn the OCU. How could she have let this bloodbath happen?

"Put down the blade," the nearest Rakshasa growled, "and I will kill you *before* I eat you."

Camille answered him with a fireball in the mouth, but he used his shield to knock it away from him.

Dozens of pairs of eyes blazed at her. Hungry. Waiting for the kill.

Time was up.

Outside, her friends were dying.

Behind her, Elana was about to be ripped to pieces.

"I have to fix this," she whispered over the rumbling growls of the Rakshasa.

No more thought than that.

She thrust her gold-laced hand toward the floor, opened herself up, and called for fire. At the same time, she tried to protect herself and keep a shield over Elana.

The Rakshasa nearest her let out a blood-squelching cry and lunged toward her, swinging his broadsword.

He seemed to be moving in slow motion. Camille was looking at him, seeing him coming, but she wasn't hearing him anymore.

All she was hearing was fire's endless, insatiable roar.

His sword came down at her, slicing toward her belly, but the chamber floor was shaking, shaking so hard, and still she pulled and pulled, begging the fire to help her, touching all the hot metal rushing beneath the city in the earth's molten channels.

The Rakshasa's sword froze midstroke as liquid ore

blasted through the floor and coated him in a huge, amorphous blob of heat and fire.

The back chamber doors broke open, and Bengal fighters spilled in. Camille saw them, couldn't help them. The metal covered them in a simmering blanket of bronze and silver and gold and iron and so many more types, she couldn't even name them.

The gouts of liquid ore blew from floor to ceiling like a beautiful moving light show, but from somewhere came a steady whisper.

Stop.

That's what it sounded like.

Stop.

Stop.

Camille struggled to regain her own awareness, her sense of separateness from the fire she was touching. Her left hand vibrated so hard she felt like every bone in her body was about to jar loose.

Stop.

Elana's voice.

She was hearing it with her ears, not just her mind.

Stop.

Stop.

Camille released the energy, letting it flow back through her, down into the earth and the channels awaiting its return.

The world seemed to go eerily silent except for the *drip-drip-drip* of the solidifying metal. The stench of burned fur and flesh was enough to make her gag.

The chamber looked like something from a pharaoh's tomb, completely encased in metal, every inch of it coated except for where Camille was standing and holding Elana behind her. The molten metal hadn't touched them.

Elana cried softly behind her, and Camille could tell she was shaking. Anyone would, reliving a nightmare like this.

So many big lumps of metal, all through the chamber. Each one Rakshasa Eldest—except there at the end, she remembered, the Bengal fighters.

Something happened inside her, a bleakness, a hopelessness, and she turned to Elana. "Oh, Goddess. How many of your people did I kill?"

"I don't know," Elana whispered. "Many. I sense few alive in these—these tombs."

Camille's mind came back to reality a little more, but she didn't want it to. Too much clarity. Too much logic. A was adding to B, and C was becoming clear. Camille raked her fingers down the sides of her face. "Did I make a tidal wave?"

Elana's white eyes glistened up at her, full of tears.

"I don't know," Elana whispered again.

Appalled with herself, with everything she had likely just visited on the world, Camille had no idea what to do. Getting Elana out was the only thing that made the slightest bit of sense. She was getting ready to pick Elana up and carry her free of this death chamber when a bellow of absolute rage met her ears.

Camille barely had time to turn toward the main room again before Tarek hurtled into the chamber in tiger form. His golden fur rippled in the odd lighting as he slid across the smooth metal.

Three Created flanked him, and Eldest and Created alike pelted straight toward Camille.

She felt nothing at all. No fear. No rage. Not even a flicker in her heart rate.

On reflex, she stretched out her gold-laced hand, heated metal on the floor in front of her, and blasted Tarek with the liquid before he could reach them. His fur caught fire and he burned, and she coated him with more and more metal as the Created gave ground but kept coming at her from different angles.

Shouts rang out behind the demons, and two broke off pursuit and turned to face whatever was challenging them. Camille saw blades swinging, felt the wind, felt the earth energy.

Sibyls.

Her mind and heart were starting to wake up from what just happened, yet she couldn't accept it. She couldn't grasp that the lumps of metal all around her used to be living creatures. Demons, yes, evil, yes—but not all. Some were Bengals.

And what had happened elsewhere in the world because of what she had done?

How many people were dying right this very moment, just because she'd wanted to save her own life?

Survival instinct, her mind told her. *Every creature has it.*

Wrong, her heart said.

She heard the echo of Elana's desperate cry: *Stop, stop, stop.*

The Created, a huge, yellow-furred creature, loomed before her, and Camille didn't even try to defend herself. She couldn't imagine killing even this monster. She couldn't kill anything right now. Maybe her body would shield Elana.

The Created jerked and its paws flew upward as the tip of a broadsword emerged from its chest.

"Hey," John shouted to the nearest group of Sibyls.

Two jogged over. Camille dully recognized Maggie Cregan. She watched, stomach roiling, as Maggie beheaded the Created and scorched its ashes. Karin Maros used her wind energy to sweep the ashes of the thing's body out one door, and she sent the ashes of its head out another door.

Camille heard all this, saw it all, registered it like she was watching a movie instead of living it.

John was here.

And somebody had been nice enough to give him clothes and body armor and a sword.

She should be feeling a rush of joy so great it lifted her straight through the ceiling. He was alive and he was here, and she was—

Missing in action.

Maggie's sword tried to swipe at John, then Camille, before she got it under control.

"Thanks," John said.

"Not a problem," Karin told him, and the two Sibyls took off back toward the tunnels.

John faced Camille. "Sorry I was a little late to the fight. Your quad hit me with one hell of a surge of elemental energy and woke up my brain—kind of like shock paddles to the head. What happened to Elana?"

Camille kept staring at John, but she did manage to tug Elana out from behind her.

He stared at her like he was amazed. "Ben's in the tunnels," he said to Elana. "A lot of your fighters have disappeared."

"You will need to check each of these mounds." Elana pointed at the metal lumps all over the room, lumps she couldn't even see, keeping her face turned away from Camille. "Many will be dead, but some will have living creatures within—either Rakshasa Eldest or my Bengal fighters. Perhaps some can be saved."

John whipped out his cell and relayed this information to Duncan and the OCU. He plugged one ear for a second and nodded like Duncan could see him. "Yeah, right here, alive and in one piece, both of them. Tell the department thanks for the help with Seneca's men. Did you find that old shithead?"

Camille watched as John frowned.

He listened a little longer, then said, "It was the damnedest thing. The demon-handlers and all those sorcerers just up and quit. Ran away. Good thing, because without the Asmodai and all that elemental disruption, we could take the Created in teams. There was nobody to direct them, and I don't think that bunch could think for themselves."

Just then Ben appeared in the chamber doorway, sword still drawn and dripping with gore.

More dead, Camille's thoughts whispered. *More wounded. More damaged.*

Camille couldn't control where her mind was going with her thoughts. When Elana moved away from her, heading for Ben, she wanted to cry, and she didn't even know why.

From somewhere far off, she heard Bela shouting, Dio swearing at something, and water splashing against a wall.

"Come here, beautiful," John said, wrapping her up in his arms, and for the briefest second Camille could feel him, his muscle, his heat, his heartbeat. She could smell the fresh, faintly spicy scent she knew was his. She let herself press her face into him, hug him back.

"I love you," she told him, and she meant it. She loved him. She loved Bela and Dio and Andy. She cared deeply for Elana, and she thought she loved Ona, too. Poor Ona. So much made sense to Camille now, in ways it never had before.

"I love you," John murmured in her ear, and she felt that like a tickle in her mind, like a tingle in her chest and gold-laced hand. "Tell me you're okay, Camille. I need to know."

But Camille couldn't give him what he asked for.

Her quad was getting closer. Everyone she knew. Coming here. They wanted to see her. They wanted to see what she'd done.

She couldn't face that.

She pressed her face deeper into John's chest.

"I'm sorry," she told John.

He held on tighter. "Wait a minute. What are you—? No, you're not—"

"I'm sorry," she told him again.

Then Camille let herself sink away into the earth and just disappear.

The man and woman in OCU SWAT gear carried their bags through the silent aqueduct chamber, which was deserted now except for the sentry at the main door. The dark visors of their helmeted face masks reflected the metal tombs of the once great and terrifying race of Rakshasa demons. The few Bengals who'd survived had been extracted and were being treated at unknown locations.

"Smells like cat piss," the woman said, her bag rattling as she bounced it off her knee.

The man responded only with a "Shh."

He surveyed the heaps of metal, searching them with elemental senses most OCU officers didn't possess. The Eldest, all but a few, were already dead. They must not have had time to assume flame form to shield themselves from this terrible attack, so they were gone from the earth now, forevermore. In some ways a blessing, but in many ways a pity.

Likely the Sibyls and OCU thought these few survivors were deceased, so faint were their heartbeats and traces. It took a special elemental gift to pick up such small signs of life. Soon enough they would finish their slow burns beneath the metal casing, and go to whatever maker claimed tiger demons as his own.

The man gripped the handles of his small black satchel and kept searching, but the woman pointed toward the front of the room. "He's up there and he's still alive. Barely."

The man glanced over his shoulder at the sentry and sent some elemental energy his way, enough to make the guard crumple to his knees. He'd wake in a few hours, which was plenty of time for what they needed to do.

The two approached the metal lump containing the crippled, dying body of Tarek, the Rakshasa *culla*.

This tomb was sloppier than the rest, cobbled and splashed instead of applied in a single sheet. The man knew it was because Tarek had been out in the tunnels when the fire Sibyl Camille Fitzgerald took out his entire race. She must have used recycled metal from the chamber floor to trap Tarek when he came for her.

"Come on," the woman said, reaching for the man's hand.

He smiled. Took her slender fingers in his.

The two of them focused their talents on the metal, melting it away, sheet by sheet, careful to do no more damage to the demon within.

Soon enough, they could see his golden-furred face, though he didn't have much fur left to him. Angry burn welts, bleeding cuts, lumps of molten ore affixed to his scalded skin. These were elemental wounds, and they would never heal, at least not completely.

The man pulled off his helmet, letting the demon see his face.

Tarek's dark eyes went wide with helpless fury.

Griffen leaned in, making sure his blond hair and blue eyes made an impression. Then he gave Tarek his most sympathetic look, because he did feel some sympathy for the trapped, damaged animal.

"You poor bastard," he said. "This is what happens when you make enemies, now, isn't it?"

Of course Griffen had had his own aims when he "worked" for Tarek. Of course he'd been chasing his own angles—but the demon never should have touched his sister. Rebecca was sacrosanct. Nobody put hands on her. She had special gifts, and one day he would find the right breeding partner for her. Matched with the right male, she might just give birth to a child with skills even more powerful than their own. Constant striving for perfection—that's the way their father would have wanted it.

Griffen heard clinks and rattles as Rebecca unwound the elemental cuffs from her bag, then got to work unfolding the very official morgue body bag. Tarek could see these things, and somehow his eyes got even wider.

"We'll keep your pain to a minimum." Griffen took a syringe out of his own satchel. "And if you're polite and cooperative, we'll probably even feed you more than once a week."

As Rebecca cuffed the demon's twisted arms, Griffen gave the beast a shot so he wouldn't start howling. On the off chance Tarek died before they could get him back to the holding cell they had prepared for him, Griffen went ahead and took a full complement of blood and saliva samples. That was the kicker about the kind of research and production they were planning. A live donor was required.

After Griffen packed his precious samples in the satchel, he and Rebecca lifted the cuffed and bound demon out of his metal prison, placed him in the body bag, and zipped him up tight. One of them could have done it—neither of them had the paltry strength of regular humans—but if anyone was watching, a move like that might give them away. Sometimes appearances were everything. The van they had waiting outside even had the proper insignias and initials stenciled onto it so nobody would question two officers carrying the bag to the back of the van, placing it in the hold, then driving away.

"Don't you worry," Griffen told Tarek as they hauled him out of the chamber, only banging him on a few of the metal tombs as they passed. "This time things will go better, Tarek. I'm going to make sure we do this right."

(41)

John Cole had never known a longer, more frustrating two weeks in his entire life. Camille was somewhere out in the world alone and hurting, thinking God only knew what about herself, and he could do exactly nothing about it.

He sat in the living room of the brownstone on the leather sofa where Camille always liked to be, his arms folded, staring into the dark, swirling projective mirrors like one of them might tell him a secret. Maybe a few of them would blink to life and show him scenes with Camille in them.

Wherever she'd gone, it wasn't in New York City, not unless she'd come up with her own muting charms. Every Sibyl who could twitch, hobble, or move had been out looking—and even Sibyls from other cities had pitched in to help. Elana had explained that in addition to Camille's deep emotional shock at killing so many living things at once, innocent and guilty alike, she was likely suffering from severe aftereffects from the projective energy itself. If her senses weren't still numbed, her emotions and thoughts were, so she was vulnerable. Maybe even helpless.

And that *killed* him.

Even the Sibyl Mothers had offered to help. Once. But they'd barely gotten out of Bela's living room alive. John didn't expect they'd be back anytime soon.

The kitchen door opened and closed softly, and John heard no further noise, so he knew it was Elana. Sure enough, the tiny little woman crossed to one of the leather chairs and took a seat opposite from him, her back to the mirrors over her head.

"Nothing from this morning's patrols?" she asked, her lyrical voice as soft and grandmotherly as ever.

"Nothing," he said, feeling the word like a weight on his heart. *Camille. Beautiful. You've got to give me a clue. Just one hint and I'll take it from there.* That's what he'd tell her if he had three seconds to get her a message.

Elana turned her head, listening for sounds, then focused her attention back on John. "Where are the others?"

He glanced at his watch. "They should be coming in from Jersey in a few."

He couldn't help noticing the faint undertones of lily everywhere in the house when there wasn't too much activity stirring stuff up. He still had pretty sharp senses, even though they didn't rise to Spider-Man level now, at least not completely.

Elana seemed to go away in her head for a few seconds, and when she came back, she said, "I don't think Camille is anywhere close to here, John."

"I don't think so, either, but it makes them feel better to look. Sometimes it makes me feel better, too." Elana couldn't see his face, so he didn't worry about his scowl or the fact he'd picked up one of Andy's empty cans off the floor. If he crushed it up real good, he could probably get off a pretty good pitch at one of those mirrors.

"She'll return when she's able," Elana said.

"Yeah? And after your, ah, bad experience in Rakshasa killing, how long was it before you were willing to face people again?"

Elana gave this some thought. "Two centuries, give or take—but I lost my quad. Camille didn't."

Two hundred years. John left that alone for now. He had a demon's body, so theoretically he could live as long as any Sibyl, and he'd wait as long as it took—but he didn't want to wait that long. Two hundred years without Camille would make the world a dark, dead place to him, and he just couldn't fathom that.

Something had been nagging at his mind a little, so he took this rare moment when the house was Sibyl-free to ask Elana about it. "I'm sorry if this is intrusive, but after what you just said about losing your quad . . . You didn't lose them all. Ona made it, and you knew she was still alive. Why did you never go see her?"

Elana reacted to this with pain, as he'd figured she would, but also with some shame and even humility. "I feared my presence would bring her only heartache, and hers the same for me." Her head turned in the general direction of the projective mirrors. "Keara held that against me. She's always had a soft spot for Ona."

"Keara." John wasn't sure he heard that bit correctly. "*Mother* Keara? Hate to disillusion you, but there's nothing soft about that sawed-off piece of gristle."

Elana's laugh was brief but genuine. "She wasn't always a blustery old woman, John, any more than I was. When Keara was a girl, she was tender and much maligned by her peers because she wasn't easy on the eye. Ona gave her comfort more than once in those tunnels down below Motherhouse Ireland."

Answers that raised more questions. Were all ancient Sibyls good at that trick? "How do you know that?"

"Because I have an unusual connection to Ona, perhaps because of the ways we joined our energies. I've been able now and again to have glimpses of Ona's life and thoughts, to see images she's seeing, especially when she's more emotional." Elana's chin dipped toward her chest. The shame was winning out now. "I should have gone to see her. I have no valid excuses."

He shrugged, more for his benefit than Elana's. "You could go now. Nothing's stopping you."

"Perhaps I will, once we locate Camille." Elana turned in her chair, seemingly to keep the projective mirrors more squarely at her back. "Truth be told, I've been very selfish and afraid on that point, seeing Ona again, and I still am."

John had some understanding of this from his battle experiences, so he left it alone. Besides, he didn't want to keep at this until he got angry—but not because it would set off the demon in his head. Those days were over. Camille had killed Strada's essence, just burned it right out of him, and Elana had confirmed that before beginning her work with Jack Blackmore and the OCU, integrating her few surviving Bengal fighters into their advisory and ancillary forces. If the Bengals had good control over their form, Jack was getting identities for them and opening doors to get them into police academies. Ben was taking this route. He was a natural for police work, and John hoped he'd stay with New York's unit. Duncan was spending most of his time at headquarters these days, helping out the Lowell brothers with their demon integration lessons.

The chimes over the front door gave a soft ring, and John couldn't help his reaction. His heart jumped like crazy, and he stared at the door thinking, *Maybe . . .*

Until he heard Dio tell Andy to get the hell off her foot, and Maggie Cregan laughing at both of them.

Bela came through the door first, with Sheila Gray and Karin Maros behind her. Maggie and Dio and Andy brought up the rear, arguing about what area they should cover next. All the Sibyls had on jeans and sweatshirts, to better blend in with the background when they conducted their day searches.

"I think we'd have better luck in Ireland," Maggie told Dio. "Maybe she's taking a sabbatical in the bogs, or one of the monasteries and convents closer to Dublin."

"If I wanted to hide out, I wouldn't go to Ireland," Dio said. "I'd go someplace nobody would think to look, not in a million years."

Old ground. They'd been covering it for days, and it wasn't getting them anywhere.

Elana waited for the women to get inside, her head turning, tracking the sound of one voice in particular. Andy came straight to her and knelt beside her, and Elana rubbed the top of Andy's head like she was a good-luck charm. "Do you need anything?" Andy asked.

"Your laughter is a comfort," Elana said, and smiled at her. "Perhaps tonight you could create me a new sandwich for dinner. I like adventures."

Bela, Dio, and the East Ranger group eyed Elana like she might be missing a few straws in her bale. John still had indigestion from something Andy had fed him the night before. Elana and Andy were getting on well, though. Andy was having quarters prepared at Motherhouse Kérkira for Elana, and John suspected that one day very soon the old woman would finally get to go home again, truly go home, and be among her own.

Any Bengals she had been caring for who couldn't or didn't want to stay in the city and work with the OCU or live out in the world on their own would go to the island with her. John figured the mix of creatures and personalities would make that Motherhouse even more unique than it already was.

A shiver of motion caught his eye, and he glanced at the big mirror over Elana's head. He motioned to Maggie Cregan, and as the chimes over the communication platform gave a ring, he asked, "Is that thing doing whatever it does?"

"It is," Maggie said with some trepidation, her gaze darting to Bela, Dio, and Andy. "Somebody's coming through from Motherhouse Ireland, and whoever it is, she's strong enough not to need assistance on this end."

The room went crypt-quiet as John stood, his heart doing that funny thing again.

Please. He stared at the mirror, then the table. Camille's whole quad was gazing at the same spot, waiting. Hoping just like he was.

Please, please . . .

The smoke on the mirror broke and the surface went clear. In one split second, John saw a big stone chamber and a figure in green robes—and a split second later, the woman in green robes was standing on the table in the brownstone's living room.

He got to be disappointed again, because whoever it was, she was half Camille's height and giving off smoke like a pipe on fire. Then he got to be pissed when the woman pushed back her green hood and ropes of gray hair spilled over her aged, hunched shoulders.

Mother Keara stared him down first and managed a semi-polite nod.

"The only points I'm giving you are for not showing up armed," he said, thinking about going downstairs. He didn't need this kind of bullshit right now.

Mother Keara didn't come back at him and she didn't try to speak to Dio, which said a little for her intelligence, even if her sanity was questionable for coming here in the first place. The old woman turned on the platform until she was facing Bela, Andy, and Elana.

"I wasn't certain when it first happened, but I'm sure now, because I've looked in every corner." Mother Keara gestured back toward the mirror open on Motherhouse Ireland's communications chamber. "Wherever Camille went, she took Ona with her, if that helps you any in yer figurin'. Neither of them used the chamber to transport themselves, so we've no way of tellin' you more."

Andy shrugged, and Bela shook her head. "We'll give it some thought." Then, grudgingly, since Mother Keara had some history with her, "Thank you for coming to tell us yourself."

John glanced at Elana, and his instincts gave a little jangle. Her expression had gone even more distant and flat, but that might be because Mother Keara was in the room with her. His expression probably looked pretty distant and flat, too.

Mother Keara turned to leave, but she spotted Maggie Cregan standing back near the front door with her crew, like they might be about to make a break for it if things got rough.

"You," Mother Keara said, pointing at her. "What have you found?"

Maggie seemed stunned by the question, but she had enough spice to answer. "Nothing. Why would I have more luck than anyone else?"

Mother Keara stared at her, shock mingling with a tinge of disgust. "You gave that sword of yours plenty of Camille's blood in your youth. It ought to have quite a taste for her by now."

Maggie's mouth came open, and Bela looked like somebody had just kicked her right in the ass. John felt like somebody had kicked him, too.

He was about to ask Mother Keara more about how that sword worked, but the old fire Sibyl walked right off the communications platform into thin air, her image appearing in the projective mirror as she crossed the platform at Motherhouse Ireland. A few seconds later the mirror went dark and started its swirling again.

"Easy come, easy go," Dio said, and Bela had to catch Dio's wrist before she let go of the throwing knife she'd pulled out to shatter the mirror behind Mother Keara.

Bela pulled Dio around with her to face Maggie. "Does

that have any merit—about the sword? It does remember whom it's cut, and it does try to find them in battle, right?"

"Yes, all of that's right." Maggie was frowning so deeply John knew she wasn't blowing this off at all. "Whether or not we can use it to find her, I honestly don't know. I've only dealt with it in close quarters, but I know some of my ancestors used it to track escaped criminals. They'd cut everyone sent to the jails, just so the blade would know their taste."

"It has to be projective in some way," Bela said, and everybody hesitated.

John thought the connection was pretty clear now. Projective energy equaled huge power—and huge danger. As far as anybody knew, Camille hadn't caused any tsunamis with what she did to kill the Rakshasa, but six buildings in Harlem had fallen into a sinkhole that city engineers swore shouldn't—couldn't—exist. But it did now.

"Could you bring the blade down to the lab?" Bela asked Maggie. "Maybe if we can study the energy a little bit, we could—"

"That won't be necessary." Elana got to her feet. She was holding Andy's hand but looking away from everyone, at the wall to the left of John's head. Slowly Elana oriented her face back toward John, and she was more tense that he'd ever seen her.

His heart got going again with its funny pounding, and the hope started to rise. The stupid hope. The crazy hope. But this time disappointment didn't follow.

"If Ona's with Camille," Elana said, her voice slow and halting, like she couldn't quite believe she was committing herself to this, "then I think I know exactly where they are."

"Can you do it?" John asked, trying not to sound like

a teenager with his eagerness. "Can you face going there to take me to her?"

"That's a question you should ask yourself, John." She looked away from him-again. "For me, this will be a trip to heaven. It's you who'll be going to hell."

Camille stood in her favorite silk nightgown in the orchard, letting the cherry blossoms swirl around her like pink butterflies as the sun came up soft and warm and exactly right for the day. The flower kisses on her skin, especially the hand now branded with gold forever, helped her relax and feel real again, and she needed the sun like she needed her fire.

This place really was amazing. She couldn't imagine how Ona and her quad had built these fantastic, ethereal gardens in a desert, but she supposed exiles had plenty of time to come up with miracles, like self-sustaining irrigation systems, elemental temperature controls, and rudimentary muting charms, so human eyes never saw the paradise they created.

When most people walked into the Valley of the Gods, they saw only ruins, desert sand, and the remnant metal sarcophagi from the first defeat of the Rakshasa. They never got to walk across the lush grass or wander in the virtual rain forest that had grown in the centuries since Ona and Elana were forced to leave their quad's handiwork behind.

The Sibyls never put us out, Ona had explained in one of her moments of lucidity. *Save for Motherhouse Antilla and Motherhouse Russia, the Dark Crescent Sisterhood wasn't that organized yet. After Doya accidentally brought that mountain down outside that Russian village and Elana made it flood on the mainland in Greece while we were visiting, the Mothers just . . . suggested we take some time apart from all the others.*

So they had come here, far from any civilization, and built the beginnings of what could have become a Motherhouse in its own right, a different kind of Motherhouse for girls with elemental sentience.

Camille raised her arms and watched the petals dance along her skin.

Ona, Elana, and the rest of their quad might have formed a safe haven for women like Camille—but the Rakshasa knew enough to fear them above all other Sibyls. The demons brought their murderous attack to the Valley of the Gods, and everything was left in ruins. All that normal eyes could see, anyway.

Ona had been better since Camille brought her here. She'd even been up more days than not, cleaning and re-organizing the two little stone houses they had been able to salvage from the weeds and fallen trees and branches.

As for her, she was feeling rested and stronger, though she still had no essence-level sense of what she should do next. Soon enough that answer would be simple: go home.

This was Elana's heaven. It was Ona's heaven.

But it wasn't Camille's.

She missed her quad. She really missed John. How she'd face any of them, how she'd find words to discuss any of what had happened, how she'd go back to fighting and killing when those things felt abhorrent to her now—these were answers she didn't have. Not yet.

Camille lowered her arms as more cherry blossoms brushed her cheeks. A light, spicy scent carried through the flowers, something familiar, but very much out of place in the secret gardens of the Valley of the Gods.

She wasn't sure if her mind was playing tricks on her, but her gold-laced hand gave a whispery tingle. Her heart started to beat, not scared, no, never afraid, just hopeful when she didn't have any right to hope.

Camille turned, and he was standing only a few feet

from her, a vision in the cherry blossoms. A vision wearing jeans and a black NYPD T-shirt.

John looked pale and rattled, and Camille couldn't quite believe he'd found her, much less been willing to stride into his own personal torture chamber to get to her. He had horrible nightmares about this place, and he probably had no idea where to fit the chaotic, overgrown gardens he'd never seen in those terrible dreams.

She wanted to go to him, wanted that more than anything, but she couldn't read him past the distress lingering at his edges. His green eyes studied her, wide and dark, full of confusion and uncertainty.

"Your quad's fine and they want you back real soon," he said. "Nobody's angry. Everybody understands."

He didn't say, *Everybody but me,* but she saw it in his face.

"I—" she started, but faltered.

What did she really want to say?

I'm sorry.

I think I'm more sane now.

I'm here.

I love you.

I want to put my arms around you.

All of those things. So she said them, one at a time, watching him for any sign of reaction.

John let her finish, and he just kept looking at her. Another long few seconds crept by before he said. "You, standing in that rain of cherry blossoms, no question you're the most amazing woman I've ever seen."

Camille's throat got dry and tight. Petals landed on her shoulders, her face, and they were landing on John, too, dropping into his dark hair like otherworldly decorations. She lifted her gold-laced hand for him to see, in case he hadn't noticed it in their few minutes back at the aqueduct before she . . . before she'd gone back on her word to him and run away to this place.

"Fancy jewelry." John glanced at the hand from a couple of angles. "Better watch out or you'll be starting trends. Is it dangerous?"

"It might be."

He nodded. Let it go. She could tell her strange new filigree tattoo didn't bother him at all, but whatever he was about to say, it was making him nervous.

"I couldn't figure out what kind of universe would make me come back here, to the place where all my troubles began, but now I know that it's a fair one. A merciful one." John curled his fingers, then let them relax again, and he seemed to be letting go of the past with every word he spoke. "If having you in my life is the trade-off for everything I had to go through, then I'd say that's a square deal."

"John—"

He held up his hand, then lowered it, and lowered his head, too. When he spoke, each word was careful, and she knew he had opened his heart wide. "Do you really want me, Camille? Because I can't stand to hold you again, then have to let you go."

The ache in his voice nearly melted her heart, and it definitely melted away the last of her insecurities and worries. Camille ran the few steps to John, and she wrapped her arms around his neck as he picked her straight up off the ground and held her against him.

"Don't ever let me go again," she said. "I wanted to tell you that the first time you ever held me, and the next time, and the time after that."

"If I'd gotten those instructions, I damned sure would have followed them." He kissed her neck. "You need to quit holding back on me."

"I want to kiss you. I want to make love to you. I want you to touch me until I can't even breathe. How's that?"

"Better." He kissed her lips next, slow and deep and long, and she forgot about everything beyond his

mouth, his tongue, and the cherry blossoms tickling
their ears and necks and shoulders. His hands moved
like he had a map of all the perfect places to touch and
knew exactly how much pressure to apply. She couldn't
think straight. Didn't care. All she wanted was to feel
him, taste him, and be his again.

His lips pressed harder against hers as his tongue
moved deeper, filling her up and promising hours of love-
making, days of pleasure—and she knew this man could
deliver. When he left her mouth, his lips touched her
cheeks, her nose, her forehead, then her eyes. In that low,
low voice, he said, "You're even softer than I remembered."

Camille kissed him again and nibbled at his mouth,
drunk with him, absorbed by how he felt and how she
felt now that she was finally in his arms again. "Are we
starting over, John?"

"What, and go through all that waiting again? No
way in hell. We're starting from here."

She stared at him, looking deep into his eyes, as far as
she could see. "Do I still know your soul?"

"You helped make it what it is today." He brushed her
mouth with his. "Do I know yours?"

"I think so. I hope so. I'll open it up and let you study
every inch, if that's what you want."

He went very still in her embrace. "What I want is
you, and not just here, right now. It's *after,* Camille, and
I want you forever."

She brushed flower blossoms out of his hair. "You really do believe in happily ever after, don't you?"

He kissed her again. "I believe it, and if you say yes to
being mine, I've got it."

"Yes."

"That fast?" He eyed her, starting to tease a little. "No
catches? No conditions?"

She gave it some thought. "Make love to me. Cover

me up with cherry blossoms and stay inside me for hours."

Camille felt the instant response of his body, the tightening of his muscles, the swell of hard warmth against her belly. When she looked up, she expected to see desire, maybe even happiness, but the man had his eyes closed and he was swearing under his breath.

"What? You don't want?"

"It's not that." The look he gave her was full of physical suffering and resignation. "It's just . . . well, I didn't come alone."

They found them in Ona's little stone house, and the two old Sibyls weren't talking.

Elana had her hands on Ona's face, tracing every scar, inch by inch, learning her sister Sibyl as she was today. Ona's good eye looked more focused than Camille had ever seen it, and she had her palms just above Elana's, now and again brushing her fingertips against Elana's knuckles. There was none of the awkwardness Camille would have expected, none of the hesitance. What she felt in the little stone house was joy, and relief, and life. A coming back, a reuniting, and a wholeness.

This was right in the universe. This was something that was supposed to happen.

She and John slipped out without saying a word, and together they walked back to the orchard, back to the cherry blossoms, which had formed a delightful soft carpet in the thick grass.

"Andy's taking Elana to Motherhouse Kérkira," John said. "What's going to happen to Ona then?"

Camille glanced over her shoulder, back toward the stone house. "After seeing them together again, I think Ona will go with Elana."

John's eyebrows lifted. "To live with the water Sibyls? Ona? Wouldn't that be ironic?"

"Andy has a fine sense of irony, and she's not afraid of a little conflict and emotion." Camille stopped walking in the middle of the blossoms and turned to face John. "Just look at whom she lives with. She'll find a place for Ona, and something useful for her to do, if that's what they all choose."

John put his hands on Camille's waist. "Think they'll be busy for a while back at that stone house?"

Camille's heart fluttered. "Probably."

"How does the first day of summer sound?" John's gaze was intense.

"For what?"

"For me marrying you." He picked up a handful of cherry blossoms and sprinkled them over her fingers. "I don't have the ring yet, but maybe these will do?"

She watched the petals trickle through her fingers and drift down to her bare feet. "They're perfect."

"Was that a yes?"

"I already said yes."

"But I didn't meet your conditions." He swept her up in his arms, cradling her this time, and before Camille could sort out what conditions he was talking about, he had her down in the flower petals, and she was gazing up at him, loving the tenderness she saw in his green eyes, loving the soft way he touched her, so careful and slow, making sure she had exactly what she wanted.

"Conditions," she whispered as he lowered his mouth to hers. "Conditions . . . oh, yeah. Make love to me. Cover me up with cherry blossoms and stay inside me for hours. Does that sound like a challenge to you?"

His grin came fast and warm, and he kissed her for a long, long time before his rumbling voice gave her fresh, sweet chills. "I don't walk away from challenges, beautiful. Not ever."

❲ acknowledgments ❳

I would very much like to thank my agent, Nancy Yost, for helping me get this series off the ground, then helping me stay on track. Additional and equal thanks to my understanding and patient editor, Kate Collins, for her thorough reads and excellent suggestions. It's always a stronger book when she finishes reading it and giving me her ideas. Thanks, also, to Kate's assistant, Kelli Fillingim, who keeps me from forgetting important things like when my book is due, where I'm supposed to send it, my last name, my birthday—well, you get the idea. Everyone at Random House/Ballantine works together to make the process smooth and sane for writers.

With each book I do, I find I focus more and more on my readers. I want each story to reward fans of the series and interest new readers, too. In the end, it's all about you, and I'm honored to have the chance to offer you this installment of the Dark Crescent Sisterhood.

Read below for an excerpt from
CAPTIVE HEART
by Anna Windsor

Sibyls.

Jack Blackmore stood on a rickety Greek dock staring across the sunlit waves of the Ionian Sea. He had come to paradise. He should be enjoying himself, but instead he was thinking about Sibyls.

Saul Brent, one of the few men who called Jack a friend, yanked at a rusty pull chain on the boat they were supposed to take to the island of Kérkira, but the battered skiff's engine wouldn't catch. "Son of a bitch," Saul muttered, giving the chain another jerk.

Shirtless, tattooed, and with his brown hair barely crammed into a ponytail, Saul looked more like a biker on spring break than a decorated soldier and career police officer. His years undercover for vice and narcotics seemed to be etched into his essence. Saul's swearing did nothing to ease Jack's mind, and neither did the warm air or the scents of wet sand and salt.

Sibyls were still a puzzle to him.

He didn't like puzzles.

Every time he dealt with Sibyls, he seemed to do something wrong. He didn't like wrong.

Jack frowned at paradise.

He'd fought demons easier to get along with than the Sibyl warriors of the Dark Crescent Sisterhood—especially the one he had come to Greece to see. What the hell was he doing, trying to make nice with the most unreasonable woman he'd ever met? A woman with elemental powers so vast they defied his understanding.

She'd already tried to kill him twice. Maybe the third time, she'd get the job done.

The engine caught, but Jack didn't make a move to get into the boat.

"Second thoughts?" Saul asked as he struggled with the last rope lashing their skiff to the dock.

Jack wondered if his features mirrored his career like Saul's did, if his years in the Army and gray ops, both internationally and stateside, showed like subtle scars on his face.

"No second thoughts," he said in answer to Saul's question before considering whether he was telling the truth. Jack considered himself an honest man, but he never said much about what was really on his mind. Training—and reflex.

Saul snickered as he worked the rope's last knot. "The thought of seeing her, it's got you nervous, doesn't it?"

Jack didn't answer, but he got into the skiff. He wasn't nervous. He didn't do nervous. The reason his gut was tight—well. Just a lot riding on this little visit to Motherhouse Kérkira.

"She might finally drown you this time," Saul said over the roar of the engine as he steered them into the deep blue waters of the channel.

The skiff lurched, and Jack had to catch himself on the splintery rail. Sea spray coated his face, cooling him enough to say, "She'll hear me out. She thinks more like us than like the Dark Crescent Sisterhood."

"Andy Myles stopped being a police officer the minute she snapped her pretty fingers and summoned her first tidal wave." Saul gestured behind them, in the general direction of Mount Olympus and Motherhouse Greece, home base of the air Sibyls, where they had started this little late-afternoon odyssey. "She hasn't been in training since birth like the rest of them, but she's a Sibyl now, and you haven't made many friends among the chicks in leather."

Jack thought about the elementally protected body-suits the Sibyls wore into battle, and about how the tight black leather hugged every enticing inch of Andy's body. His fingers tightened on the skiff's railing until his knuckles hurt.

Let it go.

Yeah. Because he was good at letting things go. No distractions. Not on a mission.

Saul stayed quiet for a minute or two, then came back with, "You still haven't told me what you want with her."

"I want her back in New York City." Jack made himself ease up on the boat's railing before he broke the damned thing. "I want her mind on operations and planning. I've read her notes and reports—she's one of the best analysts in the Occult Crimes Unit."

"She's a Sibyl now." Saul cut to the left and pointed them toward the island they sought. "One of the few water Sibyls on the planet. Did it ever occur to you that Andy has other shit to do? That she might not be willing to come running just because the great Jack Blackmore gives her a summons?"

Jack considered various answers, but he kept coming back to one obvious fact and the thing he couldn't stop believing about Andy Myles. "Once a cop, always a cop. If I ask her, she'll come."

Saul's brown eyes narrowed. "When you took your little sabbatical at the Sibyl Motherhouses and came back all Zen, I thought you'd changed—but you're still the same cold bastard. Everyone and everything exists just to get you what you want."

"Not what I want." Jack went back to strangling the boat's railing. "What we need."

"Who is *we* this week, Jack? The Army? The FBI? You and the little voices in your head?"

"The NYPD. The OCU." Jack didn't expect Saul to understand or even to believe him, which was a good thing, because Saul laughed his ass off as he whipped the skiff through the crystalline waters leading to the tip of Kérkira.

"You're full of shit," Saul called over the roar of the engine and the slap of the boat through the waves.

Meaning, *When you're finished with whatever has your interest, you'll leave New York City and the OCU in your rearview mirror just like you've left everywhere else.*

Probably true.

Thanks to some pretty bad shit in his childhood, Jack had no real ties, not to any person or any place. Once upon a time, the Army had saved his life. He'd become a soldier, a commander who knew who he was, where he was supposed to be, and what he was supposed to be doing. Then he watched a bunch of tiger-demons crawl out of the Valley of the Gods in Afghanistan, the blood of his unit dripping from their claws and fangs, and he lost track of life's basics even though he always warned his men never to do that.

The tiger-demons, the Rakshasa, had been his reason for existing—or at least his reason for being a single-minded, single-purposed bastard—since the Gulf War, but they were dead now. The darkness he had tracked for years had been scrubbed from the planet.

But he could always find more darkness.

New York City was as good a place as any. For now.

As if he had heard Jack's thoughts, Saul made a vicious cut with the rudder and the skiff scooted sideways. If Jack hadn't had a good grip on the rail, he'd have busted his face on the rough floorboards.

"When Andy decides to kick your ass all over the island, don't ask me for any help," Saul said. "I'm gonna hoot until I piss myself. And I'm staying on the boat. You're on your own with this one."

Jack studied the sands of the fast-approaching island as he tried to clear his mind and get ready to engage the—what? Enemy? Friendly? Hydra monster in a gorgeous redhead suit?

Damn, but the skiff's railing felt flimsy in his choke hold.

Even if Jack wasn't too sure about his own character, he had no doubt that Saul was an honest man. If Andy decided to wash Jack back to New York City, he was on his own—and Saul might very well get his chance to keep laughing.

One day you're a good cop with a decent career in New York City.

The next day you're the world's only water Sibyl, a warrior of the Dark Crescent Sisterhood sworn to protect the weak from the supernaturally strong.

And not too long after that, you're standing at the bottom of the Ionian Sea in your underwear, nose to beak with a big-ass octopus.

"Normal people don't have to deal with this shit." Andy Myles didn't dare take her eyes off the octopus to glare at her companion, a woman so ancient she looked more crusty than the debris in the shell midden under the octopus. Bubbles rose with each word, and Andy breathed in warm, salty breaths of her element, still amazed that she didn't need gills to treat water like air.

Aquahabitus. That's the fancy term for me being able to live underwater like a happy clam. See? I'm remembering more of this crap every day.

The octopus blew a load of black ink in Andy's face and scooted off across the seafloor, leaving tiny bursts of sand and rock in its wake.

Andy waved the stinky black cloud out of her face, but melanin coated her floating red curls. The effect was interesting. She had never given much thought to trying purple highlights. "Add this to the list of shit normal people don't have to deal with—what color will a wart with legs stain my hair today?"

"You frightened the octopus," Elana told Andy as her silver robes absorbed some of the coloring. "To approach water's many creatures, you must keep a broad view, a strong sense of purpose, and peace in your own heart and mind."

"Wonderful." Andy glanced down at her purple-stained underwear. "Let's not schedule any chats with sharks this week."

Elana stared at Andy, her eerie white eyes conveying nothing but acceptance. Andy wondered how much Elana saw, even though theoretically she saw nothing at all. How the hell did she stay so calm about *everything*?

"Let's finish for the day," Elana suggested. "You had quite a bit of success with the fish earlier."

"Sure. Three fin wounds and one tail in the face. I did great." Andy raised her fingers to the iron crescent moon charm she wore around her neck and watched currents rinse her curls, but shades of purple remained. Camille, the fire Sibyl in her quad, had made the charm for Andy. The metal's special properties increased Andy's aquasentience—her ability to move water through her essence and sense or track whatever the water might have touched—but of course, it couldn't do much to wash away octopus dye.

"The sea senses your unrest and it answers with its own."

"The sea senses I have no idea why I'm playing with fish instead of working with adepts or sailing back to New York City to fight with my quad." Andy let go of the necklace.

Elana sent bubbles of laughter swirling around her silver hair. "Water's creatures can teach you acceptance, my dear. They can teach you about vast freedom within vast limitations. We'll keep trying."

She offered Andy her small, wrinkled hand, and together they drifted up the slope of the seafloor, closer and closer to the sparkling blue surface above. The day had been bright and warm when they walked into the depths, and heat kissed Andy's freckled cheeks as waves gently helped the two women forward.

Her ears worked as well as her lungs when she was immersed in her element, but the world of water sounded so different from the world of air—richer, more nuanced, and unbelievably detailed. The slightest whistle carried for miles, like the swish of a tail or the crack of a tooth on a shell, and all the while, the ebb and flow of tides all over the world made a whispering *beat, beat, beat* she had come to know like her own thoughts. She had become fair at estimating how far sounds had traveled, and at judging their source and trajectory.

A slice-and-push noise caught her attention, and she glanced toward the Greek mainland. "Boat," she told Elana, but of course Elana already knew that.

"Five minutes until it arrives," Elana said.

Andy's head broke the surface. Ahead of her lay the steeply sloped beaches of Kérkira, where her Motherhouse had been hastily constructed. Andy could see its single turret peeking over the rise of the nearest hill. Elana's head didn't break through to air for a few more strides.

As they got a little closer to the beach, the small Motherhouse, tucked into a small, heavily treed valley near the ruins of old Turkish fortifications, came into clear view.

The place . . . lacked a little something. Like, maybe, sanity?

Air Sibyls, earth Sibyls, and fire Sibyls had built it all together and in one huge hurry when Andy first manifested her talent for working with water. Water Sibyls had been extinct for a thousand years, and their training facility, Motherhouse Antilla, had been destroyed in the tidal wave that wiped them out. Once Andy had started working with water, younger water Sibyls began appearing and seeking training, and these girls couldn't very well hang out in hotels, shelters, or anywhere else that couldn't tolerate a hefty dose of moisture. So Motherhouse Kérkira had been born, near Motherhouse Greece because air Sibyls had the most to offer in training a clueless water Sibyl. Air, like water, could be vast and fast-moving, difficult to control and unpredictable. Air, more than any other element, could control water, blowing it this way and that—or setting up an impenetrable moving barrier of wind to hold back an accidental tidal surge.

The common areas of the north section had gone up first, with old-style Russian architecture and heavy wooden walls and floors. The barracks in the western section had been laid together with Motherhouse Ireland's smooth Connemara marble and austere room design, while the kitchen and library in the eastern reaches had the open, airy look of carved crystal that marked Motherhouse Greece. In the middle, good old American brick and mortar formed an entry hall and a formal meeting chamber. Stone, crystal, wood, and brick—Motherhouse Kérkira had come out looking like a twisted fairy-tale castle, or something Picasso might have barfed after a particularly bad bender.

As Andy and Elana crested like tired waves on the beach, Elana moved her hands over her robes, absorbing all the moisture and dispersing its elemental components back to the universe.

"Aquaterminus." Andy named the ability before Elana could ask her to say it. "Halting the motion of water or absorbing small amounts. This demands significant energy and can be fatal if done on too large a scale."

"Excellent." Elana's small feet moved effortlessly over rocks and sand and branches as if she could see every hazard and shift in the terrain. "But I sense more unrest. Your tension increased the moment we walked out of the sea, my dear. What is it that troubles you so deeply— and so constantly?"

Andy grabbed her yellow Mother's robes off the rock where she had draped them. "For starters, I hate yellow. I think it's a stupid color for water Sibyls." She pitched the robes back into the waves, feeling satisfaction as the annoying sun-colored cloth whipped under the surface and darkened as it moved out to sea. The nervousness inside her wound tighter even though she was gazing across an endless vista of water and ornate islands. Most people thought the Ionian Islands were perfection itself, but right now they just bugged the hell out of her.

"I don't know who's on the boat," Andy added, fishing for any explanation that might turn out to be the truth about why she was so jumpy when Elana's only purpose in life seemed to be helping her learn to relax.

Elana cocked her head like she was listening to something. "Yes. There's disruption onboard the approaching skiff. I won't deny that."

Andy squinted toward the mainland and sighed. "I hadn't picked that up. Thanks. Do you sense more tension now?"

Elana ignored her sarcasm, as she usually did. "What bothered you when we left the waves?"

The cranks in Andy's depths turned again, ratcheting her muscles. She sensed rushing and overflowing in her own essence, but at the same time, her emotions choked inside. She felt like a river battling beaver dams at every bend and juncture. She needed to kick out some logjams before her brain flooded.

"I don't know. I don't . . . well, the building. The Motherhouse bothers me. You can't see it, but I've told you it's freaky." Andy smeared water out of her eyes with both hands, then remembered she could absorb it and dried off her face. "It's crowded here, and too public, and I'm worried more adepts are on the way. What if one of them makes a mistake and we flood half of Europe?"

Elana's lips curved at the edges like she might be trying to smile. "Keep going. Let it flow, Andy."

"Flow. Right. That's supposed to be my job." Andy glanced at the tattoo that had marked her right forearm since her Sibyl talents manifested. Earth, fire, air—mortar, pestle, broom—in a triangle around a dark crescent moon. Sibyls worked in fighting groups, with earth Sibyls as mortars, responsible for protecting and leading the group. Fire Sibyls worked as pestles, handling communications, and air Sibyls served as brooms, cleaning up messes, archiving events, and researching information on just about everything. When Andy joined their ranks, Sibyl tattoos all over the world had changed. The lines connecting the symbols went from straight to wavy, symbolizing the role of water Sibyls in a fighting group.

Flow.

She was supposed to attend to the emotional flow and growth of her group.

Whatever the hell *that* meant.

"I'm a cop and a warrior, Elana." She lowered her arm, lifted her chin, and blinked at the sudden glare of sunlight off the too-blue sea. "I shoot things. I don't flow."

"The longer you live in water, the more water will live in you. Release, Andy." Elana put her paper-soft hands on Andy's bare belly. Her dark, damp skin seemed to glitter in all the sunlight. "Tell me all of what's bothering you. Don't think. Don't censor. Just let yourself flow."

Andy closed her eyes. The beat of the tides swelled in her mind, the gentle pressure of Elana's hand focused her, and she was able to come up with the next pain on her list. "I miss my quad."

"Bela, Camille, and Dio are brilliant fighting partners." Elana's voice seemed as hypnotic and rhythmic as the waves. "I'm sure they miss you these summer months when you have to be away. What else?"

Andy listened to the water around her, tried to let it wash through her and break free everything crammed in her chest and throat. The air smelled like evergreen and fish and brine. "The beach bothers me. Stupid as this might sound, it feels wrong."

Elana said nothing. Andy kept her eyes closed, listening to the waves dance with the beach. "The trees bother me. They don't . . . they don't speak to the water like I want them to."

Andy wondered if Elana was thinking she was screwy, but the old woman just asked, "And?"

And . . .

Great. She was starting to relax a little more, but only because she didn't have the energy to fight with more than one emotion at the same time. Gently, she moved Elana's fingers away from her and opened her eyes. "It's everything, okay? It's the whole place. I sort of hate it. No, I actually do hate it. I'll never get peaceful here without regular shipments of Valium, coffee, and all the chocolate I can eat."

Elana's hands came together like a young child clapping. "Good. I agree."

Andy wasn't sure she heard that right. "What?"

"This is not the right location for our Motherhouse." Elana's white eyes brightened with emotion. "The Motherhouse we water Sibyls build for ourselves—it won't be here."

Andy stared at Elana. It had felt like a miracle, finding a single surviving water Sibyl from time before time, fully trained and able to *really* teach her what it meant to live with water in her soul. Now she was worrying that Elana's ancient mind might be running dry after all.

Warm breezes teased Andy's stained hair and under-wear, and the afternoon sun baked her freckles. "Build a Motherhouse," she said. "You and me?"

Elana gestured toward Motherhouse Disastro. "We have the adepts. They'll help."

Now Andy's mouth came open. "We have five teenagers, twenty-two kids, and three infants. Think the babies can hammer a nail?"

"And we have Ona," Elana said like she hadn't heard a word Andy spoke. Her robes and hair were completely dry, and she seemed enraptured by whatever she could see in her mind.

Desperate to make Elana talk sense, Andy said, "Ona's a renegade fire Sibyl who barely talks to anyone but you. And she sort of destroyed the last Motherhouse. And fire Sibyls burn shit up and want everything made of rock. And, and—she's as old as you are!"

Elana held up two fingers. "Two years older."

Andy smacked the side of her own head, sending a spray of water over the sand and rocks. "Does that matter when you're a thousand, for God's sake?"

Elana paused. "It's still surprising to hear you call on God instead of the Goddess."

"I'm from the American South and I didn't grow up a Sibyl. The whole Goddess thing—I'm ambivalent." Andy dried off her hands and legs in sheer frustration, soaking the water into her essence and firing it back at the ocean in a fast, arcing plume. "Assuming I go for the insanity of be-lieving we can build our own Motherhouse, where would we put it?"

Elana faced her, her scarred face serious but kind, with that ever-present relaxation she seemed to have when they visited any beach. "Where our hearts take us."

"That really helps." Andy drew in more water and shot it out over the sea, using her palm to target the stream.

Aquakinesis. She needed a lot more practice with that ability, but she felt a small release every time she did it. Nothing like a little violence to get a girl's pulse back to normal.

"When the time is right, the place will call to us," Elana said. "We'll both know."

Just the thought of moving her Sibyl training facility to some new and unknown location, never mind building a Motherhouse—Andy wasn't sure how she was supposed to ever find any peace now.

"Don't die," she told Elana. "There's no way I can fight alongside my quad in New York, figure out all this crap, and build a Motherhouse by myself."

Elana's shrug made Andy want to bury herself headfirst in the sand. "I'll live forever if nothing kills me."

Andy grimaced because Elana was referring to the fact that not only was she one of the oldest Sibyls in the world, she was also the only half-demon Sibyl . . . ever. Tiger demons known as Rakshasa had attacked her and infected her a long time ago, but she had survived and lived to help drive the bastards off the face of the planet—twice. Andy felt like she had to protect Elana at all costs, but that would be damned hard if Elana didn't quit putting herself on the front lines of demon battles.

"Our disruption has arrived." Elana pointed in the direction of the docks, and Andy saw a man striding toward them.

Weird.

Usually the locals who knew about Motherhouse Salvador Dalí's Worst Nightmare wouldn't let anybody approach this end of the island unescorted, much less march right up their private beach to bang on the front door. Which, for the record, was as ugly as the rest of the place, though Motherhouse Russia was quite proud of the carved wolf's-head door handle.

How had some guy managed to—

Andy looked closer.

The man had coal-colored hair and stoic, handsome features almost too perfectly aligned to be real instead of some Renaissance painter's fantasy. Those features were familiar, but what she really recognized was his scowl. And who could miss the totally out of place *Men in Black* suit and the dark sunglasses?

Him.

Here.

Of all places.

Oh, yeah, *this* was really going to help her relax and focus on learning healing and flow and all that other water Sibyl crap.

"Fuck me." Andy put her hand on Elana's shoulder. "It's Jack Blackmore. Think anybody would care if I drowned him?"

**OTHER HARD CASE CRIME BOOKS
YOU WILL ENJOY:**

GRIFTER'S GAME *by Lawrence Block*
FADE TO BLONDE *by Max Phillips*
TOP OF THE HEAP *by Erle Stanley Gardner*
LITTLE GIRL LOST *by Richard Aleas*
TWO FOR THE MONEY *by Max Allan Collins*
THE CONFESSION *by Domenic Stansberry*
HOME IS THE SAILOR *by Day Keene*
KISS HER GOODBYE *by Allan Guthrie*
361 *by Donald E. Westlake*
PLUNDER OF THE SUN *by David Dodge*
BRANDED WOMAN *by Wade Miller*
DUTCH UNCLE *by Peter Pavia*
THE COLORADO KID *by Stephen King*
THE GIRL WITH THE LONG GREEN HEART
by Lawrence Block
THE GUTTER AND THE GRAVE *by Ed McBain*
NIGHT WALKER *by Donald Hamilton*
A TOUCH OF DEATH *by Charles Williams*
SAY IT WITH BULLETS *by Richard Powell*
WITNESS TO MYSELF *by Seymour Shubin*
BUST *by Ken Bruen and Jason Starr*
STRAIGHT CUT *by Madison Smartt Bell*

They kicked the lock off the door and came in with their hands full of shotguns. Two of them, in black hats and anonymous black raincoats with the collars turned up. Also black handkerchiefs across their faces, like stagecoach robbers.

Grofield had been sitting there going over a play he thought they might do this summer. He'd come back to the motel, got himself a bite to eat, called the airport to arrange for a morning flight to Indianapolis via St. Louis, and had been sitting there ever since with the play open on the writing desk in front of him. Then they kicked the lock off the door and came in and pointed shotguns at him, and he dropped his red pencil, put his hands up in the air, and said, "I'm on your side."

"On your feet," the tall one said.

Grofield got to his feet. He kept his hands over his head.

The tall one kept a shotgun pointed at him while the short one searched the room. Finally the short one stepped back and picked his shotgun off the bed and said, "It isn't here."

The tall one said to Grofield, "Where is it?"

"I don't know."

"Don't waste time, Jack, we're not playin' a game."

"I didn't think you were. Not with guns, and kicking the door in and all."

"You got your choice," the short one said. "You can be alive and poor, or dead and rich."

"I'm sorry," Grofield said.

They looked at one another. "Turn around," the short one said. "Face the wall."

Grofield turned around and faced the wall. He knew what was coming, and hunched his head down into his neck. It didn't do any good. The lights went out very painfully...

"Whatever Stark writes, I read. He's a stylist, a pro, and I thoroughly enjoy his attitude."
—*Elmore Leonard*

"Donald Westlake's Parker novels are among the small number of books I read over and over. Forget all that crap you've been telling yourself about *War and Peace* and Proust—these are the books you'll want on that desert island."
—*Lawrence Block*

"Nobody does the noir thriller better than Richard Stark…His lean style and hard-edged characters, not exactly likable, but always compelling, provide a welcome return to the hard-bitten days of yore."
—*San Diego Union Tribune*

"Gritty and chillingly noir…[Westlake] succeeds in demonstrating his total mastery of crime fiction."
—*Booklist*

"If you're new to Stark's work, think of all the comic Dortmunder capers he's written under his real name—Donald E. Westlake—but with as baleful an absence of humor as in *The Ax*."
—*Kirkus Reviews*

"Among the greatest hard-boiled writing of all time."
—*London Financial Times*

"A brilliant invention."
—*New York Review of Books*

"[*Lemons Never Lie* is] a sucker punch to the groin."
—*Badazz Mofo Magazine*

Raves For the Work of
RICHARD STARK!

"[A] book by this guy is cause for happiness."
— *Stephen King*

"To me, Richard Stark is the Prince of Noir."
— *Martin Cruz Smith*

"Brilliant…Donald E. Westlake (aka Richard Stark) knows how to freeze the blood."
— *Terrence Rafferty, GQ*

"The neo-hero: the ruthless, unrepentant, single-minded operator in a humorless and amoral world…No one depicts this scene with greater clarity than Richard Stark."
— *The New York Times*

"Energy and imagination light up virtually every page, as does some of the best hard-boiled prose ever to grace the noir genre."
— *Publishers Weekly*

"As Donald E. Westlake or Richard Stark, this crime novelist gives the best lines to the bad guys."
— *Time*

"Westlake knows precisely how to grab a reader, draw him or her into the story, and then slowly tighten his grip until escape is impossible."
— *Washington Post Book World*